'The perfect book to ...
Heat

'Lovers of romance will relish this tale of friendship,
fun and flirting set in beautiful New York.'
My Weekly

'Morgan excels in balancing the sweet
and sexy to create the perfect blend.'
Booklist

'A gorgeously sparkly romance about letting
go and learning to love again.'
Julia Williams, bestselling author
of *Coming Home for Christmas*

'Full of romance and sparkle'
Lovereading

'Morgan is a magician with words'
RT Book Reviews

'Definitely looking forward to more from Sarah Morgan'
Smexy Books

'Morgan's novel delivers the classic
sweep-you-off-your-feet romantic experience.'
Publisher's Weekly

'Perfect chick-lit'
BEST Magazine

'Her dynamic prose like narrative is eloquent,
the laugh-out-loud humor lightens the load and
both her big-city and small-town settings are perfect'
RT Book Reviews

THE NO.1 BESTSELLING AUTHOR

SARAH MORGAN

Moonlight over Manhattan

ONE PLACE. MANY STORIES

This novel is entirely a work of fiction. The names, characters
and incidents portrayed in it are the work of the author's
imagination. Any resemblance to actual persons, living or
dead, events or localities is entirely coincidental.

HQ
An imprint of HarperCollins*Publishers* Ltd.
1 London Bridge Street
London SE1 9GF

This paperback edition 2017

1

First published in Great Britain by
HQ, an imprint of HarperCollins*Publishers* Ltd. 2017

Copyright © Sarah Morgan 2017

Sarah Morgan asserts the moral right to be
identified as the authors of this work
A catalogue record for this book is
available from the British Library

ISBN: 978-1-848-45667-9

Printed and bound by
CPI Group (UK) Ltd, Croydon, CR0 4YY

All rights reserved. No part of this publication maybe reproduced,
stored in a retrieval system, or transmitted, in any form or by any means,
electronic, mechanical, photocopying, recording or otherwise,
without the prior permission of the publishers.

This book is sold subject to the condition that it shall not, by way of trade
or otherwise, be lent, re-sold, hired out or otherwise circulated without
the publisher
that in which
con

Our p
recyclab
forests.
the leg

LANCASHIRE COUNTY LIBRARY	
3011813605773 8	
Askews & Holts	09-Oct-2017
AF ROM	£7.99
NST	

Dear Reader

One of my favorite quotes (and I've used it in the front of this book) is from Eleanor Roosevelt, who said 'do one thing every day that scares you'.

That quote is perfect for the heroine of this story. Harriet is a twin, and she is the shy twin. Life wasn't easy for her growing up and now her confident twin sister has moved out of their apartment, she is forced to make a new life for herself. And it's hard. She knows she has to push herself out of her comfort zone, and so resolves to do one thing every day that challenges her.

Like most people, Harriet is a mixture of strength and vulnerability and I loved watching her grow in confidence and find her own path.

As some of you know, I wrote a number of medical romances before writing longer books, and I still can't resist a sexy doctor. So my hero in this story, Dr. Ethan Black, works in the emergency department (as I did, many years ago before I changed careers and started writing stories while wearing my pajamas.) He is my favorite type of hero – strong, kind, smart and patient. I don't blame Harriet for falling in love with him (I hope you do too!), but in the end loving Ethan becomes her greatest challenge of all.

This is a story about pushing the boundaries. It's about courage, friendship and of course romance, all against the snowy, sparkly backdrop of New York City.

I hope you love it.

Sarah
xxx

To Nora, Laura, Ruth, Mary, Kat and Janeen for the laughs, friendship and great memories.

"Do one thing every day that scares you."

Eleanor Roosevelt

CHAPTER ONE

THIS WASN'T HOW a date was supposed to end.

If she'd known she was going to have to climb out of the window of the ladies' room, she wouldn't have chosen tonight to wear insanely high heels. Why hadn't she spent more time learning to balance before leaving her apartment?

She'd never been a high heel sort of person, which was *exactly* why she was now wearing a pair of skyscraper stilettos. Another thing ticked off the list she'd made of Things Harriet Knight Wouldn't Normally Do.

It was an embarrassingly long list, compiled one lonely October night when she'd realized that the reason she was sitting in the apartment on her own, talking to the animals she fostered, was that she lived her life safely cocooned inside her comfort zone. At this rate she was going to die alone, surrounded by a hundred dogs and cats.

Here lies Harriet, who knew a lot about hair balls, but not a whole lot about the other kind.

A life of sin would have been more exciting, but she'd

picked up the wrong rule book when she was born. As a
child she'd learned how to hide. How to make herself small,
if not exactly invisible. Ever since then she'd trodden the
safest path, and she'd done it while wearing sensible shoes.
Plenty of people, including her twin sister and her brother,
would say she had good reason for that. Whatever reasons
lay in her past, she lived a small life and she was uncomfortably aware that she kept it that way through choice.

The *F* word loomed big in her world.

Not the curse. She wasn't the sort of person who cursed.
For her, the *F* word was *Fear*.

Fear of humiliation, fear of failing, fear of what other
people thought of her, and all those fears originated from
fear of her father.

She was tired of the *F* word.

She didn't want to live life alone, which was why she'd
decided that for Christmas she was giving herself a new gift.

Courage.

She didn't want to look back on her life in fifty years'
time and wonder about the things she might have done had
she been braver. She didn't want to feel regret. During a
happy Thanksgiving spent with Daniel and his soon-to-be
wife, Molly, she'd distilled her fear list to a challenge a day.

Challenge Harriet.

She was going on a quest to find the confidence that
eluded her and if she couldn't find it then she'd fake it.

For the month between Thanksgiving and Christmas, she
would do one thing every day that scared her, or at least
made her uncomfortable. It had to be something that made
her think *I don't want to do that*.

For one month, she would make a point of doing the opposite of what she would usually do.

A month of putting herself through her own kind of hell.

She was going to emerge from the challenge a new, improved version of herself. Stronger. Bolder. More confident. More—everything.

Which was why she was now hanging out of a bathroom window being supported by her new best friend Natalie. Luckily for her, the restaurant wasn't on the roof terrace.

"Take your shoes off," Natalie advised. "I'll drop them down to you."

"They'll impale me or knock me unconscious. It might be safer to keep them on my feet, Natalie." There were days when she questioned the benefits of being sensible, but right now she wasn't sure if it stopped her having fun or if it kept her alive.

"Call me Nat. If I'm helping you escape, we might as well drop the formalities. And you can't keep those shoes on your feet. You'll injure yourself when you land. And give me your purse."

Harriet clung to it. This was New York City. She would no more hand her purse to a stranger than she would walk naked through Central Park. It went against every instinct she had. She was the type of person who looked twice before she crossed the road, who checked the lock on her door before she went to sleep. She wasn't a risk-taker.

Which was exactly why she should do it.

Forcing down the side of her that wanted to clutch the purse to her chest and never let it go, she thrust it at Nat. "Take it. And drop it down to me." She eased one leg out of the window, ignoring the voice of anxiety that rang loud in her head. *What if she didn't? What if she ran off with it? Used all her credit cards? Stole her identity?*

If Nat wanted to steal her identity, she was welcome to it.

She was more than ready to be someone else. Particularly after the evening she'd just had.

Being herself wasn't working out so well.

Through the open window she could hear the roar of traffic, the cacophony of horns, the squealing of brakes, the background rumble that was New York City. Harriet had lived here all her life. She knew virtually every street and every building. Manhattan was as familiar to her as her own living room, if considerably larger.

Nat took her shoes from her. "Try not to rip your coat. Great coat, by the way. Love the color, Harriet."

"The coat is new. I bought it especially for this date because I had high hopes. Which proves that an optimistic nature can be a disadvantage."

"I think it's lovely to be optimistic. Optimists are like Christmas lights. They brighten everything around them. Are you really a twin? That's very cool."

Today's challenge had been *Don't be reserved with strangers*. She was fine when she got to know someone, but often she didn't even make it past those first excruciatingly awkward stages. She was determined to change that.

Given that she and Natalie had met precisely thirty minutes earlier when she'd served her a delicious-looking shrimp salad, she was satisfied she'd made at least some progress. She hadn't clammed up or responded in monosyllables as she frequently did with people she didn't know. Most important of all she hadn't stammered, which she took as evidence that she'd finally learned to control the speech fluency issues that had blighted her life until her twenties. It had been years now since she'd stumbled her way through a sentence and even stressful situations didn't seem to trigger it, so there was no excuse for being so cautious with strangers.

All in all, a good result. And part of that was down to the support of her sister.

"It is cool being a twin. Very cool."

Nat gave a wistful sigh. "She's your best friend, right? You share everything? Confidences. Shoes..."

"Most things." The truth was that, until recently, she'd been the one to do most of the sharing. Fliss found it hard to open up, even to Harriet, but lately she'd been trying hard to change.

And Harriet was trying to change too. She'd told her twin she didn't need protecting, and now she had to prove it to herself.

Being a twin had many advantages, but one of the disadvantages was that it made you lazy. Or maybe *complacent* would be a better word. She'd never had to worry too much about navigating the stormy waters of the friendship pool because her best friend had always been right there by her side. Whatever life had thrown at them, and it had thrown plenty, she and Fliss had been a unit. Other people had good friendships but nothing, *nothing*, came close to the wonder of having a twin.

When it came to sisters, she'd won the lottery.

Nat tucked Harriet's purse under her arm. "So you share an apartment?"

"We did. Not anymore." Harriet wondered how it was some people could talk and talk without stopping. How long before the man sitting inside the restaurant came looking for her? "She's living in the Hamptons now." Not a million miles away, but it might as well have been a million miles. "She fell in love."

"Great for her I guess, but you must miss her like crazy."

That was an understatement.

The impact on Harriet had been huge, and her emotions were conflicted. She was thrilled to see her twin so happy but, for the first time in her life, she was now living alone. Waking up alone. Doing everything alone.

At first it had felt strange and a little scary, like the first time you rode a bike without training wheels. It also made her feel a little vulnerable, like going out for a walk in a blizzard and realizing you'd left your coat behind.

But this was now the reality of her life.

She woke in the mornings to silence instead of Fliss's off-key singing. She missed her sister's energy, her fierce loyalty, her dependability. She even missed tripping over her shoes, which had been habitually strewn across the floor.

Most of all she missed the easy camaraderie of being with someone who knew you. Someone you trusted implicitly.

A lump formed in her throat. "I should go before he comes looking for me. I cannot believe I'm climbing out of a window to get away from a man I only met thirty minutes ago. This is not the kind of thing I do."

Neither was online dating, which was why she'd forced herself to try it.

This was her third date, and the other two had been almost as bad.

The first man had reminded her of her father. He'd been loud, opinionated and in love with the sound of his own voice. Overwhelmed, Harriet had retreated into herself, but in this instance it hadn't mattered because it had been clear he had no interest in her opinions. The second man had taken her to an expensive restaurant and then disappeared after dessert, leaving her with a check big enough to ensure she would always remember him, and as for the third—well, he was currently sitting at the table in the window waiting for her to return from the bathroom so they could fall in love and live happily ever after. And in his case "ever after" wasn't likely to be long because despite his claim that he was in his prime, it was clear he was already long past retirement age.

She would have called time on the date and walked out of the front door if she hadn't had a feeling he would follow her. Something about him made her feel uneasy. And anyway, climbing out of the window of a ladies' room was definitely something she would never do.

In terms of Challenge Harriet, it had been a successful evening.

In terms of romance, not so much.

Right now, dying surrounded by dogs and cats was looking like the better option.

"Go." Nat opened the window wider and her expression brightened. "It's snowing! We're going to have a white Christmas."

Snowing?

Harriet stared at the lazy swirl of snowflakes. "It's not Christmas for another month."

"But it's going to be a white Christmas, I feel it. There is nowhere more magical than New York in the snow. I love the holidays, don't you?"

Harriet opened her mouth and closed it again. Normally her answer would have been yes. She adored the holidays and the emphasis on family, even if hers was restricted to siblings. But this year she'd decided she was going to spend Christmas without them. And that was going to be the biggest challenge of all. She had the best part of a month of practice to build up to the big one.

"I really should be going."

"You should. I don't want your body to be discovered frozen to the sidewalk. Go. And don't fall in the Dumpster."

"Falling into the Dumpster would be a step up from everything else that has happened this evening." Harriet glanced down. It wasn't far and anyway, how much further could she fall? She felt as if she'd already hit rock bottom. "Maybe I should go back and explain that he wasn't what I was expecting. Then I could walk out the front door and not risk walking home with a twisted ankle and food wrappers stuck to my new coat."

"No." Nat shook her head. "Don't even think about it. The guy is creepy. I've told you, you're the third woman he's brought here this week. And there's something not quite right about the way he looked at you. As if you were going to be dessert."

She'd thought the same thing.

Her instincts had been shrieking at her, but part of Challenge Harriet was learning to ignore her instincts.

"It seems rude."

"This is New York. You have to be street-smart. I'm going to keep him distracted until you're a safe distance away." Nat glanced toward the door, as if she was afraid the man might burst in at any moment. "I couldn't believe it when he started calling you babycheeks. I have to ask this—why did you agree to meet him? What was it about him that attracted you? You're the third gorgeous woman he's brought here this week. Does he have some special quality? What made you agree to choose him?"

"I didn't choose him. I chose the guy in his online dating

profile. I suspect he may have reality issues." She thought back to the moment he'd sat down opposite her. He had so obviously *not* been the person in his profile that she'd smiled politely and told him she was waiting for someone.

Instead of apologizing and moving on, he'd sat down in the chair opposite her. "You must be Harriet? Dog lover, cake lover. I love an affectionate woman who knows her way around a kitchen. We're going to do just fine together."

That was the moment Harriet had known for sure she wasn't cut out for online dating.

Why, oh why had she used her real name? Fliss would have made something up. Probably something outrageous.

Nat looked fascinated. "What did his dating profile say?"

"That he was in his thirties." She thought of the thick shock of white hair and the wrinkled brow. The yellowed teeth and the graying fuzz on his jaw. But the worst thing had been the way he'd leered at her.

"Thirty? He must be at least twice that. Or maybe he's like a dog where each year is seven years. That would make him—" she wrinkled her nose "—two hundred and ten in human years. Jeez, that's old."

"He was sixty-eight," Harriet said. "He told me he feels thirty inside. And his profile said that he works in investment, but when I questioned that he confessed that he's investing his pension."

Nat doubled over laughing and Harriet shook her head. She felt weary. And stupid.

"After three dates, I've lost my sense of humor. That's it. I'm done."

All she wanted was fun and a little human company. Was that too much to ask?

"You decided to give love a chance. Nothing wrong

with that. But someone like you shouldn't struggle to meet people. What's your job? Don't you meet anyone through work?"

"I'm a dog walker. I spend my day with handsome, four-legged animals. They are always who you think they are. Although having said that I do walk a terrier who thinks he's a Rottweiler. That does create some issues."

Maybe she should stick with dogs.

She'd proved to herself that she could do the whole on-line dating thing if she had to. She'd ticked it off her list. It was victory of a sort.

Nat opened the window wider. "Report him to the dating site so he doesn't put any more unsuspecting women in the position of having to jump out the window. And look on the bright side. At least he didn't scam you out of your life savings." She checked the street. "You're clear."

"Nice meeting you, Nat. And thank you for everything."

"If a woman can't help another woman in trouble, where would we be? Come back soon."

Harriet felt a tug deep inside.

Friendship. That was perhaps the only *F* word she liked.

Feeling a flash of regret that she would never be going anywhere near this restaurant ever again, because she genuinely liked Natalie, Harriet held her breath and dropped onto the sidewalk.

She felt her ankle twist and a sharp, agonizing pain shot up her leg.

"You okay?" Nat dropped her shoes and her purse and Harriet winced as they thudded into her lap. It seemed that the only thing she was taking away from this date was bruises.

"Never better."

Victory, she thought, was both painful and undignified.

The window above her closed and Harriet was immediately aware of two things. First, that putting weight on her ankle was agony. Second, that unless she wanted to hobble home in bare feet, she was going to have to put on the stilettos she'd borrowed from the pile of shoes Fliss had left behind.

Gingerly, she slid the shoe onto her foot and sucked in a breath as pain shot through her ankle.

For the first time in her life she used the *F* word to express something other than fear.

Another box ticked in project Challenge Harriet.

CHAPTER TWO

ACROSS TOWN IN the trauma suite of one of New York's most prestigious hospitals, Dr. Ethan Black and the rest of the trauma team smoothly and efficiently cut away the ripped, bloodied clothing of the unconscious man to expose the damage beneath. And the damage was plenty. Enough to test the skills of the team and ensure that their patient would remember this night for the rest of his life.

As far as Ethan was concerned, motorcycles were one of the world's worst inventions. Certainly the worst mode of transport. Many of the patients brought in following motorcycle injuries were male, and a high proportion had multiple injuries. This man was no exception. He'd been wearing a helmet, but that hadn't prevented him from sustaining what looked like a severe head injury.

"Intubate him and get a line in—" He assessed the damage as he worked, issuing instructions.

The team was gathered around, finding coherence in something that to an outsider would have seemed like chaos.

Each person had a role, and each person was clear about what that role was. Of all the places in the hospital it was here, in the emergency room, that the teamwork was the strongest.

"He lost control and hit an oncoming car."

Screaming came from the corridor outside, followed by a torrent of abuse delivered at a high enough pitch to shatter windows.

One of the residents winced. Ethan didn't react. There were days when he wondered if he'd actually become desensitized to other people's responses to crisis. Working in the emergency room brought you into contact with the most extreme of human emotions and distorted your view of both humanity and reality. His normal would be someone else's horror movie. He'd learned early in his career not to talk about his day in a social situation unless the people present were all medical. These days he was too busy to find himself in too many social situations. Between his clinical responsibilities as attending physician in the emergency room and his research interests, his day was full. The price he'd paid for that was an apartment he rarely saw and an ex-wife.

"Is someone caring for the woman on the end of that scream?"

"She's not the patient. She just saw her boyfriend knifed. He's in Trauma 2 with multiple facial lacerations."

"Someone show her to the waiting room. Calm her down." Ethan took a closer look at the man's leg, assessing the damage. "Whatever it takes to stop the screaming."

"We don't know how serious the injuries are."

"All the more reason to project calm. Reassure her that her boyfriend is in good hands and getting the best treatment."

It was a typical Saturday night. Maybe he should have trained as an ob-gyn, Ethan thought as he continued to assess the patient. Then he would have been there for the high point of people's lives instead of the low. He would have facilitated birth, instead of fighting to prevent death. He could have celebrated with patients. Instead his Saturday night was invariably spent surrounded by people at crisis point. The victims of traffic accidents, gunshot victims, stabbings, drug addicts looking for a fix—the list was endless and varied.

And the truth was he loved it.

He loved variety and challenge. As a Level 1 Trauma Unit, they had both in copious amounts.

They stabilized the patient sufficiently to send him for a CT scan. Ethan knew that until they had the results of that scan, they wouldn't be able to assess the extent of his head injury.

He also knew that it was difficult to predict what the scan would show. He'd had patients with minimal visible damage who turned out to have massive internal bleeding and others, like this man as it later turned out, who had a surprisingly minor internal bleed.

He paged the neurosurgeons and spoke to the man's girl-friend, who had arrived in a panic, wearing a coat over her pajamas and terror in her eyes. In the emergency room everything was concentrated and intense, including emotions. He'd seen big guys who prided themselves on being tough, break down and sob like a child. He'd seen people pray when they didn't believe in God.

He'd seen it all.

"Is he going to die?"

He handled the same question several times a day, and

he was rarely in a position to give a definitive answer. "He is in good hands. We'll be able to give you more information when we see the results of the scan." He was kind and calm, reassuring her that whatever could be done was being done. He knew how important it was to know that the person you loved was receiving the very best care, so he took time to explain what was happening and to suggest she call someone to come and be with her.

When the man was finally handed over to the neurosurgical team, Ethan ripped off his gloves and washed his hands. He probably wouldn't see the patient again. The man was gone from his life, and he'd probably never know about the part Ethan had played in keeping him alive.

Later, he might check on his progress but more often than not he was too busy focusing on the next priority to come through the door to think about those been and gone.

Susan, his colleague, nudged him out of the way and stripped off her gloves too. "That was exciting. Are you ever tempted to take a job in primary care? You could live in a cute small town where you're caring for three generations of the same family. Grandma, Grandpa, parents and a big bunch of grandkids. You'd spend your day telling them to give up smoking and lose weight. Probably never see a drop of blood."

"It was what my father did." And Ethan had never wanted that. His choices were the focus of lively arguments whenever he was home. His grandfather kept telling him he was missing out by not following a family through from birth to death. Ethan argued that he was the one who kept them alive so that they could go back to their families.

"All these months we've worked together and I never

knew that about you." Susan scrubbed her hands. "So you come from two generations of doctors?"

They'd worked together for over a year but almost all their conversation had been about the present. The ER was like that. You lived in the moment in every sense.

"Three generations. My father and grandfather both worked in primary care. They had a practice in upstate New York." He'd sat, five years old, in the waiting room watching as a steady stream of people trooped through the door to speak to his dad. There had been times when he'd wondered if the only way to see his father was to get sick.

"And your mother?"

"She's a pediatrician."

"Jeez, Black, I had no idea. So it's in the DNA." Susan yanked a paper towel from the dispenser so vigorously she almost removed it from the wall. "Well, that explains it."

"That explains what?"

"Why you always act like you have something to prove."

Ethan frowned. Was that true? No. It certainly wasn't true. "I don't have anything to prove."

"You've got a lot to live up to." She gave him a sympathetic look. "Why didn't you join them? Doctors Black, Black and Black. That's one hell of a lot of Black right there. Don't tell me, you just love the warm fuzzy feelings that come from working in the emergency room." Through the door they heard the woman yell *fuck you* and exchanged a wry smile. "All those cute patients enveloping you with endless love and gratitude—"

"Gratitude? Wait—I think that did happen to me once, a couple of years ago. Give me a moment while I cast my mind back."

He didn't feel as if he had to live up to anything.

Susan was wrong about that. He walked his own path, for his own reasons.

"You must have been hallucinating. Lack of sleep does that for you. So if the rare dose of gratitude isn't what does it, it must be the patients who curse you, throw up on your boots and tell you you're the worst doctor that ever graced god's earth and that they're going to sue the hell out of you. That works for you?"

The humor got them through days that were fraught with tension.

It sustained them through the darker shifts, through witnessing trauma that would leave the average man on the street in need of therapy.

Everyone in the trauma team found their own way of dealing with it.

They knew, as most people didn't, that a life could change in an instant. That there was no such thing as a secure future.

"I love that side of it. And then there's the constant buzz of working with adoring, respectful colleagues like you."

"You want adoring? Pick a different woman."

"I wish I could."

Susan patted his arm. "In fact I do adore you. Not because you're cute and built, although you are, but because you know what you're doing and around here competence is as close as it gets to an aphrodisiac. And maybe that's driven by a desire to be better than your daddy or your granddaddy, but I love it all the same."

He shot her an incredulous look. "Are you hitting on me?"

"Hey, I want to be with a man who is good with his hands and who knows what he's doing. What's wrong with that?" Her eyes twinkled and he knew she was winding him up.

"We are still talking about work?"

"Sure. What else? I'm married to my job, same as you. I promised myself to the ER in sickness and in health, for richer and for poorer and I can tell you that living in New York City the emphasis is definitely on poorer. But don't worry—I wouldn't be able to stay awake long enough to have sex with you. When I leave this place I fall unconscious the moment I arrive home and I'm not waking up for anyone. Not even you, blue eyes. So if you're not here for the love and positive feedback, it has to be because you're an adrenaline junkie."

"Maybe I am." It was true that he enjoyed the fast pace, the unpredictability, the adrenaline rush that came with not knowing what would come through the doors next. Emergency medicine was often like a puzzle and he enjoyed the intellectual stimulation of figuring out where the pieces fit and what the picture was. He also enjoyed helping people, although these days the doctor-patient relationship had changed. Now it was all patient satisfaction scores and other metrics that appeared to have little to do with practicing good medicine. There were days when it was hard to stay in touch with the reasons he'd wanted to be a doctor in the first place.

Susan stuffed the towel into the bin. "Know what I love most? When someone comes in all bandaged up and you never know what you're going to find when you unwrap it. Man, I love the suspense. Will it be a cut the size of a pinhead or will the finger fall off?"

"You're ghoulish, Parker."

"I am. Are you telling me you don't like that part?"

"I like fixing people." He glanced up as one of the interns walked into the room. "Problems?"

"Where do you want me to start? There are around sixty of them currently waiting, most of them drunk. We have a guy who fell off the table during his office party and hurt his back."

Ethan frowned. "It's not even December."

"They celebrate early. I don't think he needs an MRI but he's consulted Dr. Search Engine and is insisting on having one and if I don't arrange it he is going to sue me for every cent I'm worth. Do you think it would put him off if I tell him the size of my college loans?"

Susan waved a hand. "Ethan will handle it. He's great at steering people toward the right decision. And if that doesn't work he's good at playing Bad Cop."

Ethan raised an eyebrow. "Bad Cop? Seriously?"

"Hey, it's a compliment. Not many patients get one past you."

Backache, headache, toothache—all commonly appeared in the department, along with demands for prescription pain meds. Most of the experienced staff could sense when they were being played, but for less experienced staff it was a constant challenge to maintain the right balance between compassion and suspicion.

Still pondering the Bad Cop label, Ethan walked to the door but his progress toward the patient was interrupted by the arrival of another patient, this time a forty-year-old man who had suffered chest pains at work and a cardiac arrest in the ambulance. As a result, it was another thirty minutes before Ethan made it to the man with the back injury, by which time the atmosphere in the room was hostile.

"Finally!" The man stank of alcohol. "I've been waiting ages to see someone."

Alcohol and fear. They saw plenty of both in the emergency room. It was a toxic mix.

Ethan checked the records. "It says here that you were seen within ten minutes of arriving in the department, Mr. Rice."

"By a nurse. That doesn't count. And then by an intern, and he knew less than I do."

"The nurse who saw you is experienced."

"You're the one in charge so it's you I want, but you took your sweet time."

"We had an emergency, Mr. Rice."

"You're saying I'm not an emergency? I was here first! What makes him more important than me?"

The fact that he'd been clinically dead on arrival?

"How can I help you, Mr. Rice?" He kept it calm, always calm, knowing that in an already tense environment a situation could escalate with supersonic speed. The one thing they didn't need in the department was a bigger dose of tension.

"I want a fucking MRI," the man slurred. "And I want it now, not in ten years' time. Do it, or I'll sue you."

It was an all-too-familiar scenario. Patients who had looked up their symptoms on the internet and were convinced they knew not only the diagnosis but every investigation that should be performed. There was nothing worse than an amateur who thought he was an expert.

And the threats and the abuse were just two of the reasons emergency room staff had a high burnout rate. You had to learn to handle it, or it would wear you down like the ocean wore away at rocks until they crumbled.

In the crazy period between Thanksgiving and Christmas, it was only going to get worse.

Anyone who thought it was the season of goodwill, should have spent a day working with Ethan. His head was throbbing.

If he'd been one of his patients, he would have demanded a CAT scan.

"Dr. Black?" One of the residents hovered in the doorway and Ethan gave him a quick nod, indicating he'd be there as soon as he could.

As attending physician, everyone looked to him for answers. Residents, interns, ancillary staff, nurses, pharmacists, patients. He was expected to know it all.

Right now all he knew was that he wanted to get home. It had been a long, miserable shift and that didn't seem likely to change anytime soon.

He examined the man thoroughly and explained calmly and clearly why an MRI wasn't necessary.

That went down as well as he'd thought it would.

Some doctors ran the tests because at least then the patient left happy. Ethan refused to do that.

As he listened to a tirade describing him as inhuman, incompetent and a disgrace to the medical profession, he switched off. Switching off his emotions was the easy part for him now. Switching them back on again—well, that was more of a challenge, a fact borne out by his disastrous relationship record.

He let the abuse flow over him, but didn't budge in his decision. He'd decided a long time before that he wasn't going to let his decision-making be ruled by bullying or patient satisfaction scores. He did what was best for his patients, and that didn't include subjecting them to unnecessary testing or drugs that would have no impact or, worse, a negative impact on their condition.

"Dr. Black?" Tony Roberts, one of the most senior pediatricians in the hospital, was standing in the doorway. "I need your help urgently."

Ethan issued instructions to the resident caring for the patient and excused himself.

"What's the problem, Tony? You have an emergency?"

"I do." Tony looked serious. "Tell me, do you believe in Santa Claus?"

"Excuse me?" Ethan gave him an incredulous look and then laughed. "If Santa existed, he'd probably threaten me for pointing out that not only should he lose a few pounds for the good of his health, but that if he intends to ride in a horse-drawn vehicle at an altitude in excess of thirty thousand feet he should probably be wearing a safety helmet. Or at least leathers."

"Santa in leather? Mmm, me likey," Susan murmured as she passed on her way to speak to the triage nurse.

Tony grinned. "Just the cynical answer I expected from you, Black, which is why I'm here. I am going to give you an opportunity you never thought would come your way."

"A year's sabbatical in Hawaii on full pay?"

"Better. I'm going to change your life." Tony slapped him on the shoulder and Ethan wondered if he should point out that after a shift in the ER it wouldn't take much to knock him flat.

"If I don't get to the next patient fast, my life will be changed. I'll be fighting a lawsuit. Can we make this quick, Tony?"

"You know Santa visits the children's ward every Christmas?"

"I didn't, but I do now. That's great. I'm sure the kids love it." It was a world far removed from the one he inhabited.

"They do. Santa is—" Tony glanced around and lowered his voice. "Santa is actually Rob Baxter, one of the pediatricians."

"No kidding. And I thought he was real." Ethan signed a request that an intern thrust under his nose. "That's the last of my illusions shattered. You have broken my heart. I might have to go home and lie down."

"Forget it." Susan was passing again, this time in the other direction. "No one lies down in this place. Unless they're dead. When you're dead, you get to lie down and only after we've tried to resuscitate you."

Tony watched her go. "Is she always like this?"

"Yes. Comedy is all part of the service. Laughter cures all ills, hadn't you heard? What did you want, Tony? I thought you said it was an emergency."

"It is. Rob Baxter ruptured his Achilles running in Central Park. He's going to be off his feet until after Christmas. This is close to a crisis for the pediatric department, but even more of a crisis because he is Santa and we don't have a backup."

"Why are you telling me this? You want me to take a look at his Achilles? Ask Viola. She's a brilliant surgeon."

"I don't need a surgeon. I need a backup Santa."

Ethan looked at him blankly. "I don't know any Santas."

"Santas are made, not born." Tony lowered his voice. "We want you to be Santa this year. Will you do it?"

"Me?" Ethan wondered if he'd misheard. "I'm not a pediatrician."

Tony leaned closer. "You may not know this, but Santa doesn't actually have to operate or make any clinical decisions. He smiles and hands out presents."

"Sounds like my average working day," Ethan said, "only

here they want you to hand out MRIs and prescription pain meds. Gift-wrapped Vicodin is this year's must-have."

"You are cynical and jaded."

"I'm a realist, which is precisely why I'm not qualified to deal with wide-eyed children who still believe in Santa."

"Which is exactly why you should do it. It will remind you of all the reasons you went into medicine in the first place. Your heart will melt, Dr. Scrooge."

"He doesn't have a heart," Susan muttered, eavesdropping shamelessly.

Ethan glanced at her in exasperation. "Don't you have patients to see? Lives to save?"

"Just hanging around to hear your answer, boss. If you're going from Scrooge to Santa, I need to know about it. In fact, I want to be there to watch. I'd work Christmas just to see it."

"You're already working Christmas. And I'm not qualified to be Santa. Why would you think I'd agree to this?"

Tony looked at him thoughtfully. "You get to make a child's day. It doesn't get any better than that. Think about it. I'll call you in a week or so. It's an easy and rewarding job." He strode out of the department, leaving Ethan staring after him.

"Dr. Scrooge," Susan said. "How cute is that."

"Not cute at all." Surely Tony couldn't be serious? He was the last person in the world who should play Santa with wide-eyed believing children.

He noticed one of the interns hovering. "Problems?"

"Young woman with an ankle injury. Badly swollen and bruised. I'm not sure whether to x-ray or not. Dr. Marshall is busy or I would have asked him."

"Is she on the hunt for Vicodin?"

"I think she's genuine."

Because Ethan knew the young doctor didn't have the experience to know if someone was genuine or not, he followed him through the department. Vicodin was an effective painkiller. It was also a commonly used recreational drug, and he'd ceased to be surprised at the lengths some people would go to get a prescription. He didn't want anyone dispensing strong painkillers to someone who was simply hoping to get high from Vicodin.

His first thought when he saw her was that she was out of place among the rainbow of humanity that decorated the halls of the emergency room on a Saturday night. Her hair was long, and the color of creamy buttermilk. Her features were delicate and her mouth was a curve of glossy pink. She was wearing one shoe with a heel so high it could have doubled as a weapon. The other she held in her hand.

Her ankle was already turning blue.

How did women expect to wear heels like that and not damage themselves? That shoe was an accident waiting to happen. And although she seemed normal enough, he knew better than to let appearances dull his radar for trouble. A few years before, a student had presented with toothache, which had turned out to be a way to get pain meds. She'd overdosed a few days later and been brought into the emergency room.

Ethan had been present for her second visit, although not her first. It was a lesson he'd never forgotten.

"Miss Knight? I'm Dr. Black. Can you tell me what happened?"

It must have been a great party, he thought as he examined the ankle.

"I twisted it. I'm sorry to bother you when you're so

busy." She sounded more than a little embarrassed, which made a change from the two patients he'd seen immediately before her, who had taken his care as their God-given right.

He wondered what she was doing here on her own on a Saturday night. She was all dressed up, so he doubted she'd spent the evening on her own.

He guessed she was mid to late twenties. Thirty possibly, although she had one of those faces that was difficult to put an age to. With makeup she could look a little older. Without, she could pass as a college student. Her eyes were blue and her gaze warm and friendly, which made a refreshing change.

Generally speaking, he didn't see a lot of warm and friendly during his working day.

"How did you twist it?" Understanding the mechanism of the injury was one of the most helpful ways of piecing together a picture of the injury. "Dancing?"

"No. Not dancing. I wasn't wearing shoes when I twisted it."

He watched in fascination as her cheeks reddened.

It had been a while since he'd seen anyone blush.

"So how did you do it?" Realizing she might think he was after details for his own entertainment, he clarified. "The more details you give me, the easier it is for me to assess the injury."

"I jumped from a window. It wasn't far to the ground but I landed awkwardly and my ankle turned."

She'd jumped from a window?

"You're a bit of a risk-taker?"

She gave a wry smile. "My idea of risk is reading my Kindle in the bath so no, I don't think I'd describe myself as a risk-taker."

Ethan's senses were back on alert. Instead of thinking possible addict, or potential adrenaline junkie, he was thinking possible abuse victim. "So why did you jump?" He softened his tone, trying to convey with his voice and actions that he could be trusted.

"I needed to get away from someone." She must have seen something change in his expression because she shook her head quickly. "I can see what you're thinking, but I wasn't being threatened. It really was an accident."

"Jumping from a window isn't usually an accident." Unless she was intoxicated, but he didn't smell alcohol and she seemed perfectly composed. More composed than most of the people around her. The ER on a Saturday night wasn't a pretty sight. "Why not leave by the front door?"

Her gaze slid from his. "It's a long story."

And one she obviously didn't intend to share.

Ethan thought through his options. They saw plenty of domestic abuse incidents in the ER, and they had a duty to offer a place of safety and whatever support was needed. But he'd also learned that not everyone wanted to be helped. That it was a process. "Miss Knight—"

"You don't need to worry. I was on a date, if you must know, and it wasn't going well. My mistake."

"You jumped to get away from your date?"

She stared at a point beyond his shoulder. "He wasn't exactly the way his profile described him."

"You'd never met him before?" And now he was thinking trafficking. And maybe he'd been wrong about her age and she was closer to twenty than thirty.

He checked the form and saw from her date of birth that his first guess had been the correct one. She was twenty-nine.

"I was trying online dating. It didn't go quite the way I

thought it would. Oh, this is so embarrassing." She rubbed her fingers over her forehead. "He lied on his profile, and I didn't even realize people did that. Which makes me stupid, I know. And naive. And yes, maybe it also makes me a risk-taker, even if I'm an unintentional risk-taker. And I'm horribly bad at it."

He was still focused on her first words. "Lied?"

"He used a photo from thirty years ago and claimed to be all kinds of things he wasn't." She squared her shoulders. "I found him a little creepy. I had a bad feeling about the whole thing so I decided to make an exit where he couldn't see me. I didn't want him to follow me home. You don't need to hear this, do you?" She leaned down to rub her ankle and her hair slid forward, obscuring her features.

For a moment he stared at it, that curtain of shiny gold.

He breathed in a waft of her perfume. Floral. Subtle. So subtle he wondered if what he was smelling was her shampoo.

He never became emotionally involved with his patients. These days he didn't become emotionally involved in anything much, but for some reason he felt a spurt of anger toward the nameless guy who had lied to this woman.

"Why the window?" He dragged his gaze from her hair and focused on her ankle, examining it carefully. "Why not go out through the front door? Or even the kitchen or the rear entrance?"

"The kitchen was in sight of our table. I was worried he'd follow me. And to be honest I wasn't thinking about much except getting away. Pathetic, I know. Is it broken?"

"It doesn't seem to be." Ethan straightened. The injury was real enough. Her hurt was real enough, and he suspected it extended a whole lot further than a bruised ankle.

"I don't think you need an X-ray, but if it gets worse you should come back or contact your primary care provider."

He waited for her to argue with him about the need for an X-ray, but she simply nodded.

"Good. Thank you."

It was such an unusual response he repeated himself to check she'd heard him correctly. "I don't think an X-ray is necessary."

"I understand. I probably shouldn't have wasted your time, but I didn't want to make it worse by doing something I shouldn't. I'm grateful to you, and I'm relieved it isn't broken."

She was accepting his professional judgment just like that?

No arguing? No cursing? No questioning him or threatening to sue him?

"You can use whatever pain meds you have in your cabinet at home."

This was the point where a large proportion of his patients demanded something only available on prescription.

Or maybe he really was turning into a cynic.

Maybe he needed a vacation.

He had one coming, the week before Christmas. A week in a luxury cabin in Vermont.

He met up every year with family and friends and this year he needed the break more than ever. He loved his job but the relentlessness and the pressure took its toll.

"I don't need pain meds. I wanted to check it isn't broken, that's all. I walk a lot in my job." She gave him a sweet smile that fused his brain.

In his time in the ER he'd dealt with panic, hysteria,

abuse and shock. He was comfortable with all those emotional reactions. He even understood them.

He had no idea how to respond to a smile like hers.

She struggled to her feet and he had to stop himself from reaching out to help her.

"What's your job?" The question had clinical relevance. Nothing to do with the fact that he wanted to know more about her.

"I run a dog-walking business. I need to be able to get around and I don't want to make it worse."

A dog-walking business.

He looked at the freckles that dusted her nose.

He could imagine her walking dogs. And believing in Santa.

"If dog walking is your livelihood, you might want to steer clear of stilettos in the future."

"Yes, it was a stupid idea. A whim. I've been trying to do things I don't normally do, and—" She broke off and shook her head. "You don't need to hear this. You're busy and I'm taking up your time. Thank you for everything."

This one patient had thanked him more in the past five minutes than he'd been thanked in the past five weeks from all his other patients combined.

Not only that, but she hadn't questioned his clinical judgment.

Ethan, who was never surprised by a patient, was surprised.

And intrigued.

He wanted to ask why she'd been trying to do things she wouldn't normally do. Why she'd chosen to wear stilettos. *Why she'd had dinner with a man she'd met online.*

Instead he kept it professional. He talked to her about

rest, ice, compression and elevation, the whole time feeling guilty that he'd doubted her.

He wondered when, exactly, he'd started being so suspicious of human nature.

He definitely needed a vacation.

CHAPTER THREE

"IT WAS THE worst evening of my life. I need a do-over." Harriet eased her injured ankle onto the sofa as she talked to her sister on the phone. "And to cap it all I ended up in the emergency room, where Dr. Hot-but-Disapproving obviously decided I was a hooker." She could still see the wary look on his face, as if he wasn't sure whether her career choice was entirely savory.

On days when she had her arms full of slobbery dogs, she wondered that herself.

"He was hot? Tell me more."

"Seriously? I tell you I met up with creepy stalker guy and jumped from a window into a Dumpster and the only part you want to talk about is the doctor in the emergency room?"

"If he was hot, yes. Did you ask him on a date?"

For someone who claimed not to be interested in romance, her twin thought a lot about men.

"No, I did not ask him on a date."

"I thought you were trying to challenge yourself."

"I have limits. Hitting on a doctor who is treating me in the emergency room is one of them."

"You should have grabbed him and landed a smacker on his lips."

Harriet imagined the horror on his face. "And then I would have been calling you from a cell where the NYPD locked me up overnight for assault. Wait—are you *laughing*?"

"Maybe. A little." Fliss choked. "Is there footage of the whole window episode? I'd love to see it."

"I hope there isn't, because it's not something I want to relive." The painful throb of her ankle was all the reminder she needed. That and the steady hum of embarrassment that grew louder whenever she thought back to that moment in the hospital.

"I'm proud of you!"

"Why?"

"Because it's *so* not you."

"That much is true." Harriet wiggled her ankle and wondered how long it would take for the swelling to subside. The last thing she needed in her job was any injury that inhibited her walking. "It's the last time I take Molly's advice on anything. She was the one who told me to try online dating."

"It was great advice. She's a relationship expert. She knows everything."

Harriet thought about the three dates she'd endured recently. "Not everything."

"She tamed our untamable brother. That proves she knows everything."

"It's not the best approach for someone who has a problem with strangers. I'm not at my best when I don't know people."

"If you can't walk, how will you manage with the business?"

"I'm reassigning my walks for the next two days."

"Do you need me to make some calls?"

"No, I've done them."

"Dog walkers and clients?"

"All done."

"Even Mrs. Langdon?"

Ella Langdon was the editor of a major glossy magazine and she was terrifying to deal with. Before calling her, Harriet had to give herself a talking-to.

"Even Mrs. Langdon. She used her disapproving voice but on the whole the call wasn't a total nightmare." And she hadn't stuttered. Which was the most important thing. Although it hadn't happened in a long while, she still lived in fear that it would happen when she least wanted it to. As a child her stammer had alienated her from those around her. Without her twin, she wasn't sure how she would have survived.

"I'm impressed. It's like talking to a whole new Harriet. And as soon as your ankle is healed you'll be out there dating again."

"I don't think so. Internet dating is not for me. And why would it be? How are you supposed to find someone you like from a brief character sketch? And people present the things they want you to see. It's all so *fake*." And she hated that. What was the point? If you couldn't be honest with another person for two hours, how did you stand a hope of making it through forty or fifty years together? Maybe she was being unrealistic expecting a relationship to last forever. Maybe she was horribly old-fashioned.

Her morale was at rock bottom. A few months ago she

would have shared that fact with her sister, but now she kept it to herself. There was an ache behind her ribs. She wasn't sure if it was indigestion or a concentration of feelings she didn't know what to do with. "Anyway, it's irrelevant because I won't be going anywhere for the next few days. How are things in the Hamptons? How is Grams? Seth?"

"Things are good. Grams is busy with her friends—you know what she's like. She has a more active social life than anyone I know. And Seth is often working, but so am I. Walking on the beach is bliss, and there is so much more business here than I ever imagined."

And when it came to finding business, Fliss had a nose like a terrier.

"Without you the Bark Rangers wouldn't exist."

"Hey, I might have set the thing up but you keep it rolling. Clients love you. Dogs love you." Fliss paused. "Are you sure you won't spend Christmas with us? I haven't spent Christmas without you for my whole life. I'm going to miss you so much. It's going to be weird."

"It will be lovely." *Now who was being fake?* "You'll be with Seth's family."

"But you're invited too. I wish you would come."

Harriet thought about spending Christmas with a bunch of people she didn't know. Fliss would feel obliged to keep an eye on her. It would be excruciating. And anyway this, she'd decided, would be the biggest challenge of all. Christmas without her twin. It was like cutting the umbilical cord. If she could survive this, she could survive anything. It would be confidence building.

Providing she survived.

"I want to stay in the city. I love Manhattan at Christmas." That much was true. It was her favorite time of year to be walking around the city. She lingered by store windows and watched people stagger along Fifth Avenue weighed down by bags and gifts. "They're forecasting more snow. It will be magical. I *love* snow, although knowing my luck, I'll probably slip and sprain my other ankle."

"You might see Dr. Hot again."

"And if that happened he'd probably be thinking *why can't this woman learn to walk.*"

She'd thought about him a lot since that night. He'd had the most intense blue eyes. Tired blue eyes. She couldn't begin to imagine how much stamina it took to do his job, to deal with the heaving mass of people in the waiting room and the life-and-death emergencies that were brought in with a fanfare of discordant sirens and flashing lights.

While sitting in the waiting room, she'd had plenty of time to watch him in action.

She'd noticed other staff stopping him to ask him questions, but she'd also noticed that he'd taken the time to talk to an old lady who had appeared lost and confused.

It had seemed to her in that brief moment of watching that he was everything to everybody.

The last thing he needed was a second visit from her.

By the time she ended the call with her sister it was dark outside.

The apartment felt emptier and quieter than ever.

"Christmas never used to be my best time of year when I was growing up." She tipped food into the bowl for Teddy, the dachshund she was fostering for the local animal shelter. She loved dachshunds. They were lively and playful and unusually devoted. She adored Teddy's affectionate nature, his silliness and the way he burrowed under her bedcovers. She even loved the way he stubbornly refused to go outdoors when it was raining. "You know how some people love it? It's their favorite holiday and they can't wait for it to come around. They start decorating right after Thanksgiving and they love everything that goes with it. That's not me. Growing up, I always dreaded it. Do you have any idea what school is like for people who can't sing or talk fluently? Nightmare. Instead of daily humiliation among the small group of people I mixed with, I had giant public humiliation. Worst of all was the year I had to sing 'Silent Night' as a solo. It should have been renamed Stammering Night."

Teddy put his ears forward and tilted his head, sympathizing.

The great thing about dogs, Harriet thought, was that they always sympathized. It didn't matter what the problem was. Teddy might not understand the words, but Harriet knew he understood the sentiment. She'd often wondered how it was that dogs could be so much more sensitive than humans.

"It wasn't everyone. Mostly it was Johnny Hill. He was captain of the football team and he made my life hell."

Teddy thrust his nose into her palm and gave her a comforting lick.

"Fliss punched him. She had to have eight stitches in her head and she was suspended for a while. She was always protecting me. Which was great, but I guess it stopped me learning to do it for myself."

Teddy whined.

"Tomorrow you'll be going to your forever home." She stroked his silky fur, telling herself it was for the best. For Teddy, at least. "And that's fine. I'm good with that, I really am. I just want what's best for you and this is definitely what's best for you."

Teddy put his head in her lap, looking sorrowful. She

could almost convince herself he understood every word she was saying.

"You're going to be the perfect Christmas gift for them. The family has a weekend home upstate with forty-two acres. Imagine what you can do with that after living here with me. You won't have to pee on the same tree twice. You'll be able to dig, and we both know how much you love digging. And I'm going to be fine. After a day or two, I won't even notice you're not here."

She was even lying to the dog now.

What was wrong with her?

Teddy looked at her and she dropped to her knees, wincing as pain shot through her ankle.

"Give me a hug, you lovely thing."

Teddy launched himself at her chest and she cuddled him, comforted by the warmth of his body. The people adopting Teddy were one lucky family.

"The doctor said I need to ice my ankle. Fancy watching some TV on the sofa? How about *Gilmore Girls*?"

Teddy wagged his tail.

One day, Harriet thought as she limped to the sofa with him in her arms, she was going to snuggle on the sofa with someone who didn't have four legs and a wagging tail. Someone as caring and sympathetic as a dog, but with more physical appeal.

Maybe even a gorgeous doctor with blue eyes.

She rolled her eyes. Why did she keep thinking about him? He'd had physical appeal, that was undeniable. But there had been something remote and inaccessible about him, as if he'd drawn a barrier between himself and his patients.

Hot he might be, but he wasn't her type at all.

A FEW DAYS later Ethan was woken by his phone.

He reached out to grab it and knocked it on the floor.

Emitting curses learned from years in the ER, he retrieved it from under the table and answered it.

"Black."

"Ethan?"

"Debra?" Recognizing his sister's voice, he tried to force himself awake. "Everything all right?"

"No." Her voice sounded thickened. "There's been an accident."

"Who? Where?" He sat up, still in that state of disorientation that followed being woken from deep sleep.

"It's Karen. She's been hit by a car."

"What?" Ethan stood up, fully awake now. He was used to delivering bad news. Less accustomed to receiving it. His niece, Karen, was in her first year of college in California and had been having a great time. He adored her, probably because he'd long since accepted that he was unlikely to have children of his own. His sister was ten years older and the birth of her daughter, Karen, when he was sixteen years old had been a highlight. In some ways he was more like an older brother to her than an uncle. "What's her condition? Do you want me to call the hospital and talk to the medical team?"

"I've already spoken with them. They're discharging soon but she won't be able to put weight on her leg for a couple of weeks. Mark is still in the Far East. He'll fly straight to San Francisco but it will take him a long time to get there. I need to leave today. I've booked a flight for this afternoon."

Ethan glanced at the time. "I'll come with you."

"You can't do that. You'll be working."

It was true. "Family is more important. I'm coming. I'll

make it work." He tried not to think about the colleagues he'd be letting down or the research work that was waiting for him. If his sister needed him, she needed him. As far as he was concerned, that was the end of it.

"I can do this on my own, but you have no idea what it means to me that you offered."

"Debra—"

"No. I mean it. I can do this."

"If you don't want me to come with you, what can I do? There has to be something."

There was a pause. "Is that a genuine offer?"

"Of course." Ethan checked the time and decided it wasn't worth going back to sleep again. "What do you need?"

"I need you to take Madi for a few days. Maybe more than a few days. It could be a week or more before we're home."

"Madi?" It took Ethan a moment to work out who she was talking about. His sister only had one child. "You mean the dog?"

"I suppose Madi is a dog, although we think of her more as one of the family. She has remarkably human charac-teristics."

"You want me to look after the dog?" Ethan jammed his fingers into his hair. "No. Just—no, Debs."

"You said you'd help. You said 'anything.'"

"Anything but that!"

"You were willing to fly to California, but you won't take my dog?! This is so much easier."

"Not for me. I'm out of this apartment twenty hours out of twenty-four."

"All the more reason to have Madi for a week or two. She will give you something to come home to."

Ethan had a strong suspicion she'd give him a few things to come home to, none of which would be welcome.

"There's a reason I don't own a dog, Deb. And that reason is that I'm not in a position to give an animal the care and attention it deserves."

"This is an emergency. I wouldn't be asking otherwise. I don't know how long I'll be on the West Coast. Karen needs me—" her voice wobbled "—please, Ethan. I promise Madi will be no trouble at all."

It was the wobble in her voice that did it.

He couldn't remember ever seeing his big sister cry. Not even when he'd put a frog in her backpack when she was twelve.

He felt himself weaken. *Dammit.* "Why can't you put it in doggy day care? Or overnight care—a dog hotel—whatever it is people do with their pets."

What did people do with their pets? It wasn't something he'd ever thought about.

"We tried that for a night when Mark won that award and had to go to Chicago. We made a weekend of it and put her in overnight boarding, but Madi almost scratched her fur out she was so stressed. Now we make a point of going places where we can take her with us. She'd be so much happier with human company."

Not if the human was him. "I'm not great company after a day in the ER. I think I have what they call compassion fatigue."

"She doesn't need compassion. All she needs is food, walks and occasional company. I want to keep her routine as close to normal as possible so I'm going to continue with the dog walker while I'm away."

"Dog walker?"

"I use a company called the Bark Rangers. They cover the whole of the East Side of Manhattan so they won't have any problems coming to your apartment instead of mine. Easy. And she's a lovely girl."

"Who is a lovely girl?"

"Harriet. My dog walker. Actually I don't suppose *girl* is the right word. She must be late twenties."

He didn't care how old she was. "So she walks the dog for one hour a day—"

"Two. She'll come twice."

"Two hours a day. What happens to the dog for the other twenty-two hours?"

"Will you stop calling her 'the dog'? You're going to hurt her feelings."

"Yet another reason not to leave her with your cold unfeeling brother. If she's that sensitive, you don't want to leave her with someone as insensitive as me."

"You're a doctor. You're not insensitive."

"I have it on expert authority that I'm insensitive."

"If this is about your ex-wife—"

"Her name is Alison, we are on excellent terms and her comment was entirely justified. I *am* insensitive. And I know nothing about dogs."

"It's not complicated, Ethan. You feed them, you walk them. If you could bring yourself to talk to her, she'd probably appreciate that too."

"And what's she going to do the rest of the time?"

"She will happily sleep in her crate."

Ethan glanced round his apartment. Nothing had been moved since the cleaning service had been there two days previously. Mostly because he hadn't been here, either. One way to ensure you didn't make a mess of your home was to never be in it. "Are you sure that's what she'll do?"

"Yes. And if you do this it will stop Karen worrying. Madi is her dog." His sister, sensing weakness, pounced. "The whole family thanks you."

Ethan knew he was beaten. And truthfully he was too worried about his niece to dwell on the practicalities of caring for a dog. "Call me with an update as soon as you get there. And if you're not happy with what they've told her at the hospital let me know and I'll make some calls. I know a few people around there."

"You know everyone."

"We meet at medical conferences. It's a surprisingly small world. What time will you be dropping off this dog?"

"On my way to the airport. I'll walk her before I leave her with you, and we need to arrange for Harriet to meet you later. When works for you?"

None of it worked for him.

"Tonight? I'll try and get away early."

"Good. I'll give her my key to your apartment in case you're late, then she can go ahead and walk Madi. Practice saying her name, Ethan. Madi. Not 'the dog.' Madi."

"I need to go. I have two hours to dogproof—sorry, I mean Madi-proof—my home."

"You won't need to. She's very civilized."

"She's a dog."

"You're going to love her."

Ethan doubted it. Life, he knew, was rarely that simple.

CHAPTER FOUR

"MRS. SULLIVAN?" HARRIET paused in the doorway of the apartment, the key in her hand, an array of bags at her feet. Her ankle throbbed, but not as much as it had a few days earlier. Hopefully that was a good sign. "It's me! Harriet. Are you there? You didn't answer the door and I didn't want to make you jump."

"Harriet?" Glenys Sullivan appeared in the doorway of the kitchen, holding tightly to a walker. "Harvey and I were worried about you, sweetheart. You're late."

"I'm moving a little slower today." Harriet closed the door. She was worried about Glenys too. She'd lost weight since her husband had died ten months earlier and Harriet knew she was struggling. As a result she'd taken to dropping in whenever she was passing. And if sometimes "passing" meant taking a detour, that was fine with her. She didn't often see her clients once the dog-walking arrangements were confirmed, so she enjoyed the interaction. "I took a bit of a tumble a few days ago and I've been off my feet. Silly me."

Glenys had lived in the same sunny apartment on the Upper East Side for almost five decades, surrounded by her books, her furniture and her collection of china dogs.

"You fell? Is it icy out there?"

"Not yet, but it's coming. They're forecasting snow and my fingers are freezing. I need to find my gloves." Harriet carried the bags through to the kitchen, ignoring the pain in her ankle. She'd rested it for a couple of days, icing it as the doctor had instructed. It still hurt but she was tired of being trapped in her apartment and she'd wanted to check on Glenys. "I didn't want you to find yourself with an empty fridge. It's crazy out there. People are clearing the shelves and we've had around four snowflakes so far." She bent to make a fuss over Harvey, an eight-year-old West Highland terrier she'd been walking for two years. Often she handed walks to their reliable team of dog walkers, but there were a few she did herself and Harvey was one of them. He was sweet-tempered and smart. Harriet adored him.

"I remember the storm of 2006, we had twenty-eight inches of snow, but even that wasn't as bad as the blizzard of 1888."

Harriet straightened. "You weren't alive in 1888, Glenys."

"My great-grandmother used to talk about it. The railroads were blocked by drifts. Some of the commuters were trapped for days. You could walk across the East River from Brooklyn to Manhattan. Can you imagine that?"

"No. Hopefully it's not going to be that bad this time, but if it is you're not going to starve." Harriet pushed the last of the canned food into the cupboard. "Did you eat lunch today?"

"I ate a big lunch."

"Are you telling me the truth?"

"No, but I don't want to worry you. Truth is, I wasn't hungry."

Harriet made a tutting sound. "You need to eat, Glenys. You have to keep your strength up."

"What do I need strength for? I never leave this apartment. My bones aren't fit for much."

"Did you get to the doctor? Did you tell him your pain is worse?" She unloaded the bags into the fridge, automatically checking the dates on the few items already in there. She ditched a cheese covered in mold and some tomatoes that looked as if they were about to turn themselves into puree.

"He said the pain is worse because my arthritis is worse. He also said I need to keep moving. Which makes no sense. How am I supposed to keep moving if my arthritis is worse? They don't know anything, these doctors."

Harriet thought about the doctor she'd seen in the emergency room and the way other people had deferred to him.

He'd known plenty.

Dr. E. Black.

She wondered what the *E* stood for. Edward? Elliot?

She grabbed a carton of eggs and some fresh cheese and closed the fridge door. "If your doctor thinks you need to move, then you need to move."

Evan? Earl?

"Easier said than done. I'm afraid my legs might give out on me. If that happened, I'd drop on the sidewalk and everyone would just step over me."

"So you need to walk with someone you know. Like me. It would give you a little confidence to have someone to grab if you needed to."

"You're here to walk my dog. Not me. You're a dog walker, not a human walker."

"I walk some humans. Exceptional humans, like you. We can take Harvey together." Harriet broke three eggs into a bowl and whisked them together with fresh herbs she'd grown on her windowsill. "He'd love the attention. Can you imagine him out walking with two women? What a boost to his self-esteem."

"His self-esteem doesn't need a boost. He already thinks he's king. What are you doing?"

"I'm making you a delicious omelet. I'm not taking you walking unless you have food in your tummy." Harriet tipped the eggs into a skillet and turned up the heat. "I'm adding a little cheese and spinach. Good for your bones."

"My bones are beyond help. I don't think I can walk today, honey."

"Just a short walk," Harriet coaxed. "A few steps. One block."

Glenys sighed. "You're a bully."

"I know." Harriet punched the air with her fist and Glenys laughed.

"You shouldn't be wasting your time with a decrepit old lady."

"I love your company and I love to cook. Since Fliss moved out, I only have myself to cook for and it's boring." Harriet tipped a perfect omelet onto a plate and added a chunk of crusty bread. "Now sit down and eat."

"I hate eating alone."

"You're not eating alone." Harriet cut a slice of bread for herself and tried not to think what it would do to her thighs. It wasn't as if anyone but her was going to see her thighs. Suppressing that depressing thought, she reached for the butter. "I'm eating too."

"So did you take your ankle to the doctor?"

"I went to the ER. And wasted their time as it turned out, because it wasn't broken." She took a bite of bread and made a mental note to bake some chocolate chip cookies for her next visit. Everyone loved her chocolate chip cookies. The original recipe had been her grandmother's but Harriet had made a few small adjustments over time. It was as close as she had ever come to rebellion.

No I will not use one spoonful of vanilla. I'm using two, so take that.

Pitiful.

Glenys poked at her eggs. "That's not a waste of anyone's time. What if it had been broken?"

"My life would have been made difficult." She thought of the array of people in the waiting room. It had been horribly crowded and it wasn't even snowy yet. "I'm guessing that department gets super busy in the winter so I'm going to watch where I tread."

"Tell me more about the sexy doctor in the emergency room who looked at your ankle."

"I never said he was sexy."

"Doctors are always sexy. Doesn't matter how they look, just being a doctor makes them sexy. Was he dark or blond?"

"Eat your eggs and I'll tell you." She waited while Glenys ate a forkful. "Dark. Black hair, blue eyes."

"The *best* combination. My Charlie had blue eyes. It was the first thing I noticed about him."

"It was the first thing I noticed too." That and the fact that his eyes had been tired. Not tired from lack of sleep, more tired from life.

Maybe that was what working in the ER did for you. It had to take a toll. It would have drained her, dealing with so many people in trouble. Handling all that pain and anxiety.

"Maybe it's a sign." Glenys took another small mouthful of omelet. "The start of a perfect relationship. Maybe you'll be together forever."

Harriet laughed. "Unless I break the other ankle, I won't be seeing him again. And maybe he was sexy, but he didn't smile enough for me. He was a little intimidating if I'm honest."

"That's probably the way he handles the job. They deal with such a range of problems in the emergency room. I know because my Darren used to be an EMT and the stories he told would make your toes curl."

Darren was Glenys's oldest son. He lived in California and Glenys hadn't seen him since the funeral.

Harriet often wondered how it was that families came to be so scattered. It felt wrong to her. She longed to belong to a big family who lived close enough to be in and out of each other's lives all the time. Drop in for coffee? Yes, please. Find yourself cooking dinner for twelve? Harriet couldn't think of anything better. This Christmas Fliss would be spending Christmas Day with Seth's family in their home in upstate New York, her brother Daniel was traveling with Molly to see her father for the first time in ages and their mother was traveling the world. Harriet was the only one not traveling anywhere.

She'd be in Manhattan. On her own. Perusing the glittering store windows. On her own. Ice-skating. On her own. Eating Christmas dinner. On her own.

She watched as Glenys forced down another mouthful of omelet. "What are you doing for Christmas Day?"

"Staying in and waiting for Santa."

Harriet grinned. "Do you want to come and wait for him in my apartment? I'm a good cook."

"Well, I know that." Glenys took another mouthful of omelet. "Are you inviting the handsome doctor?"

"No, I'm definitely not inviting the handsome doctor. Judging from the questions he asked me, he thought I was either a hooker or an addict." And she didn't blame him for that. It hadn't been her best evening and her two hours spent in the waiting room of the emergency room hadn't enhanced it.

"They get a lot of those in the emergency room too. I bet you were a breath of fresh air. Show me your ankle."

"I can't. It's buried under four layers of wool because it's cold out there."

"But he was attractive?"

Harriet sighed. "Yes, he was attractive and yes part of me wonders why I can't meet someone like him in real life."

"The ER is about as real as it gets."

"You know what I mean. In a situation that could actually end in a date. Not that it would work out because if it ever happened I'd be too shy to open my mouth. I can't get past that first awkward meeting stage."

"You say plenty to me."

"But I've known you for years. I feel relaxed with you. Most men aren't willing to stick around for that long while I get comfortable enough to actually engage in conversation." She put her fork down. "I need to find a way to skip the 'getting to know you' part."

"That's why so many of the best marriages happen between friends. People who have known each other forever. Friends to lovers. It's my favorite theme in books and movies."

"It sounds like a great theory, but unfortunately I don't have any male friends I've known for thirty years who might be willing to marry me."

"Didn't your brother have any friends?"

"They always hit on my sister. I was the quiet one."

"Oh, honey, quiet can be good. Quiet doesn't mean you don't have important things to say. Just that you might take your time saying them."

"Maybe. But most people don't wait around long enough to hear it."

"Are you trying to tell me you've never had boyfriends?"

"I've had a few. Couple of boys in college. Uneventful and definitely not exciting. Then I dated the accountant who moved into the apartment above ours."

"And how was that?"

"He seemed interested in every figure but mine," Harriet said gloomily. "And since then—do you count the guy at Molly's Salsa dancing class she tried to set me up with?"

"I don't know. Do you think he counts?"

"We danced twice. I enjoyed it because dancing meant I didn't have to talk to him. I did warn you that my dating history isn't impressive." She watched as Glenys ate the omelet, each mouthful slower than the last. She knew that since Charlie died Glenys had to force herself to eat. Force herself to get up in the morning. Force herself to get dressed. "Do you have a warm coat and gloves? I'm going to take Harvey out for a short walk, and you're coming with me. No arguments."

"You're supposed to walk my dog, not care for me."

"You'd be doing me a favor. It's easy to talk to you, and I could use the company."

"Harriet Knight, you're such a sweet girl."

Harriet winced. "I don't want to be a sweet girl. I want to be a badass."

Glenys laughed. "That word sounds plain wrong coming from your lips."

"What do you mean? I said the *F* word last Saturday. When I landed in a heap and bust my ankle—I said it. Out loud, in public. They probably heard me in Washington Square."

"Shocking, but it's not enough." Glenys gave a placid smile and put her fork down. "Now, if you'd grabbed that sexy doctor and planted one on him, that might have improved your badass credentials."

"Fliss said the same thing. Are you two colluding? I'll say what I said to her—he would have had me arrested for assault." As it was, he'd seemed surprised at some of the things she'd said. As if he'd been expecting something different.

She couldn't even begin to imagine what it was like to work in a department like that. In the short time she'd spent in the waiting room, she'd heard people yelling abuse and several of them had been drunk. It had made her feel more than a little uncomfortable. How must it feel to handle that day after day? That was one of the things she loved most about working with dogs. They were always so thrilled to see you. There was nothing better than a wagging tail to lift the spirits, nothing more motivational than an excited bark. Dr. E. Black didn't have that when he went to work. She suspected there was a distinct shortage of wagging tails in his life.

She watched as Glenys finished the omelet, policing every mouthful. Then she got Harvey ready for his walk. She maneuvered him into his little red coat, attached his leash and helped Glenys find her coat and her gloves.

It was true that if she'd taken the dog on her own the walk would have been finished in half the time, but that wasn't what life was about for Harriet.

Glenys needed to maintain her independence and no one else was going to help her.

They walked slowly down the street, admiring the decorations in the store windows.

"I love this time of year." Harriet slid her arm through Glenys's. "It's so buzzy and exciting."

Glenys was concentrating on where she put her feet. "At my age, it's just another day."

"What? No, you can't think that way. I won't let you. I hope you've written to Santa."

"Does he deliver new hips or new husbands?"

"Maybe. If you don't write, you'll never know."

"Maybe I should try online dating."

"It didn't work for me, but no reason why it shouldn't work for you. Go for it, but don't ask me for help with your profile. I'm too honest. You need to present yourself as a twenty-year-old pole dancer."

Glenys tightened her grip on Harriet's arm. "Next time, I'm writing your profile. No more nice girl Harriet. How are your adventures going? What was today's challenge?"

She'd told Glenys about her determination to stretch herself.

"I called someone who is always rude to me." She was careful not to mention any names. "Normally Fliss does it."

"If she's rude, why do you keep her as a client?"

"I never said she was a client."

"Honey, life is too short to hang on to friends who are rude to you so it has to be a client."

"She has two dogs and a huge network of wealthy friends.

Fliss says we can't afford to lose her." Although if it had been left to Harriet she would have done exactly that months ago. Life was too short to have rude clients too.

"So you let her say bad things to you?"

"It's not that she says bad things, exactly. It's more that she's one of those people who thinks no one can possibly understand how busy and appalling her life is. So she is infuriated when I talk slowly. But I'm afraid of speeding up in case I stammer." Harriet paused as they passed a side street. "She makes me feel small. Not small as in slim and attractive. Small as in less. She makes me feel incompetent, even though I know I'm not. She reminds me of Mrs. Dancer, my fourth grade teacher."

"I'm assuming that's not a good thing."

"I wasn't the type to talk much in class, so she used to single me out. *Harriet Knight*—" she imitated Mrs. Dancer's sarcasm "—*I presume you do have a voice? We'd all love to hear it.*"

"I don't see why not talking all the time should be a disadvantage in life."

But Harriet wasn't listening. She was looking at the man huddled against the wall next to a Dumpster. She looked at his shoulders, hunched against the wind, and at the defeated look on his face. "Billy?" She checked that Glenys was steady on her feet, and hurried across to him. "I thought I recognized you. What are you doing here?" She crouched down and put her hand on his arm.

"Trying to stay warm."

"It is a cold one. Tonight is going to be worse. Can you go to the shelter? Anywhere?" She dug her hand into her pocket and pulled out a couple of granola bars. "Can I get you a hot chocolate? Tea?" She talked to him for a while, fetched him tea from the food cart nearby.

When she finally returned to Glenys, her friend was frowning.

"Didn't your mama teach you not to talk to strangers?"

"Billy isn't a stranger. I see him every time I walk Harvey. He used to be a university professor, then he had an accident and became addicted to painkillers." Was that why the doctor in the ER had made a point of telling her he wouldn't write her a prescription? Presumably he knew how easy it was for pain management to turn to addiction. "He lost his job, couldn't pay medical bills."

"How do you know all that?"

"We started talking one day in the summer when I was walking Valentine, Molly's Dalmatian."

"So you can't talk to a guy you're dating, but you can talk to a stranger on the street?"

"He wasn't exactly a stranger. I have been walking past him every night for eight months. We always said hello. He was so polite. Then we started saying more than hello. I got to know him a little. Do you know that sometimes, when it's freezing cold, he rides the train all night, from the Bronx to Brooklyn? How sad is that." It depressed her that people had to do that to stay warm in New York's freezing winter. To stay alive. "Anyone can end up homeless."

"You must have talked to him for a long time to know so much."

"I did. He was lonely." She paused. "And I guess I was a little lonely too. I was getting used to being in the apartment without Fliss."

Glenys patted her on the arm. "You miss her. I understand. I miss my Charlie. It's the little things, isn't it? Charlie always used to make the coffee in the morning. Now I do it and I can never get it quite right. And he fixed anything that went wrong in the apartment. He was handy like that."

Harriet realized she had to stop moaning.

Glenys had suffered a serious loss. She hadn't *lost* Fliss. Her sister was still in her life.

"I do miss her, but it was always going to happen one day. The alternative would have been living together until we were ninety, sharing false teeth, and that wouldn't have been great, either. Since Fliss moved out, I don't have anyone to cook for." She didn't confess that some days she made huge batches of her chocolate chip cookies, or her granola bars, and distributed them to anyone who was interested. And she knew, with brutal honesty, that she was doing it as much for her as for them. She needed to feel needed, and since Fliss had moved out and Daniel had become involved with Molly, she rarely felt needed. She missed having someone to fuss over, to cook for and nurture. There were few people she felt able to admit that to, but Glenys was one of them. "I'm not ambitious in the way Fliss is. I mean, I love our business, but what I love about it is the lifestyle. The dogs. Being outdoors. Doing something I love. Fliss likes the success of it, the growth, the bottom line. We're different like that."

"You're different in lots of ways. Fliss is always in a hurry. She never has time to chat the way you do."

Harriet sprang to the defense of her sister. "Because she's building the business. We have the Bark Rangers because of her."

Glenys stopped walking and Harriet looked at her in alarm. "What's wrong? Is your hip hurting?"

"No. Right now it's my heart that's hurting, and you're the

one hurting it. Your problem is that you don't see your own qualities." Glenys waggled her finger. "The Bark Rangers is as much about you as it is about your sister."

Fliss had said the same thing.

"It was her idea. She's the one who handles all the new business."

"But why do you think people come to you for dog walking? Because of you." Glenys patted her arm. "Because everyone in Manhattan with a brain and a dog knows that Harriet Knight is the person they want. Customer service. Individual attention. Caring. That's what it's about. That's why the Bark Rangers is a success. You are to dog walking what Tiffany's is to jewelers. You are diamond and white gold. The best."

Harriet was touched and ridiculously flattered. "What do you know about Tiffany's?"

"I was young once. I used to stand outside that store dreaming, like so many women before me. And then Charlie made my dreams come true. And he didn't do it by walking into Tiffany's and spending all his money. Love isn't a diamond. You can't buy what we had, and that's what you want too. Love. Nothing wrong with that, honey. You show me the person who doesn't want love in their life, and I'll show you a liar." Glenys started walking again, Harvey trotting by her side.

"What makes you so wise?"

"Age and experience."

After two blocks Harriet insisted they turn round, afraid that Glenys might overdo it.

"It's enough for one day. I don't want to tire you out, and I have another dog to walk before I go home."

"Are you sure you should be doing this much walking?"

"I'm doing a favor for a client who has had a family emergency. She has left Madi, her dog, with her brother and I promised to walk him. This was fun. We'll do it again tomorrow."

"If my joints haven't seized up. So what *are* you doing for the holidays, pumpkin? Have you decided?"

Harriet kept her eyes straight ahead. "You're coming. I'm already planning the menu."

Glenys gave her a keen look. "You're not staying with Fliss?"

"She's invited me, but I don't know Seth's family and it's their first Christmas all together and I know Fliss is a little nervous—"

"All the more reason to have you there."

"No." Harriet shook her head. "She doesn't need her twin, she needs Seth. She has a new family now."

"You don't throw out your old family just because you have a new one. You blend them together, like that cookie mixture you're so good at."

"For some things, yes, but not always and at Christmas it feels like an intrusion. And it will be good for me to spend Christmas without my family. I'm way too dependent on them. I'll probably watch back-to-back Christmas movies and gorge myself on unhealthy food. I'm hoping you'll join me."

"What about your grandmother? Can't you stay with her?"

"I'm staying right here. I'll still be walking dogs if people need me. Providing the snow isn't too bad." She glanced up at the sky. "Do you think they'll be right this time? Will it be a big fall?"

"Maybe. It's the holidays, Harriet. At your age you should be out partying."

"I can hurt my ankle when I'm not partying. Imagine the damage I could do if I started partying. Never been much of a party person, Glenys. You're talking to the woman who can't even walk confidently in high heels."

"I worry about you coming out here alone at night. It isn't safe."

"That's good. I'm trying to be less safe. Stepping out of my comfort zone. Is Darren coming to see you at all over the holidays?"

"Not this year. He's going to visit Karen's parents in Arizona. They'll probably cook the turkey by leaving it out in the sun for half an hour." They'd reached Glenys's apartment block and the doorman smiled and held the door open.

"Please come to me." Harriet gave her a quick hug. "It will be so much fun. Bring Harvey."

"You're a kind girl, Harriet Knight, but you don't want to spend your holidays with a creaky old bird like me."

"I do. And if you can't come to me, I'll bring the turkey to you. One creaky old bird to another."

"You're a soft touch."

"I don't think so."

"I know—" Glenys nudged her "—we could both slip on the ice and spend Christmas Day in the emergency room with that sexy doctor of yours. It's warm, and we'd have plenty of good company."

"He's not my sexy doctor, and I don't think he'd be amused to see me twice in the same month."

But if Santa wanted to drop a man like him down her chimney, that really would make for a perfect Christmas.

CHAPTER FIVE

THE SNOW CONTINUED to fall.

In the emergency room, Ethan was busier than ever.

Before he'd left for work, his sister had arrived at his apartment with Madi. He'd been surprised by how calm and well behaved the dog was. Over Thanksgiving her behavior had been close to manic but his sister assured him she'd been overexcited because of the number of people in the house.

It was certainly true that today she seemed like a different dog.

If she carried on like this, they just might make it through.

"So the dog walker—"

"Her name is Harriet, Ethan. Why are you so bad with names?"

"Because people move through my department so quickly I don't need to remember them. I don't care about their names or their ambitions. I fix them. That's it. So Harriet—" *Harriet, Harriet,* he repeated to himself "—will be coming twice a day? What about snow? Is that going to keep her away?"

"She has never let me down in two years. She'll be here. I stopped by her apartment on the way here and gave her your key."

"You gave my key to a stranger. Thanks."

"She's not a stranger. She's a lifesaver—yours. Make sure you're home to meet her later."

Satisfied that Madi's needs were going to be met by someone, if not by him, Ethan focused on his work.

His first patient was a forty-five-year-old male who had suffered chest pains while shoveling snow.

The first responders at the scene had already transmitted the twelve-lead EKG. Someone showed it to Ethan and he instructed them to page the on-call interventional cardiologist.

Moments later the man arrived in the department.

"I was clearing the snow from the steps and I started to feel funny," he told Ethan. "My chest was kind of tight, like someone was squeezing it. And I thought I was being a wimp, so I carried on. But then my wife appears at the top of the steps and she says, 'Mike, you're whiter than the damn snow.' She called 911."

"Good decision. I've already checked the EKG the first responders sent through and it shows that you're having a heart attack." Ethan saw the fear in the man's eyes and placed a hand on his shoulder. "You're in good hands, Michael. We're going to take good care of you and I've called the cardiologists." He turned to the team. "Can we get a repeat EKG? We need two large-bore IVs and let's get him on a nitro drip. We need to prepare him for the cath lab." He turned back to his patient, explained what was happening and questioned him carefully.

"I can't believe it's my heart. I feel pathetic. It was just a bit of snow. How the hell can this happen?"

"You're underestimating the physical demands of shoveling snow, especially heavy snow like the storm we had last night." Ethan slotted his stethoscope into his ears and listened to the man's chest. "It can be as demanding as a sprint, except that clearing snow usually lasts longer. Maybe a better comparison would be a heavy session on the treadmill. And the combination of cold and physical exertion increases the load on your heart. You probably had a spike in your blood pressure. At least you had the good sense to stop and call 911. We see plenty of folks who keep going, who think they're being weak and don't stop. You stopped. That was smart."

"You're sure it's a heart attack?"

Ethan showed him the EKG. "This shows that you're having what we call a STEMI. That stands for an ST Elevation Myocardial Infarction. We're going to keep you attached to a heart monitor for now and send you for an angiogram."

They prepared him for transfer to the cardiac catheterization lab, placing a portable monitor and oxygen tank on the bed.

One of the less experienced interns looked stunned. "Shoveling snow? If he'd been a walk-in I would have assumed he'd pulled a muscle."

"If someone comes in with chest pains after they've been shoveling snow, assume it's a heart attack. He needs PCI in the cardiac catheterization lab. We aim for a door-to-balloon time of ninety minutes or less."

"Ethan? Could you take a look at this?" The triage nurse called him over and Ethan moved on to the next patient.

It was a busy day. His mind was taken up by the demands of his job. His patients.

He didn't give his sister or her dog a single thought.

HARRIET TUGGED HER wool hat further over her ears and checked the address twice. Normally she picked Madi up from Debra's house, but her client was flying to the West Coast for a couple of weeks to deal with a family emergency and had left Madi with her brother. He lived in the West Village, which was technically out of the area the Bark Rangers covered, but Harriet told herself this was an exception. She went where her clients went, and if Madi was staying in the west side of lower Manhattan then that was where Harriet would go. It would require some redesigning of her schedule because she wouldn't be able to handle the walks on the Upper East Side, but they had enough dog walkers in that area to ensure that she should be able to accommodate this latest change of plan.

The temperature had plummeted and an icy wind bit through her clothing. The promised snow had finally started falling.

Harriet was wearing her weatherproof coat and her weatherproof trousers, but still she was shivering.

Debra wanted Harriet to walk Madi twice a day, every day.

"My brother is wonderful and I adore him, but he has no clue about dogs. I've promised him you will walk Madi and do whatever is needed. He's a doctor. Busy. I don't want Madi to be a bother."

Knowing Madi as well as she did, Harriet didn't hold out much hope in that direction.

It wasn't that Madi was a bother exactly, more that she was acting in a way representative of the breed. Madi was a spaniel, a working dog, intelligent and inquisitive. Harriet adored her, but she hadn't found her particularly adaptable. She wasn't convinced she would respond to a change of environment as smoothly as Debra was anticipating.

It was probably a good thing Debra's brother was a doctor. Presumably he'd be patient and caring and adept at handling difficult situations.

Someone patient and kind was exactly what Madi needed to help her settle into her new home.

She checked the address again. This part of Manhattan was a maze of winding streets. There were bookstores and bistros, bars and coffee houses. It was an area rich in history, with cobblestone streets lined with brownstones and beautiful town houses. It was also an easy place to get lost.

According to Debra, her brother lived in a two-bedroom, two-bathroom duplex loft apartment.

By the time Harriet found the apartment block, the light was fading and the tips of her fingers were numb.

She planned to take Madi for a half-hour walk, although she wasn't particularly looking forward to it. Not only was her ankle throbbing, but it was never great for the dogs when it had been snowing. The streets were mucky and winter was always hard on the dogs' paws. She constantly thought about the dogs, about their welfare and what she could do to make their lives the best they could be.

Fliss said it was the reason they had a thriving client base, but Harriet never thought about that side of it. She didn't do it for the owners, she did it for the animals. Their comfort and happiness was what mattered to her and if that led to a happy owner, then that was a bonus.

Snow or no snow, Madi needed the exercise. Debra had given her the key, and the moment she opened the door to the apartment she knew something was wrong.

She'd fostered enough pets to sense disaster when it was close by.

She had no idea what the apartment looked like normally, but she guessed it was nothing like this.

Cushions lay scattered on the floor, their stuffing surrounding them like clouds. Toilet paper was festooned over the furniture like giant ribbons.

Staring at the mess in dismay and disbelief, Harriet walked through to the kitchen.

There, on top of a mound of dried pasta sat Madi, looking guilty.

"Oh dear. Did you do this? All by yourself? Boy, are you in trouble, young lady. And a bag of flour too. You've been busy." Harriet eyed the snow-like substance covering everything in sight. She dropped her bag, dragged off her hat and her coat and tried to work out where to start. Take the dog out first? Clear up?

She decided that Madi had to be her priority. She'd never known the animal to behave badly before, which had to mean she was distressed. Clearing up could wait. "Poor Madi. What happened? Were you bored? Scared? Is this a very strange place?" She stooped to make a fuss over the dog. She pulled her onto her lap and removed pieces of pasta from her fur. "Don't worry. I'm here now and everything is going to be fine."

"I don't think so. In fact I'd say everything is far from fine." An icy voice came from the doorway and Harriet turned her head quickly. She hadn't heard anyone else enter the apartment, and neither had Madi, who wriggled off her lap and bolted for safety, scattering pasta and rice.

The man in the doorway topped six foot, the collar of his long coat turned up against the bitter winter chill, his eyes a steely blue.

Blue eyes. Ice-blue, to go with the icy voice.

She recognized those eyes, and the handsome face, and her heart skipped a beat. It made her feel a little dizzy, but she was comforted by the fact that if she collapsed in front of him he'd know what to do about it.

Why hadn't it occurred to her that Debra's brother might be the doctor who had treated her?

Dr. E. Black.

Not Edward, but Ethan.

Broad shoulders hunched, he scanned the wreckage of his kitchen and his living room with incredulity. "What the *hell* happened here?"

It was a fair question but she wished he'd asked it in a less threatening tone.

Harriet dragged herself back from the land of dreams to uncomfortable reality.

"I'm guessing Madi didn't appreciate being left alone all day in a strange environment. The poor thing was scared."

"The 'poor thing'? What about my poor apartment?"

He strode into the apartment, slamming the door behind him. The noise echoed around them and was the final straw for Madi, who fled behind the kitchen island.

Harriet was about to go to her when there was a knock on his door. Cursing under his breath, Ethan went back to it and dragged it open.

A woman stood there. Harriet guessed she was in her

seventies. Her hair was the color of the bag of flour Madi had just exploded over the floor and walls. She was slightly bent and barely reached Ethan's chest, but the look she gave him was fierce.

"Dr. Black." She peered at him over the top of her glasses. "We appreciate how hard you work and your contribution to society. I'd even go so far as to say you're something of a hero around here, but that doesn't change the fact that your dog has been howling all day. I'm sorry, but we cannot tolerate it."

"Howling?" His bemused response made it clear he had no idea how a dog might respond if left alone in a strange apartment all day.

Harriet knew.

She looked questioningly at Madi, who looked back with sorrowful eyes.

"Howling. It has driven us all crazy. As you know, well-mannered dogs *are* allowed in this building, but—" She broke off, her attention caught by something over his shoulder. "Oh *my*—whatever has happened?"

"I have yet to work that out, Mrs. Crouch. When I find out, you'll be the first to know."

"Have you had a break-in? An intruder? Because—"

"No break-in. My intruder has four legs. He's my sister's dog. She had to fly to San Francisco because my niece has been in a serious accident. I'm helping her out."

Harriet frowned.

Did he not realize Madi was a girl?

Mrs. Crouch seemed to soften a fraction. "I'm sorry to hear that. I know how close you are to your family. How is she doing?"

"I haven't called the hospital yet. I'm going to do that in a moment." He raked his fingers through his hair, still damp from the snow. "I apologize for the howling, it won't happen again. I understand your frustration and I share it. I'd be grateful for your patience while I fix this, and you have my word that I *will* fix it."

Mrs. Crouch melted. She patted him on the arm. "Don't you worry, Dr. Black. We can cope with a little howling if that's what it takes. Call your sister. You must be worrying to death. I'm sorry to have bothered you at such a difficult time."

Harriet blinked. He'd turned her from attack to apology with a few sentences.

He probably had a wealth of experience dealing with difficult situations in the emergency room, but still that was a particularly smooth performance. He'd been kind, polite and caring.

The man was wasted as a doctor. He should be a hostage negotiator.

Which was a relief, because for a moment there he'd made her a little nervous.

By the time he finally closed the door again, Harriet had relaxed a little. That feeling lasted until he turned back to her and she saw that the dangerous glint in his eyes was back.

Whatever restraint had prevailed when he'd talked to his neighbor appeared to have abandoned him. And she knew why. Mrs. Crouch wasn't the focus of his anger.

That seemed to be reserved for Harriet, although she had no idea why he should be holding her responsible. She wasn't the one who had burst the bag of flour and thrown pasta and toilet paper around his apartment.

Whatever the reason, he was angry, and she wasn't good with angry men.

Part of her wanted to follow Madi and hide behind the sofa but she stood her ground and reminded herself that he had reason to be a little annoyed, but he shouldn't be angry with *her*.

"You're the dog sitter my sister talked about?" His words were clipped and she swallowed.

"I'm not a sitter. I'm a dog walker, and yes, I'm—"

"So if you're a dog walker, why didn't you walk the damn dog?"

It felt as if all the air had been sucked out of the room.

Harriet had to force herself to inhale. "Excuse me?"

"If your job was to walk the dog, why didn't you do it?" The anger in his voice rattled her composure so badly it took her a moment to respond.

"I arrived five minutes before you did. My plan was to take Madi out and then clear up."

"Two walks." He spoke between his teeth, as if he didn't dare move his lips in case a torrent of heated words flowed out and scalded them both. "Debra said she'd arranged for you to walk the dog twice a day."

"That's true, but she told me not to come this morning because she'd make sure Madi was walked and settled before leaving her."

He scanned the rooms, his expression one of naked incredulity. "Does she *look* settled to you?"

Madi whined.

"Could you lower your voice? You're making her nervous." *Not only Madi.* Ignoring the fact that her heart was thumping and her palms were sweaty, she stood up and crossed the room to Madi. "It's okay, baby. Don't be scared.

There's nothing to be scared of." She was talking to herself as much as the dog.

"It most certainly is *not* 'okay.' What did you say your name was again?"

It felt a little better with Madi in her arms. She could feel the warmth of her body through her sleek fur. The rapid pounding of her little heart. She was sure hers was doing the same.

"Harriet. Harriet Knight."

"Well, Miss Knight, I have had a long and testing day so you'll have to forgive me if I'm not altogether delighted to return home and find my apartment trashed."

"I wouldn't describe it as *trashed* exactly—"

"No?" He stared at the pasta that carpeted the floor. "How would you describe that? What even happened to it?"

"I'm guessing she was interested in the contents of the bag so she decided to take a closer look. While she's living with you it's probably a good idea to put food away in the cupboards so it's secure. I'll deal with it." Technically it wasn't part of her job, but she didn't want him to be angry with Madi.

"And what happens tomorrow?" He prowled across the apartment, advancing on her with an ominous sense of purpose. "And the day after that? Am I going to be coming home to this every day?"

"I d-d—" She tried to respond but she couldn't get the word out. It was stuck. Blocked. Horror washed over her. Horror and embarrassment. Had that really just happened? Yes, it had. She'd stammered. After all these years of never stammering once, she'd stammered. She tried again. "I d-d-d."

No. *No!*

Madi gave a yelp of protest and Harriet realized it was because she was squeezing the dog a little too tightly.

She relaxed her grip and forced herself to breathe.

Why had this happened now? But she knew the answer to that, of course. It was because Ethan Black was yelling at her. She wasn't good with angry people. Or maybe the stress of continually pushing herself out of her comfort zone was getting to her. Yes, maybe it was that.

Thankfully, he didn't seem to have noticed her speech issues. He was too preoccupied by the mess in his apartment.

She swallowed, hoping that it was just a blip. She wanted to try speaking again to test that theory.

"There are days when I'm rarely home. Debra assured me the dog would be no problem."

"Madi was b-b-b-ored." Not a blip. Now that the stammering had started, she didn't seem able to stop it. Mortified, Harriet decided the only option was to stop talking. She had to get out of here and try and calm herself down. Had to work out what had gone wrong.

She felt like a teenager again, terrified to speak in case the words jammed in her mouth.

Terrified of impatient glances or, worse, pity.

It didn't matter what Ethan Black thought of her, she couldn't sort herself out with him scowling at her.

She scrambled to her feet, grabbed Madi's lead and her coat and took her to the door, grabbing her own coat on the way.

"Where are you going?"

"Walk." She used a single word and didn't hang around for a longer conversation. She fled.

This was one challenge too far.

CHAPTER SIX

ETHAN STARED AT the closed door in frustration and disbelief.

Walk? Walk where? It was snowing outside and the temperature was dropping. Not to mention the fact that they'd been in the middle of a conversation about how to handle the dog.

The dog.

It occurred to him that a stranger had just walked out of his apartment with his sister's beloved pet.

"Dammit." He ran his hand over his face. What was he supposed to do now?

She'd taken the dog. His sister's dog, who was his responsibility. And by the look on her face, she wasn't intending to return in a hurry. Maybe not at all.

Why had she run out like that?

Guilt flashed through him and he ran through the conversation in his mind.

He'd walked through the door, seen the mess and—

Yelled.

He winced, hit by a stab of regret and remorse. He'd definitely yelled.

And something about her had changed when he'd done that.

She'd been tense and defensive and then she'd stammered.

He thought back, remembering the look of dismay on her face.

At the time he hadn't thought anything of it, mostly because he'd been too focused on his own emotions. He'd registered the disfluency in her speech, but ignored it.

Now he remembered the flash of panic and mortification in her eyes, as if something dire and desperate had happened.

Her appalled reaction told him this was something she fought against. He'd dated a speech-language pathologist for a while when he was an intern, and he remembered her telling him that stressful situations could sometimes trigger a relapse in people who generally had the condition under control.

What if he'd caused the stressful situation?

What if Harriet Knight didn't normally stammer?

He probably shouldn't have yelled at her, but he'd had a seriously bad day and returning to find his apartment looking like the inside of a garbage disposal unit hadn't helped. Surely she could see that?

And he hadn't been yelling at *her* exactly. He'd been yelling generally.

His attempt to justify his behavior had no impact on his guilt levels because the truth was none of it was her fault.

He was about to work out whether he should go after them or not, when his phone rang.

He saw from the caller display that it was his sister in California.

Great.

Perfect timing.

His concern for his niece eclipsing his worry about the dog, Ethan answered the phone.

He was relieved when Debra told him everything was going smoothly.

"Good."

"How about you? How is Madi? Has she been good today? Is she settling in?"

Ethan looked round his wrecked apartment. Neither his sister nor his niece needed anything else to be anxious about. And he certainly didn't dare confess that right now he didn't even know where their precious dog was. He had to hope Harriet returned with her. If she didn't—well, he'd worry about that when it happened. "She seems to be settling fine."

"And Harriet showed up on time? Well, of course she did. I don't know why I'm even asking that. Harriet is the most reliable person on the planet. Isn't she gorgeous?"

Ethan thought of the way she'd scolded him for upsetting the dog. "Charming."

"I knew you'd like her. I don't know why this didn't occur to me before but she'd be *perfect* for you."

"What?! Debs—"

"Just trying to turbo boost your romantic life."

"My romantic life is fine, thanks."

"No, your sex life is fine. Your romantic life is dead."

Ethan rolled his eyes. "I draw the line at talking about sex with my sister. And I have all the romance I want, or need."

"Yeah, yeah, I know. You were married. Been there, tried

that, yada yada. But just because you and Alison ended up on the rocks doesn't mean you can't try again. I don't know Harriet that well but I love what I know and I would have said you're *exactly* her type."

Ethan doubted Harriet would agree.

He'd never met a woman more eager to get away from him.

The more he thought about it, the more he was convinced that he was the reason she'd fled the apartment in such a hurry.

The odd thing was that she seemed familiar, and yet for the life of him he couldn't think why. He didn't own a dog, and he wasn't the type of guy who forgot the women he dated. Could she be a friend of a friend? Someone he'd met in a group?

He asked a few more questions about his niece, ended the call and poured himself a whiskey. He drank it neat, but it did nothing to salve his conscience.

He had a right to be annoyed, but he didn't have a right to make her the target of his frustration.

Since when had he been a bully?

To work off his tension, he grabbed two large garbage bags and started cleaning the apartment. He tried to look on the positive side. At least the dog didn't seem to have bathroom issues. There was no water damage. Nothing lasting. The dog—he had to remember to call it Madi. Madi Madi—hadn't peed.

But what if tomorrow she did?

What if tomorrow she took her boredom out on his sofa? And if she carried on howling it would make him unpopular with his neighbors. He didn't have time to deal with aggravation in his private life. Hopefully Harriet would return with the dog, but even if she did the problem wouldn't be solved. There was tomorrow to think about. And the next day.

He took his frustrations out on the cleaning and didn't stop until the place was shining. No one would have guessed a dog had ever entered his apartment.

He'd cleared up the last of the mess when the doorman called up to tell him Harriet was downstairs.

Despite the fact that he was about to let the perpetrator of the mess back into his apartment, Ethan felt nothing but relief.

She'd returned with the dog and saved him difficult explanations and more stress.

He opened the door and Harriet walked straight past him, keeping her head down.

Ethan closed the door carefully, knowing he had a situation far more complicated to unravel than the one with Mrs. Crouch.

What was the best approach? Should he raise the fact that she'd stammered? Should he apologize or would that embarrass her more? No, it was probably better to pretend he hadn't noticed. He'd keep his apology general.

"I apologize for shouting. Not that it's an excuse, but I had a difficult day."

Finally she looked at him, and her eyes were accusatory and angry. "So did Madi."

He tried again. "I meant that my day was difficult before I arrived home. I work in the emergency room. I lost a patient." The moments the word left his lips, he regretted them. Why had he said that? Death was part of his job. He dealt with it in his own way, and his way never involved sharing his feelings with other people. What was he hoping for? Sympathy? Or was he simply offering up an excuse for his behavior, hoping for forgiveness.

"I'm sorry to hear that." She unclipped Madi's lead and eased her out of her coat. Her gaze was a little less fierce. "That must be difficult to handle. I guess every day is difficult for you."

"Forget it. I shouldn't have said anything. It's not an excuse."

"I would think it would be almost impossible to forget it. And I don't see it as an excuse. It's an explanation and I'm grateful for it." She removed Madi's coat and then sat on the floor, opened the backpack she was carrying and carefully cleaned the dog's paws.

Ethan felt more and more guilty. "I appreciate the effort you're taking, but you don't have to do that. Turns out I'm pretty good at cleaning up."

"I'm not doing it for you, I'm doing it for her. The snow is bad for the dog. They use salt and other de-icers and it irritates their paws."

Ethan, who rarely felt out of his depth, felt totally at a loss. "I never knew that."

She glanced at him briefly. "It seems there's a lot you don't know about dogs, Dr. Black."

"Ethan. You clean the paws of every dog you walk?"

"If I think it's necessary, yes." She dealt with the final paw, taking her time, meticulous and careful. "Just as you probably take the blood pressure of every patient you see, if you think it's necessary."

She was telling him that what she did was important too. He got the message.

"So why do you think Madi—" he emphasized the name,

hoping to earn his way back into her favor "—tried to destroy my home?"

"I don't think she was trying to destroy your home. I think she was expressing boredom. Or fear." Having dried and checked the last of Madi's paws, she stood up. "Spaniels are an active breed, and they crave companionship. They need to be well trained. Behavioral problems are not uncommon. What we have to do is evaluate the cause of the behavior. She's in an unfamiliar environment. I suspect that's all it is."

All?

Ethan thought back to the carnage he'd witnessed. He opened his mouth to suggest she might be minimizing the problem and then closed it again. "So what do you suggest?"

"She needs to be shown patience and kindness and then she'll be fine."

"That's it? Are you sure? What if you're wrong?"

Her eyes narrowed. "When I came to the ER the other night, I didn't question your professional opinion, Dr. Black. You told me I didn't need an X-ray. I accepted your judgment."

When I came to the ER...

That was where he'd seen her before. Of course. The girl with the injured ankle. And she was right. She hadn't questioned his opinion.

He felt thoroughly put in his place. And he noticed that she was no longer stammering. Nor did she seem afraid or intimidated.

"I remember now. That explains why you look familiar. How is your ankle?"

"It's improving, but I did as you instructed." She said it pointedly and he took the point.

"So what, in your professional opinion, am I going to do with this dog to settle her down? How do I care for her?"

"You can't care for her. It wouldn't be fair."

Ethan breathed a sigh of relief. "I'm glad you appreciate that. It's more than my sister did. I have a busy, responsible job and it certainly isn't fair on me to expect—"

"I was talking about Madi." Her gaze was steady on his. "It isn't fair on Madi to be with someone so unsympathetic and ignorant of her needs. And I can't teach you. You don't have the patience for it."

Ethan was taken aback. "I work in the emergency room. I have more patience—and patients—than you can possibly imagine."

"The difference is that your patients matter to you," she said. "I don't believe Madi matters. I think you agreed to do this because you love your sister, but loving your sister is not enough. You have to love Madi too, not just tolerate her. Dogs have an instinct for how someone is feeling. Let's be honest, Dr. Black, you're not a dog person."

"What does 'not a dog person' look like?"

"They look pretty much like you. They keep their distance from the animal, sometimes it's because they're afraid—"

"I'm not afraid of dogs." *She thought he was a coward?*

"—and sometimes it's because people simply don't like dogs, which is perfectly fine with me—" her tone suggested it wasn't fine with her at all "—as long as they don't try and care for a dog. You have a dog to care for, and the only solution I can come up with is that I will take Madi with me."

"Take her? Take her where?"

"Home. I'll call a cab and I can take Madi and all her food and belongings over to my apartment."

"I can't let you do that. I don't even know you."

"Madi knows me." Offering her support to that statement, Madi pressed close to Harriet, licking her face adoringly.

Ethan tried not to think about all the potential pathogens she was spreading. "Are you allowed pets in your apartment?"

"I would *never* live anywhere that wouldn't let me keep a dog. I often foster animals for the animal shelter."

And now she wanted to take Madi. She was offering to remove his problem.

He was sorely tempted to let her do exactly that, but then he remembered his promise to his sister.

He thought about Karen, lying in hospital anxious about her dog.

"I can't let you do that."

"You don't have a choice, Dr. Black, because I'm not leaving Madi here with you."

Had Debra really said Harriet was gentle and mild?

Clearly she didn't know her well.

He breathed deeply. "Can we start this again? I had a long day. A difficult day. I returned home to mayhem. I've needed an adjustment period, that's true, and it's also true that I have almost no experience caring for animals, but this dog is precious to my sister and my niece and I will do whatever it takes to make her happy while she's staying with me." He couldn't believe he'd just said that. "But I'm going to need you to help me because, as you rightly say, I know nothing about dogs. And before you think that disqualifies me from caring for her, I should emphasize that I'm a quick learner."

"I don't think it's in Madi's best interests to stay here."

She stared at him for a long time and he sensed she was trying to read him.

"Look—have you eaten?"

"Excuse me?"

"Have you had dinner? It's late. I'm hungry and I worked right through without lunch. My job doesn't leave much time for food or bathroom breaks. You might as well join me and we can talk this through. I need to convince you I can be a good temporary home for Madi, but I can't do that while you're sitting there covered in snow glaring at me as if I'm an axe murderer. So let's have dinner." Why was she still staring at him? And why did she look so horrified? "I'm hungry. You must be too."

There was a pause.

"I—I don't think that's a g-g-g—" She broke off, visibly dismayed.

He wanted to tell her that it wasn't a big deal. He almost finished her sentence but then remembered his old girlfriend telling him it was the worst thing you could do for someone who stammered.

So he stayed silent and waited. Listened.

When it came to clearing up the mess left by a dog he'd lost his cool, but with this he had endless patience.

There was a tense silence.

Still he waited. He saw her throat move as she swallowed. Saw her draw in a breath and brace herself to try again, like a swimmer about to plunge into deep water that had already tried to drown her once.

"—sensible." She changed the word and it came out smoothly, but he didn't see relief in her eyes. He saw embarrassment.

"I've made you nervous because I barked at you." He

wondered whether to be blunt or tactful. He went with blunt. "You stammered, and I'm guessing that was because of me." The deepening color in her cheeks told him he was right. "You mostly have it under control, is that right? And then I walked in here with my big mouth and my insensitive ways and it came back."

There was a pause and for a moment he thought she wasn't going to reply.

"Y-yes."

Knowing that made him feel almost as bad as she did.

"Why? What is it about me that triggered it?"

"You were angry. I'm not g-g-g—" She stopped, frustration in her eyes.

He could feel her agony. He witnessed people's agony daily, but witnessing it and being the cause of it were two different things. This time he was feeling it with her and it was a profoundly uncomfortable experience. Clearly he wasn't as emotionally numbed as he'd thought. He had his usual urge to fix it, but this time he wasn't dealing with blood or broken bones. He'd inflicted damage for which there was no easy fix.

She took another couple of breaths and tried again. "Angry people upset me." She stooped to pick up her bag, stuffing everything back inside. "It doesn't matter."

"It matters, and not just because you're going to be helping me with Madi. We're going to figure this out."

"I c-c-c—" She closed her eyes briefly. "Can't work with you."

He felt a flash of concern.

If Harriet refused to help him then he was in *serious* trouble.

"I handled the situation badly. I'm sorry and I want us to

start again. You weren't mad with Madi when she destroyed my apartment. You understood that there was something going on underneath. That she was upset." On impulse, he dropped into a crouch and held out his hand to Madi. "Come here, girl."

The dog looked at him warily and he couldn't exactly blame her.

Obviously deciding his contrition was genuine, she trotted across to him.

He stroked his hand over her head, feeling silken fur under his palm. "Good girl. Lovely girl. Most beautiful dog in the world." Madi sat down and looked at him. Ethan looked at Harriet. "If she's ready to give me another chance, surely you can too?"

Harriet straightened and slid her bag onto her shoulder. "That's a low trick, Dr.—"

"Ethan." He said it softly. "My name is Ethan. And it's not a trick. Stay for dinner. Dinner and one conversation. That's all I'm asking."

CHAPTER SEVEN

DINNER?

It had taken all her willpower to bring Madi back to the apartment. Given the choice, she would have taken the dog straight home. Then she would have called Debra and suggested that her brother, no matter how skilled he was in the hospital setting, wasn't good with animals.

But she knew, deep down, that her prime reason for doing it wouldn't have been about Madi. It would have been about her.

She'd stammered. Not only that, instead of standing her ground and using all the strategies she'd learned as a child, she'd run away. That depressed her almost as much as the knowledge that she'd retreated when she should have advanced.

Ethan Black was still waiting for her answer. "I understand your dilemma. I'm the cause of your stammer, so why would you stay? But, Harriet, that's on me. I'm the one with the issue here, not you."

He didn't get it. And why would he? This was *huge*.

She felt as if she'd regressed fifteen years. Was this a one-off? Would it keep happening now? Would she be unable to speak without worrying if the words were going to come out the way she wanted them to? Would it be like school, when there were times when she'd only spoken if she absolutely had to?

She was desperate to call her twin and talk it through, but that wasn't an option. She couldn't tell her sister that she wanted to be independent one minute, and then call her in hysterics the next.

She had to find a way through this. But how, when the feeling of panic was a tight ball in the center of her chest?

And she realized with a flash of insight that the "challenges" she'd been setting herself hadn't really been challenges at all. Where was the challenge in walking in high heels? Who even *cared* if she could walk in high heels?

This was the challenge. Staying where she was, when all she wanted to do was leave.

Saying yes to dinner when her lips wanted to say no.

"I d-d—" Hot with humiliation, she almost turned away and gave up but something inside her kept her feet glued to the floor.

She met Ethan's gaze and braced herself for sympathy or, worse, pity, but saw neither.

"This isn't my area of expertise," he said. "If you'd slashed yourself with a knife or fallen out of a window, I'm your man, but I'm not afraid to admit I'm out of my depth here. Tell me how I can help you."

He was asking how he could help.

No one ever did that.

They finished her sentences. They made assumptions.

They talked over her. They gave up waiting for her to say whatever it was she was trying to say.

Ethan did none of those things.

"You c-c-c—" The frustration almost made her burst, but Ethan waited quietly. Patiently.

The one thing she didn't associate her stammer with was patience. Not her own, or other people's. But Ethan was patient. She didn't get the sense that he was itching to get on with the next thing. Which was unusual. Nor did she get the impression that he was judging her the way most people did. So many people seemed unable to accept any variation on their view of "normal." As a child she'd discovered that anything that made you different, made you stand out, also made you a target. In the jungle of the playground, differences were seen as weaknesses, and weaknesses were rarely celebrated. People thought she was gentle, but Harriet knew that wasn't accurate. She wasn't particularly gentle, whatever that meant, except perhaps with animals. She was tolerant. She accepted differences. And it seemed that despite his earlier anger, Ethan Black did too. Recognizing that diffused some of the tension building inside her. "You can't help me." This time the words came out unrestricted.

He paused. "In the past, what would you have done that has helped?"

Breathing. Relaxation. She'd even tried hypnosis once, but she wasn't going to tell him that. Instead she breathed, forcing herself to relax. She was *not* going to walk out. If she walked out she would lose all respect for herself.

She was going to stay. Talk to him. Have dinner.

That was today's Challenge Harriet.

And it was probably the biggest challenge she could have given herself.

He walked to the fridge, pulled out a bottle of white wine and then removed two glasses from a cabinet.

He poured the wine and then held out a glass to her.

She took it from him. "Thank you."

This time the words came out smoothly, and she felt weak with relief.

Maybe this would be okay. Maybe this wasn't a disaster.

He leaned against the counter, the subdued lighting in the kitchen creating a false air of intimacy. It bathed the apartment with a soothing glow that nudged the edge of romantic.

Or maybe that was just the way her mind worked.

Ethan Black would probably be appalled had he been able to read her thoughts.

She wasn't a fool. She was well aware that he wasn't interested in her personally. What he was doing was managing a situation he believed he had caused. She was employed by his sister, who, presumably, he didn't want to upset. More importantly, he needed her to help with Madi. After the vanishing act she had pulled earlier, presumably he was afraid she might walk out and not return.

If he'd known her, he would have known that wasn't a possibility.

Harriet would never leave a dog in a situation she felt was bad for them, and although she had no doubt Ethan was a good person and a great doctor, she wasn't convinced he was good for Madi.

In reality it wasn't his fault that she wasn't good with strangers.

That was her problem. She was the one who had to deal with it.

She tried to relax the tense knot in her stomach. She tried telling herself he wasn't a stranger. Not only had he treated her ankle, he was Debra's brother and she'd known Debra for years. He hadn't shouted because he was angry with her. He'd shouted because he was angry with himself. Because he hadn't been able to save that patient.

She couldn't even begin to imagine how that must feel. She wanted to ask him, but right now he was focused on her.

"How long has it been?"

Taking a slow, deep breath and looking directly at him, she tried again to speak. "A few years." The words emerged with no problem. No barrier.

"Years?" Ethan put his wineglass down slowly. "Then I'm doubly sorry."

"Why?"

"Because I triggered something you had under control."

"It's my stammer. Not your fault."

"We both know that's not true. I was rude, which is inexcusable. I made you anxious."

"I find it difficult to talk to people I don't know. I'm not good with strangers. I'm shy—" She hated saying it. Immediately she wanted to follow up by saying that shy wasn't the same as weak. "And I have no idea why I just told you that. The one thing I don't do is divulge personal information to people I don't know."

"I'm a doctor. It's different."

Was that it? Maybe it was.

He sat down on one of the chairs by the kitchen island and gestured for her to do the same.

"Did you see a speech therapist?"

"For a while. Maybe I should do it again."

"I don't think you need that. You just need to relax and take your time. And not hang out with guys like me." His tone was dry. "You're not alone, you know. Aristotle had a stammer. So did Charles Darwin."

"King George VI."

"Marilyn Monroe."

She raised her eyebrows. "Really? I didn't know."

"There's an interview where she talks about it. So how do you manage with your job? Aren't you constantly required to talk to strangers?"

"Yes, but my sister does that part. New business, bookings, she handles that side of things." She slid onto the chair next to him, her fingers grasping her wineglass. She didn't trust her own powers of speech, and it was an awful feeling. She wasn't sure if alcohol would make it worse or better. "I live life in my comfort zone."

"That wasn't how it seemed the other night when I saw you in the emergency room."

"That was me trying to leave my comfort zone. You saw how it turned out." *Oh what the heck.* She took a gulp of wine and felt it slide into her veins. The words were loose and flowing again. She could almost pretend she'd imagined what had happened. Almost, but not quite. It had happened. And it could happen again. Maybe on one level she'd always known that, but she'd gotten complacent. But maybe complacency was a good thing. Worrying, anxiety, made it worse. "I think we'd both agree I'm a work in progress."

"But you went on a date with a stranger. You didn't stammer?"

She put her glass down. "He didn't give me a chance to talk. But I did manage about four short sentences, which was more than I managed on the date before him."

His eyes gleamed and he leaned forward to top up her wine. "Sounds as if you've had some thrilling dates."

"The best." She found herself smiling too. She also found herself wishing someone like Ethan had been her blind date, which made no sense at all because less than half an hour earlier she'd left the apartment and braved snow rather than stay in the same space as him. "I'm done with it now."

"You've finished dating? Aren't you a little young to give up on love?"

Why was he asking her so many questions?

He'd shown more interest in her than the three men she'd dated put together.

"I'm not giving up on love. I'm giving up on internet dating." She hadn't thought about it until that moment, but she realized she meant it. After the last guy, she'd never believe anything she read about anyone again. She needed to be able to look into their eyes and judge whether they seemed honest or not. "Which probably means no more dating at all. It's not easy meeting people."

"That's true."

She hadn't expected him to agree with her. "You must meet people all the time at the hospital."

"Not really. I don't date patients, obviously, and most of my colleagues are too busy to even think about connecting socially, even if we could get past the awkwardness of dating someone you see every day."

She'd always assumed that dating was easy for everyone else. That she was the only one who found the whole thing daunting and overwhelming.

Harriet wondered if she still counted as a patient, and then wondered why she was even thinking that.

She'd assumed someone like him would be married with two cute kids.

It hadn't occurred to her he'd be single.

What was wrong with the world?

Unsettled by her own thought processes she made a joke. "Maybe *you* should try internet dating. Put 'doctor' down and you'll be inundated. Especially when people realize you actually *are* a doctor."

"I'm nobody's idea of a dream date, Harriet."

He would have been her dream date.

Where had that thought come from? Flustered, she took a sip of her wine, reminding herself that he didn't like dogs. She could never be with anyone who didn't like dogs, even if he was a good listener and had eyes that made her think of blue skies and long summer days.

"You're too hard on yourself. Shrek would seem like a dream date compared to the last three guys I met."

"I've never been compared to Shrek before. I may need therapy to get over that one."

At least he had a sense of humor. "You said you lost a patient. How do you handle that?"

The worst thing she handled in her working day was misbehaving dogs and inclement weather.

"Tonight I handled it by losing my temper with you." His tone was dry, his words self-deprecating. "Normally? I deal with it by filing it away as part of the job. It's not something I usually talk about. I can't believe I did. I assume it was a pathetic attempt on my part to induce a pity response that might lead to forgiveness."

She loved his honesty. Her respect for him grew. "People don't expect doctors to show their feelings. Which must make it hard. You're supposed to be caring, but still detached. How does that even work?"

"Sometimes it doesn't. Generally it's easier in the emergency room. The people I see are strangers. I don't have the connection with them that doctors in other specialties might. My father works in primary care, and there are some families he has been seeing for thirty years. When he loses a patient he grieves right along with the family. I learned to handle my feelings a long time ago. Most doctors do. You learn to put up emotional boundaries."

"But putting up boundaries doesn't mean you're not feeling it, does it? When you walked through that door earlier you were on edge. Irritable and upset. That's why you lost your temper over nothing."

"I'm willing to concede that I was wrong in my response to the situation, but I will not admit that the destruction of my apartment was nothing."

Harriet finished her wine. "I'm sitting here because you told me you had lost a patient. If you're now telling me that it had no effect on you, I'm going to walk through that door and I'll be taking Madi with me."

"My sister was so wrong about you. She told me you were gentle. She never mentioned you were ruthless and capable of blackmail." He reached to top up her glass again but she shook her head and covered the glass with her fingers.

"No more. It's cold out there. I don't want to slip and bang my head on the way home. I especially don't want to be taken to the emergency room."

He put the bottle down. "Because now you know I work there."

"No, because you're not on duty tonight." She spoke without thinking and saw the surprise flicker across his face. She was surprised too. *No more wine, Harriet.* "I mean because you're obviously a good doctor. No other reason. And I'm only ruthless when it comes to protecting animals."

He looked at her for a moment and then stood up. "I'll order the food. Is there anything you don't eat?"

"No, but if you tell me what there is in your fridge I can cook it. I'm a good cook."

"In that case you are definitely going to cook for me one day, but tonight I was thinking more of takeout." He pulled open a drawer and spread a selection of flyers in front of her. "There's a Thai restaurant round the corner where the food is so good it makes you want to move to the Far East. Or we could go with pizza if you prefer."

"Thai sounds delicious, but the menu looks baffling." And the prices high. Their business was doing well, but there had been enough years where they'd scraped by to make Harriet balk at the idea of spending hard-earned dollars on food she could produce herself.

"If you don't have any allergies, you can leave it with me." He picked up the phone. The fact that he ordered without a pause and without once consulting the menu told her that he frequently made the same call.

She remembered seeing him in action in the hospital and sensed he was used to giving orders. Also to knowing what he was doing.

"Isn't every day bad where you work?"

"Some are worse than others. Today was particularly difficult, and there were complicating circumstances."

"You see a lot of things." Things she probably couldn't imagine, least of all deal with on a daily basis.

"The people who come through the department are often under a tremendous amount of stress. They're anxious and scared, and that can translate into aggression. People want things done right away, and when that doesn't happen they're not happy."

They're not happy. "That's an understatement, right?"

He gave a half smile. "Yes. And we prioritize patients according to medical need, not the order that they walk into the department. That's always a tough one for people to understand."

"They think their injury is bad, but you're seeing someone far worse." She nodded. "You must handle a lot of abuse."

"ER workers are an easy target." He reached into a drawer and pulled out forks. "I pride myself in being skilled at diffusing anger. I spend all day managing other people's emotions. It seems as if when I walked through that door tonight I forgot to manage my own."

"It must have been the final straw coming home to the mess Madi created."

He closed the drawer. "Tell me honestly—is this what I'm going to expect every day? Break the bad news to me gently."

Harriet glanced at Madi, who was happily gnawing her toy, oblivious to the chaos she'd caused. "She seems settled now. Hopefully it will continue. What time do you leave for work tomorrow?"

Until that moment she hadn't made up her mind that she was going to go through with this, but their short conversation had revealed a lot about him.

Despite what had happened earlier, she suspected it took a lot to make him lose control of his emotions. He was the sort who would keep his head under pressure. She wondered what exactly had happened with the patient he'd lost. What had driven him so close to the edge? What was different about this day?

"Tomorrow? 6:00 a.m."

"You need to take her out before you leave. You don't need to walk her, just take her out to pee. Then I'll come at nine." Harriet pulled out her phone and typed a note for herself. "What time will you be home?"

"Difficult to say." He checked his schedule on his phone. "In theory, five p.m. But it could be anytime. Do I seriously have to take her out if you're coming at nine?"

"If you don't want her to wet your oak floor and ruin it, then yes. I don't want to leave Madi on her own for more than a few hours, so instead of nine I'll come at nine thirty, and then I'll come back at two thirty. That should work."

He spread his hands in a gesture of surrender. "Whatever you say. You're the expert."

She wondered if he was making fun of her but his expression was deadly serious. "I'll take her out for some fresh air and exercise, always assuming the snow isn't too deep, and then I'll spend time with her here."

"And you can do that? How many other dogs do you walk in the day?"

"It varies. Tomorrow I have a pretty busy day, but I can pass at least two of my walks on to another dog walker, so that's what I'll do. Until she's happier, Madi is my priority. I can bring some paperwork and do it in your apartment, if you're comfortable with that."

"Anything! I owe you in a big way. Thank you."

"I'm not—"

"I know." He interrupted her with a wry smile. "You're not doing it for me. You're doing it for the dog."

"Madi. I'm doing it for Madi."

"You're as sensitive as my sister. She *is* a dog. Why can't I call her that?"

"Probably for the same reason people don't call you 'the human.' It's not overly friendly."

The food arrived and Ethan spread the cartons across the kitchen island and handed her a plate.

"Help yourself. And tell me more about your business."

"Why?"

"Because I'm interested."

"What do you want to know? We walk dogs. We cover the whole of the East Side of Manhattan." And she was proud of that. Proud of the way they'd built their business from nothing.

"Presumably you don't do it all by yourself. You mentioned a sister—"

"Fliss. We're twins. We run it together."

"And you employ dog walkers?" He spooned noodles onto her plate. "How does that work?"

"They're often college students. Sometimes people who are retired. We don't really care about the background. The important thing is that they love dogs and are responsible. Our business is built on our ability to deliver a top quality service to our clients."

"So how many dogs do you walk at a time?"

"We only offer solo walks. It's a personal service. Easier to meet the needs of the dog that way."

"And you take them to the park?"

"It varies." She twisted the noodles onto her fork. "Sometimes we take them to the park, but that doesn't work for all dogs. Sometimes we just take them for walks around the neighborhood."

"So tomorrow—do I have to bathe Madi when I come in after a walk? Clean out her paws? Because I have no idea how to do that."

He was a guy who spent his days handling life-threatening situations and he was thrown by a little dog. "Just wipe her down. I'll do the rest when I arrive."

"And you *will* arrive? You're not going to leave me in the lurch to punish me for my earlier behavior?"

"I wouldn't do that to Madi."

He pulled a face. "So you're doing it because you're afraid to leave her in my care. I shouted at you, and now you think I'm beyond hope as a dog owner, and possibly even as a human being. Can you forgive me?"

She tried not to smile. "I don't know, Dr. Black. I have yet to make up my mind about you. I'll let you know when I do."

CHAPTER EIGHT

HARRIET RODE THE SUBWAY, and then walked the rest of the way to her apartment. She was desperate to whip out her phone and search for "recurrence of stammering," but it was freezing cold and she told herself that impatience wasn't a decent trade-off for possible frostbite.

Anxious to do some research, her heart sank when she arrived home to find Daniel waiting outside her apartment.

Normally she would have been pleased to see her brother, but he was one of the few people who was likely to be able to see beneath the fake smile and want to know what had happened.

And she didn't want to talk about it.

She wanted to deal with this herself, preferably by opening her laptop and doing research. She needed answers.

Why had it come back? Did the fact that it had come back briefly mean that it might come back again?

When? Under what circumstances?

Maybe the evening had ended well enough but still it felt like a huge setback.

If she'd stammered tonight, then she could stammer again.

It was something she hadn't had to think about in a long while.

Should she contact a speech therapist? Ethan didn't seem to think she should, but she wasn't convinced.

She had a thousand questions churning inside her but she knew if she voiced any of this aloud to Daniel he'd go into overprotective mode, so she filed away her questions even though it almost killed her to do it.

"Isn't this a bit late for you to visit? Normally you drop round when you're hungry." And her brother had done that less and less since he'd fallen in love with Molly. Given that the only thing she'd thought her brother was ever going to be wedded to was his single status, she found it encouraging that he was now crazily in love.

If he could find someone in the crazy tapestry of humans that populated Manhattan then surely there was hope for her too?

"Molly and I were taking the dogs for a walk and we thought we'd drop by and see how you're doing. Haven't heard from you in a while."

Because she'd been trying to be more independent.

"I'm good. Busy." She opened the door to her apartment. "Where is Molly? And where are the dogs?"

"She stepped outside to take a call and took the dogs with her. What are you doing walking round Manhattan this late?"

"It's not late, Dan." She hung up her coat. "It's only nine o'clock."

"You've been on another date?"

Molly thought about the evening she'd had. "Not exactly."

"Fliss told me your last date didn't go so well. I don't like the idea of you meeting strangers. Why didn't you call me?" He scowled at her. "I would have come to your rescue."

Which was why she hadn't called. She'd wanted to rescue herself.

Whatever trouble she found herself in, she wanted to be the one to find the way out.

"I handled it."

"Since when did you walk dogs this late?"

She might not have a father who cared about her, but her brother more than made up for that lack of parental concern.

"Since my client went away and left a dog who is finding it hard to settle in her temporary home."

Daniel strolled through to her kitchen and opened the fridge, totally at home in her apartment. "I'm surprised you didn't just bring it back here. You used to do that when we were kids. I hid that kitten under my bed for a week, remember?"

"I remember." She'd found it in one of the backstreets, injured and abandoned by its mother. She'd guessed it was no more than a few weeks old and she'd smuggled it home under her sweater and hid it in a box under the bed, where she'd cared for it until it was stronger. She intended to keep it, and hoped her brother would find a way to help her figure that out. Daniel always found a way to work with the circumstances. It was the reason he was such a great lawyer.

"You made me walk with you to the vet's so that you could ask for advice. That was when I realized you would do just about anything for an animal, even if it meant making Dad crazy." He pulled out a beer. "This has my name on it."

Harriet rolled her eyes, put her bag down and closed the shutters.

He was right, of course. If her father had known, he would have killed her.

And she'd cared about that, but not as much as she'd cared about that kitten. She knew how it felt to be vulnerable, and she was determined to be the protector as often as she was the protected.

She heard the thunder of paws, a bark, and then Molly burst through the door with two large dogs.

"I'm going to buy a sled—" she panted, hauling on their leads "—and these two can pull it. Work off some of that excess energy. It could be a whole new way of commuting in the snow."

Daniel snapped the top off the beer and pulled a second one from the fridge. "It's not a new way if you live in Greenland. It's a way of life."

"Do you ever stop being a lawyer?"

Daniel handed her a beer and took a mouthful of his own. "That's not being a lawyer. That's general knowledge."

"You always have to lay out the facts!"

"Ah, in that case I definitely wasn't being a lawyer. At best we lawyers are selective with our facts." Ignoring the dogs, he tugged Molly against him and kissed her long and hard. She sank against him and for a moment they blended, a perfect unit.

Watching them, Harriet felt an ache behind her ribs.

Great.

Love was all around her. Or that was how it seemed.

She wasn't going to be envious. She loved Daniel. She loved Molly. She was genuinely happy for them.

And jealous.

She was jealous. Jealous of her brother and jealous of her twin.

What did that say about her?

Annoyed with herself for not being the person she wanted to be, she dropped to her knees and hugged Valentine, Molly's Dalmatian. "Who's a gorgeous boy?" Valentine answered that with an enthusiastic wag of his tail and Brutus, Daniel's German shepherd, head-butted Harriet, vying for her attention. Harriet lost her balance and thumped down on the floor. It seemed she wasn't the only one who had a jealous streak. "You're gorgeous too. Even when you knock me on my butt."

Molly eased away from Daniel. "He's not that gorgeous." She dropped the backpack she was carrying and pulled off her coat, still balancing the beer in her hand. "He rolled in snow and he's soaked. Sit, Brutus. So tell me what happened with that last guy you dated, Harriet. He sounded great. Are you seeing him again? How did the date end?"

With her climbing out of the window and spraining her ankle.

Harriet decided not to tell them that. Some things were best left unsaid. Molly was a psychologist and she had a tendency to try and analyze everything. Harriet didn't want her analyzing this. "It didn't pan out."

"No? Shame. I had high hopes." Molly dragged a towel out of her bag and rubbed Brutus's fur. "So who is next? What's new?"

What's new was that she'd stammered. After years of not stammering, she'd stammered.

The feelings churned inside her, a toxic mix of panic and disappointment.

Dating had always been a challenge for her, but now it

seemed as if she'd slipped back to the bottom of a mountain she'd been climbing. It felt huge, but so far she hadn't had time to absorb it properly. How was she ever going to get to know someone if she couldn't get past that first awkward meeting?

She could have talked to Molly, and Molly would have known exactly the right thing to say. But she wasn't ready to talk about that with anyone yet.

"I'm taking a break from dating." To change the subject, she looked at her brother's suit. "You've been in court?"

"I have. Custody hearing."

"I hate that you're so busy."

Daniel raised his eyebrows. "This is my livelihood."

"I know, but whenever I talk to you I get the feeling everyone is in a miserable relationship."

"Don't listen to him." Molly rubbed Valentine's paws with a towel. "Talking to Daniel is like watching the news. You come away thinking the world is ending. It distorts your view of reality, which is that every day, all over the world, people are doing good things for other people and those things are never made public."

Daniel finished his beer. "You have an almost ridiculous faith in human nature. How are we even together?"

"Because you can't care for your dog without my help."

Harriet bent to stroke Brutus, who she'd fostered for a short while until Daniel had given him a home. "Don't start or I'll worry about you both."

"You don't need to worry about us." Molly stood up and kissed Daniel. "Are you going to tell her our news or shall I?"

"Tell her what?"

Molly scowled and Valentine was on his feet in an instant. "See? My dog senses when you make me unhappy. Better watch it, Mr. Heartbreaker, or you will be covered in teeth marks."

"Promises, promises."

Knowing that the banter could have gone on forever, Harriet interrupted. "What's your news?"

"We've fixed a date." Molly looked pleased with herself. "For our wedding. We're getting married in May, and we're having the wedding in Central Park because that's where we met. Cherry blossom. Blue skies—"

"—you in your running shoes with your hair pulled back in a tail." Daniel grinned at her. "I like it that way. It's sexy."

"I'm wearing a long white dress."

"In the park?" Daniel winced. "Are we leaving the dogs at home?"

"No!"

"Then I don't recommend a long white dress."

Harriet interrupted again. "Congratulations. I'm so happy for you." And she was, she really was. They were perfect together, just as Fliss and Seth were perfect together. Two by two. Everyone was in pairs.

Except for her.

She was one.

Alone.

Molly hugged her. "Will you be my bridesmaid? You and Fliss?"

"Of course. Thank you."

Daniel sprawled on her sofa, watching her closely. "This place is quiet without Fliss."

It was horribly quiet.

"I've been too busy with work to notice. And fostering animals keeps the place pretty noisy."

Daniel glanced around. "I don't see animals."

Her brother didn't miss a thing. "I had Teddy until recently. He went to his forever home." She watched as Valentine lay down on the floor. Brutus joined him. Molly and Daniel had met while walking the dogs and now the two dogs were inseparable. "So are you working on anything exciting right now?"

"The usual. Handling people's toxic marriages. Why anyone bothers I have no idea, but I guess people's optimism and fairy-tale belief in the power of Happy Ever After keeps me in business, so who am I to question it?"

Molly gave him a look. "You're marrying me. You shouldn't question it."

"You are my Snow White."

"I hate apples."

"My Cinderella?"

"She was great at cleaning, and I'm crap."

"Rapunzel? No, your hair is the wrong color and too short. Beauty? No, because that would make me the beast."

"Which is how you're known in impolite circles."

Daniel glanced at his watch. "I'm hungry. We thought we could order pizza. Molly?"

Pizza?

She thought of the small mountain of Thai food she'd consumed with Ethan.

And all the questions stacked up in her head, waiting to be answered.

"I've eaten, but you go ahead." In truth it was nice to see her brother, and it felt good to have the apartment filled with noise, laughter and dogs.

Maybe she needed to get a dog of her own.

It was something she'd considered a few times and rejected because she wanted to keep herself free to foster animals from the shelter when necessary. But now she was starting to rethink that plan.

"What did you cook? Any leftovers in the fridge? You're the best cook on the planet."

Harriet paused. "I didn't say I cooked. I said I ate."

"So you *did* go on a date?" Molly looked interested.

"It wasn't a date. I was dealing with some issues settling a dog, it got late, so he offered me something to eat. He'd worked a long day and he was tired. It was no big deal."

"He? And is 'he' a lawyer?"

"He's a doctor."

Molly slapped her hand on the arm of the sofa, making the dogs jump. "Perfect! I've always said that someone in the medical profession would suit you well. Smart, caring—"

"This is not a personal relationship, it's a professional one."

"Yeah? But apart from right at the beginning, you don't often see your clients, do you?"

"That's true, but this is different. He is struggling with the dog."

"And you're helping him." Molly smiled. "That's good."

"Molly—"

"Don't fight her," Daniel advised. "She will make a relationship out of a box of tissues and a candle if those are the only items in the room. She can't help herself. This is a DNA situation."

Harriet smiled. "You think matchmaking is in her DNA? It's an inherited trait, like blue eyes?"

"No. In our house DNA means Do Not Argue."

Molly raised an eyebrow. "Something you know little about, Daniel Knight."

Harriet gave up. "You guys are cute, but I have an early start and should really get some sleep."

Daniel stood up. "You're walking this guy's dog again tomorrow?"

"Twice. Morning and afternoon, so that we don't leave her on her own for long. I have three other walks besides Madi."

"Who is this doctor? Give me his name," Daniel said casually. "I'll check him out."

"You will not check him out." Harriet gave him a push. "I don't walk into your courtroom and embarrass you, so don't do it to me."

"I just want to check he's not going to hurt you."

It was no wonder she struggled to step out of her comfort zone. Her brother and sister had virtually locked her in there.

"He's a client, Daniel. The only way he can hurt me is if he doesn't settle his invoices on time."

"And what are you going to do if the dog doesn't behave?"

"She will. I'm sure Madi will be fine now."

CHAPTER NINE

Madi howled all night.

She started as soon as the lights went out, and Ethan dragged himself out of bed and tried talking to her, but that simply made her howl more.

He prided himself on being able to calm panicking humans, but it seemed that when it came to dogs he didn't have what it took.

His head throbbing, he let her out of the crate to try and find out what was wrong and she shot past him, up the stairs into his bedroom.

"You have got to be kidding me."

By the time he walked into the room, she was curled up in the middle of his bed looking as if she belonged there.

"No way. This is not happening." He tugged at her collar and she somehow dug herself into the mattress, refusing to move. In the end Ethan picked her up and carried her back to the crate. "*This* is where you sleep."

Why did anyone choose to have a dog?

Life was tough enough already. Why add in an extra layer of complication?

He found it incomprehensible.

His sister would have observed that he was the one who was incomprehensible.

You need something in your life other than work, Ethan.

His ex-wife would have agreed.

It was also the reason they were now divorced.

Madi lay down and Ethan felt a rush of relief.

All right. Maybe caring for a dog wasn't so hard after all. You just needed to be firm and in command.

His smug feeling lasted until he turned the lights off.

Madi barked again, but this time the barking was interspersed with pitiful howls.

Conscious of the other inhabitants of his apartment block, Ethan let out a string of curses. What was he supposed to do? If he left her, he'd have his neighbors complaining. But he couldn't spend the entire night getting up every five minutes. To deal with the challenges of his job, he had to be rested.

Throwing off the covers, he stomped downstairs again and tried being firm. This time he didn't take her out of her crate.

Madi's barking grew louder and more frantic.

Willing to do just about anything to get a few hours' rest and avoid a complaint from his neighbors, Ethan let her out of the crate.

She sped upstairs to the bedroom.

Ethan followed and shook his head in disbelief when he saw her curled up in exactly the same place as last time.

The middle of the bed.

What was he supposed to do?

"You can stay here this once." He couldn't believe he was saying it. "Tomorrow I'm taking advice from Harriet on how to get you to sleep in your own bed. You should know I don't often have overnight guests, so this is not going to become a habit. Are we clear?"

Madi lay with her head on her paws, comfortable and settled.

"I'll take that as a yes." Ethan pushed her across to make room, slid into bed. "I hope you don't snore. I need my sleep. I need to be awake to do my job well."

He was talking to himself.

Madi was already asleep.

Ethan finally drifted off too.

When the alarm finally cut the threads on sleep, he didn't feel as if he'd had any rest at all.

Madi was still asleep next to him.

Unbelievable, he thought as he dragged on his clothes.

Outside it was still dark, which wasn't unusual. He spent most of the winter going forward and backward to work in the dark. The only light he saw was artificial. What *was* unusual was starting the day feeling worse than he'd felt when it had ended.

He took the dog outside as instructed and almost froze on the sidewalk as a frigid arctic blast of icy air wrapped itself round him.

Harriet was going to walk dogs in this all day? How did she do it?

She was obviously a lot tougher than she looked.

He went back to his apartment, gave Madi a cursory rub with an old towel and then got ready for work.

As he was about to leave the apartment, he took a final look at the dog.

"You're going to sit there and be a good girl. Harriet will be here soon."

Madi followed him to the door, staying close to his side.

"No, you are staying here and I am going to work. Do you understand?"

Madi wagged her tail.

"I'm taking that to be a yes."

Hopeful that now that she'd had a comfortable night, she'd behave herself during the day, he left for work.

He arrived at the hospital to find the place in chaos.

There had been a fire in a warehouse close by and the department was crammed with patients suffering from burns and smoke inhalation.

Ethan dived into the deep end and forgot about Madi. He forgot about Harriet, his sister and even his niece.

His entire focus was his patients, which made it all the more surprising when he arrived home ten hours later to find Harriet still in his apartment.

The place looked exactly the way he'd left it. There was no pasta explosion, no flour avalanche, no visible signs that anything was amiss. Madi was lying on the floor, chewing her toy bone. The only clue that everything was not as smooth as it seemed, was Harriet's presence and the expression on her face.

"What?" He removed his coat, showering the floor with snowflakes. He knew she'd planned to leave well before he arrived home, so presumably things weren't as smooth as they appeared on the surface. "I take my bad news like a shot of tequila—fast and undiluted, so don't hold back."

"Madi wasn't altogether happy today."

"Given your ability to smooth rough edges, I'm translating that to mean things were really bad. How bad?"

Harriet sighed. "She doesn't like being left alone. She was fine when I took her for her walk this morning, but when I returned this afternoon she'd been howling and barking for the entire time she was left on her own. She has separation anxiety."

"How do you know?"

"Because I met Judy in the stairwell."

"Who is Judy?"

Harriet looked puzzled. "She came to your door last night. You spoke to her."

"Are you talking about Mrs. Crouch?" He'd lived here for six years and he hadn't known her first name was Judy. Even if he *had* known, he wouldn't have felt comfortable using it. Mrs. Crouch wasn't a first name person, although it seemed Harriet had managed to crack through the formality. "She complained?"

"She didn't exactly *complain*. But we both agreed it couldn't continue. She came in and I made her tea. I hope you don't mind."

Ethan tried to imagine the austere Mrs. Crouch sitting on his sofa sipping tea.

"You're a surprising woman, Harriet Knight. Mrs. Crouch isn't known for her tolerance or her desire to communicate." Something for which he'd frequently been grateful when he returned home in the early hours from the hospital and met her in the elevator.

"She's probably a little shy with people before she gets to know them. I know all about that. And she has lived on her own since her husband died, so that probably doesn't help. You lose a little confidence, I think. I've seen it happen with Glenys."

"Who is Glenys?"

"One of my clients. I walk Harvey for her."

"Harvey?"

"The detail doesn't matter. What matters is that Judy is probably suffering in the way Glenys is. It's lonely for her. And of course she rarely sees Margaret—"

"Wait—who is Margaret?"

"Her daughter. She lives in Austin, Texas. She moved there eight years ago, two years before Bill died. And Margaret has just had a baby."

Ethan was struggling to keep up. He hadn't even known Mrs. Crouch had a daughter. "Bill was her husband?"

"Yes, and naturally Judy is a little upset at the thought of not seeing Charlene."

"Charlene?"

"Her first grandchild."

"I can't believe this."

"Why? My grandmother once told me that having grandchildren was the highlight of her life. Unlike when you're a parent, you don't have the responsibility. You can simply have fun with them."

"That's not the part I can't believe. What I can't believe is that she told you all this voluntarily."

"Well, of course she told me voluntarily." Harriet lifted her eyebrows. "Or maybe you think I tied her to the sofa and tortured her with Earl Grey tea?"

"I've never known her to be particularly forthcoming."

"Have you even tried talking to her?"

"I—" It was a fair question. Ethan ran his hand over the back of his neck. "Honestly? No. Our communication is mostly monosyllabic greetings when we run into each other in the elevator. Usually when I bump into her I'm either in a rush to get to work, or comatose returning from work." He hadn't known she'd lost her husband, that she lived alone or that she had a daughter.

He was fairly sure his ex-wife wouldn't have known that, either.

But Harriet knew.

"I always feel if there's a problem the best way to handle it is conversation, and conversations are best conducted in a comfortable environment not in a drafty corridor. So I invited her in."

"You told me you find it difficult to talk to strangers."

"I do, but in this instance we bonded over our concern for Madi. Did you know Judy has a Shih Tzu?"

"A—what?" Was that a disease he hadn't heard of?

"A Shih Tzu—it's a breed of dog."

"No. I didn't know that." Ethan flung his coat across the nearest chair. "I'm learning from you every day."

"Turns out she's finding it hard to walk it herself, so I've promised to take him out as I'm in the building anyway with Madi."

"So apart from being Mrs. Crouch's new best friend and picking up some business along the way, what else happened?"

Harriet hesitated. "Judy wasn't super happy about the howling."

"I'm not super happy, either." Ethan gave Madi a look, and she looked right back. He was learning that dogs had particularly expressive faces. "She howled for most of the night."

"Oh no!" Harriet sounded appalled. "The poor thing."

Ethan leaned against the kitchen counter, not sure whether to be amused or exasperated. "Don't I deserve a tiny scrap of sympathy?"

"Were you anxious and frightened?"

He held her gaze. "I was terrified. I cried all night. Shivered and sobbed like a baby."

Her eyes narrowed. "Somehow I can't picture that."

"Well, maybe not *sobbed*, exactly, that would have required energy and I didn't have any. I don't know why. Oh wait, it was because I had a dog howling in my ear when I should have been sleeping."

Harriet knelt on the floor and hugged Madi. "Were you scared in a strange place? Were you uncomfortable?"

"I can assure you she slept in maximum comfort in the middle of my king-size bed. Someone needs to teach her to share."

"The topic of where to sleep in a king-size bed isn't generally covered at dog obedience." Harriet stood up. "You shouldn't have let her sleep on your bed. That's bad."

"Tell me about it."

"You're teaching her bad habits."

"She came to me with those habits fully formed."

"She should have slept in her crate."

Ethan folded his arms. "And if you have any useful tips on how to persuade her to do that, I'm listening."

"Did you try soothing her with your voice?"

"I tried everything short of pouring her a whiskey and singing her a lullaby."

Harriet gave him an exasperated look. "How did she end up on your bed?"

"I opened the crate and she ran. She clearly has some sort of inbuilt radar for supreme comfort."

"Why didn't you speak to her firmly and take her back?"

"I did. Several times. But she started howling, and having to move apartments because my neighbors hate me is a high price to pay for a few nights helping my sister. I had to be fit for work today so in the end I left her where she was."

"In the middle of the bed?"

"Yes." He glared at Madi. "You need to rethink your sleeping habits."

Madi wagged her tail.

"Oh—" Harriet pressed her hand to her chest and he frowned.

"What's wrong? Indigestion? Chest pain?"

"No, I—" she said, and let her hand drop, "it's *you*. You're teasing her."

"Teasing? I was scolding her."

"You were teasing her, and she knows you were teasing her because she's wagging her tail."

"Then she clearly isn't well tuned in to the subtleties of body language."

"You like her."

Ethan ignored that. "Have you been here all afternoon?"

"You like her."

He sighed. "She's not completely awful. Compared to some of the humans I meet, she's pretty cute. Now answer my question."

"Yes, I've been here since four o'clock. I didn't like to leave her. It didn't seem fair."

"Thank you." He lifted his hand. "And before you say anything, I know you are talking about the dog, not me. That's fine. You're right, it isn't fair. But life rarely is and in the meantime we have to find an option that works for all of us, because we can't carry on like this. She's cute, but she is wrecking my life. I have to be able to concentrate at work, so if you have any suggestions I'd love to hear them."

The irony of it didn't escape him. He was used to making split-second decisions in a fast-moving, tense working environment but he had no idea what to do about this unexpected disruption to his life.

Was he going to be sleeping with the dog until his sister returned?

"I don't suppose you'd consider working shorter days until she is settled?" The way she said it made it obvious that she didn't think for one moment he would consider it.

And she was right.

Ethan thought about the throng of people in the emergency room and his already overstretched colleagues. "Not an option. Can you come more often?"

"You want me to come three times a day? I suppose I could, but I'm not sure that will help. It won't solve the fact that she'll be alone in between those times."

"Could you put her in your backpack and take her with you on your other walks?"

Her eyes widened. "She's a dog, Ethan. Not a sandwich lunch."

"I've seen people carry dogs in handbags."

Her head turned toward Madi. "She's not a large dog by most standards, but she wouldn't fit into any bag I've ever seen. That's not an option, either." She hesitated. "I know you're not super keen on the idea, but I could take her home with me."

"No." Ethan shook his head and then realized how rude his response probably seemed. "Don't be offended. It's not that I don't want to. Frankly, it would be the best option all round but Debra wanted me to take her. I can't go against her wishes. I said I'd give Madi a home, and I'll give her a home. We have to find another way. And taking her back to your place won't work if the problem is that she wants company."

Far from being offended, her gaze softened. "I'm not offended. I'm impressed at your loyalty and the fact that you do what you say you're going to do. Plenty of people don't." She looked at Madi. "I suppose we will have to go with the three walks a day option and see how we get on. But I'll need to get Debra's approval because it will cost—"

"Cost doesn't matter. I'll pay. Let's not bother Debra with this. And before you say anything, it's not simply because I don't want her to know I'm inept. She has a lot on her plate right now and I don't want her worrying. But you don't think three walks a day will work, do you? And if you do more it will hardly be worth you leaving." He stared at her, wondering why that option hadn't occurred to him before. "That's it."

"Excuse me?"

"It's not worth you leaving. So you could stay. Dog sitting. I have a comfortable guest room with its own bathroom. You can treat the place like home."

"Wait! Slow down." Something that looked like panic flashed across her face. "We don't offer dog sitting. Solo walks only."

"It's snowing. They are forecasting more. What if you're not able to get here one day? I will lose my job and my home. And where would Madi and I live then?"

"Are you trying to guilt-trip me?"

"Whatever it takes."

"You're seriously suggesting I stay here?" She said it slowly, as if she couldn't quite believe what he was asking her to do.

He couldn't quite believe it, either.

"Yes, and believe me that's not something I do lightly." He made the joke but she didn't laugh. She looked anxious and undecided.

"I c-c-c—"

Can't.

Dammit. He'd stressed her. *Again.*

She shook her head in frustration. "No."

He noticed she'd chosen a different way to say the same thing. It was a common strategy among people who stammered. One word sticks, lead with a different word.

"You're not comfortable staying in a stranger's apartment, particularly when the stranger is still there. I get that. But this is an emergency. You're looking at a desperate man. I cannot be my best self at work if I'm up all night with a howling dog. And I'm not a stranger. This is our third meeting. Our relationship has already lasted longer than some marriages." He was relieved to see her smile. "For the sake of my sanity, my sofa, and most of all for Madi, please move in. You can bring whatever you need to run your business here."

"Again, no."

"Harriet, I'm begging you." On impulse he bent and scooped up Madi, trying not to drop her as she wriggled and tried to lick his face. "And, more importantly, Madi is begging you too."

"That's manipulative."

"It's the truth. Will you do it?"

CHAPTER TEN

SHE HAD TO be crazy, Harriet thought as she packed her things into a large suitcase the following morning.

She could have stayed in the comfort and security of her apartment. It was what she wanted. Christmas was approaching. She wanted to make the place cozy and festive. Decorate. Put things in place to make sure she felt comfortable and able to enjoy herself. Pad her world with comfort to keep out the psychological chill of spending the holidays without her family.

She didn't want to stay in a stranger's apartment.

Which was *exactly* why she was doing this.

Spending a few nights with Ethan Black would be the ultimate challenge, which was why the first thing she stuffed into her suitcase were three of her favorite books. She had a feeling she was going to need the comfort.

Resisting the temptation to call him and tell him she'd changed her mind, she added sweaters, several pairs of pants and a couple of shirts.

She removed a dress from the hanger and then paused. Why would she need a dress?

She was going to be walking dogs. Doing what she always did. She wasn't going to need a dress.

She was putting it back on the hanger when her phone rang.

It was Fliss.

"Hi there." Harriet tucked the phone between her ear and her shoulder as she thrust the dress back into her crowded closet space. "Everything okay?"

"Never better. How about you? You have snow!"

"We do." Thinking of it made Harriet stuff two extra pairs of thick socks into her packing.

"Are you having trouble getting around? Any cancellations?"

"Not so far." She picked up her favorite pair of boots and a spare scarf. "By the way, I'm moving my base of operations a few blocks south. I'm dog sitting for a while." She said it casually, even though she knew there was no hope that Fliss would leave it at that.

"You're *what*? You mean overnight? You said you would never do that. I've been trying to talk you into it for months. Who requested it? It must have been one of our special clients for you to say yes."

"It was Debra." She told herself that Debra was the ultimate beneficiary, so it wasn't exactly a lie. "This is a one-off, special circumstance. Her daughter is in hospital."

"You told me. And Madi was staying with her brother, and you agreed to walk twice a day. It's right here in our schedule. So where does staying the night fit into all that? What were the special circumstances?"

"Madi is having problems settling."

"Problems?"

Harriet wrapped her running shoes in a bag and tucked them into the side of the case. "She's wrecking the apartment when she's left."

"Well, dogs are social animals."

"I know, but knowing doesn't help me solve the problem. Worse, she's barking and howling. This guy has neighbors, and he wants to carry on living there after Madi has gone." Harriet switched the phone to her other shoulder and started pushing underwear into the corners of her case. "She's not settling at night, either. She's howling."

"So you're moving in. With a stranger."

"Not a stranger. He's Debra's brother, which is as good as having a reference. And he's a doctor."

"I didn't know there were different categories of stranger."

"It's not as if I haven't met him. We've talked a couple of times." Harriet decided not to mention the dinner they'd shared.

"Just because he's a doctor, doesn't mean he's a saint. Think of Dr. Jekyll and Mr. Hyde."

"Fictional characters don't count."

"Some people say Jack the Ripper was a surgeon."

"You are so comforting." Harriet packed her pajamas. "I don't think Debra's brother is a serial killer."

"Serial killers have relatives, you know."

"He is not a serial killer. I've met him several times. Remember that trip to the hospital I took when I sprained my ankle?"

"Are you telling me this guy is Dr. Hot?"

"Your name, not mine."

"Well, why didn't you say so right away? Now I approve. Harriet Knight, congratulations. I never thought I'd see you moving in with a man you barely know. You are officially on your way to being a bad girl."

Harriet rolled her eyes. Her inner GPS never took her anywhere near that particular destination. "He's not even going to be there. He spends most of his life at work. That's the reason we have a problem. Madi is struggling being on her own all day so I'm going to base myself there so that I can give her a little more attention and see if I can settle her down."

"So you are moving into a stranger's apartment to care for a dog."

"That's right."

"That's all it is?"

"Of course. What else?"

"I've always said you'd make the perfect doctor's wife."

"That's insane." Harriet stood up. "You talk as if doctors are one homogeneous being instead of individual people. And this guy doesn't seem like the relationship type."

"What have you packed to sleep in? Do *not* wear that old T-shirt with *I love dogs* on it."

"It's my favorite T-shirt and I do love dogs. It's honest nightwear."

"It's not something you need to emblazon on your breasts when you're spending the night with a sexy guy."

"I never said he was sexy."

"Is he?"

Harriet thought about the way he'd waited patiently while she'd struggled to get her words out. He hadn't once tried to finish her sentence. True, he'd yelled but only that once and even she had to admit his frustration had been justified. And he'd apologized. She didn't know many people who were big enough to apologize.

He'd let Madi sleep on his bed when she was distressed.
And the way he'd picked her up—

She sighed. "He's sexy."

"Whoa. Never heard you say that about a guy before. What do you like about him most? Shoulders? Abs? Great eyes?"

"He's a good listener."

"I'm talking about what makes him sexy."

"So am I. That's what makes him sexy to me. I like the fact that he didn't interrupt me. He didn't try to—" She stopped just in time. She wasn't ready to tell Fliss that her stammer had come back. She wanted to deal with it by herself. "He didn't try to dominate the conversation in the way some guys do."

"So what you're saying is that he's totally unfortunate looking, but a nice person?"

Harriet laughed. "That's not what I'm saying. But looks don't matter, do they? My first internet dating experience kept checking his reflection on his phone."

"Gross."

"Exactly. And what Ethan looks like is irrelevant because this isn't a date, it's work. I'm doing this for Madi and for Debra. And for him, because he cannot make life-and-death decisions after three hours' sleep."

"I have been trying to talk you into dog sitting for ages. This is great."

"This is a one-off. Don't get any ideas." Harriet could almost see Fliss making notes and plans. Next she'd be sending an email with suggestions for expanding their business into dog sitting and she really didn't want that.

"I can't believe you're doing this."

Harriet tried to close her bulging case. "I can't believe it, either. But I'm doing it for Madi."

For the dog. For Debra.

Not for any other reason.

CHAPTER ELEVEN

"LIFE WOULD BE so much easier if I was better with people." Harriet slowed her pace so that Glenys could keep up. The drop in temperature didn't seem to have kept people inside. The streets were busier than ever and there was a buzz of expectation in the air that increased as they drew closer to Christmas.

Across Manhattan, the stores unveiled their holiday displays and people traveled especially to admire the store windows.

Harriet liked to wait until after dark and then wander along Madison Avenue, Lexington and Fifth Avenue.

When they were growing up, her mother had taken her and Fliss to see the store windows and Harriet remembered the special buzz that had come from being just the three of them. Without her father there, she hadn't been so afraid to speak.

Glenys patted her arm. "What are you talking about? You're wonderful with people."

"Not really, although I'm better one-on-one than I am in a crowd. But I want to be the sort of person who can bound into a room and be the life and soul of a party. It must be great to feel that comfortable and confident." She watched as Harvey picked his way over the snow. "I'm a coward."

Glenys stopped walking. "Oh no, honey. You're nothing of the sort. You are brave."

Harriet thought about the number of times she'd almost called Ethan Black and canceled. "I'm really not."

"Think about it—" Glenys waggled her gloved finger. "Is it hard for Fliss to bounce into a room and talk to everyone?"

"No. She does it naturally." And it was a skill she'd always envied. There were so many days when she wished she were more like her sister.

"So what's brave about that? She does it without a second thought. Brave is walking into that room when it's the last thing you want to do. Brave is putting yourself out there when you'd rather hide away in the safety of your apartment. Brave is what you're doing. Moving in with a guy you hardly know to protect that innocent little dog."

"You're freaking me out, Glenys. You're making it sound like the biggest risk."

"It's going to be fine," Glenys said, her voice devoid of conviction. "You're brave as a lion, honey."

Harriet didn't feel particularly lionlike as she hauled her suitcase across town to Ethan's apartment in the West Village.

Unlike the rest of Manhattan, where the streets were laid out in an ordered, logical grid, here they meandered and curved. It was easy to get lost, particularly as Harriet didn't know this area as well as the rest of Manhattan. She walked past an organic bakery, a craft store and an artsy boutique all decked out for the holidays with garlands of holly leaves and twinkling lights. Now, with the cobbled streets hidden under layers of snow, it felt as if she'd stepped straight into the pages of a Dickens novel.

She reached Ethan's apartment block and took the elevator to the top floor.

He'd already left for work and there was no sign of Madi.

Concerned, Harriet dumped her suitcase in the living room and sprinted upstairs.

Madi was sprawled in the middle of his bed, her eyes closed.

Harriet shook her head in disapproval. "You are a bad girl."

Madi opened her eyes, then sprang off the bed and gave Harriet an ecstatic welcome.

"You are not allowed to sleep on his bed. Are you listening to me?"

Madi wagged her tail.

"You have to behave. I'm not taking any nonsense from you."

It was the first time she'd had the chance to take a proper look at his apartment. The first time she'd come here it had been dark, and yesterday she'd been too busy focusing on the fact he wanted her to dog sit to pay any attention to her surroundings.

But now she looked.

The sun-filled living room had high ceilings and exposed brick walls. There was a large wood-burning fireplace, and three oversize windows faced west and offered a view of the Hudson River.

Harriet walked across to the window. From her own apartment she saw other buildings. Brick walls, trimmed with iron fire escapes. If she stood on a chair and craned her neck she could just about see the tops of a few trees in Central Park. Her view was nothing like this.

She gazed for a moment and then turned back to the room.

A large leather sofa faced a fireplace that was flanked with bookcases. They ran the whole length of the wall and reached up to the ceiling.

For Harriet, a bookcase was too much of a draw to simply walk past without giving it attention.

Curious, she stepped forward to read some of the spines.

Dickens and Dostoyevsky nestled alongside modern authors such as Stephen King. There were medical textbooks, books on music and art history. If she'd had to compile a character study of the owner of the apartment based on the contents of his bookshelves, she would have struggled.

What it told her was that Ethan Black read what he wanted to read. The books on the shelves hadn't been chosen to impress, but were a haphazard catalog of the owner's varied tastes and interests.

Two large armchairs sat invitingly on either side of the fireplace and on the coffee table in between them there were more books and a few medical journals. A photographic book on Prague, a biography of a leading politician and a book on motivation written by a gold-medal-winning skier called Tyler O'Neil.

On the shelf in front of the bookcase were several photographs. She stepped forward and took a closer look. She recognized Debra in one, with a younger girl who was presumably Ethan's niece. Next to that was a photograph of four men standing on a snowy slope in ski gear. She recognized Ethan Black. Who were the other three men? His brothers?

There was another photo with about twelve people grouped together, laughing.

Whoever they were, Ethan seemed to have a big family and lots of friends.

She felt a stab of envy. No doubt his Christmas would be full of laughter and eggnog. Not that she particularly liked eggnog, but she would have liked to have a busy, noisy Christmas.

Harriet resisted the temptation to sink into the comfortable armchair and lose herself in one of those books. Books had always been a comfort to her. More than comfort. There were times when reading came close to an addiction.

When things had been tough at home, Harriet's solution had been to remove herself from life and disappear. She'd chosen to be invisible. Sometimes physically, by hiding under the table, but sometimes psychologically by diving into a literary world unlike her own.

As a child she'd liked to sink into the pages and lose herself for hours at a time. When she was reading, she didn't just leave her own life behind, she stepped into someone else's. There were times when she'd read for hours without noticing the passage of time or the onset of darkness. When it grew too dark to read, she simply switched on her flashlight and read under the covers so that she didn't disturb her sister, who was sleeping in the next bed. At school, she carried her book around. When things were difficult, the weight of her bag would comfort her. It helped just to know the book was there, waiting for her. At various points in the day she'd feel the edges bump against her thigh, reminding her of its existence. It was like having a friend close by, telling her *I'm still here and we can spend time together later.*

Even now, more than a decade on from that difficult time

of her life, she found herself instinctively reaching for a book when she was stressed. Comfort was different things to different people. To some it was a bar of chocolate or a glass of wine, a run in the park or coffee with a friend.

To Harriet, it was a book. Now, when she was feeling uncomfortable and unsettled in a stranger's home, was one of those times.

There, on the shelf in front of her, was an elaborate edition of Charles Dickens's *A Christmas Carol*. It was one of her favorite stories, particularly at this time of year. She loved reading about Scrooge's transformation. It gave her hope.

She reached to pull it from the shelf and then paused.

If she started reading, she'd find it difficult to stop and she had work to do. Later, she could read.

Regretfully, she stepped back from the bookshelves, gazing at them the way another woman might salivate over chocolate.

Fliss had never been able to understand how the mere thought of reading could lift her spirits and make her feel excited.

Tearing her gaze away from temptation, she picked up her case and carried it upstairs.

It was a duplex apartment, and in many ways it felt more like a house. Certainly more like a house than her apartment did.

If she stopped and listened she could hear faint sounds of street noise coming from far below, but the place was remarkably quiet for Manhattan.

Even as she had the thought, Madi barked and Harriet put her case down and shook her head.

"No." She spoke firmly. "Quiet." She knew that patience and consistency were the secret to training a dog.

Madi looked at her and wagged her tail but didn't bark, so Harriet picked up her case again and hauled it upstairs.

There was a master bedroom suite that was obviously Ethan's, and she glimpsed a walk-in closet that had been cleverly converted to a mini gym. There was a rack of free weights, a bench and other pieces of exercise equipment.

So even though his nutrition left something to be desired, he did work out.

Tearing her gaze away from the big bed, she left the room and found the spare room.

It was spacious and comfortable, decorated in dark forest greens, with a rug on the oak floor. There were cushions and the bed was draped with a warm, velvety throw that invited the occupant to snuggle.

This room was much smaller than his, but large enough to house a desk by the window and have its own small bathroom. It also had another wall of bookshelves.

It was another point in his favor that Ethan was a book lover.

She put her case inside, removed her laptop from her backpack and placed it on the desk by the window.

By the time she'd settled herself down, she'd decided that she was in love with Ethan's apartment. It wasn't as big and showy as the one her brother Daniel owned on Fifth Avenue, but it was elegant and comfortable, full of sunlight and character. And books. There were books everywhere. Some of them were stacked in piles on the floor because there wasn't room on the shelves.

Who couldn't be happy living here?

Madi watched her from the doorway and she smiled at the dog.

"You picked a nice property for your time away from home. And you're a good girl. How about a walk? We could drop into a couple of stores and buy something for dinner."

The prospect of cooking in that wonderfully equipped kitchen excited her as much as the idea of having someone to cook for. She'd been cooking meals for one for the past five months.

Maybe dog sitting wasn't so bad after all.

ETHAN TOOK THE elevator to his apartment with a sense of trepidation. His head ached. He wanted to take a shower, pour himself a glass of wine and relax with a book.

If he didn't have houseguests—did the dog count as a guest?—that was exactly what he'd be doing.

It was what he *wanted* to do.

He was used to coming home and thinking only of himself.

Selfish and single-minded, his ex-wife had called it. Fortunately she'd been wired the same way, which was why their parting had been fairly amicable. They'd both been married to their jobs, which made it virtually impossible to make the other sort of marriage work.

As he opened his front door, he wondered what he would find this time. Disconsolate neighbors? A wrecked sofa? An empty food cupboard?

Braced for all of those possibilities and worse, he opened the door and paused.

The mellow sound of jazz floated through the apartment along with the most delicious smells.

He heard laughter and the sound of Harriet's voice as

she chatted. For a moment he thought she'd invited people round and felt a flash of irritation because the last thing he felt like being was sociable. But then he strolled through to the kitchen and saw that Harriet was talking to the dog, chatting confidently and without a hint of a stammer as she stirred something that simmered on the stove.

"So I need to do the accounts, but it's something I always put off." She added a spoonful of something to the pot on the stove, and then a pinch of something else. "It's one of my biggest failings. Putting off doing the things I hate. Do you ever do that?"

Ethan was about to respond, but then he remembered she wasn't talking to him. She was talking to the dog.

And she was obviously more comfortable talking to the dog than she ever was with him.

Gone was the wariness that was present whenever she talked to Ethan.

"Fliss usually does it, which is exactly why I've said I'll do it." She gave the pot another stir. "When someone always does things for you, it stops you doing them for yourself."

He barely recognized his kitchen. Overnight it had transformed from a stark, sterile barely used space into a fusion of color and scent. A freshly baked loaf of bread lay cooling on the countertop.

It was an alien scene.

Medical school had been a nonstop ingestion of fast food eaten at an even faster pace, and his short-lived marriage had consisted mostly of takeout food or meals eaten in restaurants. Early in their marriage Alison had cooked a couple of meals that had ended up in the trash when he was late home. After that, she'd given up. His sister, outspoken, had once told him their relationship had been a recipe for disaster.

Ethan had joked that neither of them knew what a recipe was.

They certainly didn't have homemaking anywhere on their priority list.

Something niggled in his brain.

He thought back to the conversation when Harriet had told him that she was single and dating.

Was that what this was? Was she playing house? And if so, what exactly was his role in this?

He felt a twinge of unease. What if she'd misunderstood his reasons for asking her to move in with him? What if she wasn't here because of Madi, but because of him?

He thought back to something Susan had said.

You're young, single and an excellent doctor, Black. That makes you a catch.

Ethan knew differently. Despite, or perhaps because of, those qualities that made him an excellent doctor, he knew he was a bad deal for any woman.

But what if Harriet didn't?

What if she thought he was just the person she'd been looking for?

She lowered the heat under the pan and turned and smiled at him. "How was your day?"

How was your day, dear?

He and Alison had never talked about their days. Partly because they'd rarely occupied the same space for long enough to indulge in any kind of conversation, and partly because in the short time they weren't working neither of them had wanted to talk about it.

He wished he'd thought this through more carefully before asking Harriet to move in.

"My day was busy." He threw his coat over the back of the nearest chair, trying to work out the best way to handle this. "I see you're all settled in."

Madi uncurled herself and trotted across to greet him, tail wagging.

He'd returned home to a woman cooking in his kitchen, and a dog.

He hadn't seen so much domesticity in one place since the last time he'd been home to visit his parents. And that had been a while.

"She's been good today, but she's been glued to my side for most of it." Harriet lifted the lid off the blue pot and stirred.

Ethan lost his train of thought. Whatever she was stirring smelled fantastic.

His mouth watered and his stomach reminded him he hadn't eaten since lunchtime.

"I wasn't expecting you to cook. You didn't have to do that."

She glanced at him, puzzled. "Excuse me?"

He decided to be honest. "Look, I appreciate the whole 'homemaking' thing, but that wasn't part of the agreement we had. Your job is to look after the dog, that's all. Not me. I'm not part of the deal here."

"The deal?"

"You only need to feed the dog. I could have been late and then the wonderful meal you've spent hours creating would have been ruined."

Comprehension dawned. Understanding was swiftly followed by annoyance.

There was a little flare of anger in her eyes. The same anger he'd seen the day he'd shouted at Madi. "You think I did this for *you*?"

"Didn't you?"

There was a pause, and he had the feeling she was choosing her words carefully.

"I'm cooking because, believe it or not, I have to eat. I have a physical job and I work long hours, often outdoors in the cold. I need fuel. And I mean real fuel, not the nutrition-free takeout food you live on that is loaded with salt, sugar and not much else." She turned away and put the spoon down on the saucer, slowly and carefully, as if she was having to fight hard not to throw it at him. "And when we made our 'agreement,' it didn't occur to me that I wouldn't be allowed to use your kitchen. I'm new to the rules of dog sitting, but I was assuming I could treat your home as my own for the duration of the job."

Realizing he'd made a huge mistake Ethan made what was intended to be a placatory gesture, but she wasn't looking. "Of course you're allowed to use my kitchen. That's not—"

"That's not, what?" She turned swiftly. "That's not what you meant? Then what did you mean? What's the problem?"

The problem was that he should have kept his big mouth shut. Again. "I may have misread the situation."

"*May* have? Just to clarify, you thought I was turning this into some sort of romantic evening with you in the starring role, is that right?"

Definitely should have kept his mouth shut. "You mentioned that you were doing online dating, that's all, and I thought—" Aware that he was making it worse, he stopped talking and she lifted an eyebrow.

"You thought? You thought I was desperate, is that right? You think you tick all the boxes if a woman is looking for a guy."

If he'd thought he was in trouble before, he was in even bigger trouble now.

He was starting to understand why she was so good at dog training. That raised eyebrow alone made him want to take refuge in the crate.

"Harriet—"

"You've had your say, now it's my turn." She turned the heat off under the pot and lifted a deep bowl from the cabinet. "If you think me cooking myself something to eat in your apartment is a sign that I'm making a move on you, then you've definitely misread the situation."

That was becoming abundantly clear. "Perhaps I should—"

"Firstly, I signed up for online dating *not* because I am desperate to meet a man but as part of Challenge Harriet. Between now and Christmas, I'm trying to challenge myself to do things I find difficult. Dating is something I find difficult. It's about me, not you. Nothing to do with you." She spooned the thick, fragrant casserole into the deep bowl and then carved herself a hunk of bread, the movements of the knife so vigorous that if he hadn't already realized he'd upset her, he would have then. It made him relieved he had chosen to speak from a safe distance.

"If we could maybe—"

"Secondly, why would you assume this meal is for you? Women do cook for themselves you know. You think when we're on our own we sob into a lonely bowl of cereal? This may come as a surprise, but cooking isn't something we only do when there is a man around." She took a plate and a spoon from one of his cupboards, added both to her tray with a clatter.

It was the most inviting, perfect-smelling, stomach teasing, tray of food he'd ever seen in his life.

Ethan had to stop himself ripping it from her hand.

"Thirdly," she said, as she added a glass of water to the tray, "even if that part of Challenge Harriet hadn't ended and I was still thinking of dating someone, you would be right at the bottom of my list."

"Why?" He asked the question before he could stop himself.

"Why what?"

"Why would I be at the bottom of your list? Plenty of women would consider a doctor to be a catch." It was clear from the look she gave him that she wasn't one of them.

"If I'm sick, I need a doctor. If I'm dating, I need a man who interests me. That's not you."

Ouch.

"Just because I'm a doctor, doesn't mean I can't be interesting. That still doesn't tell me why I'd be at the bottom of your list."

"You're the guy who yelled and made me stammer for the first time in years. I had it under control, so what you did was quite an achievement. And yes, I do realize I'm responsible for my own feelings and reactions, my soon-to-be-sister-in-law is a psychologist so I'm an expert on all that, but feelings and reactions need triggers and you were one hell of a trigger, Dr. Black. A date with you would be my idea of torture."

"You don't seem to be having much trouble with fluency right now."

"That's because I'm the one who is mad. I don't stammer when I'm mad, only when someone else is mad."

"So you're allowed to be mad, but I'm not? How is that fair?"

"Life isn't fair, Dr. Black. And I can't believe this is the first time anyone has pointed that out to you."

Without waiting for a reply, she headed for the stairs.

As she passed him, the most glorious aroma of herbs and red wine teased his senses. Right now he would have paid a month's salary for the food on that tray. He had to stop himself grabbing it.

"Wait—where are you going?"

"Given that you seem to have a problem with me being in your apartment, I'm taking my food to my room."

"You don't have to do that. There's a perfectly good table here, and the dog likes you being around."

"Right now I'd prefer my own company. And if you call Madi 'the dog' one more time I'm taking her back to my apartment." She walked away without looking back, leaving him with hunger pangs and the option of groveling or calling for takeout.

CHAPTER TWELVE

HARRIET PUT THE tray down on the desk in the bedroom, but didn't touch it.

She was too upset and angry to eat.

Upset with Ethan, and angry with herself because he'd been scarily close to the truth.

When she'd planned and cooked the meal, she *had* assumed he'd be joining her. Not because she had designs on him romantically, but because it seemed like the civilized thing to do. She'd pictured herself serving the meal, and imagined his enjoyment at finally tasting real food instead of endless takeout meals and fast food. She'd tried to make it special. She'd even had a quick look in the kitchen cabinets to see if she could find candles for the table.

Candles?

With a groan, Harriet leaned her head against the window.

How could she have been so incredibly stupid?

This was what happened when you moved outside your comfort zone, outside the circle of people who knew you well.

Creating a home wherever she went was something she did automatically. No matter where she was, she always wanted the atmosphere to be as comforting and soothing as possible. Her siblings teased her for it. They removed cushions before they sat on the sofa, ignored napkins she placed on the table.

Before Molly had arrived on the scene, when she and Fliss had still been sharing the apartment, Daniel had often dropped in for breakfast. Sundays had become her favorite day. She'd made homemade granola and stacks of fresh pancakes, and both her brother and sister had eaten so much they could barely drag themselves to the sofa.

She particularly wanted mealtimes to be relaxing, probably because growing up they had been anything but. Every meal had been fraught with tension, and for years after she'd left home Harriet had worked hard to even want to sit at a table to eat. The solution she'd found had been to make it as different from her childhood experience as possible. She enjoyed cooking, but there was so much more to her enjoyment than simply a fascination with recipes and food.

For her, cooking and eating was symbolic of something bigger. Cooking was her way of expressing love. A way of creating a warm, comforting space, and you didn't need a degree in psychology to know that the origins of her need for that were to be found in her childhood.

There had been nothing warm or comforting about her home growing up. Nothing warm or comforting about mealtimes. Sitting round the table together had been something to be endured. The atmosphere had been strained, the food nothing more than punctuation in an hour of rising stress levels.

Harriet had eaten little. As a child her weight had been on the low side of normal, not because she had food issues, but simply because she couldn't seem to push it past the lump of tension wedged in her throat and chest. She'd willed mealtimes to be over as fast as possible so she could escape back to her room. Sometimes she'd ended up under the table, hiding while the battle raged above her head.

Now, she wanted fine dining and good conversation. Instead of shouting, she wanted to hear the clink of glass and the hum of laughter. She wanted everyone relaxed and focused on the food, instead of glancing at the time and wondering how quickly they could escape.

In her later teenage years she'd used candles as a method of calming herself, and it had been easy enough to add those to a meal table.

Her brother Daniel had teased her for creating a romantic atmosphere, and she'd admitted that it had nothing at all to do with romance and everything to do with her own rituals for keeping calm in a situation she'd always found stressful.

What if she'd found candles and matches? In all probability she would have used them, and Ethan would have come home to fine dining and candlelight. She would have had a big problem explaining her way out of *that* one.

She could have told him it was the way she liked to live her life now. When she'd moved into an apartment with her sister, she'd immediately set about creating a space that felt safe and cozy. Plants, cushions, rugs—she was the one who had turned their place into a home, and although Fliss teased her and wouldn't have watered a plant if her life depended on it, Harriet knew she'd enjoyed living there too.

Up until a few months ago, she'd shared almost every aspect of her life with her twin.

And she was missing that. Because a home was so much more than four walls, some pretty throw cushions and a few healthy plants, wasn't it? A home was about the people. Atmosphere.

And right now her home was depressingly silent. She missed the feeling of coming home to someone.

Had that been part of the reason she'd accepted Ethan's invitation to stay at his place? Had she been avoiding her own? Or had she secretly hoped that something might develop between them?

Pathetic, she muttered, and sat down in the chair by the window to eat her meal. Alone.

This was what Challenge Harriet was all about. If she had a problem with the way she was living her life, then she needed to fix it. And wanting things to go back to the way they were wasn't a fix.

If she missed people then the answer was to fill her home with more people. It shouldn't matter that Fliss wasn't living with her anymore. She should simply make some calls and have people over. Maybe she should call Molly and suggest meeting for brunch. Or her friend Matilda. Except that Matilda was spending most of her time in the Hamptons with her new baby.

She needed to make new friends. Be self-sufficient and adventurous.

Maybe she ought to book a week away somewhere. She could go hiking. Get some fresh air. Snatch some time away from the city. A change of scene would be good.

She was pondering that when there was a tap on the door.

She put her spoon down, knowing this wasn't a conversation she was going to be able to avoid.

Ethan opened the door but didn't walk into the room. "If I step inside this room are you going to throw food at my head?"

"I don't know. It depends on what you say when you step in here."

"Would an apology work?" His smile was crooked. "I seem to spend my life apologizing to you. Believe it or not, I'm not usually this bad with people."

"So I bring out the worst in you?" She wasn't going to be charmed by that smile. Absolutely not.

"It's not you, so much as the circumstances." Ethan glanced down as Madi, who pushed her nose against his leg. "My life has changed quite a bit over the past couple of days. I think I'm still getting over the shock." He crouched down to stroke Madi's head. "There, Madi. Lovely Madi."

"That's not going to work this time." But at least he was trying. She relented. "It's not easy having an animal around when you're not used to it."

"It's not just Madi. I've lived on my own for a long time. I'm used to being in my own space and doing what I want to do when I want to do it."

He made living alone sound like the ultimate indulgence.

Harriet was in that position too, and so far she hated it.

"You like living on your own?"

He glanced at her. "Yes. It's easy. I don't have to think about anyone but myself. I'd be the first to admit I'm not good at compromising. Nor am I used to walking through the door to the delicious smells of home cooking. I made assumptions that were totally wrong."

His apology disarmed her as much as his honesty. She

thought about the dates she'd been on, and the lies people had told to make themselves look better. She didn't understand how relationships were ever supposed to work if people weren't honest about who they were. What was the point of pretending to be interested in reading if you never picked up a book? Why lie about what work you did, or your income or your age? If you had to pretend to be someone different, how was that ever going to work?

With that in mind, she was honest too.

"You weren't wrong. I did assume you would want to eat too. And it was stupid of me."

"Not stupid at all. A reasonable assumption that I'd be hungry, and a kind gesture to cook. You were thoughtful. And kind. And I was a jerk." He stared at the food on the tray. "What is it?"

"It's *boeuf bourguignon*. A French dish of beef marinated in wine and herbs."

"It smells good."

Discovering a wicked streak she hadn't even known she had, Harriet took another mouthful and savored it. "It tastes good. Deliciously warming after being out in the cold."

He laughed. "You're a cruel woman."

"I intended to share it with you. You made it clear I'd overstepped the mark. How does that make me cruel?"

"You want me to apologize again? Grovel?"

Harriet took another mouthful and pondered. "Yes," she said slowly, "I think I do."

"Please, Harriet, may I help myself to a bowl of your beef whatever-it's-called?"

She finished her bowl. "I don't think so."

"You don't have enough?"

"I have more than enough. But feeding you casserole

might be dangerous." She put her bowl on the tray and stood up. "I'm a seriously good cook. If the way to a man's heart is through his stomach, then you'd fall in love with me and then we'd both be in trouble because there is no way I'd ever go on a date with you." She had no idea why she was teasing him. Or was it flirting? It wasn't something she was even aware she knew how to do.

The way he smiled back at her told her he knew everything there was to know about flirting.

"My knowledge of anatomy is excellent. I know that you don't get to the heart through the stomach, so we're both safe." He left the room and she followed him.

Downstairs, she put her empty plate on the counter and watched as he served himself a generous portion of food.

Was she supposed to join him? Watch him eat?

He poured a glass of wine and handed it to her so she had little choice but to sit down at the table with him.

And now she wished she hadn't taken her food to her room, because it felt a little uncomfortable sitting here watching while he ate.

To distract herself, she looked over his shoulder to the living room of the apartment.

It was about three times the size of hers, and the high ceilings and tall windows enhanced the feeling of space. If she'd had the money, she would have chosen a place exactly like this.

Or maybe a pretty house near the water in the Hamptons. A village, where she'd walk dogs and greet everyone by name. She could call in and see her sister—

Harriet stopped the thought in midtrack.

She was building a new life now. A different life.

Fliss would always be her sister. Always be her twin. But

she was kidding herself if she thought things weren't going to change. They'd already changed.

And truthfully she wouldn't want to live in the Hamptons. She loved Manhattan.

She took a large mouthful of wine.

Ethan glanced at her. "You're quiet."

"So are you."

"I was eating." He put his fork down, his plate clear. "You're right. You're a seriously good cook. Would you really have cooked that for yourself?"

"Yes. I don't see why you need to eat boring food just because you live alone. And to be honest I haven't adjusted to being alone yet. I still think I'm cooking for two. Most days I have a ton of food left over. My freezer is bulging."

"You just broke up with someone?"

"Not exactly." Although thinking back, that was probably the way she'd made it sound. "My twin sister recently moved out of the apartment we shared."

"How long have the two of you lived together?"

Harriet took a sip of wine. "Almost all our lives. There was a brief moment between college and work where we didn't, but not for long."

"So you've always lived with her and now you're alone." He put his glass down. "That must feel strange."

"It feels like a lot of things. I guess strange is somewhere on that list." It didn't begin to describe the emotions that were churning inside her.

"So where is your sister now?"

"She's living in the Hamptons, with the man she's going to marry. For the second time."

Ethan leaned back in his chair. "They've been married before?"

"Briefly, when Fliss was eighteen. It didn't last."

"So they're doing it again? They don't learn from their mistakes?"

"Their mistake," Harriet said, "was breaking up in the first place."

"So you think getting back together is the right thing to do?"

"It's not my decision but since you asked then yes, I think it's the right thing to do. They're perfect together. They always were. Their breakup was—complicated."

"Relationships always are. Tell me about Challenge Harriet." He glanced at her. "You said you were internet dating as a challenge. What did you mean?"

"Nothing." Why on earth had she mentioned that? That particular detail of her life was far too personal to share with a stranger.

"You weren't dating because you wanted to meet someone?"

"In a way, but it was more about doing something I found difficult. I went on three dates."

"And on the last one you escaped through the window." His eyes gleamed. "That sounds like quite a challenge. Three dates, and not one of the men were interesting?"

"I'm sure there are women out there who would have found them interesting." Maybe the problem lay with her. She wasn't good on dates. Especially not first dates. When she didn't know someone she found it almost impossible to relax. Maybe, if she could conquer her initial shyness in a first date she might be able to make it through to a second date and possibly even a third.

"But you still met up with them."

"Once. No second dates."

"Three evenings of your life you'll never get back. But you made yourself do it. Are you always this hard on yourself?"

"Plenty of people use internet dating. In today's world where it's hard to meet anyone, it's a legitimate way to find a partner."

"Maybe, but you found it hard. So I wonder why you didn't find another way."

"That's why. Because I found it hard. That's why I'm doing this. Normally I live life in my comfort zone."

"Most people do. Is there anything wrong with being in your comfort zone?"

"If you don't push yourself to do the things that scare you, how will you ever find out if there's more to life than the one you're living?" She felt heat warm her cheeks. This conversation was becoming far deeper than she'd intended. Talking to strangers wasn't something she was good at. Confiding in strangers wasn't something she ever did.

The only person she'd discussed Challenge Harriet with was Glenys.

He gave her a speculative look. "Good point. And now you're making me wonder if I should rethink my life."

"You're mocking me."

"No." There was no sign of mockery in his eyes. "Most of us wake up in the morning and do the same thing we always do. Follow the same habits. Most people hate change, and only do it when it's forced on them. You are actively embracing it."

"I wouldn't exactly say I'm *embracing* it," Harriet muttered. "That implies that I'm running forward into change enthusiastically. I'm forcing myself kicking and screaming, looking for excuses to back out and generally struggling all the way."

"But you're doing it." He topped off her glass and did the same with his own. "Doing something you don't want to do takes self-discipline. I'm impressed."

He was impressed? "You're a doctor. You save lives every single day."

"I thought you weren't impressed by doctors."

"That isn't what I said. I said that being a doctor didn't increase your appeal as dating material."

"I feel thoroughly put in my place. If I ever thought being a doctor might earn me bonus points, I stand corrected." But he seemed amused rather than offended. "Thanks to you, I wouldn't even have the courage to use a dating app now. My confidence is wrecked."

He didn't look as if his confidence had ever suffered even the slightest dent.

"People whose confidence is wrecked don't smile the way you're smiling. I bet you've never suffered a single confidence wobble in your life."

"You'd be surprised. So what sort of man *would* be high on your list as a potential date?"

"Someone who shows interest in something, and someone, other than themselves I suppose."

Which he was doing.

Since he'd sat down at the table he'd done nothing but ask questions about her, something not one of her three dates had done. And he looked at her while he asked the questions, as if he was genuinely interested in hearing her answer.

She had to keep reminding herself that this wasn't a date. Which made the situation all the more ironic. None of her dates had been as interesting as this non-date. None of the men she'd met had captured her attention the way Ethan Black did. And if none of them had also caused that little kick in her pulse rate or that rush of sensation across her nerve endings she chose to ignore that.

Madi nudged her leg and gave a little whine.

Grateful for a reason to leave her thoughts behind, Harriet stood up. "She wants to go out. I'll take her for a walk."

"Now?" He glanced at his phone. "It's late. I'll come with you."

"No need." She already had Madi in her coat and was grabbing her backpack.

"You're not walking the streets of Manhattan by yourself at this time." He retrieved his coat from the back of his chair. His movements were slow and controlled, the way they'd been in the emergency room that day. As if he knew that haste was achieved by thoughtful strategy and not by panic.

She couldn't imagine Ethan panicking. She couldn't imagine him lying about who he was, or what he did. Or spending a whole evening talking about himself. He wasn't the sort who would fill a silence with words for the sake of it.

He was the sort who would take care of his sister's dog even though it meant turning his own life upside down.

That was the part that turned her heart upside down.

That was the part that made him dangerous.

"It's not that late. And I do it all the time. It's my job."

"You don't want my company?"

She wanted his company very much. That was the problem. "If you're going to come with me, you might as well have walked Madi yourself. You don't need me."

"I need you." His gaze held hers and for a crazy moment she felt a rush of awareness she couldn't remember ever feeling before.

Ethan Black needed her.

Then she remembered he needed her for her canine skills. Not for anything else.

"You don't need me."

He glanced at Madi. "You only have to look at how calm and well behaved she is to understand how much I need you. In this situation, you're the team leader."

"Excuse me?"

"In the emergency room, we have a trauma team leader. Someone who calls the shots during resuscitation. The team leader decides on the priorities, and the timing and sequence of investigations so everyone is clear what they're doing. They're not involved in the actually clinical procedures—their job is to stand back and make the decisions."

"You're the leader?"

"Yes, because that's my role. My area of expertise. Dogs fall outside my area of expertise."

She had no problem imagining him as the leader. He had a calm air of authority that would no doubt translate into calm in an otherwise tense atmosphere. The confidence and presence that she found a little intimidating would be reassuring to an injured patient and a busy staff.

Harriet attached Madi's lead. She couldn't help wishing he needed her for more than her dog-walking skills. "I hardly think you can compare the skill and complexity of what you do in the emergency room, with what I'm doing here."

"Skill is the ability to do something well. That usually involves two elements—training and practice. Being a doctor is all about training and practice. It's not magic."

She was sure there was a great deal more to it than he described, but she wasn't about to argue because Madi was looking at her anxiously and she recognized that look.

"We need to get her outside now, or she's going to have an accident and that wouldn't be good for your beautiful oak floor." She crouched down and took Madi's face in her hands. "We are going in the elevator and you are going to be a good girl. And if we meet Judy you are going to sit and not bark. Is that clear?"

Madi wagged her tail.

Harriet reached for her own coat but Ethan already had it in his hands.

He helped her on with it, and the old-fashioned gesture made her stomach flutter.

Some people would probably find reason to object to the fact that he'd helped her, also the fact that he held the door for her as she walked out of his apartment, but she thought there was nothing wrong with good old-fashioned manners.

They'd been sadly lacking in the last three men she'd dated.

As had interesting conversation.

As they stepped into the elevator she was suddenly aware of the claustrophobic nature of their surroundings. Her arm brushed against his and she felt a shock of sexual awareness. It caught her off guard and she stepped back with a murmur of apology. Their earlier misunderstanding had flavored the air with something sharp and a little dangerous. He'd put thoughts in her head that hadn't been there before. Or maybe they'd been there but she hadn't recognized them. All she knew was that if he could turn the simple act of making a meal for someone into something more complicated, what was preventing him from thinking she was brushing against him on purpose? It was a good thing he couldn't read her mind, because her mind was going to all sorts of places he certainly wasn't invited.

That brief physical encounter left her with an impression of hard muscle under the wool of his coat. Her nerve endings tingled and she kept her gaze fixed on the seam of the elevator doors, wondering what it was about elevator rides that was so excruciatingly awkward. It was the air of false intimacy, she decided. People who barely knew each other—in this case two people—forced into close proximity by limited space. Where were you supposed to look? To stare at the floor felt apologetic and she had nothing to apologize for. To maintain eye contact felt awkward, and eye contact could be as easily misread as a meal cooked for two.

Harriet continued to stare at the doors, even though there was nothing about them that deserved such close attention.

To intensify the discomfort of the moment the elevator stopped on the next floor and a woman stepped in holding hands with a man. They were laughing together, clearly enjoying a shared joke. Harriet felt a stab of envy. You only had to look at them, the eye contact, the pleasure they took in each other's company, to know they hadn't "settled."

To make room for them Harriet was forced to step back and in doing so she tripped over Madi's leash, which had somehow wound itself round her ankles.

She fell against Ethan with a thud and a gasp of apology.

His arms came up and he steadied her, his hands closing around her upper arms, holding her firm until she regained her balance and untangled her legs from the offending leash.

Keeping her hand on Ethan's broad chest for balance, she bent to free herself and saw Madi looking at her.

She could have sworn the dog had done it on purpose.

Madi the matchmaker.

It was only moments until she was back on her feet, but in those few moments she learned two things. Firstly, that Ethan's strength wasn't only restricted to his character. And secondly, that she was capable of all manner of feelings she hadn't previously encountered. Apparently her heart was capable of beating harder and faster than she'd ever thought possible, and her stomach was able to perform a strange, fluttery maneuver that she couldn't begin to describe let alone put a name to.

She wondered what Ethan was thinking.

Probably that she was clumsy, and that for an expert who supposedly did this every day, she was surprisingly slow at dodging the potential obstacle of a dog's leash.

Or maybe he wasn't thinking of her at all.

He was simply taking his sister's dog for a walk.

She was the one who was unpicking each element of the situation and analyzing it until her brain hurt.

She was the one with the problem.

CHAPTER THIRTEEN

ETHAN FOLLOWED HARRIET out into the street, for once glad of the cold air.

The elevator had felt stifling, or maybe the heat had come from inside him. He wasn't sure. All he knew was that his height had given him a perfect view of Harriet's hair. It spilled over her shoulders in a subtle blend of pale gold and buttermilk, reminding him of long, lazy summers growing up when his priority had been to do nothing.

Right now he would have been happy to do nothing with Harriet.

The thought startled him. Not just the doing nothing part, which would in itself have been enough to make those who knew him raise an eyebrow, but that she would have been his choice of companion.

She chose that moment to look at him. "What? Why the frown?"

"It's colder than I thought it would be." He said the first thing that came into his head, although in fact it was the second thing. Because she'd been the first thing. He'd been thinking about how her cheeks dimpled when she smiled, and how shiny her hair was under the lights of the elevator. He'd been thinking about how her eyes had blazed when she'd confronted him, how patient she was with Madi, and how the food she'd made had been the best thing he'd ever eaten. "Really cold."

He turned up the collar of his coat in support of his statement about the cold. And it *was* cold. There was no way he'd be caught in a lie.

"Wasn't it cold a few hours ago?"

She obviously thought his behavior was strange.

He thought it was strange too.

He knew she was still feeling awkward around him.

He knew that was entirely his fault.

He also knew that the edge of awareness he felt when he was with her was something he was going to keep to himself. He and Alison had been similar in many ways, which was why when they drifted in and out of their ill-fated marriage, neither of them had been hurt. The fact that their separation hadn't left so much as a bruise on either of them showed the depth of feeling involved.

Harriet wasn't like that. He suspected she was the type of woman who bruised easily, which meant he needed to keep well away from her.

They walked along the snowy streets, their breaths clouding the freezing air. This part of Manhattan had a small, intimate feel. Snow fell like frozen confetti, muffling street noise and carpeting the cobbled streets. In this part of the street the trees reached across and touched each other, street lamps bathing the snow with an ethereal glow.

She walked with purpose and confidence, jeans tucked

into her snow boots. He decided he preferred her like this to all dressed up in stilettos. Not because he particularly cared what she wore, but because it was obvious she cared. She seemed comfortable. A thousand times more comfortable than that night he'd first met her.

"It looks like a Christmas card." She paused under the light from the street lamp and took a photograph, then turned the camera toward Madi and took a photo of the dog. "I'll send that to Debra."

"You're sending her a photo of her dog?"

"Of course." She fiddled with her phone, her lower lip caught between her teeth as she concentrated. "All our clients love to see what their dogs are doing when they're away, and a photo is so much stronger than words."

"That photo will tell her I'm not taking good care of her dog."

She pushed her phone back into her pocket and looked up. "Not true. It will tell her you're taking excellent care of her dog."

"The fact that you're involved tells her I couldn't cope."

"The fact that I'm involved tells her you cared enough about Madi's welfare to call me. She'll be impressed."

Ethan wasn't convinced. He thought his sister was more likely to roll her eyes and make some comment about the fact that he was in charge of people's lives, and yet couldn't take care of one little dog.

He was also aware that once Debra discovered Harriet was staying in his apartment, he would be a target for more of her matchmaking efforts. His sister might not be as slick as a dating app, he thought, but she was a lot harder to delete.

Aware that he could no longer feel his fingers, he thrust his hands into his pockets. "Are you always this positive?"

"Is it being positive? I see it as the truth." She paused. "In the ER your job is to determine what a patient needs, is that right? So if a patient has a brain injury you don't handle it yourself, you call the expert in that specialty."

"That's right."

"This is no different." She waited as Madi sniffed the snow. "You called an expert. Not that I'm comparing myself to a neurosurgeon, you understand. I'm guessing you must see some pretty gross things."

"Gross is all a matter of interpretation." He watched as she cleaned up after Madi. "What you're doing now is pretty gross."

"It's part of responsible dog ownership. Have you ever had anything come into the ER that you couldn't deal with?"

"It's my job to deal with it, just as it's your job to deal with all dogs, even one you find challenging."

"It's hardly the same thing. If it's a little child, don't you get emotional?"

"Children are generally dealt with by the pediatric trauma unit. But whoever the patient, I try and detach myself emotionally because I need to be able to think clearly. Child or adult, their loved ones are relying on me to make the best decisions. I can't do that if I'm thinking about the emotional impact on the family. It doesn't help anyone."

"That sounds great in theory, but is it really that easy to do in practice?"

"Not at first. It's a skill I learned over time. Or maybe it's not a skill. Maybe it's a failing. Or maybe I just got a little too good at disconnecting and not feeling."

"So you're a block of ice inside?"

"I didn't say that." He paused. "It's not that you don't feel emotion, more that you learn to suppress it and then process it in your own way, in your own time." But he'd discovered that if you suppressed emotion enough, it seemed to disappear altogether.

"What's your way?"

"I practice karate. I'm a black belt." He saw her eyes widen.

"So you beat people up and send them to the emergency room you just left?"

"No. If I injure anyone, I try and fix them right away."

They strolled along the snowy streets, avoiding the noise and bustle of the west highway.

As the cold nipped bare flesh, he shivered. "Aren't you cold?"

"No. I spend most of my working day outdoors. I dress for the weather. You don't want to know how many layers I'm wearing." She tipped her face up to the sky. "It's snowing again."

"You say that as if it's something to be delighted about instead of an inconvenience that will no doubt bring misery to many." He saw snow and thought about the accidents it would cause, and the fact that the emergency room would be full to the brim.

"I know it can be a nuisance, but I still think there's something magical about snow, don't you?" She held out her hands and caught a snowflake, examining it the way another woman might a diamond.

Ethan was charmed, which came as a shock. These days he was rarely, if ever, charmed.

Cynical, tired and disillusioned? All the time.

Charmed? Never.

"Magical?"

"Just *seeing* snow lifts the spirits."

"I like snow when I'm skiing. In New York City, snow means the ER will be extra busy."

"I'm surprised you ski, knowing everything you know about injuries." She shrugged. "I guess you can fix yourself if you break something."

He laughed. "If only it were that easy. Fortunately, I don't plan on breaking anything."

"You ski often?"

"I'm taking a vacation the week before Christmas. My godmother is getting married and my whole family is attending the wedding, always assuming Karen is cleared to fly by then."

"Your godmother?"

"Elizabeth O'Neil. She's one of my mother's closest friends. They met while they were both doing a cookery course in Paris. They stayed friends. We used to go and stay with them every year when we were growing up. Twice, some years. Summer and winter. The family owns a resort by a lake in Vermont."

"Sounds dreamy."

"It is, although keeping it going hasn't always been easy for them. It's been in the family for three generations but it had started to decline. Michael, Elizabeth's first husband, wasn't much of a businessman from what I can gather. He died a few years ago, and Jackson, the oldest son, took it over. He has built it up into a destination resort. It's very much a family concern and always has been. His brother Tyler helps now too, but Sean, the third brother, is an orthopedic surgeon so he isn't directly involved."

"I saw the photo of you on a ski slope. I thought maybe they were your brothers."

"Growing up, we were as close as brothers. Now we see

each other a few times a year. Jackson comes up to Manhattan for business, I go there for skiing—" he shrugged
"—a few summers ago we walked part of the Appalachian
Trail together."

"And now Elizabeth is getting married again? How old
is she?"

"Sixties? I'm not good at guessing ages. You've already
discovered how tactless I can be, so don't push me on that
one."

"I think it's wonderful that she's fallen in love again. So
you're all going to the wedding?"

He'd talked to her about the business and yet the subject
that interested her most was the fact that Elizabeth was getting married again.

"We usually go at this time of year anyway. That's probably why Elizabeth fixed this date. It's before Christmas,
so not too crazy, but there should be good skiing. We've
booked out a few cabins."

"Cabins?"

"The accommodation at Snow Crystal is mostly in luxury log cabins around the lake."

"Sounds perfect. A winter wedding in a snowy forest.
That would be my dream."

The fact that she dreamed of weddings should have been
enough to send him skidding back to his apartment but for
some reason he was still standing here.

"Do you ski?"

"Never intentionally." She grinned. "Only when I lose my
balance when walking. Which happens pretty often at this
time of year." They reached the curve of Morton Street and
turned around, returning the way they'd come. "So being
a trauma doctor doesn't put you off adventurous sports?"

"No, although some things are off-limits."

"Such as?"

"I hate motorcycles."

"Did you always want to be a doctor?"

"Yes." They arrived back at his building and he held the door for her. "My father and grandfather are both doctors. Family practice in Connecticut."

"You didn't want to join them? Follow in the family footsteps?"

"I wanted something faster paced."

"Was your father angry with you for not wanting to join him?"

"Angry?" The question surprised him. "Why would he be angry?"

"Oh, because—" She gave a little shake of her head. "I thought maybe he wanted you to join him, and that you doing something different might have made him angry."

"He wanted me to do whatever it was that interested me. In my case that was trauma." He stood aside to let her walk first into the elevator. "Did you always want to own your own business?"

"No. In fact it would have been the last thing on my mind." She unwound her scarf from her neck. "I'm not that good with people and I'm not good with accounts."

"My sister says the Bark Rangers virtually own the whole of the East Side of Manhattan."

"We're doing well. Most of that is down to my sister, Fliss. She's the business brain."

He watched as she soothed Madi.

The dog had been so well behaved the whole time they'd been out he hardly recognized her as the same animal he'd met when he'd walked through the door that first day.

"Does Fliss have your sophisticated skills as an animal tamer?"

"Animal tamer?" She straightened. "Aren't you slightly exaggerating my skills?"

"Not from where I'm standing."

"I thought 'animal tamer' was reserved for someone who works in a circus, or at least with dangerous animals."

"My apartment looked like a circus when you arrived the other day and as for what's dangerous—it's all about perspective. You turned Madi from a marauding mass of teeth and fur into a well-behaved animal. She's looking at you for praise and attention all the time. She's walking close to your leg and waiting for you to give her instructions. If that isn't animal taming I don't know what is."

"She's a good girl."

He noticed that the moment they arrived in his apartment, she removed Madi's coat. The dog's comfort was always her priority.

"You love your job."

"I adore it. Don't you love yours?"

Did he love his? Ethan frowned. It was a question he hadn't asked himself in a long time. "Love is probably the wrong word. It's satisfying. Challenging. So now your sister is working from the Hamptons? You weren't tempted to join her?"

"No. I love Manhattan. I love the Hamptons too, but I wouldn't want to live there. I've worked with some of my clients for eight years. They feel like family. And this place feels like home." She took Madi to her crate and the dog settled down without argument.

"What about your real family? Are your parents still alive?"

She stroked Madi's head. "They're divorced. My mom is traveling right now so I don't see much of her."

"And your father?" The moment he asked the question he knew it was the wrong one.

Her smile faded like a light bulb on a dimmer switch. "I don't see him, either. Good night, Ethan." She stood up and walked toward the stairs without looking back, leaving him with the uncomfortable knowledge that he'd just asked the wrong question.

CHAPTER FOURTEEN

HARRIET TOOK A shower and slid into bed, even though she knew there was no chance of sleeping. Her mind was churning like the inside of a washing machine.

He'd asked her a question, that was all. Not even a particularly personal question.

And what had she done? Had she shifted the conversation to more comfortable territory? No. She'd bolted like Madi after a stick in the park.

His question might not have been personal, but she'd taken it personally. She'd let it release a flock of insecurities.

Infuriated and stressed, she reached for the book she'd tucked under her pillow.

Why was she so bad at conversation?

And why did she find it so awkward to talk about her parents?

Plenty of people had parents who were divorced. *They're divorced.* That was all she needed to say. She didn't need to deliver any more details. Ethan hadn't wanted her life history, just a normal to and fro exchange of words.

But, no. She'd had to overreact.

Still clutching the book, she rolled onto her back and stared up at the ceiling.

It had been more than a decade since she'd left home.

The mere mention of her father shouldn't send her pulse rate thumping and she certainly shouldn't find it awkward to talk about it.

Why should it bother her that she didn't see him? Why did she find that detail embarrassing?

But she knew the answer to that. Because she believed, deep in her heart, that family was something worth fighting for. That no circumstances, however dark, should succeed in tearing a family apart. And yet theirs had been torn apart and even the knowledge that it had been her father who had done the tearing didn't comfort her. If anything it made it worse, as if his desire for no contact somehow reflected on her and made her less of a person.

The truth was, her father didn't like her and she had spent her lifetime trying to adjust to that reality. But how did you adjust to something that felt so wrong? It wasn't right for a parent not to love a child. In the universe she inhabited in her head, parents loved their children unconditionally. They didn't find them irritating and seek every reason not to spend time with them.

She knew she wasn't the only one with issues.

Fliss had spent her life battling against their father's negative opinion. She'd found it almost impossible to shake off the cloak he'd draped her with when she was young.

Harriet was the same.

It didn't matter how many times she reminded herself

that it was his choice, not hers, his choice to cut all contact from his family was upsetting.

It was something she hated admitting to people, afraid that in saying *my father doesn't want to be in touch with me*, what she was really telling them was *I'm not worth knowing*.

She didn't believe that, not really, so she didn't understand why telling people felt so personal. It seemed like a failure.

She lay staring at the ceiling, unable to read or sleep.

When she heard Madi's first whine she was out of bed in an instant, hoping to reach her before she woke Ethan.

Downstairs, she found Madi whining and miserable.

"What's wrong?" She knelt by the crate and then saw one of Madi's toys halfway across the kitchen floor. "Did you lose your toy? Why aren't you sleeping?" She retrieved the toy and waited while Madi settled down. "Are you missing Debra? It's difficult when family go away and leave you, I know. You and I have a lot in common. We're both getting used to new circumstances. It isn't easy."

"Is there anything I can do to make it easier?" Ethan's voice came from behind her and she scrambled to her feet, horribly conscious that she hadn't bothered to grab a robe when she'd heard Madi whine. She was wearing her pajamas with the butterflies.

Fliss would have rolled her eyes and called it a missed opportunity.

"I'm sorry she woke you."

"I wasn't asleep. I was working on my research paper."

"At midnight?"

"It's the time I do my best thinking. Did she wake you?"

"No, I couldn't sleep."

"And that's my fault." He spoke softly, presumably so

that they didn't disturb Madi. "I'm the one who asked the tactless question. I'm sorry." He gave a humorless laugh. "I've apologized to you more in the last forty-eight hours than I ever have in my life before."

"You don't owe me an apology." She wondered if the pajamas turned transparent with the light behind them. Hopefully not. After the dinner episode, he'd probably think she was trying to seduce him. "It's not your fault that my father is a touchy subject. I need to deal with it better. That's on me, not you. The truth is my father and I don't have a great relationship." It had to be the understatement of the century. "In fact we have no relationship. And that doesn't quite fit with how I think families should be."

He was silent for a moment. "Hot chocolate? My niece tells me I make the best hot chocolate on the planet."

It wasn't the response she'd expected. Maybe that meant he didn't want to talk about it. Or maybe it meant he was being sensitive because he realized she didn't want to talk about it.

She wished her brain would stop overthinking everything.

"And no doubt you correct her by telling her that she hasn't tasted all the hot chocolate on the planet."

He strolled to the kitchen. "Believe it or not, I'm remarkably mellow around my niece. If I try hard I even manage not to be pedantic. You should say yes. Not only is it 'deliciously yummy,' I get five stars. When it comes to hot chocolate, I'm a winner. It might help you sleep."

He was wearing black jeans and a black sweater that molded to the hard swell of his biceps.

Looking at him made her more conscious that she was in her pajamas.

She wondered if she should sprint upstairs and grab a robe.

What would Fliss do?

She'd walk confidently into the kitchen and drink the hot chocolate, while happily holding a conversation about everything under the sun, that's what she'd do.

Harriet might not be able to match the conversation, but she could walk into the kitchen and drink the hot chocolate.

"How is Karen? Have you spoken to Debra today?"

"Twice. Once in a two-minute break I had between patients this morning and then again about an hour ago. Karen is doing well. Discharging her tomorrow, although it will be another few days before she can fly." He took milk from the fridge, as relaxed as she was tense. "We spoke on the phone. She was making jokes, so that was good."

He'd had no time for lunch, but he'd found time to call his sister and his niece. Twice.

Harriet's heart beat a little faster. "How long will it take her to recover?"

"She'll be in a cast for a few weeks. I'll arrange for her to see the orthopedic doctor here, so she doesn't need to stay in California. She'd be better off at home until she's more mobile. And we're all going to Vermont the week before Christmas so she will join us there, although she won't be skiing of course."

She slid onto the chair, thinking that at least her lower half was protected behind the kitchen island. She wasn't used to having anyone witness what she wore to bed. "What's it like working on Christmas Day?"

"In the ER it's pretty much like any other day. It's probably different on wards where the staff know the patients.

If you're on the kids' ward, they get a visit from Santa." He laughed and she looked at him.

"Why are you laughing?"

"Because apparently Santa has a conflict in his schedule this year so I've been asked to step in."

"They want you to be Santa?"

"I know—" he shook his head "—it's crazy."

She imagined him dressed up in a Santa suit, those blue eyes warm with kindness as he handed out gifts to sick children.

"What's crazy about it? I think that's amazing. It must be miserable being in hospital at Christmas. I mean, think how they must feel. Every kid loves Christmas, right? There's the whole tree, and the presents—but they don't have that. Instead they're frightened and missing home and their parents." Her eyes welled up at the thought of it and she saw him looking at her.

"Are you crying?"

"No!" She blinked rapidly. "But I hate to think of kids on their own in hospital at Christmas."

He gave a smile. A funny, crooked smile that somehow made him a thousand times more attractive than he was already. "I'm beginning to understand why you chose not to be a vet. You're a marshmallow, Harriet Knight."

"I am." She cleared her throat. "Not good for much."

"I wouldn't say that."

She wished she were better at reading glances because she was sure there was something she was missing in the way he was looking at her.

Or maybe he was just wondering how a marshmallow like her had made it this far in life without being squished under someone's boot.

"I get why you have to switch off emotionally when you're working, but how can you not feel for those kids?"

"Now you're trying to make me cry too?"

"No. I'm trying to show you why you should be Santa. A visit from Santa must be the one bright spot in their day. How cool is that? To be the one bright spot in someone's day?" She looked at him. "Why are you shaking your head?"

"I'm trying to remember if I ever looked at life the way you do. I'm wondering if I should be the one to break the news to you or not." He poured milk into the pan and she watched, distracted by the way he moved. It had been the same in the emergency room, she remembered. She'd noticed his eyes first, and then his hands. He had clever hands. He wasn't a man who would fumble or hesitate. She suspected those hands could handle just about anything.

The thought of what "anything" might entail distracted her and suddenly her head was full of images that made heat rush across her skin and brought the color pouring into her cheeks. It was like accidentally clicking on a link on the computer and finding the screen covered in naked bodies. It took her a moment to realize he was looking at her.

"Are you all right? You're flushed. I hope you're not about to succumb to the flu. There's a lot of it around."

She had a suspicion that the only thing she was about to succumb to was him.

"I'm good. It's warm in here, that's all." Although most of the heat was generated from her thoughts. She tried to delete the unnerving images from her brain. "You said you had news to break to me?"

He lifted two mugs from the cabinet. "Here's the thing— Santa doesn't exist, Harriet." His expression was sober. His warm, sympathetic tone made her think that if she ever had to hear bad news, she'd want it to be from him.

"I don't believe in Santa. I do believe human beings have a huge capacity to improve life for each other in a million small ways. Just as one person can make your life miserable, so can a person make your day happy. Small things matter. Going that extra mile. Like you did that night in the emergency room." Oh God, she shouldn't have said that. Now he'd realize that she'd been watching him. After the whole romantic dinner episode, he'd think she was a stalker.

He paused. "What night?"

"The night I came in with my injured ankle. There was a woman sobbing in the waiting room and you stopped and talked to her. You probably don't even remember, but I'm sure she does. She was at a really low point, and when you're low there is nothing that helps more than a kind word from a stranger." She flushed. "Ignore me. I'm talking too much."

"You're not talking too much. I'd rather people talked. It's easier to figure them out that way." He whisked chocolate into hot milk while she wondered why he would want to figure her out and whether she wanted that to happen.

"This looks elaborate. Your niece taught you to do that?"

"The first time I made it for her, she fired me."

"What was wrong with it? Too cold? Too lumpy? Too watery?"

"All those things and more. Not enough chocolate, I used the wrong milk—the list was endless. Cardiac surgery was less daunting." He put the mug down in front of her. "Of course this is made to my niece's specifications. You might not like it."

She took a cautious sip and closed her eyes. "How could anyone not like it? This is a hug in a mug. Comfort in a cup."

"A hug in a mug? Maybe you should stop walking dogs and start writing slogans." He slid into the seat opposite her. The sleeves of his sweater were pushed back, exposing forearms dusted with dark hairs. He had strong arms. The kind of arms you wanted wrapped around you in a crisis, although no doubt that wasn't generally the way he handled all the different crises that came his way during an average working day. His hair was ruffled, his eyes were tired and he was just about the sexiest guy she'd ever laid eyes on.

The apartment was quiet. The only noise was the almost silent hum of the refrigerator and the soft sound of Madi's rhythmic breathing.

Beyond the windows the snow was falling, drawing a veil over the buildings beyond.

"So when is your next date?"

The question skidded uncomfortably close to her thoughts and she took another sip of chocolate. "No more dates. I'm done."

"You're done after just three dates? Is three supposed to be a lucky number?"

"Three was the number I picked. I promised myself I'd go on three before I allowed myself to give up."

"What if the guy who is perfect for you is guy number four?"

She lowered the mug. "Honestly? I didn't expect to meet a guy who was perfect for me. It was more about trying to get better at going on a date. I'm not dating because I'm desperate for a man, Ethan. I'm dating because I find it hard and right now I'm trying to do things I find hard."

"I didn't realize dating required a certain skill level."

His comment confirmed what she already knew. That for most people, this sort of thing was easy, whereas she had to work at every step. "I find talking to strangers hard. And the hardest thing of all is dinner. People say 'hey, let's grab something to eat' as if it's nothing, but to me it's not nothing."

"Dinner is hard? Is it the atmosphere? The whole pressure of romance?"

"I'm not good when I don't know someone. It takes me a while to relax, and I never reach that point during one date." She paused, wondering how much to say. "Growing up, mealtimes were stressful. I think some of that has carried over into adulthood for me. So although a first date will always be a nightmare, a first date over dinner is a double nightmare." It was something she'd never confided to anyone before, not even Fliss, but something about Ethan made it easy to say things that were usually hard. Maybe it was the way he listened, giving her his full attention as if what she was saying was interesting and important.

Like now. His gaze hadn't once shifted from her face.

"Why mealtimes specifically?"

"Because that was the only time during the day when we were together as a family. Sounds perfect, doesn't it? Whole family round the table. I can tell you it wasn't. It was excruciating."

"Because of your family?"

"Not my whole family. My father. I stayed out of his way as much as I could, but during mealtimes there was no avoiding anything. I think sitting around the table once a day was my mom's way of trying to pretend we were a normal family even though we all knew we were anything but."

"You said your parents were divorced. So that only happened after you left home?"

"Sadly. It would have been better for everyone if it had happened sooner."

"He was abusive?" There was a slight edge to his tone that hadn't been there before.

"Verbally. He was smart with words. In his hands, words were the perfect weapon. He didn't need to raise a hand or unbuckle his belt. He could cause bruises and scars just by opening his mouth." She wrapped her hands round the mug, feeling the heat seep through and warm her palms. "Because he was good with words, it drove him insane that I wasn't. The madder he became, the more I stammered. It aggravated him to have to wait for me to get a word out, so he finished my sentences and it mostly ended up with him having a conversation with himself. So then I was silent, and that drove him mad too. Fliss and Daniel fought with him, partly to attract attention away from me. So you can imagine how peaceful mealtimes were. The rest of the time he could pretend he didn't have me as a daughter, but at mealtimes he was forced to confront the fact that I existed." She stopped, embarrassed. "I'm talking too much, which is ironic in the circumstances." Normally her problem was not talking enough, but being with Ethan seemed to have fixed that problem.

Maybe he'd spiked her hot chocolate.

"You're not talking too much." His voice was soft. "Did he get angry with your mom too? Was it all about the marriage? He didn't love her?"

"He loved her very much. That was the problem." It was a relief to talk to someone who wasn't emotionally involved. Someone who would listen, without judging. "Fliss and I only discovered that recently. My mom spent her life trying to smooth things over and please him. We always assumed she was crazy about him and that he didn't feel the same way. Turns out it was the other way round. He was crazy about her, and she didn't love him back."

"But I'm sure he loved you, deep down."

"Now who is believing in fairy tales?" But she understood why he would say that and believe it, because she'd felt that way herself for years before finally acknowledging the painful truth. "I hate to destroy your illusions of happy families, but he didn't love me. Not at all." She saw the shock and disbelief in his eyes. "You're thinking I'm wrong, but I'm not. I didn't want to believe it, either. For years I told myself it was my fault he got so mad with me. I could hardly get the words out so of course he was going to be exasperated. My stammer must have been infuriating for someone as confident as my dad. Wherever we went he owned the room. He had a personality larger than the Empire State Building. I thought that if I worked harder at it, if I tried to please him, he'd love me. He didn't. The more he yelled, the more I stammered. I blamed myself. Thought I must be difficult to love. I twisted myself into a pretzel trying to win his approval, but it never happened." She didn't mention the one, defining incident that had happened when she was eleven years old.

"Is he alive?"

"He had his first heart attack a few years ago, but yes, he's alive." And even when he'd been in hospital, rigged up to machines, he hadn't wanted to see her. There had been no signs of regret or change in his feelings. That was the moment Harriet had learned that wanting someone to love you wasn't enough. You couldn't will it to happen, or change in order to make it happen. If they didn't love you, the way you were, they were never going to love you.

"Do you see him?"

"The last time was in the summer. I won't be going again." And that would be a different kind of challenge. The challenge of choosing reality over hope. Of allowing illusions to be replaced by disillusions. "I kept trying. It felt like the right thing to do, but it makes me feel terrible and he doesn't want to see me, so I'm done with it. And I've learned to handle that." That wasn't strictly true, but she'd already told him more than she'd ever told anyone, so she decided enough was enough. "Now tell me about your parents. Judging from the photos around your apartment, you seem to have a regular family."

"I'm not sure there's any such thing as a regular family, but yes, I'm lucky with mine. My father is a doctor and so is my mother. My grandfather is a doctor. The conversation around the table can be pretty 'gross' according to my niece, and it's often lively, but it's a friendly type of arguing."

"And you wanted to be a doctor from when you were a little boy?"

"No, I wanted to be a champion downhill ski racer like my friend Tyler."

She laughed. "So why didn't you?"

"I grew up in a town in Connecticut and skied twice a year if I was lucky. Tyler grew up in Vermont and skied every hour of every day when there was snow. I had to re-think my dream." He leaned forward, his hands wrapped around the mug. "I grew up assuming I'd be a doctor. I re-member once asking my mother if there were any other jobs a person could do, because everyone I knew were doctors."

"Debra is the only one in your family who isn't a doctor?"

"She bucked the trend, but she's shared in enough con-versations that she could probably run the emergency room single-handed." He put his mug down. "Returning to our original conversation, don't you think you're a little young to be done with dating?"

"I'm definitely done with the online version. Obviously if I happen to bump into someone gorgeous while I'm walking one of the dogs who turns out to be wonderfully easy to talk to, then that's different."

"Does that happen?"

"Not usually, but it's how my brother, Daniel, met Molly." She laughed. "In fact that's not strictly true. Daniel saw Molly walking her dog in the park and decided he wanted to meet her, so he borrowed a dog from us. So although they met while walking dogs, it wasn't strictly Daniel's dog."

Ethan was laughing. "I think I like your brother."

"I like him too, although there are times when I could strangle him. But to be fair he now owns that dog and Molly is the best thing that has ever happened to him, so I've forgiven him for being manipulative."

"So happy endings all round."

"Yes. They're getting married." And she wasn't used to the idea yet. "So is Fliss." She imagined holidays together where everyone was a couple except her. And soon the children would start arriving. She'd be Aunty Harriet.

Envy, she decided, was a truly uncomfortable emotion. It said things about you that you didn't want to hear. She didn't want to be someone who was envious of the people she loved most.

"And that feels strange?"

"I'm thrilled for them. I really want them to be happy."

"Of course you do." He watched her steadily. "But you can be thrilled and happy for someone and still feel disappointed for yourself. And that's harder to cope with, because you don't feel that you're allowed to feel that way."

She sighed and finished her chocolate. "How do you know so much?"

"I spend my day around people in trouble." His gaze held hers. "You're going through a difficult transition. A major life change. And you're not happy."

Was it that obvious? "I have no reason to not be happy. It's not as if I've lost my job or had my heart broken."

"But in a way you have. You've suffered a loss. Loss of a sister you'd lived with for almost all your life. Loss of a lifestyle you loved. And loss of comfort, because everything you're doing right now feels uncomfortable and that's stressful. Constantly pushing ourselves out of our comfort zone means we're in a constant place of fight or flight."

"The irony is that of the three of us, I was the only one who wanted the whole home and family thing. I guess life is weird that way. I feel pathetic," she confessed, "because I haven't really lost her. I can call her anytime."

"But that's not the same, is it?" He hadn't moved. Hadn't touched her. And yet the tone of his voice was so comforting it felt as if he had. She wouldn't have thought the man who had shouted at her on that first evening could have been capable of such sensitivity.

"No, it's not the same." Her throat thickened. "It's all the small things. We used to talk about everything all the time. I was the person closest to her. Now that's Seth. I feel—" She swallowed. "Replaced."

"Even though you know you're not."

"Even though I know that." She was acutely conscious of his solid presence across the table from her. He sat still, listening, his arms resting on the cool granite of the countertop. His eyes were tired and he had a serious five o'clock shadow, but she'd never seen a sexier man in her life. Something stirred to life inside her. Feelings fluttered and bloomed. Feelings that shouldn't have been there because this wasn't a date.

Her gaze met his and she felt an almost electric chemistry. It buzzed across her skin and settled in her chest.

She was glad he was the one talking because right at that moment she wasn't sure she'd be able to find her voice.

"The life you loved has changed, and it wasn't your choice. It's okay to feel upset about that. It's natural. You're going through a period of adjustment. What I don't understand is why you make that harder with 'Challenge Harriet'?" Why not wait until things feel a little easier?"

"Because I always want life to be easier and that isn't how it is. My natural instinct is to stay inside and watch back-to-back episodes of *Gilmore Girls*. If I let myself, then I would walk the dogs and then come home every night and be alone. Fliss was my social life for almost all my life. All my friends are connected with my family. I love Molly, but now she's marrying Daniel. My friend Matilda has a new baby and she's spending very little time in New York. I need to get out there and grow a new life. That's what I'm doing. But the world isn't set up for shy people."

"There are advantages to being shy."

She glanced up again. "Name one."

"Shy people often have much more sophisticated observational skills. They watch and listen more than the average person, which gives them greater insight into human behavior."

"But there's not much point in having insight if you're too scared to talk to the human on the other end of the behavior. There are days when I'd like to be able to walk through a door and own the room."

"Are you opening the door first?" His eyes gleamed. "Owning the room isn't all it's cracked up to be. And it's not how much you talk, it's about what you say."

"You make it sound great, but when I was at dinner with those guys I said almost nothing. They talked the whole time."

"About themselves presumably."

"Pretty much."

"Insecurity. Trying to convince you what great guys they were. And I think you're being hard on yourself. If they talked the whole time about themselves, how were you supposed to contribute? From your description the whole evening sounds like the equivalent of—" he fished for an appropriate analogy "—conversational masturbation."

She burst out laughing. "Glenys thinks it's the equivalent of taking a two-hour selfie. I guess that's the cleaner version."

"Who is Glenys?"

"A friend. A client really, but I think of her more as a friend. Speaking of Glenys, if you don't mind I'm going to use your kitchen tomorrow to cook some meals for her. And I'll need to leave Madi with you for a few hours while I take them to her. Normally I'd take her with me, but I want to make sure Glenys goes for a walk and Madi is too bouncy."

"You walk your clients as well as your dogs?"

The idea of it made her smile. "Glenys had her hip done in the summer and she is supposed to be moving more than she is. She's scared to go out in the snow and ice, so I take her with me and we hold on to each other."

"That's—" He paused, as if he couldn't quite find the

words he needed. "Kind of you. And you cook for her. Sounds like you're a little more than a dog walker, Harriet Knight."

"I only do it for Glenys, so don't spread the word. She lives alone since her husband died and she's losing weight. I like to take her the occasional meal."

"Who cooks for you?"

"No one. But I have had dinner out three times in the past couple of weeks and the great thing about conversational masturbation is that you get to focus on the food. I had the most delicious risotto in the first place, a heavenly chocolate dessert in the second—I asked them for the recipe—and a yummy shrimp salad in the third."

"That was the one where you climbed out the window."

"That's right."

He reached for her empty mug and stood up. "My sister is back on Monday, and I'm working over the weekend, which means Friday is our last night together."

He made it sound as if their living arrangements weren't simply for the convenience of the dog.

"Oh." There was no reasonable explanation for the disappointment that thudded through her. None at all. She should be pleased to be able to get her life back to normal. "I'm pleased your niece is well enough to travel."

"I'm taking you out to dinner."

Dinner? Her heart sped forward and her stomach felt fluttery. Had that just happened? Had she misheard? No. Definitely not. He'd asked her to dinner.

So it wasn't just her who was feeling the chemistry. He was too.

She couldn't believe this was happening. *He'd actually*

asked her out. On a date. A proper date. Not one randomly assigned by some app.

A man she really liked, who liked her back and wanted to spend time with her.

She had a feeling that a date with him would be unlike any of her other dates. No sitting across from him trying to haul up her sinking heart while she pinned a fake smile on her face and tried to pretend she was interested in a monologue.

Ethan was a great listener. And she felt relaxed with him.

It promised to be an amazing evening. Possibly the first truly excellent first date of her life.

"Thanks," she croaked. "I'd like that."

He smiled. "It's the least I can do after you moved in here to help."

She went from elation to disappointment in less time than it took Madi to devour a dog treat. So it wasn't a proper date.

It was a thank-you.

Why was she such a ridiculous optimist? She needed to keep hope locked in a cupboard somewhere instead of letting it soar uncontrolled into the stratosphere.

In the meantime, she needed to hope that all her fantasies hadn't played out across her face.

"You're paying me for that. Big-time."

"I know, but you and I both know it's not about the money." He slid the mugs into the dishwasher. "We are going to dinner, and you are going to relax and talk and build your confidence. And if you stammer, who cares?"

She would care. She would care a great deal.

"So what you're suggesting is a kind of dating master class." Not even a thank-you. It was more of a training session. Great. It was becoming harder and harder to keep the smile on her face.

"If you want to call it that. You helped me out. I want to help you out."

Hope shriveled and died, probably never to be resurrected.

The chemistry she'd imagined had been on her side alone. It wasn't that he was overwhelmed by the sight of her in her butterfly pajamas. It wasn't that he wanted to rip them off and have wild sex with her on every available surface. She wasn't that sort of woman. No, she was the sort of woman men wanted to help. Not the sort they wanted to help themselves to.

Ethan was a doctor. He wanted to fix her.

Her confidence deflated like a giant balloon.

"I don't need training," she said, "because I'm not going on any more dates for a while."

"But you never know when you might need those skills. And I'd like to buy you dinner. As a thank-you."

A thank-you. She would have rather he'd sent her a card.

"I don't need thanks."

"I'm working tomorrow, so it will have to be Friday."

"We can't leave Madi."

"There's a great Italian place a block away. We'll be gone for two hours. Three at most."

Three hours. Three hours of sitting across from Ethan, knowing he was doing her a favor.

It sounded like a nightmare to her.

CHAPTER FIFTEEN

"SO HOW IS your live-in relationship?"

"It's good." Harriet wedged the phone between her ear and her shoulder as she tugged Madi's leash to coax her to lift her nose out of the snowdrift. They'd done this same walk every day for a week and both of them knew every inch of it. "She's settled down and behaving herself. She felt insecure, that's all." And she had sympathy with that.

Fliss laughed. "I wasn't asking about the dog. I was asking about the man."

"The man? What does he have to do with anything? I'm here because I'm dog sitting."

"Yes, but the owner is there with you. It's a unique situation and one which I'm hoping you will exploit."

"For me, it's all about the dog."

"Sadly, I believe you. So how is Doctor Hot-but-Disapproving?"

Harriet thought about the time she'd spent with Ethan.

The way he listened and paid attention. "He's not really disapproving."

"So now he's just hot? Interesting."

Harriet shook her head in exasperation, but she was smiling too. She realized how much she missed talking to her sister. Not even about the big things, but the small things too. How pretty Manhattan looked in the snow. How Madi had learned to sit without moving while Harriet was preparing her dinner. How she'd found the best Christmas present for Daniel—

Cramming the small details of life into a phone call wasn't the same.

"I barely see him. He's mostly at the hospital."

"He can't be at the hospital the whole time. I mean he has to come home and eat and sleep at some point surely?"

"He does, but we don't spend time together." Apart from the three hours they'd spent talking over dinner the night before, and two the night before that. Would Fliss notice the change in her tone? Probably. Harriet knew she was a hopeless liar. She needed lie training, as well as date training.

Her "date" with Ethan was hours away and after tomorrow she was probably never going to see him again. Unless she jumped out of another window and sprained her ankle. Or transformed herself into the type of woman who inspired lust instead of pity. A woman who could seduce a man with one slow blink of her eyelashes.

Dinner? Sure. Just wait while I change into my little black dress.

She was desperate to ask Fliss what she should wear on a date that wasn't a date but if she did that she knew she'd never be able to wriggle out of the inevitable questions. And frankly it was more than a little humiliating that he was taking her out in order to help her. She was almost thirty. She shouldn't need help with dating. Why couldn't he have asked her out like a normal woman?

That would have been the best thing he could have done for her confidence.

But whatever the sentiment driving the invitation, she planned to head back to the apartment soon and spend the next hour trying really hard to make it look as if she hadn't tried hard.

Fliss was still talking. "So he hasn't put his healing hands all over you yet? Shame. Have you seen him naked?"

"How are we twins? We are *so* different." And she hadn't seen him naked, but she'd started imagining it whenever he walked into the room, which was unsettling. The longer she spent with him, the more she was wishing that tonight was a proper date.

Why couldn't she meet someone like Ethan in the normal course of her life?

"You should pretend to be me for a few days. Throw off your shy self and drag him into the bedroom for some fun."

She wondered how Ethan would react if she walked into his bedroom minus the butterfly pajamas.

But she'd never do that, would she? And even if she did, it wouldn't work. You needed the personality to go with the actions and she'd never been the sort of woman to confidently strip off her clothes in front of a man without at least small signs of encouragement. "No way."

"Harriet, he is perfect for you."

"You've never met him and I've barely told you a thing about him."

"Which tells me everything I need to know. If there was nothing to tell, you'd be telling me everything."

"That makes no sense." It felt strange keeping something this big from her twin. If they'd still been sharing an apartment they would have talked about it. But things had changed, and not just because Fliss wasn't living with her anymore. Harriet bent to tug Madi's nose out of another snowdrift and reminded herself she was capable of making a decision without her sister. If they were walking to a restaurant a block away, she'd wear jeans and boots. Casual. Then he wouldn't think she was getting the wrong idea. "To answer your question, he has not put his healing hands all over me and no, I haven't seen him naked." She straightened and saw Ethan standing next to her.

Oh holy crap.

How long had he been standing there?

Her face flamed so hot she expected the snow around them to melt and turn to floodwater. Where had he appeared from? Had he heard? If he'd heard, she was doomed. "I have to go."

"Why? We've only been talking five minutes. Don't go. I promise to stop teasing you. If you don't want to talk about Dr. Sexy, we won't talk about him."

At least she hadn't put her sister on speaker.

"I'm freezing. Need to get inside. I'll call you later." She tucked the phone in her pocket and braved it out with a smile, although she didn't quite meet his eyes. "Hi. You're early." And now she sounded like a wife. *How was your day, dear? Can I fetch your slippers?* "I mean, no accidents today? Everyone in New York City is happy and healthy?"

"I wouldn't go that far." He took Madi's leash from her. "That was your sister on the phone?"

"Yes, we were catching up." Had he heard? He *must* have heard. Should she apologize or ignore it and pretend it hadn't happened? Ignore it. Definitely. "I haven't seen her in weeks. We have business to discuss." And sex, and all the other topics Fliss always insisted on covering.

Ethan brushed snow out of her hair, his touch gentle. "You couldn't have found somewhere a little warmer for your business discussions?"

No, but they could have found somewhere a lot more private.

"I'm well wrapped up." No silky lingerie for her. When she was walking around the city in winter she wore layers that wouldn't have let her down in the Arctic. "I wasn't expecting you home for a while." *Still sounding like a wife, Harriet.* Like she'd been watching the time and the window, waiting for him to come home. To his home. It wasn't her home, even though she felt more comfortable in his apartment than she did in her own right now. "I meant home as in your apartment, obviously." Finally she looked at him and realized he was unusually pale. "Are you all right?"

"I'm fine. Just a bit tired." He swayed slightly, as if it was taking all his effort to stay standing up. "Let's get inside."

"If you're tired, we could always get takeout." And part of her thought that might be easier.

"Am I that intimidating? We've been eating together and talking all week. How is this different?"

Because they were going out. Just the two of them. It was intentional, instead of incidental.

And because it wasn't a date.

How could she explain that this whole thing felt even more awkward than usual? She fully expected to stammer her way through the evening. But it seemed simpler to say yes and get it over with. That was one advantage of moving out on Monday. However embarrassing tonight was, she'd never have to see him again.

The date was today's Challenge Harriet.

Back in the apartment she tended to Madi first, and then went to shower.

In the privacy of her bathroom, she changed her sweater three times. Black? No. White? Definitely no. She'd spill something down her front. In the end she opted for a pale cashmere sweater in a soft shade of heather that had been an early Christmas gift from a client who owned a boutique. She put her hair up and decided it looked as if she was trying too hard so took it down again. She wasn't really a hair up type of person.

And it didn't really matter what she wore, did it? This wasn't a proper date. It was dating practice. Not the same thing.

Taking deep breaths, she walked out of the bedroom downstairs.

Madi was chewing her toy happily but there was no sign of Ethan.

Harriet selected one of his books from the shelf and sat down with it but she couldn't settle. She felt as if she was in the doctor's surgery waiting for a consultation she didn't want to have.

Ten minutes passed. Then twenty.

There were no sounds from upstairs.

After thirty minutes she put the book down. If he'd changed his mind he would have said so, wouldn't he?

Wishing she had more experience in non-dating etiquette, she went upstairs and paused outside the door.

Hearing nothing, she tapped lightly. "Ethan?"

There was no reply and she opened the door a crack and

saw him sprawled across the bed, still fully clothed. He hadn't even removed his coat.

His cheeks were flushed and his eyes were closed.

She felt a stab of concern. Was he that exhausted?

Thinking back, she realized he hadn't looked well earlier. She'd assumed he was just tired, but now she was wondering if it was something more. Maybe he was coming down with something.

Leaving him to sleep, she backed out of the room quietly and walked back downstairs.

The snow was coming down heavily and she thought that maybe it was a good thing that they hadn't gone out to dinner. Generally she loved the snow, but tonight the skies were clogged with it and visibility was blurred to almost nothing.

After all the stress and the dressing and undressing, she was surprised to discover that she was disappointed not to be going out.

She curled up on the sofa and read for an hour, lost in her book, Madi asleep at her feet.

It was hunger that drove her to her feet again. Hunger and an undercurrent of stress and tension, the cause of which she couldn't quite identify.

She walked to the kitchen and chopped vegetables, thinking that soup would be perfect when Ethan finally woke up hungry.

Her grandmother had taught her to cook and it had associations of comfort for Harriet. Each time she stood at the stove, she remembered standing there with her grandmother, side by side, their arms occasionally touching. A pinch of this and a touch of that. Stir, taste, stir some more. Her grandmother had cooked by instinct but it had been an excellent instinct and she'd passed that skill on to Harriet.

She'd taught her how to choose the best vegetables, how to choose the freshest fish, how a stem of asparagus should snap just so.

The summers she'd spent at her grandmother's house had been the only time Harriet had eaten properly. Mealtimes had been relaxed and fun, a celebration of the food they'd lovingly prepared together.

She took her time, and an hour later had a beautifully rich and smooth soup, but there was still no sign of Ethan. She'd eaten a bowl of soup and was halfway through the book. The apartment was eerily silent. The snow swirling beyond the windows gave the impression that they were marooned.

Marooned with Ethan Black.

Even thinking about it did strange things to her breathing, which made no sense at all. Especially given that he was currently unconscious.

She glanced at Madi. "Do you think he's okay?" The dog thumped her tail.

Harriet went to check on him again and saw that he hadn't moved.

That wasn't normal, surely?

Concerned, she stepped into the room and tentatively put her fingers on his forehead.

He was burning hot.

She snatched her hand away. "You have a fever!" Horrified, she stood for a moment, frozen by indecision, and then snapped into action. Her insecurities evaporated. She may not know much about seduction, but she knew about this. "You're sick. I have to get that coat off you. Ethan? Ethan." She gave his shoulder a gentle shake and he opened his eyes as if he had lead attached to the lids. They glittered with fever and his gaze was bleary and unfocused.

Not good.

"I have to get you out of this coat. You're burning up. Is this why you came home early from work? Why didn't you say something?"

He grunted a protest as she tried to ease his coat away from his shoulders. It was only when he resisted that she realized how strong he was. And how heavy. And almost all that weight was muscle.

This wasn't going to be easy.

"You're a doctor." She tugged and pulled until she removed the coat. It was no easy feat. He was bigger than her and much stronger. "You should know it's not good to wrap up when you have a fever. We have to cool you down."

"Go away." His teeth were chattering. "Whatever I've got, you don't want it."

She ignored him. "Help me take your sweater off. Just move a fraction, *please*, Ethan." He obviously wasn't the type who was good at following orders because he didn't move. She slid her hands up his arms, feeling rock solid muscles. He was built like a weight lifter. She tugged at his sweater, dragging it up the column of his back and trying to ease it over his shoulder.

He grunted a protest. "When I imagined you undressing me, it didn't go quite like this."

He'd imagined her undressing him? Her heart gave a little flutter and then she remembered that he had a fever. He probably didn't know what he was saying.

Great. It took delirium for a sexy guy to pay her a compliment.

"Keep the jokes until later. Is there someone you want me to call? Who is your doctor?"

"I'm the doctor—" He broke off in a dry, hacking cough. "Get out, or you'll catch it."

"I never get sick." She tugged and pulled, but he was heavy and gave her no help. By the time she'd removed his sweater she was out of breath. "Although of course now I've tempted fate and I'll probably have bubonic plague by Monday, but I'll worry about that later. Hopefully by then you'll be better and in a position to save my life. Right now I need to get your jeans off."

"Is that an indecent suggestion?" He coughed again and she winced.

"Stop talking. You sound as if you're going to cough up your lung. Why didn't you tell me you weren't feeling well?"

"I thought I'd be fine after a lie-down."

"For a doctor, you're pretty stupid."

His breathing was raspy. "I think I might have caught something."

"No kidding. You trained for all those years to tell me that?"

"You really should get out of here." He spoke as if every word was an effort.

"No, because if you die in the night I don't want that on my conscience. I already have enough scars and baggage to deal with. Carrying any more will give me spinal problems."

"How come you suddenly have so much to say for yourself? What happened to shy Harriet?"

"You're weak and can't fight back."

"You're right about that." His eyes closed. "I don't feel too good."

"Because you're burning up like a rocket launcher. Any minute now you're going to be propelled into space. Still, I guess the advantage of that is that the rest of us wouldn't catch it and to be honest it doesn't look like a whole lot of fun. We need to get the rest of these layers off you. If I undress you are you going to take it the wrong way like you did when I cooked dinner?" She reached for the hem of his T-shirt but he stopped her.

"I was an asshole."

"I'm not arguing with that. The only reason I didn't walk out and leave you to deal with Madi on your own is because I care too much about her."

"C-cold." His teeth were chattering and his body shuddering.

"You're not cold. I could barbecue ribs on your head. You need to strip. And I need to get you liquids."

"Liquids. Yes." He hacked again and slowly hauled himself to a sitting position, doubling over as she watched helplessly. She could sense his frustration, his exasperation with the weakness of his own body.

And she felt a twinge of unease.

She'd never seen anyone get so sick, so fast.

What if it wasn't the flu? What if it was something more serious? She hoped the anxiety knotting inside her didn't show on her face. How did he handle serious cases in the ER? She'd be standing there gnawing her nails down to the skin wondering what she was missing.

"Can you stand up? Could you make it to the shower? We need to cool you down."

Without answering, he lay back down and covered himself with the soft throw that lay across the bed.

Harriet pulled it off again. "I'll take that as a no, but either way I still need to get your jeans off."

"I'm not in the mood."

She took comfort from the fact he still had a sense of

humor. If he were dying of something serious, he wouldn't be laughing, would he?

She glanced at the snug fit of his jeans and felt her color rise. "Can you at least undo them?"

He moved his hands slowly and then let them fall away to his sides. "No."

Rolling her eyes, Harriet took over.

It took her two attempts to unbutton his jeans, her fingers fumbling and inept as she tried to subdue her mind's sudden determination to take her imagination to places she definitely didn't want to go.

Thankfully he seemed pretty out of it so he wasn't likely to remember her struggles to undress him.

Clenching her jaw, she pulled at his jeans, each tug revealing a little more masculinity. Taut, muscular abs, the light shadow of hair across his chest and on his thighs.

She averted her eyes from his black boxer shorts.

He was the most gorgeous man she'd ever laid eyes on. Not that she'd laid eyes on that many. Her love life had been as small and cautious as the rest of her life.

Boring, some would say and she wouldn't have argued with that.

She turned away and folded his jeans.

She was fantasizing over a half-dead guy. What was wrong with her? But she knew the answer to that, of course. Right now he was vulnerable rather than intimidating. And even half-dead, Ethan Black was sexier than any guy she'd ever met.

"Stay there and don't move. I'm going to fetch you a drink."

"Whiskey."

"Not that sort of drink. And we should try and cool you

down. I'm going to turn up the air-conditioning. Do you have any Tylenol? Ibuprofen?" She felt a flash of exasperation as she saw him shake his head. "What sort of a doctor are you?"

"The sort who lives at the hospital." He coughed again and she winced.

"I can't believe you don't even have Tylenol." She walked into his bathroom and wet a towel. "Here. Try this." She wiped it across his forchead and he shuddered.

"F-freezing."

"I'm the one who is supposed to stammer. This is role reversal."

"You're intimidating when you're in charge."

She ignored that. "Stay there. And if you try and get out of bed, I'll give you something to stammer about."

His eyes stayed closed. "You're only this brave because you know I'm too weak to resist."

It was truc.

She went into her own bedroom and removed Tylenol and ibuprofen from her packing.

Then she went downstairs and filled a jug with water.

She added ice, thinking that the evening was less stressful than dinner would have been. If they'd had dinner, he would have been the one in charge. The one with the experience and the expertise. Right now, she had the upper hand.

He was easier to handle when he was sick. He'd lost some of the cool authority that made her feel a little inadequate and him seem unapproachable.

On the other hand that wasn't a good sign.

Maybe she should do an internet search on "raging flu symptoms that come on in a matter of hours." What if it wasn't the flu? Should she call someone?

She was about to head back upstairs when she heard the buzzer.

It had to be someone who lived in the building, otherwise the doorman would have called.

In the time she'd been staying here the only person who had arrived directly at the door was Judy when she'd come to complain about the noise.

She glanced at Madi. "If that's a neighbor telling me you've been barking again you are in trouble."

Madi wagged her tail happily.

Harriet opened the door.

A woman stood there, her hair sparkling with snow.

"Hi, I—" She broke off, clearly bemused to see Harriet. "Did I get the wrong apartment? I was looking for Ethan."

Harriet's heart plummeted.

In everything Ethan had said, it hadn't occurred to her that he was dating anyone right now.

But why wouldn't he be?

Reminding herself that his love life wasn't exactly her business, she remembered her manners and opened the door. "This is the right apartment. Come in."

"No need. I don't want to disturb anything—" The other woman seemed intrigued rather than jealous and Harriet wondered why she seemed so relaxed.

"You're not disturbing anything. I'm Harriet, the dog sitter." She felt she had a responsibility to make that clear. Whatever this relationship was, she didn't want to wreck it.

"I'm Susan. Ethan has a dog?" Susan's eyes popped. "We are talking about the same Ethan? Tall. Too handsome for his own good. A touch on the arrogant side but with a heart of gold?"

She couldn't have come up with a better description herself.

"Yes. And it's not his dog. It's his sister's dog."

"Ah. That makes a lot more sense, although even I'm surprised he agreed to take on a dog. Ethan doesn't love disruption in his life."

Harriet thought about how often he'd called to see how his niece was doing. "Maybe not, but he loves his sister."

"And that," Susan said, "is the heart of gold part. I admit I'm disappointed. For a moment there I thought you were the reason he's been smiling more at work lately."

Ethan had been smiling?

"I'm looking after the dog because, as you say, he doesn't like disruption in his life. So you don't need to be worried at all."

"Why would I be worried? Oh—" Enlightenment dawned on her face and she gave a slow smile. "No. I'm a colleague, that's all. We work together. He didn't seem himself today and he hasn't answered his phone since he left the hospital so I wanted to check on him, because I know he lives alone."

Harriet wondered why that news would make her feel lighter.

"Did you say you were a doctor?"

"I am. Why? Are you sick?"

"No, but Ethan is." Harriet opened the door wider. "He's barely moved since he arrived home and he has a fever. I assume it's the flu, but I'm worried it might not be because he got sick faster than anyone I've ever seen. Could you take a look at him?"

Susan walked into the apartment and stripped off her coat. "Show me to the patient. Is he irritable and cursing you?"

"No. He's been well behaved."

"That's bad."

"It is?"

"Ethan is a guy who likes things to go his way. And he's not good at being sick. Makes him irritable as hell. If he's not irritable, that's bad." She took the stairs two a time and Harriet followed more slowly, thinking that the two of them together in the emergency room must be a force to be reckoned with.

"His room is the first on the left."

"Got it." Susan pushed open the door and stood there for a moment. "Well hell, Black, what have you done to yourself this time?"

Ethan didn't stir and Susan strode over to the bed. "Ethan?" She touched his forehead and her eyebrows rose. "You are one hot man, and for once I'm not talking about your pecs or your abs."

"I took his clothes off." Harriet had no idea why that admission should make her blush.

"Good move." As Susan put her bag down by the bed, Ethan opened his eyes.

"What are you doing here?" The words were little more than a hoarse rasp and set off a coughing fit that lasted a full minute.

"Which one of our goddamn patients gave you that?" Susan leaned forward and hauled him into a sitting position. "Harriet? Can you hold him? I need to listen to his chest."

Ethan grunted. "I don't need—"

"I'll decide what you need. Now shut up or you'll make yourself cough, and if you give it to me I'll kill you myself." Susan pulled a stethoscope out of her bag. "Harriet?"

Harriet stepped forward, wondering how she was supposed to hold him upright.

She sat on the edge of the bed and put her hands on his upper arms, trying to hold him steady, but he swayed backward, the weight of him pulling her with him and she had no choice but to wrap her arms round him and pull him toward her.

She held her breath, not because she was afraid of catching something but because she suddenly couldn't remember how to get air in and out of her lungs. She felt the pressure of his chest against hers, the width of his shoulders and the strength of his muscles.

Her face was close to his. She tried to keep her gaze fixed on the wall behind her but she couldn't help noticing the stubble that darkened his jaw and the thickness of his eyelashes. He was shockingly pale but that didn't stop her from wanting to bury her face in his neck and breathe him in.

It occurred to her that this was probably the closest she was ever going to get to Ethan Black.

Susan finished her examination and propped pillows behind him.

"When you undressed him, did you see a rash?"

"No. But I wasn't looking." She'd made a point of it. Her imagination had been active enough by itself, without adding reality into the mix.

"I'm going to give you antibiotics."

Ethan scowled. "I don't need—"

"Did I ask for your opinion? You're the patient, I'm the doctor. You're going to take them."

Harriet waited for Ethan to argue again but he seemed to have given up the fight. He lay with his eyes closed, as if the effort required to sit up had drained the last of his energy.

Susan opened her bag again and placed two small boxes by the bed. "Take two now."

"I have Tylenol," Harriet said. "Presumably he should have those?"

"Yes, and ibuprofen." Susan dug in her back again. "It will bring the fever down. You can alternate them. Are you staying here tonight? He needs someone to check on him."

Ethan opened his eyes a crack. "Don't need anyone."

"Yeah, I know that's how you prefer to live your life. Not needing anyone." Susan snapped her bag shut. "But right now, you need someone. So what you are trying to say is 'thank you.' Be nice to Harriet because if she walks out and I have to come back and sit with you, it won't be fun."

Ethan started to protest but ended up coughing again, this time so hard that even Susan frowned.

"I won't walk out," Harriet said. "I need to be here for Madi." What she didn't say was that she wouldn't have walked out anyway. She tried telling herself it was because she wouldn't leave anyone in the state Ethan was in, but even she didn't believe that.

"Hear that?" Susan stood up. "You're one step lower than a dog in her priorities. When you're better, you might want to think about that."

Ethan used language that made Harriet blink.

Susan grinned. "The great thing about the emergency room is that it extends your vocabulary." She walked to the door. "If you're worried, call me. I'm only a few blocks away. This is my number." She thrust a card into Harriet's hand.

"Thank you." Harriet followed her downstairs. "So you think it's the flu?"

"Hopefully. I don't think it's anything that requires more

than a few days in bed and some antibiotics. Don't let him order you around."

"Would you like a drink or something before you leave?"

"By drink, do you mean alcohol? Because I could get behind that idea."

Harriet removed a bottle of white from the fridge and lifted two glasses out of the cabinet.

The least Ethan could do was provide them both with a glass of decent wine. "You know him well?"

"Yes." Susan took the glass from her. "He's the best doctor I've worked with. Coolheaded. Smart. His brain works faster than anyone else's. But those same qualities that make him the best doctor I've worked with, can make you want to strangle him outside work."

Harriet blinked. "Excuse me?"

"He's used to being in charge. Giving the commands. Sometimes he finds it hard to remember he has left work."

Harriet thought of the first encounter they'd had and laughed. "That sounds right."

"He's compassionate too." Susan had already half finished her wine. "A lot of doctors in his position get cynical, but Ethan is always the one who remembers there is a person under the problem."

Harriet had a sudden burning need to find out more about Ethan. "Are you hungry? I made soup."

Susan stared at her. "You *made* soup? It's not from a tin or a carton?"

"Fresh. From real vegetables."

"Hell yes." Susan dropped her bag and walked to the kitchen, the wineglass still in her hand. "Do you have any idea how long it is since I had home-cooked food?"

"If you're anything like Ethan, I'm guessing it's been a

while." She wondered why it was doctors found it so hard to cook for themselves.

"It's been too long." Susan lifted the lid and peered into the pot. "That smells incredible. I'm going to buy a dog and have you come and live with me."

Harriet grinned. "I don't do dog sitting."

"And yet you're here." Susan ladled soup into a bowl, and leaned forward to inhale. "Man, that smells good."

"I'm doing a favor for my client."

"And is your client the dog or the owner?" Susan put her bowl on the kitchen island and sat down.

"Both, but it's the dog's needs that come first for me." Harriet put a fresh sourdough loaf in front of Susan and sat down next to her. "Originally I was supposed to be walking Madi, but she was very unsettled and almost wrecked the place so Ethan asked me to base myself here." She told Susan everything.

"So you've been living here all week." Susan finished the soup, eating as if she were starved. "That explains a lot."

"It does?" Harriet took Susan's bowl and filled it up again. The loaf of bread she'd baked that afternoon was already almost gone. Maybe she should set up a stall near the emergency room and nourish underfed doctors.

"Ignore me." Susan all but snatched the soup out of her hands. "So when is Debra back?"

"Next week." And then she'd be moving out and Harriet would never see Ethan again. It was something she found oddly depressing. "You eat quickly."

"It's one of the side effects of being a doctor. You never know when your meal will be interrupted so you learn to eat quickly." Susan finished the second bowl of soup and sat back. "That was amazing. Anytime you want to invite me to dinner, consider it a yes from me. I'll call the hospital and tell them Ethan won't be in over the weekend. Hopefully by Monday he'll be well enough to call them himself with an update. You're sure you're going to be okay here?"

"Yes. I feel better now someone qualified has taken a look at him. I was worried."

"He's going to be fine. Don't let him take advantage of you."

Susan left half an hour later, leaving Harriet alone in the apartment with Ethan.

Madi was asleep.

Her own room beckoned, the bed waiting for her.

Instead, she walked into Ethan's room.

His eyes were closed, but she could hear the faint rasp of his breathing.

She touched his forehead lightly and discovered he was still burning up.

She walked into his bathroom and dampened a washcloth. The bathroom was sleek and masculine, dark gray tiles broken up by an entire wall that was mirrored.

Everything was neatly ordered. Nothing strewn about the place, as it had been in her own bathroom when Fliss was living with her.

She placed the cloth on his forehead but this time he didn't stir.

Telling herself that the meds would take time to work, she curled up in the chair near his bed.

If he was going to die, it wasn't going to be on her watch.

CHAPTER SIXTEEN

ETHAN WOKE COUGHING several times in the night and each time Harriet helped him to sit up, forced him to drink fluids and did what she could to bring down the fever. She'd never seen anyone so ill. Despite Susan's reassurances, she didn't like leaving him on his own for long.

She tried sleeping on top of her bed with her door open so that she'd hear him if he called for her, but then she found she was listening out for him all the time and wondering if he was still breathing, so she gave up on that and made herself comfortable in the deep armchair in the corner of his room.

It was almost as comfortable as her bed, and she slept in fitful bouts, her mind hovering between wakefulness and sleep, conscious of Ethan within arm's reach. It felt strange, this intimacy between two people who barely knew each other.

It was a long night.

Every time he coughed she fetched him drinks and tried to help him sit up. When he slept, she tried to sleep.

Morning came, the weak winter sun spilling diffuse light through the window.

Ethan didn't stir and Harriet leaned closer to check he was breathing before going downstairs to make breakfast.

After a night of almost no sleep, her head throbbed and she felt as if she'd been hit over the head with a hammer.

Madi was waiting for her, tail wagging.

Deciding that she had no choice but to leave Ethan while she took the dog for a walk, she scribbled a note and left it by his bedside along with his phone.

The moment she stepped outside the apartment the cold hit her, driving away the smothering fog of sleep.

She wrapped her scarf more tightly round her neck and huddled deeper into her coat.

The city was oddly silent, all sound muffled by a fresh layer of snow.

Worried about Ethan, she kept the walk as short as she felt was fair on Madi and when she returned to the apartment Ethan still hadn't moved.

Harriet touched his forehead and decided he felt a little cooler.

That had to be a good thing, surely? As was the fact that he was finally sleeping.

The dark shadow on his jaw that had been no more than whisker grain the day before was more pronounced now, accentuating the pallor of his skin.

Halfway through the afternoon she was in the kitchen when she heard a crash from the bedroom.

She took the stairs two at a time and found Ethan clutching the end of the bed, eyeing the bathroom as if he were an explorer contemplating a long and dangerous sea voyage.

She took his arm and he leaned on her heavily, his legs almost buckling as he reached the bathroom door.

"I need to take a shower."

"Are you sure it's a good idea? You don't seem exactly steady on your feet. If you do, don't lock the door. I'll wait right here."

His blue gaze connected with hers. "You could join me. I could put my healing hands on you."

So he *had* heard.

She decided to pretend she didn't know what he was talking about. He'd had a fever when he'd overheard that conversation, hadn't he? It was amazing how fever could blur the brain.

"Don't make offers you're not capable of seeing through. And right now you're the one who needs healing. I could knock you over with a touch of my finger."

"I won't always be sick, Harriet. Then you and I are going to talk." He started to cough and she rolled her eyes.

"But right now you are sick, so let's focus on that." And once he was better, she'd be out of here.

"You're a beautiful woman."

Her heart almost stopped. "I—what did you say?"

"I said you're beautiful." His gaze dropped to her mouth and lingered there.

Her skin tingled. She felt as if she'd been electrocuted. "I've been up all night and I haven't even brushed my hair."

His mouth curved slightly. "That must be it. You look as if you just emerged from a wild night of sin."

She wanted to say that she wouldn't know sin if she fell over it, but instead she pushed him toward the bathroom.

"You're delirious. That happens with a fever. Get in the shower, Ethan, and I suggest you turn it to cold."

She made sure he was steady on his feet—because if he fell and banged his head, that would be something else she would have to fix—and backed out of the room.

She leaned against the wall and closed her eyes, forcing herself to breathe.

Beautiful? Last time she'd checked, she'd looked like a ghost. He had to be hallucinating.

During her average working day she didn't pay much attention to her appearance. She worked with dogs. Her objective was to find practical clothing that was warm in winter, and cool in summer. Sensible shoes more suitable for pounding the paths of Central Park than walking a red carpet.

Pulling herself together, she walked back into his bedroom and took advantage of the fact he wasn't there to change the bedding. Then she busied herself in her own room, made a couple of calls to clients, answered a couple of calls from dog walkers and handled a few schedule changes. And all the time she kept listening for the moment the shower was turned off. She tried not to think about the water sliding over his naked body. Tried not to think about those wide shoulders, those flat abs, his sense of humor, all that heart-melting charm under that rough exterior—

Stop it, Harriet!

She hoped he didn't pass out because she didn't want to be the one to walk into that shower and drag his body out.

She gave him ten minutes and walked back into his room.

He'd pulled on a loose black tee and a pair of trackpants. His hair stood in shiny spikes, droplets of water still clinging to his neck. He stood in the doorway of the bathroom, as if trying to make up his mind if he had what it took to get back to the bed. If she were to judge on appearances she would have said he'd used every last scrap of energy.

He watched as she piled up the pillows. "Thank you for looking after me."

"I'm doing it for Madi."

He raised an eyebrow. "The dog cares about my well-being?"

"If you die, she will be unsettled again. She needs stability."

"It's good to have a reason to cling to life." His dry tone told her he had to be feeling better.

She sent mental thanks to Susan. "Have you taken your meds?"

"I have." He walked carefully to the bed. Before that remark about her being beautiful she would have helped him, but now she decided it was safer to keep her distance. She no longer knew the rules of this relationship.

She shook her head. "You look pitiful. Do you want to sleep some more? Watch TV?"

"I don't have TV in the bedroom." He collapsed onto the freshly made bed. "The bedroom is for two things only. Sleep and—"

"Okay, I get it." She interrupted him quickly and reached for the throw. She didn't want to hear about the things that had happened in that huge bed of his. On balance she'd preferred it when he had less to say for himself.

"For a woman of almost thirty—"

"How do you know my age?" She pulled the throw over him.

"I treated you in the ER. I was going to say that for a woman of almost thirty, you're shy about sex. Tell me about your previous boyfriends."

She gave a start. "Are you delirious?"

"No, but I feel like crap and I want distraction."

"Then you don't want to talk about my boyfriends because there's not a lot of distraction there."

"There haven't been many?"

"I never really saw the point of dating for the sake of it."

"So I was right."

"About what?"

"You're not the type for casual sex."

Up until she'd met him, she would have agreed but right now she wasn't sure.

She seemed to think about nothing but sex when she was with him. Serious, casual, right now she would have taken whatever was on offer.

She was agonizingly aware of him watching her as she moved around the room.

"I suppose I'm more of a relationship sort of person."

"I guessed that about you. Tell me about the last guy you had sex with."

"Excuse me?" Her cheeks flamed. She never talked about sex with anyone. Not even her sister. Why would he ask her that question? And why now, with the sun spotlighting her every reaction?

"I'm trying to even the score. You've undressed me and seen me almost naked. That gives me certain rights."

"It gives you no rights."

"Well I'm taking them anyway. Tell me about the last guy you dated."

She picked up the clothes he'd dropped on the floor, not because she particularly felt the need to tidy, but because it made it easier to hide her face. "Charlton Morris."

"Where did you meet him, how long did it last and why

did you break up?" He started coughing again and this time she looked at him without sympathy.

"That's your punishment for asking so many questions, none of which are your business."

"I was supposed to be taking you on a training date. Consider this research."

"I don't need a training date. I don't plan on dating a man who makes me feel so uncomfortable I have to be coached to get through the evening. I want someone I'm comfortable with. How hard is that?" She threw his clothes into the laundry hamper as if they were personally responsible for her deficiencies in that area.

"Hard. It's not easy to meet people, least of all someone you feel comfortable with." He reached for his water and it was so obviously a struggle that she took pity and handed it to him.

"Sit up. And you probably need another dose of antibiotics. I like Susan, by the way. You should marry her. She'd be good for you."

He choked on the water. "I'm not marrying anyone ever again, least of all Susan."

"Why 'least of all'? She came round here after her shift to check on you. She cares about you."

"And I care about her. But all we have is friendship. If it turned to anything more we would kill each other in a day."

"You could try being less sure of yourself all the time. That might make you a little more endearing."

He put the glass down, spilling some of it. "So next time a patient is bleeding out you want me to tell him I'm not sure what I'm doing? Believe it or not, when people are sick they want to feel as if they're in good hands. They want confidence."

"Tell me about your marriage. What went wrong?" She mopped up the water he'd spilled.

"That's a personal question."

"No more personal than the ones you were asking me."

"But you didn't answer."

She shifted the pillows behind him so that he was more comfortable. "I told you about Charlton."

"You told me nothing about Charlton. Was he good in bed?"

She paused, the pillow in her hands. She didn't know whether to put it down or suffocate him with it. "I don't know. I didn't sleep with him."

"Why not?"

"Because I could never quite relax around him and I can't imagine ever going to bed with a man if I can't relax. How would that even work? Don't answer that," she said hastily, stuffing the pillow behind his back. "It was rhetorical." She reached for the throw and pulled it over his legs. "Now that you've cooled down, we need to be careful you don't get cold."

"I had no idea you knew so much about caring for someone with a fever."

"Susan gave me a list of instructions. And she called earlier to see how you were."

"So if you didn't sleep with Charlton, who was the last man you slept with?"

Harriet sighed. "I'm starting to wish Susan had found a way to knock you unconscious. Shouldn't you be resting?"

"I'll rest when you've answered my question."

"His name was Eric. He worked as a vet in our local practice. Are you done now?"

"No."

"I think I preferred it when I thought you might die."

His smile was faint, but definitely there. "That could still happen. This is a lull, brought on by an excess of painkillers and antibiotics."

"I will write your obituary. Here lies Ethan, who never knew when to stop asking tactless questions."

"So you slept with Eric. And the earth didn't move."

"I never said the earth didn't move."

"Your expression said it. Was that why you broke up?"

"No!" She picked up his glass, intending to refill it. Why were they even talking about this? "He didn't want a relationship. He wanted the sex part."

"I can understand that."

"I'm sure you can."

"No, I mean I understand him wanting to have sex with you. Any man would."

She almost dropped the glass. "Stop saying things like that."

"Why?"

"Because it makes me uncomfortable."

"Isn't that what Challenge Harriet is all about? I'm pushing you out of your comfort zone. You're welcome."

"I'm supposed to be grateful you're embarrassing me?"

"No. You're supposed to answer my questions until you're not embarrassed. It's okay to talk about sex. It's okay for women to love sex."

"I don't love sex." The words came out before she could stop them and she saw his eyes darken.

She wanted to snatch the words back because this was a conversation she definitely didn't want to have.

"So the earth really didn't move."

Not even a faint tremor, but she didn't want to admit that to him.

It seemed she didn't have to because he nodded. "Interesting. So who did make the earth move?"

"What's this sudden interest in sexual seismic activity? I really don't want to talk about this anymore."

"You're shy, so whoever is with you would need to take their time and gain your confidence before going any further. I'm guessing Eric and Charlton both jumped on you like dogs in heat."

That was exactly how it had happened.

"What happened with your wife?" If he could ask personal questions, so could she. "What went wrong?"

"She married me." He slumped back against the pillows and let his eyes close.

"Oh no, you don't get off that easily, buster." Harriet folded her arms. "If you embarrass me, then I can embarrass you."

"I'm not embarrassed. I don't particularly like talking about my marriage, that's all. No man wants to confront his failures."

"She must have contributed too. A relationship is never one-sided, even a bad one." And she'd been in a few bad ones.

"All right, let's talk about my ex-wife. I deserve it, I guess. What do you want to know?"

"Where did you meet?"

"She's a journalist. She was doing a series on real life in the ER. She interviewed me and then decided I was good on camera and she wanted to make the whole series about me."

"So you're a movie star?"

"Hardly."

"I bet you had fan mail."

He cracked open one eye. "What makes you think that?"

"Because people are naturally drawn to doctors. They work on the assumption that you're caring and a bit special. That's before they get to know you, of course."

"Kick a man when he's down."

"I will."

He gave her a sardonic look. "You don't seem to be particularly drawn to doctors."

"I could be. There's a kind of built-in attraction. The word *Doctor* says *good guy. Caring.* Able to save your life if you jump from a window and fall in the Dumpster."

"So why aren't you drawn to me?"

She was. She really was, although she suspected that had nothing to do with the fact that he was a doctor. "Because you're irritable, shouty, and you think you know it all."

"Shouty? Is that even a word?"

"It is in my world."

"I shouted at you once."

"But it was loud."

"You're never going to forgive me for that one?"

"I've forgiven you, but we were talking about attraction. I would never date someone who makes me stammer."

"That happened in the first five minutes of meeting you. I should get a free pass. And you're not stammering now."

"That's because you're weakened and not a threat to me."

"What happens when I'm fully recovered?"

"By then Debra will be back and we can both go back to our normal lives."

He frowned slightly, as if he hadn't thought that far ahead. "So you're saying you're not at all attracted to me?"

"Not at all," she lied. "Not even a tiny bit. You were telling me about your wife."

"We dated for eighteen months and were married for six. Then we both woke up one day and agreed it wasn't working. By that time we were little more than roommates. She was dedicated to her work, and I was dedicated to mine. There was no room for anything else in our lives."

Harriet felt something tug inside her. "That's sad."

"Do I look sad?"

"No. And that's what makes it even sadder."

"Not everyone needs a long-term relationship."

"You have plenty of long-term relationships. You love your sister. You obviously love your niece. You're close to your parents. You have lifelong friends you still see. Those are long-term relationships." What she didn't say was that he had more long-term relationships than she did, although she'd gathered a few more lately since Daniel met Molly and Fliss had got back together with Seth.

She wanted one of her own. She wanted to share her life with someone special. Someone who would know her. Someone who liked the way she was and didn't expect her to put on an act or pretend to be someone different. Was that too much to ask?

Ethan gave her a curious look. "Maybe what I mean is that I don't need a wife."

"You make it sound like a liability. Or an accessory. *I don't need a new coat, I'm perfectly fine with the one I already own.*"

"That's how it felt. I felt bad about myself the whole time I was married."

She couldn't imagine him feeling bad about anything. "Why?"

"Because I was focused on work and I felt guilty about that. And so did she. Our relationship felt like pressure, not pleasure."

She had to admit it didn't sound much like the relationship she was hoping to find one day. "Did you love her?"

He was silent for a moment and the simple fact that he had to think about his answer told her everything she needed to know. "Not sure," he said finally. "I thought I did, or I wouldn't have married her. We got together because we were similar in many ways, but being similar isn't necessarily a good thing. Were you in love with Eric? You said he didn't want a relationship, which implies that you did."

She wondered how he always managed to ask the questions she didn't want to answer. "I think I was in love with the idea of a relationship more than I was with Eric. I know I have to be careful. My childhood left me with a need for warmth and security in my home life. I have to be careful not to be so desperate for that type of comfort, that I make bad decisions."

"That sounds sensible, if a little clinical. Do you always think everything through carefully? Haven't you ever made a wild, wanton decision?"

"Never."

His eyes closed again. "If I didn't feel as if I'd just done ten rounds in a boxing ring, I'd do something about that. Challenge Harriet."

"Right now you're not in a position to challenge anything, Ethan."

And she wasn't sure whether to be disappointed or relieved.

CHAPTER SEVENTEEN

IT TOOK TWO days for his fever to finally come down. He slept most of the time, and each time he opened his eyes Harriet was there, checking his temperature, refreshing his water, reminding him to take his medication, rubbing his back when he was racked by coughing. Everything ached and moving from the bed seemed like an impossible task. Given that all he was doing was sleeping, he was surprised by how much he liked having her there. He wasn't used to having anyone else living in the apartment, let alone hovering in his bedroom. Usually he prized the silence, but not only was he fairly sure he wouldn't have bothered to drink anything had she not been there to hand it to him, she also created a level of background noise he found oddly comforting.

Occasionally she'd leave the room and through the drifting mist of sleep he'd hear her downstairs, talking to Madi or clattering in the kitchen. The dog adored her and followed her everywhere, and it wasn't hard to see why.

Harriet was calm, her presence soothing. Anyone would feel better around her.

Over the past forty-eight hours, even hidden behind a fog of fever, he'd learned a lot about her.

He'd learned that she sang when she cooked, that when she spoke to a client about a dog she always asked after them too. She knew them all. What they'd been doing. What their problems were. And he heard her talking to her sister and knew she was fielding questions she didn't want to answer. He learned that although she didn't seem to lie, she was more than capable of being evasive.

He'd hear an *mmm* and a *maybe* and an occasional *how are we twins when we're so different?*, but he hadn't heard her mention him since that night he'd gone down with the flu and been too sick to question what he'd overheard.

And being ill had taught him another thing about her.

It had taught him that Harriet Knight was the kindest person he'd ever met.

He drifted off to sleep again and when he woke in the evening, two days after he'd all but dragged himself into his bed, delicious smells were wafting up the stairs. It was dark outside and the snow fell steadily outside his window. He felt a twinge of guilt, because he knew the emergency room would be busy, his colleagues having to pull together to find a way to fill the hole created by his absence.

"You're awake." Harriet appeared in the doorway, as she had done hundreds of times over the past few days. She'd taken a shower and changed into jeans and a soft sweater.

Ethan had to fight the urge to pull her into bed with him. "What's that amazing smell?"

"It's Madi's dinner." She topped up his water glass and must have seen the disappointment on his face because she gave a half smile. "I'm kidding. It's chicken soup. My grandmother's recipe. It's perfect for tempting the appetite in people who aren't well. I used to look forward to being sick so she would make this soup for me. And before you start reading too much into that, I should tell you it's my favorite soup. I made it for myself."

He knew that wasn't true.

Food, he realized now, was her way of showing care and love. He also knew that if he didn't play his cards right, he wouldn't be eating the soup.

"So you're not planning on sharing it?"

"Maybe." She held the glass out. "Drink. You're dehydrated."

Everything she did was calm and quiet, from the way she moved around the room, to the way she did what she could to make things better for him.

Her generosity floored him. He knew he was miserly with his feelings. He kept them inside, safe from harm. It was part of the mechanism he'd developed to protect him from the job. He'd learned to keep his emotions locked away, but there were times when he wondered whether he'd maybe done too good a job. In order to stay focused and effective he didn't let himself feel. When he was younger, before experience and older colleagues had given him more wisdom, he'd allowed his job to get to him. He'd reached a point where he was considering a change in career, but before he'd made the final decision he'd gone home for the weekend and talked with his parents and grandfather.

He'd come away from that weekend feeling supported and, more importantly, with some useful strategies for coping with the inevitable stress of his profession.

He remembered whole weekends growing up when his

father would barely talk. His mother would never ask what was wrong. Instead she was a quiet, supportive presence, providing what comfort she could while his father worked through whatever trauma or issue was bothering him. She hadn't demanded that he cheer up, or that he talk about whatever it was that was stressing him. But she'd made it clear that she was there if he needed her.

Harriet had the same soothing, undemanding quality.

It crossed his mind that her good nature and kindness would make her an easy person to take advantage of, and he felt a shaft of discomfort, wondering if that was what he'd been doing. First he'd pressured her to move in and look after Madi, and now she was looking after him.

And she was looking after him a bit too well.

She'd barely left his side for the past few days and now she'd cooked him a meal.

"Chicken soup? Homemade from an actual chicken?" He took the glass, noticing that her nails were short and neat.

"It's hard to make chicken soup from any other animal."

"When did you go shopping?"

"Earlier. You were asleep. I had to take Madi out anyway." She dismissed it as nothing and knowing that he was the reason she felt the need to do that, he felt a stab of guilt.

"Is Madi all right?"

"Better than you. Do you still have a fever?"

He noticed that she asked him this time, instead of touching his forehead to find out for herself. She didn't look at him much, either. Something had changed and he wasn't sure what. "I'm feeling better. Thanks to you."

"It had nothing to do with me. It was a combination of medication, sleep and time."

It was partly true, but he knew that her working so hard to

keep his fever down and make him comfortable had played a huge part in his recovery. She'd been patient and kind when he'd felt like death and he made a mental note to be more sympathetic next time a patient visited the emergency room with the flu.

He tried to stand up, frustrated that his legs still felt as if they'd been filled with concrete. Cursing, he sank back down onto the edge of the bed again. "Who invented flu?"

"Someone who decided that even a confident man needs to be laid low once in a while. It's good for you to be reminded that you're not all-powerful."

Powerful?

If he'd had the energy, he would have laughed out loud.

She hesitated for a fraction of a second and then stepped toward him. "Do you need help?"

He probably could have managed, but he didn't tell her that. Instead he put his arm round her shoulders and leaned on her. She smelled of strawberry and sunshine. Unable to help himself he leaned in a little closer, his attention caught by the golden sheen of her hair.

She turned her head to look at him and the movement caused her hair to brush against his cheek and suddenly he found it hard to breathe.

Her eyes held his in wordless communication.

Sexual awareness rippled through him, the sudden tension in the atmosphere closing in like a force field. The room, the outside world, faded into the background. There was only her.

He knew he should pull back. He knew this was dangerous, but he couldn't bring himself to be the one to break the connection.

He had to remind himself of all the things she'd said to

him in the dark of the night. About how she'd wanted a relationship and Eric hadn't.

Harriet deserved the best, and he knew for sure he wasn't the best.

"What are you doing?" Her face was so close to his that all he could see was the blue of her eyes.

"I'm leaning on you. You offered." And her mouth was right there. Right there.

But her mouth wasn't on offer. None of her was. Not to him.

"Are you sure you're not capable of walking by yourself?"

"Definitely not." He staggered a bit to prove his point, knowing that he was taking advantage of her good nature.

By the time they reached the bathroom he felt as if he needed to lie down for a month. That, he thought, was his punishment for pretending to be weaker than he was. Now he really did feel as weak as he'd pretended to feel.

He braced his arm against the door frame, frustrated by the lethargy that threatened to floor him. "I'm not sure I can make it downstairs to eat."

"No worries. I'll bring it up on a tray." She touched his face with her palm, her eyes warm with sympathy. "Do you feel horrid?"

"Yes." And that was probably a good thing, he thought, or he might have done something he would definitely have regretted later.

The moment she sensed weakness, she lowered the barriers.

It was the only good thing about being ill.

He took a shower and when he walked back into the bedroom she was standing there holding a tray.

"Chair or bed?"

Unable to help himself, he gave her a wicked smile. "Which would you prefer?"

She gave him a look that made him wonder if she'd ever taught kindergarten. "I can walk out anytime and take my soup with me."

"Bed." He slid back under the covers and she placed the tray on his legs, the weight of it pressing down through the covers. "Stay and talk. I promise to behave."

"I have to do my accounts."

"If you're prioritizing accounts over me then I'm truly put in my place."

"I don't want to do them, but I have to. Honestly, I hate it. I'm not good at it. Fliss is."

He picked up the spoon. "Then why not let her do it?"

"Because she can do it easily and I can't." She said it as if it was obvious.

"Why do something you're not good at, if it's a strength of your sister's?"

"Challenge Harriet."

"There's a difference between doing something that scares you, and something that doesn't play to your skills." He took a mouthful of soup and closed his eyes. "This is incredible."

"I'll pass your compliments to my grandmother."

"Tell me about her."

"She has a beautiful beach house in the Hamptons." She sat down on the chair, but on the edge as if she hadn't quite decided whether to stay or not. "We used to spend the summer with her. It was my favorite time."

"Because you love the beach?"

"Because my father wasn't there."

He thought about the summers he'd spent with his father, and how much he'd taken the stability of their family life for granted.

"Your childhood was difficult. It's not surprising you want a peaceful family life now."

"I'd rather be on my own than with the wrong person. Or someone who doesn't love you. That's worse, I think. That's the situation my parents were in." A strand of hair slid forward and curved round her cheek. "I wish I'd known a bit more about their situation when I was growing up. It might have helped me understand."

"You think that excuses your father's behavior?"

"No. But I think it helps explain it. I used to think it was about me. But now I see it was about him."

Judging from her unhappy expression, that revelation hadn't brought her a whole lot of comfort.

"Tell me about summers with your grandmother."

"It was easy being with her. Grams never minded if my words stuck in my mouth, if I wasn't fluent. She waited until I'd said whatever it was I wanted to say. With her I felt normal. And summers there were the way I'd always imagined a family should be. Lots of laughter, friendly arguing, no tension. When I was with her, I didn't feel like the disappointment of the family."

"That's how you felt?"

"It was hard not to. Daniel and Fliss were both brilliant at everything. They always had top marks. Fliss used to scribble her assignments on the school bus and she'd get an A every time. I'd work for hours, with help, and still only get a B. I've always had to try harder than everyone else."

"But you didn't feel like that with your grandmother?"

"She made sure we spent time together. She was the one who taught me to cook. It made me feel special. When you're a twin, you're often lumped together as if you're one person. It's 'you girls,' or 'the two of you.' It's hard to be an individual, particularly when you look identical to someone else."

"Did the two of you ever switch places and fool people?"

"Occasionally. I'm a terrible liar, so fooling people was never something I was good at."

He noticed the way she used her hands when she talked, and the way her face lit up when she talked about her grandmother.

There was so much more to Harriet Knight than was visible on first acquaintance.

And he wanted to know more.

"Surely you didn't only cook in the Hamptons. What happened when you were at home in New York?"

"I spent as much time in my room as I could."

That revealing statement told him everything he needed to know about her childhood.

It made him want to hold her and wipe out the memories.

"Your grandmother taught you well." He finished his soup and put the spoon down.

"Can I ask you something?"

It occurred to him that Harriet Knight was the only woman he knew who would seek permission to ask him something that was obviously going to be uncomfortable.

"After making soup like that you can ask me anything." And because of the shine in her blue eyes, and the way she was looking at him.

"Will you agree to be Santa?"

Of all the questions he'd anticipated, that hadn't been on the list.

"Why do you care?"

"I think it would be wonderful."

"Are you offering to dress up as my elf?"

"If you'd like me to."

"It's Christmas Day. Don't you have anything better to do on Christmas Day? Aren't you seeing your sister? Your brother?"

"Not this year. Daniel is going away with Molly, and Fliss is spending Christmas with Seth's folks. I'm staying by myself." She said it brightly, as if she couldn't imagine anything more exciting than being on her own for the holidays.

He felt a stab of anger. "They didn't invite you?"

"Oh yes, they invited me. But I've never spent a Christmas without them before and I thought I should."

She'd chosen to spend Christmas on her own? He was trying to understand why someone like her would do a thing like that, when the answer came to him.

"Challenge Harriet?"

"Yes."

It didn't sound like a challenge to him. It sounded brutal. "Harriet, this is—" He broke off and started again. "Why deprive yourself of family, when family is so important to you?"

"That's why." She stood up. "Because I need to know I can survive by myself."

Survival sounded like a pretty brutal goal too.

Telling himself it was none of his business, he changed the subject. "My sister is coming tomorrow to pick up Madi. I'm hoping to be back at work."

"Ethan, you could barely walk to the bathroom."

"I'll take a cab to the hospital."

"I don't know much about the ER, but I assume the doctors aren't supposed to be sicker than the patients."

"I'm improving by the hour. My cough is better. By to-morrow I'll be fine."

She opened her mouth as if she intended to argue, and then closed it again. "Great. If you tell me what time I'll make sure I'm here when they arrive. And I'll move out after that."

He had no idea why the prospect of that made him feel disappointed. "No hurry."

She paused, her hands on the tray, a strand of hair sliding forward. "If Madi isn't here, why would I stay?"

It was a fair question.

Because his apartment was a whole lot nicer with her in it?

Because having her around lifted his mood?

Because she was gorgeous?

Any one of those replies would have earned him one of her questioning looks, so he didn't give voice to any of them.

"All I meant was that you don't need to rush off. There's no pressure. I'm grateful for what you've done. Move at your convenience."

"Right." She straightened and picked up his tray without looking at him. "I'll do that."

MONDAY MORNING CAME too quickly.

Harriet packed her things into her case with the same ab-sence of enthusiasm she'd felt when she'd packed to come here, which made no sense. She'd moved in as a favor to a client and for Madi. Her services were no longer needed.

Crazy as it was to admit it, she'd enjoyed the weekend. Crazy and a little selfish maybe, because Ethan had been sick. There had been something comforting about being just the two of them, closeted in his apartment while snow fell outside the window. It was as if they'd stepped out of their lives for a moment and inhabited a different world.

She was disappointed that it was over. She'd enjoyed the quietness of it, the coziness.

Oh who was she kidding?

She'd also enjoyed spending all that time with him. She'd enjoyed their conversation, those shared glances, the way it felt when his fingers brushed against hers and the way his gaze followed her round the room.

And then there was that moment when he'd leaned on her a little too heavily. She'd been convinced he was about to kiss her, but he hadn't.

Why?

She zipped her case with so much vigor she almost broke it.

A man like Ethan Black didn't hang around asking for permission. If he'd wanted to kiss her he would have done it. *She wished he had.*

"Ugh." Cross with herself, she hauled her suitcase to the door.

She'd come here to do a job, and she'd done that job.

Time to go home.

Time to get on with her real life. Not her dream life.

She was going to miss Madi. The dog was adorable. Bouncy, fun and endlessly affectionate.

But most of all she was going to miss Ethan.

CHAPTER EIGHTEEN

"So what's going on?" Susan rested her hips against the desk as Ethan studied the scan in front of him.

"He's had a bleed—" Ethan pointed at it with his pen but she shook her head.

"I meant with you."

"Me?" Dragging his gaze from the scan, he turned to look at her. "What do you mean?"

"You seem different."

Ethan leaned back in his chair. "Different? In what way am I different? I had the flu. I may have lost weight."

"You poor, pathetic baby. No, it's not that. You're more relaxed. More like the old Ethan."

"There was an old Ethan?" That was news to him.

"When I first met you, you were fun. Occasionally you even made me laugh. Lately you've gotten more serious."

"You may not have noticed, but this is a serious job we do here. Life and death. That kind of thing."

"All the more reason to enjoy the life part. So come on."

She nudged him so violently he wondered if he should be concerned about internal injuries.

"Come on, what?"

"Tell me the truth. It's Harriet, isn't it?"

"What is?"

"The reason you're suddenly mellow. She has softened all your rough edges. Living with her is good for you."

"I'm not living with her."

"Are you sure about that? Because last time I called by your apartment she had her things in the room next to yours. And she was mopping your fevered brow and looking like she gave a damn whether you lived or died."

"She was dog sitting."

"Right. Now you mention it, I remember seeing a dog." Susan folded her arms. "Cute little black-and-white spaniel. But you seemed to be the one getting all the attention."

"I was sick."

"Yeah, well you won't find me arguing with that."

"She moved out a week ago."

"That is a damn shame." She leaned toward him. "Listen carefully, Dr. Hot, because I'm about to tell you something for free. Any woman who doesn't want to kill a man when he's sick is a keeper."

"Maybe she did want to kill me. Can we maybe talk about something—"

"No. We're talking about this. Why did she move out?"

"Because my sister came and collected Madi."

"Madi?" Susan frowned. "Who the hell is Madi? Oh, you mean the dog?"

"Do not call her 'the dog' in front of Harriet," Ethan muttered and Susan grinned.

"She really has whipped you into shape. So the dog left, and you let Harriet leave too."

"I've told you—she was there as dog sitter. Without a dog to sit with, there wasn't much of a reason for her to stay."

"And you couldn't think of a reason? What has happened to your brain?"

"My brain is good, thank you. She has her own home. Her own life."

Susan shook her head. "Your lack of creativity is depressing. Have you called her since she moved out?"

"Why would I call her?" He'd intended to take her on a date, but then he'd gone down with the flu. And it wouldn't have been a real date anyway. He'd been offering to do her a favor, that was all. Help her out, to make up for all the help she'd given him.

He ignored the small side of him that said he was lying to himself. That dinner with Harriet would have been a really good way to spend an evening.

It wasn't as if he hadn't eaten dinner with her before. They'd eaten together most nights when he was home in time. Admittedly it had been casual, sitting at the kitchen island, chatting about what had happened during their day. No romantic lighting or dressing up. But he'd enjoyed it. In fact he'd enjoyed being with Harriet more than he could remember being with anyone in a long time.

There was something calming about her.

"To say thank you, to check how she's doing, to ask her to dinner—I don't know. You're the man with the reputation with women, although clearly that reputation is not well deserved if you let her get away from you."

"Excuse me?"

"Gorgeous girl, right there in your apartment, mopping your fevered brow, and you didn't ravish her?"

"Ravish? What sort of word is *ravish*? It might have escaped your notice but I had trouble dragging myself to the bathroom for the first forty-eight hours. Ravishing anyone was beyond my capabilities." *But he'd thought about it.*

"Feeble," Susan muttered, visibly disgusted with his lack of motivation. "I really liked her, Ethan. I liked Alison, but the two of you together were just so wrong it was painful to watch. Not that I'm an expert, but if everyone on the planet had died of a hideous plague and you were the only two left, I would have suggested you both occupy different continents. You and Alison used to stand there comparing schedules. It made my unromantic heart break watching you. Now Harriet—" she lingered over the name "—she's totally different. I don't have many girlfriends. Don't have the time but if I had one, I'd pick someone like Harriet. Fun, loyal, kind, great cook. And this is the part I don't get—she moves into your house, takes care of your dog, generally improves your quality of life and then you wave her goodbye without even giving her the kiss of life?"

"She left my apartment conscious and breathing. She didn't need the kiss of life."

"For a smart guy, you're stupid when it comes to women."

"Knowing I'm not the right guy for her doesn't make me stupid."

But who would be? Not Eric, it seemed. Or Charlton. And how was she going to meet the right guy? She'd admitted she was giving up on internet dating, so what was she going to do? Hope to bump into someone in the park? It didn't sound like a reliable strategy to him, especially for someone who was shy with people she didn't know.

He thought about that first evening, when she'd stammered her way through their first encounter, and then remembered subsequent evenings when she'd been confident and comfortable.

All she needed to do was find a way to get through those few awkward hours when you first met someone. Once she relaxed, she had no problem. And he'd intended to help her with that part. He was the master of keeping things superficial. He could keep conversation skimming across the water like a hovercraft, never delving deeper. He preferred it that way.

Susan was scowling at him. "What makes you think you're not the right guy?"

"Harriet deserves the best."

"Jeez, Black." She studied him for a moment. "I can't believe the stuff you tell yourself."

"What do you mean?"

"When you say 'she deserves the best,' what you're really saying is 'she and I could be good together and that scares the shit out of me so I'm going to do that man thing of pretending it isn't happening and hope it all goes away.'"

"That's not what I'm saying."

"No? Then call her up."

"Why would I call her up?"

"Because it would be the smart move, and you're supposed to be smart. Unless I'm right about you being scared. Unless you're afraid you might actually fall for her, because that would be awkward, wouldn't it?"

"That's not it."

"Then what?"

He frowned. "Maybe I don't want to hurt her. She's the

type of person who spends her life looking after vulnerable creatures."

Susan rolled her eyes. "That doesn't make her vulnerable herself. Does she seem like a fragile flower? I don't think so. She can make up her own mind about whether you're trouble or not. Let her decide if you're worth taking a risk over."

Ethan thought about what he knew about her childhood. No, she certainly wasn't a delicate flower. But she had been hurt. And he disagreed that she wasn't vulnerable. He suspected she was extremely vulnerable. "She's a good, decent person."

"Right. But that doesn't make her weak, you butthead. What are you saying? You'd rather date someone bad and indecent?"

Ethan grasped the opportunity to change the subject. "Now you mention it, that does sound like fun." He broke off as a nurse hurried across to him.

"Dr. Black? You're needed in Trauma 1."

Ethan stood up, relieved to have an excuse to escape the inquisition.

He strode down the corridor, Susan's voice followed him.

"Call her, Black. Or I'll call her myself and fix the two of you up."

"I don't have a reason to call her."

He paused in midstride.

Or maybe he did...

HARRIET WALKED THROUGH the snowy expanse of Central Park with Brutus and Valentine. The two dogs adored each other so she was always happy to walk them together whenever Daniel and Molly needed her to. Brutus lived up to his name, an exuberant, slightly overbearing German shepherd whereas Valentine, a handsome Dalmatian, was sleek and cool. He never tugged on his lead and occasionally glanced over his shoulder to check Harriet was okay. He was a beautiful dog, and always drew glances wherever he went and not only because of his heart-shaped nose. Molly always claimed it was his nose that inspired his name, but Harriet wasn't sure she believed her. Before Molly had met Daniel, she'd been totally off men.

Harriet had never felt that way, but she did often wonder how on earth you were supposed to meet someone you'd like to spend the rest of your life with. With almost all the men she'd met it had been a struggle to make it to the end of the date. The last one had lasted all of forty minutes. Clocking up forty years seemed ambitious.

But things had changed overnight for Molly. Maybe that could happen to her too.

She wondered what Ethan was doing. Working, probably. Saving a life.

Whereas she was walking dogs.

She hadn't even had a chance to say a proper goodbye. She'd been so exhausted after her weekend of playing nurse, she'd fallen asleep on the bed when she'd finished packing and woken to discover he'd left for work.

He'd left her a note. Two words, scrawled in bold black ink. They were close to illegible, but after five minutes of staring at the letters, puzzled, she'd finally decided it said *thank you*.

Was he thanking her for taking care of Madi, or him?

She was surprised he'd found the energy to return to work so soon, but Ethan Black wasn't the type of guy to languish in bed for long.

She'd gathered the last of her things, and shortly after

that Debra had arrived with Karen. It had been a crazy, emotional few moments during which Madi temporarily forgot all the manners Harriet had taught her over the previous week. Ecstatic, the little dog had returned home and so had Harriet.

And that, Harriet thought, was the end of that.

Madi was happy, Debra was happy, Ethan was most certainly happy.

The only person who would have liked the situation to carry on indefinitely, was Harriet.

She watched as Brutus and Valentine tumbled together on the snow, apparently indifferent to the cold.

After a good walk, she returned them to Molly, who had now moved into Daniel's Fifth Avenue apartment and had been catching up on some work.

"You're an angel." Molly hugged her. "Do you want to come in? I've made tea."

Molly was British and seemed to think hot tea was some kind of life-giving liquid. Harriet wondered how that worked for Daniel, who thought good wine was the most important liquid.

"I should probably get home. I haven't had a chance to unpack and sort out my apartment." The thought of it wasn't exactly thrilling. There would be no Madi. And no Ethan.

Maybe it was time for her to get a life.

It was certainly time for her to think about getting a dog of her own.

"One cup." Molly all but pulled her inside. "I haven't seen you for a couple of weeks. I want to hear all about the sexy doctor you've been living with."

"You've been talking to Fliss?" In her family, nothing was a secret it seemed. And Molly was as good as family.

Molly eyed her. "We might have exchanged a few words."

"I was dog sitting." She glanced round the apartment, feeling a twinge of envy as she noticed the huge fir tree covered in sparkling lights. "I love your tree. How did you talk Daniel into that?"

"I didn't." Molly put a mug of tea in front of her. "I bought it without checking with him. So much harder to protest once something is done, don't you think?"

Harriet laughed. "Daniel never decorates."

"He does now. Or rather I do, and he raises an eyebrow but says nothing. I love decorating for the holidays." Molly thrust a book into her hands. "You need to read this."

Harriet glanced at the book. "*Mate for Life*—I already have your book. I've read it cover to cover at least three times. I can pretty much recite the chapters. Right now I'd be happy to mate for five minutes. Mating for life seems an overly ambitious objective."

"What I'm trying to say is that I think Ethan is perfect for you. If you apply some of the criteria I outline in my book, you'll see what I mean. He's responsible, kind, caring and he has leadership skills—"

"How do you know? You've never even met him." Harriet kicked off her shoes and flopped onto the sofa, unable to resist the opportunity to talk about Ethan. Molly knew plenty about relationships. Maybe she could put her head back together. "You've spent too much time talking to my sister, that's all."

"Not just that." Molly grinned. "I might have spent a morning watching his series filmed in the ER."

"A whole morning?"

"It was meant to be a quick look, but he's very watchable."

She knew exactly how watchable he was. She'd spent the past week watching him in person.

"I haven't seen it."

"Well let's put it this way, if I'm ever in an accident I want him running the show."

Molly fanned herself, but before Harriet could respond the door opened and her brother strolled in. Brutus charged at him. He fielded the dog with one hand while disposing of his coat with the other.

Harriet was still getting used to seeing her brother wrestling with a dog. It was almost as alien as seeing him in love with a woman.

"Hey, babe." Daniel gave Molly a long, appreciative kiss and Harriet rolled her eyes and slid her shoes on. She was happy for both of them, but if there was one thing she wasn't in the mood for it was witnessing an excess of togetherness.

"And this," she muttered, "is why I'm leaving the two of you alone. So that you can mate for life without witnesses."

Daniel released Molly and gave Harriet a hug. "How are you doing?"

"Great," Harriet lied, ignoring the question in Molly's eyes. "Never better. But looking at your apartment makes me realize I'm nowhere near ready for Christmas. So I'm going home right now to decorate my own apartment."

That part wasn't a lie.

The first step to not dying alone surrounded by foster dogs was to take care of herself. And taking care included the little things.

Or maybe not so little, she thought half an hour later as she studied the tall fir tree propped against the wall in a side street off Fifth Avenue.

"You don't have anything a little smaller?"

"A week ago I had every size you can imagine. They're all gone. That's it, lady. Take it or leave it." The man selling trees looked grumpy, which took away some of the magic. Surely selling Christmas trees should be a happy experience?

She blew on her fingers and stamped her feet to keep warm. Maybe she should have planned this more carefully instead of being spontaneous.

Practical Harriet would have walked away. The tree was too big for her apartment. She lived alone. Why did she need a tree that big? Why did she need a tree at all?

Because she was tired of being practical Harriet.

She wanted to be rash, impulsive Harriet.

"I'll take it." She spoke loudly, as if volume somehow made her decision more permanent.

She almost changed her mind when he told her the price, but she handed over what seemed like an obscene number of dollars.

She was now the owner of a large Christmas tree, which was almost certainly not going to fit into her apartment. And now she had a new problem. How to get it home.

She was going to have to drag it, which probably wasn't going to do much for its appearance.

"I hope you're hardy." She pushed her hand through the spiky branches and tried to grab the trunk. "You're going to need to be, living with me."

The man went from grumpy to alarmed. "I'm not living with you."

"I was talking to the tree."

His expression told her everything she needed to know about his feelings toward women who talked to trees.

She talked to dogs all the time. Why not trees?

All the same, it was time to get out of here before his moody expression removed the gloss from her very expensive purchase.

She tried picking it up, but couldn't see where she was going, so she put it down again and started dragging it by the trunk.

Great. At this rate the tree would arrive at her apartment already decorated with whatever was lying on the streets of New York and that wouldn't be pretty.

"Do you need help with that?" A deep, male voice came from behind her and she turned and saw Ethan Black. His coat hugged his broad shoulders and the collar was turned up against the wind, but what really drew her attention was his smile. It creased his cheeks and warmed his eyes until looking at him made her feel warm too. Madi was next to him, wagging her tail.

"Ethan? Madi? I—" Delight gave way to concern and she dropped the tree and the branches scraped her leg accusingly. "Is something wrong? Is Karen okay? Did the journey make her worse?"

"Nothing is wrong, and Karen is doing fine."

She stooped to make a fuss over the dog. "So why do you have Madi?"

"Would you believe me if I said I missed her?"

Was he winding her up? This was the man who had almost had a panic attack when he'd first seen Madi in his apartment. "You—" She cleared her throat and straightened up. "Seriously?"

"You have no idea how empty my apartment feels."

She knew exactly how empty his apartment probably felt because hers was the same. The difference was that she'd never like it that way, whereas he had.

"You mean how tidy it is. And quiet, because you've had no complaints from your neighbors."

His smile widened. "That's part of it."

What was the other part? "So you borrowed Madi."

"Karen and Debra have driven to the airport to meet my brother-in-law. He's been on a business trip. I said I'd take the dog and drop her round later."

Because that was what families did. They helped each other, even when they had a job as punishing as Ethan's.

She noticed the sheen of his hair and the width of his shoulders. Her heart gave a flutter. "Aren't you a little out of your way?"

"I wanted to see you. I wanted to check on how you're doing."

So it was a charity call.

Her heart rhythm slowly returned to normal. "I'm doing fine, thanks. Why wouldn't I be? You didn't need to check on me."

"No more jumping out of restaurant bathrooms?"

"Just the one time." She stooped to pick up the tree again, wondering why he'd bothered traipsing across town to ask her that.

"If you take Madi, I'll carry that up to your apartment." He held Madi's lead out to her and she paused.

She wasn't sure she wanted Ethan in her apartment. So far it was an Ethan-free space. The only memories of him there were the ones in her head and she was struggling to erase those. She didn't need him spreading himself around the rest of her life.

On the other hand, if he helped her, it would solve the very real problem of how she was going to get the tree where it needed to go.

"Thanks." She took Madi's lead and dug in her pocket for her keys.

"Do you have an old blanket? Or a sheet?"

"I have one I use for the dogs."

"Fetch it, and we'll wrap the tree in it. Trust me, it will work."

She did trust him, and it did work.

Twenty minutes later, the tree was safely installed in her apartment with almost all of its needles still attached. Ethan, it turned out, was as competent with misbehaving Christmas trees as he was with sick patients.

"It's magnificent." And Harriet was relieved. For a moment there she thought she might have blown a significant chunk of her earnings on a tree she couldn't actually get to her apartment. She'd had visions of spending Christmas outside in the street with her tree. "Now I can make the place festive. Thank you *so* much."

She expected Ethan to leave, but instead he took off his coat and laid it carefully over the back of one of her chairs. Then he dropped into a crouch and wiped Madi's paws with a scrap of something he removed from his pocket.

Harriet watched. Was her mouth open?

It should have been, because she couldn't have been more surprised if he'd come here to tell her he'd opened a pet sanctuary.

He glanced up at her. "What's wrong?"

"You're cleaning her paws."

"Isn't that what I'm supposed to do when she's been walking in the snow?"

"Yes, but—" She gulped. "What is that you're using?"

"It's a washcloth. I grabbed it when I was leaving the

apartment." He rose to his feet. "Is there a problem? Am I doing something wrong?"

No. He was doing everything right. *That* was the problem. "You're not doing anything wrong." And it might have helped her a bit if he had. "She looks happy."

"She's pleased to be home with her family, and who can blame her. Nice place you have here."

Was he kidding? "It's a tenth of the size of yours."

"It's charming. Really comfortable." He scanned her bookshelves and she stiffened, hoping she hadn't left her copy of *Mate For Life* anywhere visible. That would make for an awkward conversation.

Well, Dr. Hot, my soon-to-be sister-in-law thinks you're perfect.

"Would you like a drink or something?"

It was so polite. So formal.

She was trying to forget that she'd undressed him down to his boxer briefs. Trying to forget she knew exactly what lay under that wool coat and thick black sweater.

He probably didn't even remember that she'd been the one to remove his clothes.

In fact she wasn't sure what he remembered.

Neither of them had ever mentioned that moment in the depths of the night when he'd almost kissed her.

It would have been easy enough to decide she'd imagined it, but she knew she hadn't. She definitely hadn't imagined it, but it was entirely possible that he'd been delirious at the time.

"I'd love a drink." He turned from studying the books on the top shelf. "What do you have?"

"Soda. Wine." She was starting to feel flustered now because she didn't really know what this was. Was it a duty call? A social call? Their relationship was strange. Loaded with intimacy, even though they'd never been intimate. "I have beer, because Daniel drinks it."

"Beer would be great. So where are your decorations?"

"Why?"

"Because I'll help you." He studied the tree. "It's tall. You're going to need help getting the decorations near the top."

"You're offering to help me decorate the tree? You, Dr. Scrooge, who won't be Santa for the kids?"

"That's different." His gaze held hers for a long moment while the air around them was suddenly thickened by something thrilling and dangerous. "Where are your decorations?"

On edge, she fetched the box from under her bed, and together they decorated the tree.

She was agonizingly aware of every move he made.

It felt strange having him in her apartment.

"How was work? Are you fully recovered?"

"I'm tired, but doing okay. Thanks to you. I suspect my recovery wouldn't have been so swift if you hadn't been there making everything easy for me." He took a silver decoration from her hand, his fingers brushing against hers. "I owe you dinner."

"You don't owe me anything."

"Have you been on a date since you moved out of my apartment?"

She slid the decoration onto the tree. "It's only been a week. Give me time."

"In other words, no. I finish early tomorrow. I'll pick you up at seven."

"Ethan—"

"Don't argue. I want to take you to dinner."

The question "why" hovered on her lips, but she didn't say it because she already knew the answer. He'd promised, and he was a man of his word. Knowing that, she decided it was better to go along with this and get it out of the way. Then both of them could get on with their lives, debt free.

"Fine. Great. Dinner. Where do you want me to meet you?"

"I'll pick you up." He finished hanging the decorations and stepped back. "It's looking good. Now all you need is gifts."

"I have a whole heap of them ready to be wrapped."

"Then you're all ready for the holidays. Still planning to spend it alone?"

"I won't be alone. Just not with my family. I'm cooking lunch for Glenys and I plan on going over to the animal shelter for a few hours to help out. They struggle to find people on Christmas Day."

"The animal shelter?"

"I foster for them, and occasionally help out walking and socializing the animals."

"Socializing?"

"Some of these animals haven't had happy lives. It increases the likelihood of finding a forever family if they have some positive experiences with people."

"And that's the goal?" His gaze held hers. "Finding a forever family?"

Why was he looking at her like that?

And what had happened to her voice? It had been working perfectly fine a few moments earlier.

"Yes. We try and find good homes for them where they're loved and wanted."

And that, she thought, was exactly what she wanted for herself.

CHAPTER NINETEEN

THE RESTAURANT WAS COZY, warm and decorated for Christmas. Candles flickered in the center of the tables and fairy lights were strung around the low beams.

As Harriet slid into her seat by the window, she felt oddly nervous. She wasn't sure she was going to be able to eat anything. This pretend date was turning out to be more stressful than a real date, and the reason was that *this* was the date she really wanted to be on.

The only one that had ever mattered.

Ethan Black was the first man in a long time she'd been excited to spend time with.

She'd spent close to an hour making her hair smooth and applying makeup that was hopefully going to look as if she hadn't tried too hard.

When he'd picked her up from her apartment she'd been wearing neutral lip gloss, but she'd chewed it off in the first five minutes and she didn't want to risk reapplying it in case he saw her and misinterpreted the gesture. If he'd thought her cooking for him on the first night had been a romantic gesture, then presumably lip gloss would be tantamount to a proposal.

He sat opposite her, watching her expectantly, but she had absolutely no idea what he was expecting.

Hopefully not riveting conversation because her mind had emptied the moment she'd opened the door and seen him standing there. He filled her doorway with his broad shoulders and sexy smile and for a moment she'd been unable to catch her breath, as if she'd run up four flights of stairs carrying a load of shopping.

She still felt that way, and she had no idea what to say.

When she'd started internet dating she'd compiled a list of conversation topics. The weather, travel, books, life goals—she called them emergency silence fillers. So far she hadn't needed to use them because the men she'd dated had been happy enough to fill silence to the point of overflowing until she'd been ready to beg them to stop talking.

Ethan was different.

The moment they were seated, he leaned forward. "Tonight, there is only one rule."

There were rules? "Which is?"

"No escaping through the bathroom window." Humor glinted in his eyes. "If something I say offends you, tell me. Don't jump."

"I promise."

And just like that the tension was broken. Everything that followed was easy.

Ethan was calm, relaxed and entertaining. His idea of conversation wasn't to deliver a monologue, but to engage her on whatever topic he raised. He asked her opinion and listened to her answers, and before she knew it she was talking about everything under the sun, from subjects she'd struggled with at school, to how being a twin had been the best thing that could have happened to her. She told him about the time Fliss had beaten up Johnny Hill because he'd refused to stop bullying her about her stammer. She'd been suspended from school as a result, and still had a scar on her head to show for it. And she told him about her parents' divorce, and how she wished it had happened years before it did, and how she'd thought Daniel would never get married and how thrilled she was that he'd met Molly, who was wonderful and knew everything about relationships (even though she'd avoided having one of her own until she'd met Daniel) and had even had a book published.

And all the time she talked she was aware of Ethan listening, adding the occasional comment or observation, making sure her water glass was filled and that she was enjoying the food.

They ate grilled shrimp and zucchini, followed by a delicious chicken dish, but she barely noticed the food because she was either talking or listening. And for Harriet, the night wasn't about food. It was all about the man sitting across from her.

She told him about her summers in the Hamptons. About the puppy her grandmother had rescued when Harriet was nine, and how she'd taken care of it herself for two months. How she'd asked her mother if they could take the puppy home, but been told her father would never allow it. And she talked about more recent events, when she'd had to work hard to persuade Fliss to open up to her.

Ethan told her about growing up in a family of doctors. How people had knocked on the door on a Sunday when they were in trouble, how the phone never stopped ringing.

It was a totally different experience from her other dates when she hadn't been remotely interested in the person sitting across from her. Then, all she'd thought about was getting away as fast as possible. This time all she could think about was that she didn't want the evening to end.

She realized that far from not talking, she'd done nothing *but* talk and she clamped her mouth shut, embarrassed.

He gave her a searching look. "What's wrong?"

What was wrong was that she didn't want this date to be pretend. She wanted it to be real. She wanted to be sitting across from him, hearing about his day and talking while she told him about hers.

And then she wanted to go home with him, rip all his clothes off, and do things Harriet Knight had never done in her life before.

She thought about the night she'd undressed him, the glimpse of his hard strong body. She couldn't stop thinking about it.

"Harriet?"

"Sorry? What? Yes—" *Please don't let her have said any of that out loud.* "What did you say?"

"I asked what was wrong."

She'd got her fantasy mixed up with reality, that was what was wrong. "I realized I've been doing that thing I hate. Talking nonstop without coming up for air."

"You weren't talking nonstop. I talked too."

"Not as much." And she was mortified. He'd probably been thinking all the things she'd been thinking when she sat across from those men who didn't know when to be quiet. "Why didn't you stop me?"

"Because I found it interesting. I find *you* interesting. I didn't want to stop you."

"It was a monologue." She knew her cheeks were pink. This was why she didn't use blush. Combined with her own natural tendency to color up at the slightest hint of an awkward situation, she'd end up looking like a clown.

"It was not a monologue, but it did give me an insight into who you are. I feel I know you a little better now, which is good."

"A little better? I gave you my whole life history. You know everything there is to know. Apart from the fact I had appendicitis when I was eight."

He smiled. "Good to have your medical history too. Any allergies?"

"You mean apart from online dating?"

Why was it good that he knew her better? Why? What was the point?

What happened next? If she really fumbled her way through it perhaps he'd decide she needed more practice and date her again. If she was clever about it, it could wind up being her longest relationship ever.

Dessert arrived, a whipped confection of cream and she stared at it, thinking that it was like her life right now, sweet and perfect. But you couldn't live on dessert, could you? And she wasn't going to have a date like this again.

The candlclight sent flickers of light across his face, highlighting his lean, handsome features and those blue eyes that saw far too much. There was a faint hint of amusement in the curve of his mouth. She wished all dates could be as easy and relaxed as this one. She wished every moment of her life could feel like this, as if she were on the verge of something exciting and incredible.

She was enjoying herself so much she never wanted the evening to end.

Her head was spinning and she knew it wasn't just as a result of the wine she'd drunk. It was being with Ethan.

She wondered what he'd be like in bed.

Confident.

Skilled.

Her face flamed. "Debra adores you. She used to talk about you all the time when I went round there. Her brother, the doctor. She's very proud. You're lucky being part of such a close family."

"You're close to your sister and brother."

"Yes, but right now—" She broke off, feeling disloyal talking about it. She adored Fliss and Daniel, but they didn't seem to understand that she didn't need them to fix her life all the time. "They're both super protective, and when I was younger I was grateful for that. But sometimes now it gets to be an issue. If I'm struggling with something, Fliss wants to fix it and Daniel wants to take out an immediate lawsuit. They don't understand that if something needs fixing, I need to fix it for myself. And if it can't be fixed, then I need to adjust the way I'm thinking to accept that."

"Is this what Challenge Harriet is all about? Are you sending a message to your family?"

"No. Challenge Harriet is for me." She finished her wine, wondering how much to say. "The thing is, in the last year both of them have fallen in love. I'm not sure Fliss ever fell out of love, but that's another story. And because they're in love, they feel guilty. They feel that they're excluding me and the easiest way to fix that is by finding someone for me too. It would stop them worrying about me."

He nodded. "So what you're saying is that they've been pairing you up. Is that why you started internet dating?"

"Molly suggested it, but I'd already thought it was a good

idea simply because it was the last thing in the world I wanted to do. Why are you laughing?"

"Because every other person I know avoids doing the last thing in the world they want to do. That's why it's called the last thing. And what you're describing just seems to be the natural order of things. Siblings want you to be as happy as they are. Parents want grandchildren."

Hers didn't. Her mother had finally started living the life she wanted to live and was traveling all over the world. Her father had made it clear that he didn't want his children in his life, so it seemed doubtful he'd want grandchildren. "But Debra has already given your parents grandchildren."

"My point exactly." He waved his spoon. "Apparently it's different. She has fulfilled her duty, but I haven't."

"Don't you want children?"

Oh God, she was talking about having children with a man she wasn't even dating.

Nice one, Harriet.

She may not know much about what constituted great conversation during a date but she was pretty confident this wasn't it.

"Forget I said that." She put her glass down. "How are you feeling? You've fully recovered?"

"You already asked me that. And why are we supposed to forget what you said?"

"Because the subject isn't exactly suitable for two people on a pretend date."

He paused, his gaze fixed on hers. "Right. Pretend date." Something in his tone made her look at him closely.

"If the objective was for you to help me find suitably neutral topics, I've failed dismally. I did warn you. I'm not good on dates."

"But as you keep telling me, this isn't a proper date." Calm, he topped up her wineglass. "This is two friends having dinner and catching up on news. You were asking me about children, although that seems like a surprising question given that you've already seen how useless I was with a dog."

"You weren't useless. I think you were lovely with Madi. If you ignore that first day when you were tired and not expecting to find your home disrupted, you were very patient and tolerant about having a very lively dog in your apartment."

"You always see the best in people."

"Not always. In fact I don't think I'm good with people at all. And sometimes I'm trying to see the best because I just don't want to believe that people can be so unkind. But you only have to spend a couple of hours working in the animal shelter to know that humans aren't all good."

"Do they pay you to work there?"

"I volunteer. I don't spend much time at the actual shelter. Not as much as I'd like because I'm mostly busy with the business. Often I just drop by when they have animals that need fostering."

"So you take them and give them back. That surprises me."

Clearly he didn't know her very well. "I would never refuse a vulnerable animal a home if I was able to provide it."

"That isn't the part that surprises me. The part that surprises me is that you'd give them back."

"I can't keep them all."

"But you would if you could. And I bet you hate it." His voice was soft. "I bet you really hate giving them back."

"Yes. And I've never had a pet of my own because between the dog walking and the fostering it's just too complicated, but now I'm starting to think I really want that." It was the first time she'd mentioned it to anyone. It probably should have felt strange that Ethan was the first person she'd mentioned it to, but it didn't. "I want a dog that's mine, that I don't hand back when I've walked him for an hour, or when I've fed him by hand and he's old enough to go to his forever home."

"So are you going to do it?"

"I don't know. I only just started thinking about it, but yes. I think I will. I want to. I need to work out how I'd handle it. What compromises I'd need to make."

"Nowhere near as many compromises as you'd need to make if you were living with someone. Speaking of which, why does Fliss think I'd be perfect for you?"

She almost dropped her spoon. "Excuse me?"

"I overheard your sister asking if I'd had my hands all over you."

"You heard that? Oh that's *bad*." Dying inside, Harriet covered her face with her hands. "Get me out of here. Dinner is over. So is my dignity." She heard his soft laugh and slowly let her hands drop. "You're laughing at me? That's cruel. Now I finally believe you're heartless."

"I'm not laughing at you."

"No? Because it seemed that way from where I'm sitting."

"I assumed you knew I'd heard that. You were very flustered."

"I thought you might have overheard, but I was hoping you were too delirious to remember. And then you never mentioned it again."

"You were taking care of me. I was afraid that if I mentioned it you might abandon me in my hour of need."

Harriet poked at her food, keeping her eyes on her plate. If she'd ever had a more embarrassing moment, she couldn't remember it. "I wouldn't have abandoned you."

There was a pause. "No," he said slowly. "You wouldn't do that. That's not the kind of person you are."

She pushed her plate away. "Okay, this is awkward."

"How is it awkward?"

"Because now I know you overheard my sister's ridiculous suggestions I have absolutely no clue what to say to you."

"We laugh about it. We share sympathetic notes about siblings who interfere. Debra does it to me all the time."

She risked a glance at him. "She does?"

"Yes. It's a shocker. I've lost count of the number of women she's tried to fix me up with. *Ethan*," he said, in a perfect imitation of his sister's accent, "*I've found a girl who would be perfect for you.*"

Harriet laughed. "That's it. That's what my sister does. How do you handle it?"

"Sometimes I'll play along with it for the duration of the phone call because I love my sister. If it happens too often, I'm rude."

"Does that work?"

"Nothing works for long. Sometimes I end the call. If I'm desperate, I pretend I have to go save a life. Don't ever tell her that or I won't examine your ankle next time you leap out of a window."

"So who was the last woman she wanted to fix you up with?"

There was a pause. "You."

Harriet stared at him, stunned. "She—what? Oh, that's awful. Now I'm even more embarrassed."

"Why is it awful? She thinks you're the perfect person to cure me of my wicked bachelor ways and heal my supposedly bruised heart. It's one hell of a brief for any woman, even one who likes a challenge."

"Is your heart bruised?"

"I don't know. I don't think so. I haven't been able to find it in a while."

She wondered how he could possibly think he didn't have a heart when she saw evidence of his kindness and caring all the time.

"That's why she wanted me to come and walk Madi?" A horrible thought occurred to her. "Karen really did have an accident? The whole thing wasn't an elaborate setup?"

"It wasn't a setup. My sister is an opportunist, not a sadist. And she's an excellent mother."

"So did she leave you alone when you told her you weren't interested?"

He finished his wine and put the glass down slowly. "Who said I wasn't interested?"

Her heart suddenly doubled its rhythm and her limbs felt as if they'd been turned to liquid. "You. You said you weren't interested in women."

"That's not what I said. I said I wasn't interested in marrying a second time. Not quite the same thing. I'm not a monk, Harriet." He sounded amused. "I have relationships. Just not the kind that end in marriage. And that's the kind you're hoping for."

Right now she was willing to take any kind if he featured in the starring role.

She wanted to ask if he'd be interested in a relationship if all she wanted was wild, passionate sex.

Was that a bit ambitious? Did she even know how to have wild, passionate sex?

She wasn't sure if she'd be able to relax and let go enough to ever find out.

Except that with him, she thought she might. He was capable and kind, strong and sure, and she found him sexier than any man she'd ever met. Being with him made her feel something she'd never felt before, and she liked it. He made her feel interesting, feminine, fun. He made her feel alive.

His gaze met hers and she felt a streak of longing, a burst of blind lust that obliterated all other thoughts and feelings. All the sounds around them faded to nothing. There was just him, and the way he made her feel. She realized she'd underestimated the power of sexual attraction. Or maybe she'd just never felt it before. Not like this. This shivery, delicious thrill. The stomach-knotting sense of anticipation that turned need into desperation.

One thing was sure—after tonight, it was going to be even harder to go on a bad date because now she knew what a good one looked like.

"Let's get out of here." His voice was rough and connected with something deep inside her.

She had no idea what they were going to do once they left the restaurant, but whatever it was she was going with it. The decision was made without her even being conscious that she'd made it.

If this was the only date with him she was ever going to have, she was going to make it a night to remember.

CHAPTER TWENTY

THEY TOOK A cab back to her apartment.

Although she kept her eyes fixed ahead, he could feel her tension. She was so still she barely seemed to be breathing.

Wondering if she was nervous, he reached out and covered her hand, closing his gloved fingers around hers.

She sent him a glance that told him she wasn't nervous. He'd expected indecision and doubt, but there was no sign of either and everything he saw in her eyes made him want her even more than he already did.

The evening hadn't exactly gone the way he'd planned. As for what happened next—

He'd intended to see her safely to her door and then leave. That would have been the safe, sensible thing to do but when they reached the front door of her apartment building she turned to him.

There was something in her eyes he hadn't expected to see. A challenge. He wasn't sure if she was challenging herself or him.

"Do you want to come in?" She sounded breathless, as if they'd both sprinted the length of Fifth Avenue instead of cruising in the warmth of a cab.

Did he want to go in with her? The answer was yes, but whether he should was a different question altogether.

What was she thinking?

What was going on in her head?

It was snowing again, and he reached out and brushed the flakes from her hair. Had he ever felt temptation like this? If he had he couldn't remember it. Selfish and single-minded, Alison had called him. And maybe it was true, because he was about to be selfish again. "You're not the sort to invite a man in after a first date."

"Maybe I am. Maybe I want to be."

"So is this another Challenge Harriet?"

"I don't know. But I do know that if you want to come in, then I'd like that."

She was so straightforward. So honest. It was one of the things he loved about her. *Liked*, he corrected himself quickly. *Liked*, not loved.

He quieted his conscience by reminding himself that she wasn't a child. She was a woman with a mind of her own, and it seemed that mind had been made up. Who was he to talk her out of doing something they both wanted? And it wasn't as if it was complicated.

What he wanted was simple.

Driven by a need he couldn't quite identify, he cupped her face in his hands, taking his time.

The whole time she'd been living in his apartment, he'd thought about kissing her. By the time she'd moved out, he'd found it hard to think about anything else.

None of his thoughts had come close to reality.

The moment his mouth touched hers, he realized that there was nothing simple about this. Nothing simple about his relationship with Harriet. Nothing simple about the chemistry that burned through them, or the way she made him feel.

Her lips were cool and soft and he felt them part under the pressure of his. He kept it gentle, exploring her mouth with slow easy kisses intended to relax her, but they created nothing but a delicious, dangerous tension and slow and easy swiftly turned into raw and passionate. After five seconds of kissing her he was so aroused that for a moment he forgot that they were standing outside her apartment in full view of anyone who happened to pass.

Not that many people were passing. It was a winter night in New York City and most people were tucked away inside.

Ethan had his own internal warmth, all of it generated by kissing Harriet. He felt her arms wrap round his neck and her body press against his. If she was undecided about what should happen next, there were no outward signs of it.

Above them the sky was inky dark but the street was bathed by the ghostly wash of lamplight. He felt the snow, light as the air it floated through and he felt her sway and then wrap her arms round his neck and press closer. She molded herself against him, delivering hot, melting kisses that burned through the last of his doubts. He could feel her soft curves through her coat, felt temptation and promise. He also felt her shiver.

It was the shivering that cut through the brain-clouding desire.

He rubbed his hands down her arms and then folded her close, using his body to protect her from the icy bite of the winter air.

She felt fragile, but he knew she wasn't fragile.

"It's cold." Although right now he didn't feel cold. He felt nothing but heat.

She stayed in the shelter of his arms, her forehead resting on his chest so that all he could see was the top of her head.

He had a feeling she was making a decision about something, hovering on the edge of something, not sure whether to step forward or not. He probably should have stepped back, but he didn't want to.

For a moment she said nothing, and then she lifted her head. Her eyes shone with anticipation. "It *is* cold. Shall we go inside?"

She was inviting him in and it was obvious that she had more than coffee and warmth in mind.

A better man than him would have refused. He probably should have refused. But somehow he found himself following her up the stairs to her apartment. She'd added a few more festive touches since he'd helped her with the Christmas tree—a bowl of silver pinecones, strings of Christmas lights that added warmth to the welcome.

Apart from books, his apartment was minimalist. So minimalist that his sister teased him that if anyone broke in they'd leave empty-handed because they'd assume the place was unoccupied. Standing in Harriet's cozy apartment he wondered whether perhaps he should buy a few cushions. Maybe a plant or two. A rug like the one she had, in muted shades of green?

There was no overhead lighting, just lamps that bathed the room in a golden glow, picking out the sunlit yellow walls and the blue sofas. Fresh flowers provided a bright splash of color on a day when the world outside the window was winter white. It was like being outdoors on a sunny day. Just stepping over the threshold instantly made a person feel better.

"Would you like a drink?"

He wondered if she was having second thoughts.

"Not unless you do." What he wanted was her. Shy, or not shy, he didn't give a damn as long as she was naked and with him all the way.

They exchanged a single look and then she was in his arms again and he was kissing her as if this was going to be the last thing they ever did on this earth. They crashed into the door, their combined weight slamming it shut and he braced his arm against it, caging her.

She breathed his name against his lips, then fumbled with his coat and he took over, dealing with buttons as he crushed her against the door and claimed her mouth with his. They kissed as if they had no choice in the matter, as if it were life-giving, as essential as breathing. They kissed without pausing or breaking off as they undressed. Her hair clung to the wool of his coat and he pushed it away from her face, his fingers sliding through snow-dampened strands of scented silk as he devoured her mouth with his.

His coat hit the floor first, then hers, closely followed by the rest of their clothes.

He'd promised himself that if this ever happened he'd take his time and savor every second, but now there was nothing but urgency and desperation as if by slowing down he might lose the moment or, worse, lose her. He caught a glimpse of creamy flesh, a flash of gold, the peep of dusky pink and he didn't know whether to look or touch. All he knew was that he didn't want this to stop.

He had no idea what would happen tomorrow but right now, today, she was all he wanted.

"Bedroom," he groaned, and she pushed at his chest, gesturing vaguely with her hand.

Drunk with desire, they stumbled across the apartment to her bed and tumbled, crushing her beneath him. Heat and desire escalated to alarming levels. He kissed his way down her body, his tongue slowly tracing the rosy pink tips of her breasts. It was like being plunged straight into summer. Strawberries and cream. Sunshine and warmth. Her breathing grew choppy. Soft gasps turned to low moans, sweet sounds as he found all her sensitive places, leaving no part of her untouched or unexplored.

"Ethan, Ethan," she murmured his name, shifting against the sheets, as he took liberties, shifting their relationship from one of friendship to deep intimacy.

And then he realized his wallet, with the one essential item he needed, was on the floor of the living room in his pocket.

In that one, brief moment he finally understood why people occasionally chose to be reckless.

It took all his willpower to drag himself away from her, especially as she protested.

"Don't move," he muttered, glancing at her splayed body the way a starving man might view his first home-cooked meal in a year.

He moved with the swift efficiency and focus honed and sharpened by years in the ER, and was back before she'd even had a chance to lift her head.

She stared at him, her gaze unfocused.

"Ethan—"

"I know—I know, baby." He pushed her thighs apart and slid his hand under her bottom, lifting her. She moved with him, her body a graceful arch, and he was about to thrust

deep when he remembered what she'd said about not enjoying sex very much. However desperate he was feeling,
he was determined she was going to enjoy this. More than
enjoy it, so he forced himself to back off and instead of
entering her, he pushed her legs wider and kissed his way
down to the golden shadows of her thighs, using his tongue
to taste and tease, licking into her until she was crying his
name and couldn't stay still unless he held her. Finally, after
he'd driven her half-mad, he eased himself over her, taking
his time, holding back. He entered her slowly, by degrees,
keeping his rhythm gentle and careful. He drew her arms
above her head and locked his fingers with hers, holding
her hands and her gaze as each thrust took him deeper. He
felt her close around him, felt her flesh ripple against the
sensual invasion, and even though it half killed him to do
it, he forced himself to pause.

"Are you okay?" Somehow he asked the question and she
nodded, cheeks flushed, eyes fixed on his as if he was the
only stable thing in a shifting universe.

He eased deeper, keeping the same steady rhythm, and
he felt the change in her, felt her body open to his and then
close around him in silken intimacy. He paused, dropped
his head to her shoulder, trying to delay his own release,
but she was moving her hips, urging him on and whatever
control he had slipped away from him. It was wild and
crazy, so all-consuming that everything else faded into
the background.

He heard her cry out and felt her nails dig hard into his
shoulders. Then she tightened around him, her body ensuring that any attempt on his part to hold back would be fruit-
less. She called out his name as her climax tipped him over
the edge and sent him into a free fall of pleasure.

SHE LAY SECURELY wrapped in the circle of his arms, feeling weak and sated. Her heart was still hammering and her skin was warm and damp against his. If there had ever been a more perfect moment she couldn't remember it. She couldn't believe that he was here, in her bed, solid, strong and real.

She hadn't planned to end the evening in bed with him, but nothing had ever felt more natural. Maybe she was better at stepping out of her comfort zone than she'd first thought.

Maybe she really could be bad-girl Harriet.

Or maybe not.

She'd promised herself she wasn't going to read anything into this but it turned out it wasn't as easy to control her mind as she'd thought.

"So—" She was out of breath. "If that was lesson one of your dating master class, what happens in lesson two?"

His eyes were closed. "Give me a minute, and I'll show you. Lesson two might be about to run into lesson one."

She snuggled closer, making the most of the fact that he was here in her bed. "So—sex after a first date. Does that qualify me for bad-girl status?"

"I don't know, but if it didn't I have a few ideas of what I could do to you to help you earn that badge. Happy to help you live out your bad-girl fantasy."

"You're all heart."

He opened his eyes. "Definitely not that."

"You really think you don't have a heart?"

She didn't know how he could possibly think that given what she knew about him.

He had more heart than any man she'd ever met.

He brushed her cheek with his fingers. "I don't seem to find it easy to feel anymore. Early in my career I struggled with feeling too much. Every damn day I'd come home emotionally drained and I learned to manage it, but the price I paid is that now I don't seem to be able to switch it on again easily."

"But you did when you were married?"

"No. That was part of the problem. And Alison was the same. She was a news reporter. Some of the things she saw in the newsroom, raw footage, were probably almost as bad as the stuff I was seeing. And it has an effect on you. You learn to detach. You have to. It's how you continue to function and do the job you're supposed to do. But the downside is that you can't just switch it on and off again. You don't just flick a switch and become a normal human being again."

"You seem like a normal human being to me. And I don't know how you do what you do." She was humbled by it. She knew there was no way she would be able to cope with the emotional pressures of his job, let alone the rest of it.

"Hey, I don't know how you do what you do."

She laughed. "I walk dogs, Ethan. That is not rocket science."

"It is to someone like me. I'd find the responsibility terrifying. I'd bring them all back dead or injured."

"This from someone who spends his days saving the lives of someone's loved one, although having seen you with a dog, I'm not going to argue with the point you make." She rested her head on his chest and smiled as she felt his fingers gently stroke her hair. "You were right, by the way. This is my first ever one-night stand. If I'd known how much fun it was I might not have waited so long."

And she wondered why, when it felt like that, anyone would ever stop at one night.

She hated the idea that she'd never have a night like that again.

Was that how it was for Fliss? Daniel?

No. They were in love. It was different.

Ethan was silent for a moment. "I hate to break it to you, but that wasn't a one-night stand."

"It wasn't?"

"No. Have I just ruined your bad-girl status?"

"I don't know. I guess that depends on what happens next."

He turned his head and trailed his mouth across her jaw and upward, his lips lingering on the corner of her mouth. She felt his hands cup her cheeks and then his mouth, firm, coaxing and then demanding, slow expert kisses that demolished her ability to think.

"Ethan—"

He lifted his mouth from hers just enough to speak. "I don't know where this is going. I don't know what this even is, but right now I'm not sure I'm ever going to let you out of my bed again."

She didn't know where it was going, either, and she didn't care.

She was dizzy with it.

She loved the shape of his mouth. The firm lines and the way the corners tilted when he smiled.

"This is my bed. We're in my bed."

"In that case you're going to have to call someone to have me forcibly removed. In fact I'm not sure I'm going to move again. When I find the energy to pick up my phone, I'm going to call work and resign. We can both stay here until we die of thirst or starvation." He slid his hand over her hip and lower, lingering on the junction of her thighs.

She caught her breath and arched against his seeking fingers, her body heavy with sensation and saturated with need. She'd never felt this way about anyone before. Not ever. Never felt this all-consuming, intimate connection with a man.

His touch was sure and skilled and she wondered how it was that he could know exactly what she wanted and needed when she hadn't said a word. The only sounds that came from her lips were soft moans of pleasure and he captured them with his mouth, intensifying sensation with kisses that blew her mind.

And in the back of her mind, the only part that hadn't blown a fuse, a question began to form.

If this wasn't a one-night stand, what was it?

CHAPTER TWENTY-ONE

SHE WALKED ON AIR, her smile so wide that people turned their heads to look at her as she walked the dogs, curious as to what had made her so happy.

She could have told them in one word.

Ethan.

Ethan, Ethan, Ethan.

"You look as if Christmas came early," Glenys said as they walked slowly along Fifth Avenue. "So it's going well then with the doctor?"

"Oh—" Harriet blinked. Was it that obvious? "Well, he's working a lot of the time of course, but we've seen each other occasionally." And each time had been better than the last. She never would have believed dating could be so *easy*.

"I knew right from the beginning that he was the one for you."

Harriet felt her heart skip. "I don't believe in 'the one.' How can there only be one person for us? What if 'the one' lives in Peru and I'm in New York? How am I supposed to find him? I don't think my internal GPS is that reliable."

"You found him, didn't you? Life has a way of sending us to the right place at the right time."

"You think spraining my ankle was all part of some master plan? Because that wasn't even the start of it. If it hadn't been for the dog sitting, I never would have seen him again."

"Maybe. Maybe not." Glenys was cryptic.

Harriet sidestepped a patch of ice. "Be careful here. How's your hip?"

"Much better thanks to you. The doctor says all the walking has been good for me."

"I'm pleased to hear it."

"Are you seeing him later?"

"Your doctor?"

"No, *your* doctor, honey." Glenys gave her a saucy wink and Harriet rolled her eyes.

"You're worse than my sister." And she was conscious that she had yet to tell Fliss what was happening. But what *was* happening exactly? She didn't know, which was why she was avoiding the conversation. Fliss would turn it into more than it was and Harriet didn't want that.

"We love you, that's all. We want you to be happy. You're like a granddaughter to me. If you didn't already have a grandmother who loves you, I'd try and officially adopt you. Because of your chocolate chip cookies of course. Not for any other reason."

Harriet stopped and hugged her. "I promise you a lifetime supply."

"Have you cooked for that man of yours yet? Because if you have, he's a goner. He'd soon give up all this 'never getting married again' nonsense if he knew the way you cooked."

"I cooked a little when I was in his apartment, but everyday stuff. Nothing special." After that painfully embarrassing incident on the first night, she'd kept the food simple. No one could read seduction into spaghetti with red sauce.

"What are you waiting for? Seduce his taste buds. Blow his mind."

"Funny you should say that because tonight I'm really going all out to impress him." She'd been planning the menu all week. It was ambitious and potentially full of things that could go wrong, but she wanted the evening to be special.

Ethan only had one more week in the city before he left for his ski trip and she wanted to make sure he went away thinking of her.

Back in her apartment she chopped, sautéed and did all the initial preparation for the meal.

Telling herself that she was just killing time, she went onto YouTube and watched an episode on life in the ER, with Ethan in the starring role. She could see why they'd decided to make a series. He was movie-star handsome, but not in an inaccessible movie-star way. He seemed human. Real. And he seemed cool and calm no matter what came through the doors of the ER. Drunks, knife wounds, gunshot wounds—he dealt with it all. It didn't surprise her to discover he had a huge female fan base. Of course he did.

When the scenes on the screen became too graphic, she clicked off and then on impulse searched for the name of his ex-wife.

She clicked on a clip of Alison reporting from Africa. There she was in the dust and the heat looking cool and elegant in khaki and crisp white, her hair a sleek bob. Apparently neither the heat nor the pressure was allowed to affect her performance.

She spoke directly to the camera about the current political situation. She was poised and eloquent. Not a single *um*.

This woman had never stammered in her life. She spoke clearly and without pause, the words emerging with an almost musical fluency. Harriet watched, transfixed and dismayed. She wanted to switch it off, but she couldn't stop watching. For her, the words, certain letters, could so easily be jammed. Trapped in her mouth. Sometimes she'd practice speaking in front of the mirror, but talking to herself didn't present the same challenge as talking to a stranger. She'd learned that most people preferred to talk than to listen so she often stayed silent, even though she knew by doing so she'd be labeled quiet or shy. There had been so many times when Fliss and Daniel had leaped in, taking on the role of understudy when her brain and mouth had refused to perform as expected.

It made her feel vulnerable to know her tongue could still let her down. Speech was a fundamental part of a person. And maybe it was wrong, but people judged.

Having thoroughly depressed herself, she flipped her laptop shut and stood up.

Alison was lovely, and eloquent, but Ethan wasn't with her anymore.

She wasn't going to feel envy about a relationship that no longer existed.

If anything she felt sad for him. Because, personal feelings aside, anytime a marriage failed was sad.

She distracted herself by cooking the perfect meal.

Ethan had said he'd be home by seven, so she planned to eat at 7:30 to allow him time to be late.

She switched on the Christmas tree lights, lit two of her favorite cinnamon and orange scented candles.

Humming along to carols, she prepared the duck and slid it into the oven.

By seven thirty everything was ready but there was no sign of Ethan.

She stared at her phone. Should she call? No. If he wanted to call her, he'd call. He didn't exactly have a nine to five job, did he?

She poured herself a glass of red wine and stood by the window.

It had finally stopped snowing but the city was bathed in an ethereal glow.

Her phone told her it was past eight, but still there was no sign of him.

What had possessed her to cook a soufflé?

Maybe she should ditch it and serve smoked salmon instead.

After an hour she poured herself another glass of wine.

After two hours she was starting to get seriously worried.

Maybe he'd had second thoughts. Maybe cooking dinner at home sent the wrong signals.

THERE WERE DAYS when he loved his job. Today wasn't one of them.

"Remind me. Why do I spend my Saturday nights in this place?" Susan ripped off her gloves. "I could be at the theatre or having sex with a hot guy. I could be having a life instead of always being in on the worst moments of someone else's."

They'd lost the patient and it had been a harrowing few hours.

Ethan was exhausted. He knew the rest of the team was too.

Each member would go home and process the loss in the way that best suited them. Some might use counseling, some might reach for the bottle, some might just bury it deep and keep going. All of them would analyze. They'd go over every step of the care they'd given, looking for holes.

In this case there hadn't been any.

He knew they'd done everything that they could have done and that the odds had been stacked against them.

The man had been drunk when the car he'd been driving had rammed into a wall. The car had caught fire, something that happened more in the movies than in real life but in this case the guy had been unlucky, as was the woman he'd hit with the car before he'd made contact with the wall. His passenger had crawled from the wreckage moments before the car had exploded. The driver had been brought in with most of his skin toasted and his aorta severed. His friend had walked away with nothing more than a cut finger.

Alcohol and *driving*. Two words that shouldn't ever appear in the same sentence, Ethan thought as he watched Susan try and haul her emotions back inside. She kept up a stream of her usual black humor, but it was different from usual and Ethan knew why. He knew what most people didn't. That her husband had been killed by a drunk driver. He knew that this case wasn't just professional for her, it was personal.

He also knew it would take her a few days to get back to her normal self. In the meantime he'd help all he could.

"You'd hate living a normal life."

"I don't think so." She looked tired and for once there was no sign of the humor or banter that characterized their relationship. "This place shows you the worst side of humans."

"Maybe. Or maybe it shows you the truth about humans."

"Jeez, Black, that's depressing. You need someone to lighten your dark side. Go to the theatre. Do something happy. Speaking of which, how is Harriet?"

He decided a little teasing might be good for her. "Who?"

"Cut me some slack. If I can't have my own sex life, I'm going to enjoy yours."

"What makes you think I have a sex life?" He could already see that he'd pulled her away from that dark, dark place. Not completely, but at least she seemed to be clear of the edge.

"You smile more."

"You're thinking of someone else. There's nothing to smile about here."

"True, which makes it all the more appealing when you do smile." She patted his hand. "Don't think I don't know what you're doing."

"What am I doing?"

She sighed. "You're being a good friend, that's what. And I'm grateful for it. And relieved to know you're human."

"Who said I was human?" They'd get through it, Ethan thought. They'd find a way through this bad day the way they'd found their way through all the others.

The department was swarming with cops looking for answers.

Ethan wasn't sure they'd find any other than the obvious.

The driver had a blood alcohol so far over the legal limit it was a wonder he'd focused enough to pick up his car keys and drive. But he had, and that answered the question of what they were all doing here. *Why* he'd thought consuming that level of alcohol was a good idea was a question that was beyond Ethan's understanding.

He was about to suggest to Susan that they grab a quick coffee, when a man appeared in the doorway.

Ethan recognized him as the passenger of the car, and it seemed he was as drunk as his friend had been. It showed in his eyes. In the way he walked. There was a scrape on his cheek and his left hand was bandaged.

"Who's in charge?" He slurred his words. "Are you the doctor?"

Ethan knew trouble when he saw it and he was looking at it now.

"I'm Doctor Black. Let me take you somewhere more private where we can talk."

The man lifted his finger and pointed to Ethan, stabbing the air. "You killed Nick. *You fucking killed my brother.*"

"You're upset. I understand that. We did everything that could humanly be done. Unfortunately Nick's injuries were serious and life-threatening." Ethan spoke calmly, trying to diffuse the situation, but reasoning and logic weren't much use when a man had that much alcohol in his system.

The man's gaze transferred to Susan and the anger in his face turned into something uglier.

"You're the bitch who had her hands on him when he was brought in. I saw you."

Susan opened her mouth to reply, but never got a chance.

It happened so quickly that afterward it was hard to recall the exact sequence of events. One minute they were talking and the next minute Ethan saw the quick flash of a blade as the guy pulled a knife. He moved fast, but so did Ethan. Without thinking he put himself in front of Susan and felt a flash of white heat and agony as the blade connected with his arm. With a neat move he hooked his leg behind the other man and dropped him to the ground. He went down hard, arms and legs flailing. The noise must have alerted security because moments later the room was crawling with cops and hospital security.

"Get a medical team in here," one of the cops called and Ethan shook his head.

"It's all right." His voice sounded gruff. "It's just a superficial wound." And then he realized they weren't looking at him, they were looking at Susan.

She'd collapsed to the ground and Ethan saw a red stain darkening and spreading across her scrubs.

"Jesus, no. Susan." He was by her side in an instant, dimly aware that one of the nurses was tying something around his arm to stop the bleeding.

Susan's eyes flickered open. "Trying to be a hero again. You're bleeding."

Nowhere near as much as she was.

He couldn't work it out. Couldn't work out how she was the one lying on the floor bleeding out. And then he realized the man must have somehow managed to get one last stab in before Ethan had floored him.

"The things you do to get attention." His voice shook as he lifted her scrubs and saw the knife wound and the steady pump of blood. Mentally running through all the vital organs the man might have hit on his quest to take revenge for his brother's death, Ethan barked out orders.

Get a line in. Let's do an abdominal ultrasound. Call the surgeons.

It was automatic, another case—except that this wasn't another case. This was Susan. Susan, who worked by his side every day. Who he trusted with his life. Who had trusted him with hers. It tore at his gut and his heart.

The team swarmed round Susan and the next few minutes passed in a blur of action.

Liver? Spleen? Ethan examined her, scanned her abdomen, watched her blood pressure dip and her pulse accelerate.

He didn't like the way she looked. Her skin was waxy pale and her pulse thready. "How soon until we can get her into the OR?"

"Couple of minutes."

It was the longest couple of minutes of his life. His hands were covered in her blood.

She opened her eyes again but this time he could see it was an effort.

"Hey there." He gave her his best reassuring smile. "You're going to be fine."

"You're a terrible liar." Her eyes closed. Her voice was faint. "I'm going to die right here in my own department and your ugly face is the last thing I'll see. There's no justice."

"You're not going to die. It will ruin my reputation if you die. Time for the surgeons to take over and find out whether he hit something important." He started to straighten up when she reached out and caught his arm.

"Promise me something, Ethan." This time her tone was serious. Her face was white and he felt fear lurch from his chest to his throat. This was how people felt every day in this department, but not him. He was always on the other side of it. He was the one fixing, reassuring, dealing. He wasn't the one worrying. Until now.

"Anything."

"If I live, I get to be godmother to your children."

If I live.

"I don't have children."

"But you will, one day. Two children and a dog. White picket fence. Maybe a rosebush."

His laugh was shaky. "Don't you ever give up?"

"Promise me."

"I promise. If I ever have children, you're godmother. It's a deal."

It was only later, when he'd washed Susan's blood from his fingers and gone to sit on one of the hard plastic chairs near the operating room, that he realized he'd forgotten to call Harriet. A glance at his phone told him he was four hours late for their date.

She'd cooked him a special dinner, which no doubt was now congealed and ruined.

It had happened many times when he'd first got together with Alison, which was why they'd resorted to eating out. Solo eating in a restaurant wasn't as frustrating as laboring for hours over food that was scraped into the trash.

This was the first time it had happened with Harriet.

He pulled out a phone but couldn't face talking to anyone, so instead of calling he sent a text. Brief. Factual.

He'd deal with the fallout later.

How to ruin a relationship before it started.

A short time later he felt a hand on his shoulder and one of the nurses handed him a cup of coffee. Not the sort people gathered in coffee bars to drink. The vile-tasting stuff the hospital produced to make sure no one lingered longer than they had to.

He managed to thank her, although he was thanking her more for the sentiment than the actual coffee. He didn't know its exact chemical makeup, but he doubted it had ever seen a coffee bean.

He knew he wasn't the only one waiting for news of

Susan, but he was the only one waiting outside the operating room. The police came to talk to him, hospital staff came and went, sent him sympathetic glances, murmured the occasional word, but mostly left him alone. They probably would have let him inside if he'd asked, but he wasn't sure he could cope with that much reality right now.

He felt as if the edges of his world had blurred. Right now he was both doctor, and concerned friend. The doctor side of him kept thinking about all the various scenarios that could be taking place inside the operating room. The friend kept thinking about how he and Susan had been chatting only minutes before the man had appeared in the room.

He felt a hand on his shoulder again. He looked up expecting to see a nurse and was surprised to see Harriet.

Her coat was buttoned unevenly and she wasn't wearing gloves. She'd obviously left the apartment in a hurry.

"I came as soon as I got your text."

She'd come in person? It hadn't even crossed his mind that she'd do that. "I'm sorry."

"For what?"

"The ruined dinner. I should have called, not sent a text."

"Do you really think I care about that? In the circumstances I'm surprised you even managed to text. How is she doing? Any news?" She sat down next to him on another of the hard plastic chairs that seemed to have been chosen for their discomfort. It was a place no one would choose to linger, as if the painful psychology of waiting had somehow oozed into the furniture.

He was still processing the fact Harriet was here, sitting in the uncomfortable chair next to his. "No news. But why are you here?"

"Isn't that what friendship is? Supporting another friend in trouble?"

He stared down at his hands, trying not to think about Susan's blood. "I'm fine. I don't need support."

"I know. Dr. Tough. So big and strong you don't feel anything. You've told me that before. But I'm not here for you. I'm here for Susan. I liked her. A lot. I want to be here when she wakes up. She might need chicken soup or something." She looked at the coffee in his hand. "I don't think you should drink that."

He stared at the drink and realized his hand was shaking. Dr. Tough? Not so much. Maybe he had more feelings left than he'd thought. "It's caffeine. It will do the job."

"Of poisoning you? If it's caffeine you need, I can do better." She reached into her bag and pulled out a flask. The liquid she poured into the cup was strong and black and tasted like heaven.

"What did you put in this? I've never tasted anything like it before."

"It's coffee. Real coffee. I grind the beans fresh. I thought you might need it."

He did.

He drank two cups and felt the caffeine kick through his veins, firing him up. Maybe he should grind his own coffee beans too, if this was how the finished product tasted.

Unfortunately the sudden energy boost also kick-started his brain. He should have seen it coming. The moment the man had appeared in the door with his eyes glittering like LED lights, he should have got Susan out of the room. He should have moved faster. He should have called security straight off, but the whole incident had taken—what? Less than thirty seconds he was guessing. How the man had smuggled a knife past security he had no idea.

"How serious is it?"

"Too soon to say. The wound was pretty deep and it was close to some vital organs." And he didn't want to think about the possibilities or he'd drive himself insane. He was about to ask if there was any more coffee in her flask when she took the cup from his hand and topped it up.

He wondered how it was that she always seemed to know exactly what he needed.

She put the flask back in her bag. "When did you last eat?"

"I don't know. Lunch?" His memory of the day was cloudy. The last hour had eclipsed everything. "In fact I think I missed lunch. I had caffeine at some point." One hastily drunk cup of disgusting hospital coffee that had scalded his tongue and made him question his choices.

Harriet reached into her bag again and this time put a food container on his lap. "If we're going to be here all night, you're going to need to eat. You fainting from hunger won't help Susan."

He thought back to the first night she'd cooked for him in his apartment. Before he'd known better, he'd thought it was a romantic gesture. Now he understood that, for Harriet, cooking wasn't a gesture of romantic interest but of comfort. That first night she'd been stressed and comforting herself by cooking, but she also comforted others. Chicken soup for him. Same for Susan when she'd visited. Cookies to Glenys. The sandwich she'd brought him wasn't her making a point that he'd ruined dinner. It wasn't her trying to win his heart. It was her trying to make things better. "I'm not hungry. Will you be offended if I don't eat it?"

"No, but maybe take one bite." Her tone was soft and coaxing. "It's duck. The bread is from a sourdough loaf I made this morning. You couldn't make it to dinner, so I brought dinner to you although not quite in the format originally planned."

He took one bite to please her, but after one bite he discovered he was starving. And having eaten, he felt better.

The bread was the best sourdough he'd tasted outside of San Francisco. A perfect crust and chewy center.

He glanced along the corridor, knowing it would be a while until they had news of any sort. "This is a restricted area. I'm surprised they didn't try and stop you."

"They did." Her cheeks turned pink. "I may have told a lie."

"I thought you were no good at lying?"

"Apparently I'm getting better. I said I was Susan's cousin and that you'd called me."

He could imagine her standing there, channeling all her energies into telling a lie. Challenge Harriet. "In that case you've definitely earned bad-girl status."

"I think so."

"There's only one problem—Susan doesn't have any family."

Harriet folded her hands in her lap and didn't move from her chair. "She does now."

Something sprang to life inside him, something he hadn't felt in a long time.

"You're a good person, Harriet Knight."

"I think what you meant to say was that I'm a badass, kick-ass serious piece of work."

He couldn't help it. He laughed. Out loud. Here in the stark hospital corridor, where the air seemed to be filled with nothing but tension. "If you're going to say those words, you need to have an expression that matches it."

"At least I didn't stammer. Lucky for me, *badass* isn't a word I stammer over. I think it might spoil the effect. Can you imagine? B-b-badass doesn't sound right, does it?"

He was still smiling when she covered his hand with hers.

"They told me you were hurt too. Are you in a lot of pain?"

He'd barely thought about his arm. At some point someone had checked it and dressed it. "It's a scratch, that's all. I was trying to stop him getting to Susan. I still can't quite work out how he did."

"And because he did, you're blaming yourself."

"It was my fault." He ran his hand over his face. "I should have anticipated it. Should have stopped it."

"How? Are you a mind reader? Bad things happen, Ethan. It's life."

He knew about life. He saw it every day, just as he dealt with the consequences of the bad things.

He wondered why she was still here, in this soulless place that no one would ever visit through choice.

She was as out of place as a gerbera daisy in a garbage heap.

"You should go home."

"Do you want me to go? Because of course if you want me to, then I'll go. But I thought you might like company."

It was true that he'd barely noticed the thirty minutes that had elapsed since her arrival.

He opened his mouth to tell her she should go, but discovered he really didn't want her to.

Something about her quiet presence made it not quite so difficult to handle.

"If you could stay," he said, "that would be good. But it's going to be a long night."

She crossed her legs and settled into the chair. "I'm not going anywhere."

CHAPTER TWENTY-TWO

ETHAN WAS RIGHT about one thing. It was a long night.

"This is the first time I've been in a hospital waiting for news." He leaned his head back against the wall.

Harriet knew he was exhausted. She also knew there was no point in telling him to leave. The same inner drive that had made him agree to take his sister's dog, wouldn't allow him to leave his injured colleague.

The sandwiches she'd made were gone. So was the coffee. She wished now that she'd brought a second flask.

She delved into her bag and handed him a carefully wrapped packet.

"What's this? Don't tell me you brought dessert?"

"In a way. They're my specialty. Chocolate chip cookies. Eat them quickly. Men have been known to fight over them."

"Yeah? Give me an example."

"Two years ago at the bake sale near my grandmother's. William Duggart and Barney Townsend almost came to blows over the last one on sale. Tensions were high. William said he'd marry me if I cooked them for him for the rest of his life."

"And how old is he?"

"Eighty-six. Which, now I think about it, wasn't so different from the last man I dated."

"Unless there's something you need to tell me about how you spent your day, I'm the last man you dated." He took a bite of cookie. "Okay, this is good. Seriously good. I can see why William was prepared to marry you. These are enough to make any man contemplate giving up his single status."

Except him.

She pushed the thought away. "Anything to cheer up this horrible place. I don't know how you work here every day."

"Normally I'm on the other end of the stress. It's different."

Maybe. But did that make it easier? She wasn't convinced. "I've only been in a hospital a few times in my life."

He glanced at her. "I presume one of those times was when you injured your ankle. What happened those other times?"

"My father had a heart attack. The first one was about five years ago, and then he had another one the year after that. Fliss and I were at home when we got the call that first time. He refused to see Daniel because he blamed him for the fact that Mom eventually divorced him. He refused to see Fliss too."

"But you went to see him."

"Crazy, I know. I kept thinking maybe he'd have an epiphany and suddenly realize he loved me. He didn't." She paused, surprised at herself. "I don't know why I'm telling you this."

"It's the ambience." He gestured toward the stark corridor. "There's something about a drafty hospital corridor that encourages confidences."

"That must be it." That, and the fact that he was so easy to talk to.

"Sounds like you spent most of your childhood trying to please him."

"I did. I couldn't quite 'get' that nothing I did was ever going to please him. I annoyed him. Irritated him. And he wasn't afraid to show it. The worst time was when I had to recite a poem at school. I'd rehearsed and rehearsed. Fliss and Daniel helped me. I did it over and over again with not a single stammer. I was so proud of myself. And excited. At school I was always—" She hesitated. "I was teased for my stammer."

"You mean you were bullied." His tone was flat.

"Yes. I didn't have much confidence, so the fact that I could recite this poem—I saw it as an opportunity to show everyone I could do it without stammering. I imagined the applause. The smiles. My life changing overnight. No more accidentally bumping into me in the lunch line and knocking the contents of my tray everywhere. No more frogs in my locker."

Two nurses appeared, talking as they walked.

Ethan waited until they'd passed and the sound of footsteps had receded.

"Frogs in your locker?"

"They didn't worry me. I like animals. But I was worried about the frogs."

"Teasing—bullying—can make dysfluency worse so I'm guessing none of that helped. Tell me about the poem. I'm guessing things didn't go the way they were supposed to."

"I walked onstage, all fired up and ready to impress—"

"And?"

"And my father was right there in the front row. Fliss and Daniel were next to him looking furious and my mother had obviously been crying. We were one big happy family."

"I'm assuming he didn't turn up to support you."

"No. He never came to school events. He turned up that night because he was the biggest bully of them all." She breathed out slowly. "What he did confirmed it, although it took me years to admit that to myself. Years to admit that he didn't love me at all. It just didn't seem right or natural." She felt Ethan's fingers close over hers.

"This is one story where I'm not sure I even want to hear the ending."

"The ending is very predictable. I saw him, turned to stone, couldn't move a muscle and certainly not my vocal cords. Out of the corner of my eye I could see Daniel trying to catch my attention, trying to encourage me to look at him and not our father, but I couldn't look away. And then I decided this was the perfect time to finally make him proud. If I could recite this poem, then he'd finally love me."

"But by then you were too stressed to get a word out."

"Too stressed to say a whole word, that's true. I managed to repeat the first letter a few times and I was so mortified by all the giggling from the audience all the fight went out of me. Pathetic, I know." She hated thinking about it. Even now, years later, she wished she could turn back the clock. She would have stayed on the stage and stammered her way through the whole damn thing.

"Not pathetic at all. You were—how old?"

"Can't remember exactly. Eleven or twelve? And I made it about me. All of it. His behavior. The fact he didn't love me. All about me. And the truth is that none of it was about me.

It was never about me." She drew in a little breath. "Took me years to realize that."

There was a long pause.

"Eleven." Ethan stretched out his legs. "I don't remember much about being eleven, but I remember being thirteen and I guess it's not much different. It was all about not making a fool of yourself. You think the whole world is looking at you and thinking about you and you're scared they're going to know what a mess you are inside."

"You felt that way?" She found it hard to imagine.

"All kids feel that way. Some hide it better than others, that's all. And it takes maturity to realize most people are so busy thinking about themselves that they don't give a damn about what you're doing."

"Well, people did look at me. When having a conversation takes an extra five minutes, people tend to notice. And they're not kind."

"So what happened?"

"I stammered, died inside and fled from the stage. We all went home and Fliss was so furious she flew at him with a skillet. I swear she would have killed him if Daniel hadn't dragged her away. It was hideous."

"Sounds like it. I'm glad you had your twin and your brother."

"Yes. It made us closer. In a way we formed a little family of our own. And we've stayed close."

"I'm starting to understand what a big deal it must have been for you when your sister moved away."

"It's been a life change, that's for sure. I guess I got lazy. I stopped doing some things—tough things—for myself because Fliss and Daniel would always do it for me, and they probably did it better. If we had an awkward client it was better for Fliss to deal with it than me. I was always scared that if someone was aggressive, it would bring back my stammer."

"And then you met me, and your worst nightmares came true."

He was more dream than nightmare but she didn't say that. "It was good for me. My worst scenario happened. I survived. I got through it. And I got through it without calling my twin." She was proud of that. "Not calling Fliss was almost as big a challenge."

"Because you're used to talking to her about everything."

"Yes, and then she worries and tries to protect me. Which is great, except that I would rather protect myself. And maybe I'm not going to do it in the same way she does—"

"Beaning someone with a skillet, you mean?"

She smiled. "Her methods do tend to be physical, that's true."

He leaned his head back against the wall. "We see it here too. Abuse. Not always easy to spot. Even harder to do something about, but we try. That night you came in—"

"You thought I'd been abused."

He turned his head to look at her, his gaze direct and unsettling. "It crossed my mind. You had a vulnerable quality—I don't know how to describe it."

"That's how I look when I try and wear stilettos." She turned it into a joke. "When you can't balance, you're vulnerable."

A smile touched the edges of his mouth. "You're an impressive person, Harriet Knight."

Her heart beat a little harder. "You wouldn't say that if you'd seen me trying to climb out of that window."

He was about to say something when a woman strode toward them wearing scrubs.

Ethan was on his feet instantly. "How is she?"

Harriet stood up too, but stayed back a little, not wanting to intrude. She overheard some of it—lower grade rupture of the spleen, hematologic parameters, splenic preservation, arterial intervention—none of it made sense to her, and all of it sounded horrendous but Ethan seemed relieved, so perhaps it wasn't as bad as it sounded.

He ran his hand over his face. "Can I see her?"

"Sure. But keep it brief."

Harriet was about to sit back down on the chair to wait when he grabbed her hand.

"You should come too. She'd like that. You can promise her a bowl of your chicken soup."

Susan was in recovery and although she seemed groggy, her eyes were open. She saw Ethan and managed something close to a smile.

"Jeez, you still here? What time is it?"

"Middle of the night. I thought I'd hang around."

Susan's gaze slid to Harriet. "But you got yourself some company." Her eyes closed. "Did you tell her, Black?"

"Did I tell her what?"

"About your promise."

"I don't remember a promise. The anesthetic must have affected your memory."

"You break your promise, I'm going to come back and haunt you."

"You have to die first, and there is no way you're dying. I need you back here."

"I'm not sure that's an incentive to recover. A bowl of Harriet's soup might."

Harriet stepped forward. "As soon as you're on the ward and eating, I'll bring you some."

"You're an angel." Her eyes opened. "Do you hear that, Black? She's an angel."

"You need to rest."

"And you need to go home." She stretched her hand out to him and he took it. "Thanks, Ethan."

"That's the first time you've ever called me by name."

"It's the first time you've ever saved my life."

"Given that you're lying there, I didn't do such a great job."

"We both know that without you, I'd be dead." Her eyes closed again. "Go home. Get some sleep. But come back tomorrow. With Harriet. And soup. And don't forget your promise."

"What is this promise she keeps talking about?" Harriet asked as they walked out of the hospital into the freezing night.

"She wants to be godmother to my children."

"But you don't have—ah." Understanding dawned. "She wants you to have children. Is she in league with your sister?"

"They've never met, but they seem to be on the same wavelength. Susan seems to want me to have it all. No idea why. Ironic, coming from a loner like her."

"Not married then?"

He hesitated. "She was married. Eight years ago her husband was killed by a drunk driver while he was walking their son home from kindergarten. The car mounted the sidewalk. Their little boy was killed too."

The emotion was like a punch to her chest. "Oh, that's terrible."

"Yes. And so is drinking and then getting behind the wheel of a car."

"How do you ever get over something like that?"

"You don't. If you're lucky you learn to live alongside it. You find ways to keep going. Susan's way was to throw herself into work. I guess she feels that although she couldn't save her own family, she might be able to save someone else's."

"But she's never married again. She lives alone?"

"She has an apartment near mine."

"What is she doing for Christmas?"

He frowned. "I have no idea. Why?"

"I just wondered, that's all." Harriet paused as they reached a set of lights. "Do you want to come home with me?"

"Now? It's already almost four in the morning."

"My place is closer. And I can make you breakfast."

"Now that's an offer I can't refuse." He pulled her into his arms. "Thanks for coming tonight. I'm glad you did."

"Me too."

SUSAN MADE A remarkably swift recovery.

Three days after her surgery she was dressed and walking around her room.

"Are you sure you're supposed to be expending so much energy?" Harriet watched her doubtfully. "Shouldn't you be resting?"

"I can rest when I'm dead. Which I almost was, so I guess I already rested. Is that chicken soup?" She gazed hopefully at the container Harriet was lifting carefully out of the bag.

"It is. I added a touch of cream to give you extra calories. You'll probably lecture me about the health of your arteries."

"My arteries have never been happier, thank you." Susan took the container from her, sat down and started to eat. "I never knew food could even taste this good. If Ethan doesn't marry you, I will."

Harriet almost dropped the rest of the food. She was relieved Ethan wasn't here. "Ethan isn't going to marry anyone ever again."

"That's what he says."

"And you don't believe him." She probably should have stayed silent but the temptation to talk about him was too great.

"I don't think he knows what's good for him. I think working here has screwed him up some. It happens. And he's divorced. Ethan is big on responsibility. If you've been hanging around with him, you probably already know that. It's the reason he says yes to looking after his sister's dog even though it totally disrupts his life. It's the reason he steps in front of a crazy drunk with a knife and sits half the night in a drafty corridor waiting for news about a colleague. He holds himself to high standards. And he likes to take care of everybody. From what I've heard, it's in the genes. Rock solid family. Community people who would give you the shirt from their back. Remember that and you'll understand why he thinks he failed at marriage. Blames himself, although I can tell you now that Alison would say she was more than half to blame and if ever two people were wrong for each other, it's those two. Now you—that's a different ball game."

Harriet was about to ask how she knew Alison when she remembered that it was Ethan's ex-wife who had been part of the live "fly on the wall" documentary set in the ER.

"How is it a different ball game?"

"He's been different since he met you."

Harriet's heart bumped a little harder. She wasn't going to read anything into that. "Different in what way?"

"More approachable. More human."

"If Alison wasn't right for him, why did he marry her?"

"Now that's a question I can't answer, but if I had to guess I'd say he didn't think about it too deeply. She rocked up here one day with her blond hair and there's Ethan, all shoulders and muscle in his scrubs, saving a kid. She was gone. I saw it happen. What they should have done was screwed each other's brains out and then waved each other goodbye, but for some reason he put a ring on her finger." She stared sadly into the empty soup container. "Is this hard to make? Could an idiot cook make it? When they send me home, I want to be able to make this."

"I'll fill your freezer," Harriet promised, topping up her soup. "When are they sending you out?"

"Tomorrow if I get my way." Susan finished the soup and sat back.

"Do you like chocolate chip cookies?"

"What sort of a question is that? Who the hell doesn't like chocolate chip cookies?"

Harriet grinned and handed over a small box tied with a bow. "They're my specialty."

Susan took a bite and closed her eyes. "Man, how are you ever single?"

"I ask myself that question regularly but haven't yet come up with an answer."

"Obviously all the men in your life are batshit crazy. You ever make those fancy cupcake things? Covered in swirly icing that's basically all sugar and calories?"

"I make great cupcakes. I'll add a batch to the list of things I'm leaving in your apartment."

"I've got a better idea—" Susan brushed crumbs from her mouth "—come and live, then you can cook for me onsite. You are too good at this to be living alone."

Harriet put the empty soup container back in her bag. An idea had been growing in her mind. "What are you doing for Christmas?"

Susan slumped back against the pillows. "I was working, but now I guess I'm not. Damn. And I wanted to be at work. This place is one big party over the holidays. I hate to miss it." Her tone was sarcastic, but Harriet knew she was speaking the truth. She would rather have been at work, presumably because being at work stopped her thinking about family. The family she'd lost. It must be the worst time of year for her.

"Will you join me? I'm having a few people over."

"I appreciate the offer, but it's not my best time of year." Susan's voice was rough. "Ethan told you my sad tale?"

"Yes. And I'm so sorry." The words felt woefully inadequate, but what was the right thing to say to someone who had lost everything that mattered to them? There were no right words.

"I appreciate the invitation, but I'm not good company."

"You don't have to sing and dance. Come and sit on the sofa and let me feed you."

Susan eyed her. "Christmas is family time. Why aren't you going home to spend it with your mom and dad?"

"They divorced years ago. My mom is traveling and my dad—we're not in touch." She was surprised by how easily she said it. "He doesn't speak to me. I'm close to my sister and brother, but this year I decided I wanted to spend Christmas by myself." She paused and then on impulse told

Susan about Challenge Harriet, starting from the beginning and not stopping until she'd reached the end.

"So you're doing something you find hard every day? Jeez, that's—" Susan stared at her and Harriet shrugged.

"Stupid?"

"I was going to say inspirational. Maybe I will join you. Not staying in bed on Christmas Day could be my first Challenge Susan."

"If you have other friends you'd rather go to, don't worry," Harriet said quickly, "don't feel pressure."

"Most of my friends gave up on me a long time ago. My fault, not theirs. Work was my therapy. I didn't want sympathy or pitying glances. Eventually they gave up."

What sort of person gave up on a friend who'd suffered such an extreme blow? "In that case, I hope you'll come to me."

Susan stared at her for a moment and then grinned. "Hey, I'm going to be godmother to your children. That makes me as good as family, so maybe I will."

Harriet gave a start, remembering what Ethan had said. "Godmother?"

"Sure. He made me a deathbed promise."

"You're alive."

"Barely. I'd love to spend Christmas with you. All I need is your address. And I'll wear my loose trousers because if you're going to cook like this I'm going to need room for expansion."

ETHAN LAY SPRAWLED on Harriet's sofa, watching as she bottle-fed kittens.

"I hate to break this to you, but your badass credentials are taking a serious blow."

She nestled the kitten closer. "Just because I can bottle-feed a kitten, doesn't mean I can't be a bad girl."

"Not convinced. You'd better take me back to bed and prove it."

Instead, she carefully placed one of the kittens in his lap and handed him a bottle. "Stop talking and get to work."

Ethan felt the warmth of the tiny kitten through his jeans. "I don't know anything about feeding kittens."

"You didn't know anything about dogs, either, but Madi was pretty fond of you by the end."

"Because you were supervising." He pushed the bottle toward the kitten, who immediately latched on.

"Tilt it a little more." Harriet's hand covered his, moving it into position. "She's swallowing air."

She returned to the other kitten, scooping it up with the ease of experience and settling it carefully in her lap.

She was gentle, kind and attentive and Ethan couldn't work out for the life of him how her father could possibly not have loved her.

What sort of guy couldn't love a woman like Harriet? She didn't have a mean bone in her body. Whatever had been wrong with his marriage, there was no reason at all to take it out on his daughter.

Another person might have grown up bitter. Might have spent their lives protecting themselves.

Not Harriet. She was the most generous, giving person he'd ever met.

She sat cross-legged on the floor in a position he was pretty sure he couldn't have achieved without requiring emergency assistance afterward.

"You do yoga or something?"

"For the past fifteen years. It started as a way to relax."

Because having a stammer had been stressful. Living with her father had been stressful.

He didn't like thinking about it because thinking about it made him understand why she valued home and family so strongly and that, in turn, made him worry about what she was doing with him. Maybe she made a point of being with lost causes. "So you can do lots of fancy poses?"

"I'm pretty flexible, if that's what you mean." She glanced up, challenge in her eyes. "I can wrap my legs around my neck."

Heat and desire shot through him.

He forgot that he wasn't the right man for her.

He forgot that they wanted different things. Right then at that moment there was only one thing he wanted.

In the grip of an attack of pure lust, Ethan felt sweat sheen his brow. "No kidding."

"I'd prove it, Dr. Black, but I'm holding a kitten."

"I guess I can manage to hold two if you'd like to show me."

"Why don't I start with something less provocative?" She finished feeding the kitten, placed it on Ethan's lap and then put her hands flat on the floor. She paused for a moment, breathed and then kicked her legs into a perfect handstand, narrowly missing the tree that took pride of place in the living room.

She was poised, ramrod straight, her balance perfect. Her hair slid down and the ends brushed the floor.

He was just wondering how anyone could hold such a perfectly straight handstand for that length of time, when she lowered her legs to the floor with as much grace as she'd used to kick them up in the first place.

He was surprised all the needles were still attached to the Christmas tree.

Ethan tried to speak but had to clear his throat before any words would emerge.

"Okay, I'm impressed. Now move on to the provocative."

She arched her back and did something with her body that made him want to strip her naked and take her right there and then. He would have done it if it weren't for the kittens in his lap. They were definitely too young to witness what he had in mind.

"Enough." He shifted on the sofa and she raised an eyebrow.

"Are those kittens making you uncomfortable?"

"Nothing to do with the kittens, sweetheart." And then he saw the sparkle in her eyes and realized she knew exactly why he was feeling uncomfortable.

"I take it back. You're a bad girl. Does your twin do yoga too?"

"No." She stood up gracefully. "Yoga is too slow and calm for Fliss. She prefers kickboxing and karate." She leaned forward to take the kittens from him and her hair brushed against his cheek.

For a moment he forgot how to breathe, but then she stepped back and placed the kittens in a basket.

"I forgot to tell you—" She straightened, her cheeks flushed. "Susan is spending Christmas with me."

"You invited her? That was kind of you. Not working over Christmas would have been her kind of hell." And the fact that she'd invited her confirmed what he already knew. That Harriet Knight was the kindest person he'd ever met. "It's a tough time of year for her."

"I did it for me too. I like her. I want my friends around me."

It almost made him wish he wasn't working at Christmas.

It was two days until his vacation. Two days. Usually by this stage he couldn't wait. Usually there wasn't one single thing about New York City that he'd miss. But this time—

"What are you doing next week?"

"The usual. Walking dogs. Why?"

He wouldn't see her for over a week and then it would be Christmas and he wouldn't see her then, either. An emotion stirred to life inside him. An emotion he decided not to examine too closely.

"Come with me to Vermont. I'll teach you to ski." He knew that by inviting her he'd crossed an invisible line. A line neither of them talked about, but which both of them knew was there. Casual dating in New York City was one thing. Inviting her to share his vacation was something else entirely.

He knew it. She knew it. And it was difficult to know which of them was most surprised by the suggestion.

Her eyes widened. "Excuse me?"

Maybe she was the more surprised, given that she needed confirmation of his question.

"I'm asking you to join me. When did you last take a vacation?" As if that had any bearing at all on his reason for asking.

"I don't know. It's been a while. I had a few days in the Hamptons in the summer."

"Staying with your grandmother. Checking on your sister." She'd told him about the struggle she had persuading her twin to open up to her. "When did you last have a week that was all about you?"

"But this week is all about *you*. You've told me that." She held his gaze. "You look forward to it all year. You catch up with friends—family—it's your godmother's wedding! You can't invite me to your godmother's wedding."

"I can." He decided not to tell her how pleased his friends and family would be if he showed up with Harriet as his guest. "My invitation says plus one. You're my plus one. I'd love you to join me. Could you make some calls? Delegate some of your walks?"

"I'm not walking that many myself right now. Only Harvey, because I like to keep an eye on Glenys, but I can ask Judy to call in."

"Good. Then that's settled."

"Wait! This is—are you sure?" She sounded breathless and flustered. "This is a ski vacation and I don't know how to ski."

"I'll teach you."

"I might be terrible at it."

He pulled her into the circle of his arms. "Even if you hate it there is plenty to enjoy at Snow Crystal. Trust me on that. You'll have a great time. Luxury cabin by a frozen lake. Snowy forest. Log fire. Shelves of books, extra large bed—"

"Stop! You're making sure I can't possibly say no."

"Why would you say no?"

"Because it isn't something I've ever done before."

"Isn't that what Challenge Harriet is all about?"

"Good point. And what would I wear to a winter wedding?"

"Something warm, because knowing the O'Neil family at least part of it will be outdoors." He stayed silent, letting her chew it over, surprised by how badly he wanted her there. "Well? What do you think?"

She smiled. "I think it sounds like one big challenge. Which makes it perfect. What do I need to pack?"

CHAPTER TWENTY-THREE

THE GENEROUS FALL of snow had turned Vermont into a winter wonderland. They drove over covered bridges white with snow and through villages decked for the holidays. They passed storefronts decorated with fresh green wreaths and windows strung with sparkling lights. Harriet saw pretty clapboard homesteads and people overloaded with parcels struggling home through the snow. And then there were the mountains, their snowy peaks and forested slopes cradling the villages below.

"I never believed in love at first sight until now. It's magical," she breathed. "Like something from a Christmas fairy tale." The words caught in her throat. This was Christmas as she'd imagined it should be when she was a child and trying to escape the reality of her own.

Of course reality had been nothing like this.

In their house, Christmas had been another day to be endured. Worse, if anything, than other days because of the pressure to spend it together. Oh, they'd gone through the motions, opening presents, eating food. Sadly, her father's temper didn't take a holiday. If anything it was exacerbated when he was caged with his family. A wife he loved, but who didn't love him back. Children who understood none of it.

Would things have been different, Harriet wondered, if they'd known the truth?

Ethan was driving, his hands steady on the wheel as he tackled the increasingly challenging road conditions.

"This fall of snow is lucky for them. Good start to the winter. Are you cold?" He glanced at her briefly. "You haven't taken your hat off."

"I'm good." And she had a reason for not removing her hat. A road sign flashed past and she squinted at it. "Moose Crossing?"

"They have to cross exactly there or they get a ticket." Ethan kept a straight face and she laughed.

"I may be a city girl, but I'm not stupid."

He slowed his speed as they approached a bend in the road. "It's a warning to motorists. If there's one thing you don't want to hit around here it's a moose."

"I'm sure the moose would agree. Can't be a happy experience for him, either."

He glanced at her with a smile and a shake of his head. "Only you would think about the emotional impact on the moose."

"What were you thinking of?"

"The probable injuries incurred by the driver. I'm assuming you've never had a collision with a moose. They have long legs. If you hit one at night the likely scenario is that they come shooting through your windshield and that's one hell of a lot of animal landing on you. The result isn't pretty."

"Have you ever seen that happen?"

"Not many moose in Times Square."

"Oh funny." She pulled a face. "You worked out in the boonies, and you've visited here every year for decades. You must have had a moose encounter."

"Only when hiking."

"Are they dangerous?"

"They're probably more scared of you than you are of them." He turned down a narrow lane and she craned her neck to see through the trees.

"The lake is frozen! People are skating."

"If there's one thing Vermont has plenty of, it's ice."

"What about wildlife? Any bears I should know about?"

"They're hibernating. If you're lucky you might see white-tailed deer, snowshoe hare, coyote, bobcats and the odd porcupine." He pulled up outside a rustic gate. "We have to walk from here. It's not far."

Trees drooped under the heavy load of snow, the silence broken only when the weight of their burden became too much and it thudded to the ground in a soft avalanche of white.

Harriet stared upward feeling as if she were a million miles from her life.

Her eyes stung. She told herself it was because of the cold, but she knew she was lying.

It was because she'd never been anywhere more beautiful.

Behind her, she heard the slam of the trunk as Ethan removed their cases.

The path had been cleared recently, although judging from the layer of new snow it had snowed again since. Their footsteps were muffled and their breath clouded the freezing air. She felt the cold penetrate her gloves, stinging the tips of her fingers. She didn't care. They turned a corner and there, right in front of them, was a cabin that looked like something out of a fairy tale. A tasteful blend of wood and glass, it merged with the forest as if it were part of it. The cabin was framed by the forest and set on the shores of the lake.

Harriet admired it. "I'm beginning to understand why you come back here every year."

"This is a relatively recent development. Jackson upgraded the place when he took over. Made a few changes."

"I think the place is gorgeous."

"Wait until you see inside."

They stamped the snow from their boots and stepped through the door.

Harriet stared up at the cathedral ceiling and the glass windows that soared into the eaves. In the corner of the room a pretty iron staircase led to a sleeping "shelf" overlooking the forest.

Roughly chopped logs had been stacked in a basket next to the flickering fire and someone had hung tiny lights from the rafters, turning the whole place into the adult equivalent of a fairy grotto. Deep cushioned sofas faced each other across a rug and tall bookshelves made from reclaimed wood hugged one wall of the cabin.

It occurred to her that if she hadn't challenged herself to agree to dog sitting she never would have met Ethan, at least not properly because she didn't count the whole bruised ankle incident. And if she hadn't met Ethan, she wouldn't be here now. Which proved, once again, that Challenge Harriet paid dividends. Doing things you'd never thought of doing led to discoveries like this one.

Harriet walked across the room, feeling her feet sink into the soft rug. "I want to move in and live here forever."

"Yeah, it has that effect on people." Ethan dumped their cases by the door. "It's one of the reasons it's a success. Some of their guests have been coming back for years. Jackson could have crammed in more lodges, but he chose to keep it exclusive. Each cabin feels secluded and intimate. You wouldn't even know there was anyone else nearby. Which is handy if you feel like having sex in the hot tub on the deck. Unless that's something Harriet Knight would never do."

She turned her head and met his gaze. "It's definitely something Harriet Knight *would* do."

But first there was something she needed to show him.

Hoping she hadn't made a mistake, she slipped off her coat and finally pulled off her hat, watching him the whole time.

His eyes widened. He opened his mouth, but no words emerged.

It was the reaction she'd been hoping for.

She smiled. "I'll take that as a compliment."

He swallowed. "You had it cut?"

"No, a madman attacked me with a pair of scissors when I was in Bloomingdale's. Of course I had it cut." She stroked the ends of her hair self-consciously. It still felt strange to have short hair brushing against her jaw.

"Have you had it short before?"

"Never." And she still wasn't used to it herself. Her whole life she'd had hair down her back. Now it swung in a short cut that ended at her chin. "I was worried you might hate it."

"I love it." He crossed the room toward her. "It makes your eyes look huge. And you have *great* bones. You're beautiful—"

"Keep talking. Don't stop."

"I have to stop. I can't talk and kiss you and I really have to kiss you." He slid his fingers into her hair and brought his mouth down on hers, the intimate slide of his tongue the most erotic thing she'd ever experienced. Heat blasted through her, spreading through her body. He wrapped his arms round her, his arms strong, and she melted against him, passion consuming both of them.

She felt the hardening length of him and might have done something about it there and then if it hadn't been for the fact that from behind them came the sound of someone clearing his throat.

Ethan released her reluctantly and both of them turned toward the sound.

A man stood in the doorway of the cabin. He was dressed in ski gear and had the bluest eyes Harriet had ever seen.

"Came to check you'd settled in, but you don't seem to be having any problems on that score."

"Ty—" Ethan crossed the room and the two men greeted each other. "How's Jess?"

"She's going to be the youngest slalom champion in history." Tyler's eyes glowed with pride. "No one can catch her."

"Chip off the old block."

"Seems that way."

"And Brenna?"

"Pregnant."

Ethan grinned. "You've been busy. How does Jess feel about it?"

"She can't wait. She'll have the baby on skis before he or she can walk." Tyler's gaze rested on Harriet. "You brought a guest."

Harriet recognized him from the photo on the book jacket of the autobiography she'd found in Ethan's apartment. The front cover had been a photo of him skiing what appeared to be an almost vertical slope, and the back cover had been a photo of him holding a gold medal and laughing at the camera.

"I'm Harriet." She stretched out her hand but before Tyler could take it two large Siberian husky dogs barreled through the door, almost knocking the two men down.

"Stay! Sit," Tyler bellowed but both dogs ignored him and headed straight for Harriet.

Tyler swore fluently but Harriet stooped to greet the dogs.

"Well, aren't you *beautiful*. Gorgeous, gorgeous dogs."

Tyler exchanged an astonished glance with Ethan, who shrugged.

"Harriet loves dogs and she's good with them."

"In that case she's going to fit right in around here. I was going to apologize for their terrible manners but maybe I'll save my breath."

"They're the most beautiful dogs I've ever seen." Harriet dropped to her knees on the rug and buried her hands in the fur of the dog closest to her. "I love Siberian huskies. What are their names?"

"That's Luna. She's the one with the brain. Devoted to my daughter. Pines when she's away. The other one is Ash. He's more of a bruiser. Seems pretty taken with you. Do you have a dog back home?"

"Not my own, but I'm thinking of it." She stood up and Ash immediately head-butted her leg, annoyed to have lost her attention. "I have to find a breed suitable for apartment living. Nothing as large and bouncy as these."

"Yeah, they like to use up every inch of the forest. If you have everything you need, I'll leave the two of you to unpack. Dinner is at seven. It's family night, so no excuses accepted. We'll catch up properly then. And we'll find you boots and skis." He left, the dogs bounding ahead, and Harriet watched them go.

"Family night?"

"The O'Neils have a rule that once a week everyone eats together, no matter what is going on and how busy they are. All of them. Grandparents. Kids. Dogs. No exceptions unless you're out of the country."

She felt something uncurl inside her. "I'm not family."

"You're with me. That counts." He picked up the cases. "I'll take these through to the bedroom."

Harriet glanced up at the shelf and felt a stab of disappointment. "That's not the bedroom?"

"It's not the master suite."

"But we could sleep there?"

"It's where I sleep when I come on my own. Do you want to sleep there?"

"Yes! How can you even ask? It's like being part of the forest."

"Then let's sleep there, but we'll keep our stuff in the main bedroom. That's where the bathroom is. Do you want to take a shower before dinner?"

"Who exactly will be at dinner?"

"Most of the family, probably. Is that a problem?" His expression changed to one of understanding. "Strangers. Dinner. Your two least favorite things. But these are good people, Harriet."

"Yes." Harriet glanced down at her black jeans and her soft sweater. "Should I dress up?"

"You look great. And that sweater looks amazing with your new short hair." He pulled her against him and brought his mouth down to hers in a kiss that almost made her wish they didn't have to go to dinner. Given the choice she would have stayed right here, in this amazing cabin, and watched the snow gently layer on the trees.

She comforted herself with the knowledge that these people had dogs. How bad could they be?

All the same, she felt nervous as they walked the short distance to the main house.

As Ethan pushed open the door that led straight into the big farmhouse kitchen, Harriet saw what felt like a million pairs of eyes turned in her direction.

Ethan closed the door, locking in the heat. "This is Harriet."

"Harriet!" A woman rose to her feet, all smiles. "I'm Elizabeth O'Neil, Ethan's godmother. My three sons, Jackson, Sean and Tyler, their grandparents Walter and Alice—"

The introductions seemed to go on and on and blurred in her head. How many people were there? Nine? Ten? Was Kayla married to Jackson or was that someone else? No, the dark-haired girl was Brenna and she was pregnant, which meant she had to be Tyler's wife. And the woman talking to herself in French while she cooked was Élise, Sean's wife. Jess, Tyler's teenage daughter, was away at a training camp...

She wished they were wearing name tags.

And she wished they weren't all looking at her.

It was her turn to say something.

"G-g-g—" The word refused to leave her mouth and she

froze. No. *No!* Why now? She felt the familiar wash of panic. The usual desire to run, but Ethan was standing behind her, his body a solid wall of protection and reassurance.

And she realized she had two choices. She could run, as she'd done that night with Ethan. She could mumble her excuses and leave and no doubt the O'Neils would be very polite about it, or she could face it and find her way through it. Running was the easy way out. Running wasn't the challenge.

Staying put and trying again, that was the challenge.

She forced herself to stand still. Forced herself to breathe and take her time.

So what if her words weren't smooth? Did it really matter? This time she was *not* walking out. She was not calling her sister. She was not going to make a vow never to walk into a room with a bunch of strangers again.

She was going to deal with the issue as best she could.

She felt Ethan's hand on her shoulder and the reassuring squeeze of his fingers.

She pushed her hair away from her face, conscious of the snow dusting her head and her shoulders. And tried again, this time starting with a different word. "It's good to meet you all."

The moment the words left her lips, she felt a rush of elation.

She'd done it.

This time, she hadn't run from the obstacle. And she discovered that an obstacle didn't seem so much of an obstacle if you knew you could get to the other side.

The two Siberian huskies, Ash and Luna, came bounding across to her, as did a small miniature poodle with the sweetest face she'd ever seen.

It leaped up at her, leaving paw prints on her black jeans.

"Maple!" It was Jackson who called the dog but Harriet bent and scooped her up.

"Are you Maple? And you live with these two big bruisers? How's that working out for you?" Her words flowed, as if her previous lack of fluency had never happened.

"It's working out just fine," Tyler drawled, "because she's the one in charge. Don't let her size fool you. She's the boss."

"It is the same in our house." Élise waved the wooden spoon she was holding. "I am smaller, but I am absolutely the boss." She eyed Sean and he gave a deceptively placid smile.

"I never argue with you when you're cooking, angel."

"Those dogs shouldn't be jumping on our guest." Elizabeth fussed but Tyler waved a hand.

"Harriet is a dog lover. She's fine."

Harriet would have agreed. She was fine. *She really was fine.*

How many things had she avoided doing in case she stammered? All those phone calls. Her issues with strangers. Most of them were tied in with her anxiety about stammering and what people thought about her.

And honestly, who *cared*?

No one, just as no one seemed to care that Élise spoke with a strong French accent.

Still holding a wriggling, ecstatic Maple, Harriet joined the O'Neils at the table. She was filled with a whole new confidence. *Challenge? What challenge?* "I spend my whole day around dogs, but sadly not my own. I've been thinking of changing that. I hadn't thought of getting a miniature poodle."

"She's a rescue. Jackson found her tied to a tree—" Tyler

reached out to help himself to bread but his mother slapped his hand.

"We have a guest."

"I know we have a guest. There are napkins on the table, which only happens when we have a guest. If napkins are a sign we can't eat, I hate them more than I did before." He closed his hand over a bread roll and his mother shook her head in despair.

"What is wrong with you?"

"Nothing is wrong with me. I'm a normal healthy male and I've been on the mountain all day expending calories like there's no tomorrow. I'm starving. If I don't eat there won't be a tomorrow. Also, if I eat I can be civil to our guest. If not, I'll be unconscious and Sean will have to resuscitate me." He tore the roll in half and spread it thickly with butter.

"What makes you think I'd resuscitate you?" Sean yawned. "For the record, I'd push your body out of the way and eat your portion. And I've been operating all day, so don't look to me for sympathy."

Sean was a doctor, Harriet remembered. Orthopedic surgeon. Jackson was the businessman.

"No one looks to you for sympathy." Tyler scowled at Sean. "You're the least sympathetic doctor on the planet. God help your patients."

"Sympathy is a wasted emotion, especially since my patients are mostly unconscious."

"They have no idea how lucky they are."

"Ignore him." Elizabeth handed Brenna a deep bowl filled with the most delicious-smelling soup.

As Elizabeth served food and Sean and Tyler continued to argue, Harriet had a chance to glance around the room. There were bunches of herbs drying above the range, surfaces gleamed and everywhere she looked there were family photographs.

She noticed that the grandmother, Alice, was knitting at the table and mostly ignoring the arguing going on around her. Everyone was relaxed and comfortable.

Family night.

She felt the hard ball of tension inside her gradually melt.

This was how it should be. Love and respect simmered in the air. It was there in the teasing, in the laughter, in the listening.

This was what she wanted. She wanted a big scrubbed kitchen table with scars that showed the passage of family life. She wanted to be surrounded by this much laughter and this much love. She wanted people to be able to disagree without fear, to voice differing opinions without animosity.

She wanted family night.

Sean and Ethan started talking about some medical development and Kayla covered her ears with her hands.

"No hospital talk at the table, Sean, that's the rule."

"All I'm saying is that I was called to the ER last week to see—"

"La la la," Kayla sang loudly, "I can't hear you."

Sean rolled his eyes and gestured to Ethan, indicating that they'd grab some time later.

The door opened again and another man entered carrying an armful of logs. He was older. In his sixties, Harriet guessed, but still handsome in a rough, outdoorsy sort of way. His hair was gray and he had the kindest eyes she'd ever seen.

Elizabeth put down the plate she'd been holding. "Tom."

The look they shared excluded everyone else in the room.

Harriet knew she should look away, but she couldn't.

When had her parents ever looked at each other like that? Never.

There was a tight feeling around her heart. A sting in her throat.

"No romance at the table." Tyler covered his eyes. "Spare us."

Did Elizabeth's sons mind that their mother was marrying again? She could see how that might be a sensitive topic for them.

"Sit down, Tom." Jackson pulled out the chair next to him. "You need to eat while there's still some food."

"Don't hold back," Sean advised. "That's the way to starvation in this family."

Tom's smile indicated he was familiar with the rules of the house. He nodded at Harriet and then turned back to Elizabeth. "I fixed the shower in the Hayloft."

The conversation continued, back and forth, switching between subjects, occasionally punctuated by the dogs.

If there was tension, it was well hidden.

She felt an almost unbearable longing. She knew what she was witnessing was precious. It was love in all its different forms. Mother to child. Grandmother to child. Man to woman. Brother to brother. Husband to wife. It was all right there, a perfect web of love.

Some people might look at a mansion and covet it. They might want to fill their closet with designer labels, or travel the world.

What Harriet coveted was right here in this room.

They drew her into the conversation, asking her about herself, about the dogs, about living in New York. After only an hour in their company, she felt more at ease than she ever had with her own family.

For these people mealtimes were something to be celebrated, a chance to get together and share stories. Despite Tyler's griping about food, napkins and visible displays of affection, it was clearly an important night for them. Nothing like her own family gatherings, which had been something to endure.

By the time she and Ethan left to return to their cabin, she felt as if she'd known the O'Neils forever.

"Lovely people." She virtually danced along the path, a feat in itself given the ice.

Ethan held her hand tightly to stop her slipping. "I don't know what's happening to you, but I love it."

"What's happening is that I nailed today's challenge. I did *not* run out the door." She punched the air with her free hand and saw that he was grinning.

"I'd say you kicked your challenge in the butt."

The moment they stepped through the door of the cabin, he caught her to him and kissed her.

"I'm proud of you. You're incredible."

She kissed him back, feeling powerful and capable of anything. *Anything.* When she lowered her hands to the zipper of his jeans, he raised an eyebrow.

"Miss Knight, are you doing what I think you're doing?"

"I am." She closed her hand around his erection and heard the breath hiss through his teeth.

"The bedroom is—"

"No." She pushed him back and they both tumbled onto the rug in front of the fire. In less than ten seconds both of them were naked. It wasn't the first time they'd made love, but it was the first time she'd been in charge.

She kissed her way down his body, taking her time to explore, allowing her mouth to roam. She couldn't remember ever feeling this way before, having this fierce craving to discover. She wasn't just discovering him. She was discovering herself, and it was a heady experience. Up until recently she'd tiptoed through life, careful not to draw attention to herself. Now, there was no more tiptoeing, and she definitely had his full attention. She went where she wanted to go. Did what she wanted to do, and what she did drew a rough sound from somewhere deep in his throat.

She felt the sudden acceleration of his heart under her hand, felt the hard muscle of his abs tighten as she moved lower and took him into the heat of her mouth. She heard his breathing grow heavy and felt a whole new powerful feeling that came from knowing what she was doing was driving him wild. He fought for breath, moaned her name and she gave and gave until his hands hauled her upward and she finally moved over him, straddling him.

In the firelight she could see the bunched muscle of his shoulders and the glitter of his eyes as he focused on her face. She knew she was flushed. She knew her hair was tangled from his hands. It didn't matter to her. It certainly didn't seem to matter to him.

Murmuring that she was beautiful, incredible, driving him crazy, he gripped her hips and entered her with a slow upward thrust that filled her completely. The sheer intensity of it stole her breath. She felt her body yield to the demands of his and the thrill of the masculine invasion made her heart race and her tummy tighten. All she was aware of was him, and the hot aching need that spread through her body.

She closed her eyes.

Sex with Ethan was an intimacy she'd never known before.

And then he started to move. He moved with a slow, relentless rhythm that sent pleasure coursing through her. With each stroke he went a little higher, a little harder, urging her close and closer to the edge until there was nothing in her mind except this. She didn't care about the past. She didn't care about the future. There was only now. And he made the most of now, driving into her until her body was screaming for more, until sensation after sensation crashed down on her and the contractions of her body rippled along his shaft, taking him with her.

Somehow, much later, they made it up to the shelf and lay together looking at the snowy forest, luminous in the moonlight.

She felt dazed. Drugged. And happier than she could ever remember feeling.

Ethan stroked her arm. "I was afraid you were going to find this evening daunting. I was worried that by putting you in a room with a large number of strangers, I wasn't being fair on you."

"It was great. And I'm glad I stammered. Falling and discovering that you can get back up is good for confidence. Right now I feel as if I can do anything."

He pulled her closer. "And now you've discovered you can do anything, what's next for Challenge Harriet?"

"No idea. But I'm tired of not doing things because I'm afraid of screwing them up. I really wanted to meet your friends. Your godmother. And I loved them. I love the O'Neils." She snuggled closer. "I can see why you come back here whenever you can."

"It's a great place. At one point I even considered getting a job here."

"In the hospital where Sean works?" She tried to imagine Ethan away from the frenetic pace of New York City. "Why didn't you?"

"I enjoy where I work. The ER in a place like this would be different."

"You mean like skiing accidents and injury by moose encounter."

"That kind of thing."

"I can't believe the whole family run this business together. It's wonderful."

"It's not as picture-perfect as you might think. Jackson gave up his job to take over the place and save it from crumbling into the dirt. He could see what needed to be done to make the place a viable business in a busy market, but his grandparents didn't want change. Jackson and Walter—they locked horns a million times when he was trying to upgrade this place. In the end he brought in Kayla. She worked for a company in Manhattan. He decided an outsider who could view the whole thing without considering the emotional elements might be the answer to the problem."

"So she stayed and never left."

Ethan grinned. "It wasn't quite as smooth as that. From what Tyler told me, Kayla was a city girl and arrived in her elegant coat and heels. Took a while for her to warm up to the place. Literally."

"But she did. And she fell in love with Jackson." It sounded perfect to her. "How did Tyler meet Brenna?"

"They virtually grew up together. Brenna lived in the village."

"And they run the ski side of things?"

"Yes. They all pulled together to make this place what it is now. For a while it didn't look as if it would happen."

"But they got there in the end. They found a way." And

that was how it should be, Harriet thought. She wasn't stupid. She didn't expect picture perfect. She never had. What she'd always dreamed about was a family who stuck together and supported one another through thick and thin, as the O'Neils had. Anyone could be there for the good bits. That was the easy part. The part that mattered, the part that really tested love, was to be there for the bad. "Do they mind that their mother is marrying again?"

"They want her to be happy. It helps that they like Tom. And he fits in well. This place has been home to him forever."

"Did you bring Alison here?" She told herself that she wasn't jealous. She was interested, that was all. She wanted to know him better and somewhere deep inside her she knew the key to understanding him was to understand what had gone wrong with his marriage.

"Once. It was too quiet for her. Not enough going on. She's a city girl. And she had no interest in skiing, so that didn't help."

"You don't talk about her very often."

"There's not much to talk about. She's my ex-wife. We tried. We failed. That's it."

He condensed it into a few short sentences. A few weeks ago she might have left it at that, but she wasn't the same person she'd been a few weeks before. "Why do you see it as failure?"

"I didn't win any awards for husband of the year." He pushed her hair away from her face. "Did I mention that I love your new haircut?"

"Good. Why do you blame yourself?"

"Because I was already married to the job. I couldn't give her the relationship she wanted."

"But didn't you meet her when she was filming you in the ER?"

"Yes."

She lifted herself onto her elbow so she could look at him. "And she fell in love with the handsome hero who saved lives."

"Maybe, but that isn't what the job is. Not really. They can make it look glamorous on TV, but the reality is something different." He lay back against the pillows, taking her with him so that they snuggled together looking at the trees beyond the wall of glass. "Growing up, my dad was my hero. He was a respected part of the community. Everywhere we went, people greeted him. Going to buy a loaf of bread from the store turned into a half-hour trip instead of the ten minutes it should have been. People would stop him and ask him things and I never saw him impatient. Never once saw him turn them away or tell them to see him in clinic hours. If someone was distressed, he was there. Time and time again, I saw him step up. When a kid went under a truck at the County Fair, when a man was beating his wife and the police wanted my dad to go with them. My dad was there. And I wanted to be exactly like him. I wanted to make a difference."

"Were you ever tempted to work in the community like him?"

"No. Because I wanted my home life to be separate. I didn't want to bump into my patients every time I left the house. My parents' marriage worked because my mother understood the man he was, and she never tried to change him, not even when she was scraping burned dinners into the garbage or hosting a dinner party by herself because my dad was out helping someone else. Of course it helped that she was a doctor too."

"Why would she try and change him?"

"Because that's what usually happens."

She asked a question that had been on her mind for a while. "How long were you and Alison together before you decided to get married?"

"A year and a half. Maybe a little longer."

"And during that time you didn't stop working?"

He frowned. "Of course not."

"So she knew exactly what your job entailed when she married you."

"Your point being?"

"She could hardly blame you for doing the job you've always done. She fell in love with you because of who you are. The job is part of who you are. Did she expect you to give it up?"

"No, but I think the reality was a bit more than she expected."

"And you blamed yourself for that?"

"I worked long hours. Unpredictable hours. That's a fact. I was unreliable. That's a fact too. I missed dinner parties, journalist functions she wanted to take me to—she told me after one of our rows that the only thing she could depend on was that I wouldn't be there for her if she needed me."

"Maybe you wouldn't have been there for her socially, but if she'd needed you in any other way you would have been there."

"You seem very sure about that."

"I am. You're loyal to your friends and your family. I've seen it. And you prioritize. But your job is important. What you do is important. I don't think you were the problem. I think the way you felt about each other was the problem. A relationship is like a jigsaw, isn't it? The pieces have to fit together if it's going to work." And her parents' relationship hadn't worked. The pieces hadn't fitted. She could see that so clearly now.

His arms tightened around her. "You know a lot considering you've never been in love."

Until now. Harriet stared into the darkness, acknowledging the truth.

She loved Ethan.

It had happened gradually, without her even noticing. Maybe she'd fallen in love with him a little that day she'd first met him in the ER. Not because of the gentle way he'd examined her ankle, but because of the questions he'd asked. He'd been determined not to let her go before he'd satisfied himself that her injuries weren't the result of any kind of abuse. That was the type of man he was. He was the type of man who would look after his sister's dog even though it was the last thing he wanted to do. A man who was determined to make a difference in the world, and who would step in front of a friend even though doing so put his own life in danger. The type of man who made friendships that lasted a lifetime, and who could indulge the devil inside himself and ski a double black diamond run.

The type of man a woman could easily fall in love with.

Whenever she'd thought about it, and she'd thought about it often, she'd imagined love would be a gentle, comforting, enveloping feeling. Like bathing in warm water or being wrapped in a blanket. She hadn't expected it to feel like this. Hadn't expected the wild intoxication that felt as if she'd inhaled an illegal substance. It made her giddy. It made her want to smile at times where no smile was warranted. When she was feeding one of the dogs or occupied by some mundane task like peeling potatoes.

This wasn't how she'd thought it would be. She'd gone on dates, hoping to find love, and had never expected to find it when she wasn't looking. And yet that was what had happened. She'd fallen in love with him piece by piece, heartbeat by heartbeat. With each glance, each touch, each conversation, she'd slid deeper. She wasn't sure if she felt ecstatic or terrified.

But she knew what his reaction would be.

He'd back off. Withdraw. Protect himself, and believe he was protecting her.

He'd end the relationship.

And she wasn't ready for that. That, she thought, was a challenge too far.

So she said nothing. Simply lay in the dark with her secret, thinking of all those times she'd thought about falling in love and wondering why she'd ever thought it would be simple.

CHAPTER TWENTY-FOUR

THE WEEK FLEW PAST, in the way time always seemed to whenever something good was happening.

To Ethan's surprise, and hers, Harriet turned out to be a natural skier.

Tyler commented that the yoga and Pilates had probably helped her balance and strengthened her core muscles, but Ethan thought it had more to do with the new determination she showed in everything she did.

In the relatively short time he'd known her, he'd seen a change in her. A big change.

She had a confidence now that had been lacking in the woman he'd first met in the emergency room. The woman who had stammered and fled from his apartment had been replaced by a woman who didn't seem much inclined to flee from anything.

Now, instead of having to force herself to meet her daily challenge, she seemed to embrace it. *Bring it on.* It was as if all those days of doing the thing she found most hard had taught her that her limits didn't lie where she'd originally thought. She'd stepped outside the walls she'd built for herself and discovered a whole new world.

He'd seen it that morning when Tyler had suggested she take the chair lift up the mountain and tackle a run that would have been beyond the scope of most beginners.

There had been a brief moment when she'd thought about it and then she'd nodded and stomped her way toward the lift in her rigid boots, carrying her skis.

He'd seen the concentration on her face, the frustration when she'd fallen in an inelegant heap, and the determination with which she'd scrambled upright again. It was as if that ski run had been in some way representative of the way she intended to live her life.

Watching her made him wonder when he'd last pushed himself out of his comfort zone.

Marriage, probably.

In a serious relationship that had demanded things of him, he'd been seriously out of his comfort zone.

When he'd come here with Alison, she'd insisted that he stay by her side in case she fell. It had taken a matter of hours for her to decide skiing was an expensive form of suicide, and after that she'd resented the time he spent skiing.

I don't even get to see you when we're on vacation.

Harriet actively encouraged him to leave her and ski with Tyler.

"It will be less embarrassing for me if you're not standing there watching." She let him haul her to her feet again after yet another fall. "I plan to go up and down this run until I can do it without falling."

In the end she persuaded him to go and he and Tyler had one of the best days skiing either of them could remember.

They skied Devil's Gully, which, Ethan reflected, probably wasn't the most sensible thing he'd ever done in his life given that most of the year his fitness was honed on machines. Pounding on a treadmill and hefting weights wasn't the same as hurling yourself off a cliff and hurtling down a slope so steep it made your thighs scream and your gut churn. For the seven minutes of hair-raising descent, he'd definitely been out of his comfort zone.

He reached the bottom of the run in the same condition he'd started it, and counted himself lucky.

"You're out of condition." Tyler grinned at him. "City life is making you soft."

Halfway through the week the rest of his family arrived. First his parents, who had booked a lodge to themselves, and then his sister, who drove up from New York with her husband and Karen, who seemed to have almost fully recovered from her ordeal.

Much to Harriet's delight, Madi was with them.

The dog greeted Ethan with an enthusiasm he knew he didn't deserve.

Maybe Harriet wasn't the only one who had changed, he thought as he dropped to his haunches to play with the dog. He'd changed too.

His mother cooked and they ate in the cabin. Several times over dinner he caught his sister watching him, and knew she had questions that no doubt she wouldn't hold back from asking.

The problem was, he didn't have answers.

His decision to invite Harriet to join him on this trip had been an impulsive one. As it turned out, it had also been a good one. She charmed everyone with her kind, quiet nature and she especially charmed the dogs. They followed her around the resort as if she were the Pied Piper.

The grilling he'd been expecting came as he and his sister washed up.

"So—" Debra thrust a dripping plate into his hands. "Is there something you need to tell me?"

"Nothing." He dried the plate and placed it back in the rack. "If you're planning an interrogation, don't waste your breath."

"I like Harriet. No, that's not true. I *love* Harriet. She is a sweet, kind, dear person. If you upset her, I will kill you."

"Are you always this protective of your dog walkers?"

"I've only ever had one dog walker—" she sent him a look "—Harriet. I don't want to ever have to replace her, so don't make me choose because I tell you now if you do that, you're history."

"Nice to know where you stand on family loyalty."

She didn't laugh. Instead, she looked troubled. "Are you going to break her heart?"

"I hope not."

"So what's going on? What are your intentions? Is this about sex and a home-cooked meal? Or is it something more?"

"I don't know what it is. I'm a man. I don't analyze everything the way you do. But it's more than sex and a home-cooked meal. And as for my intentions—" Ethan took the plate from her hands "—my intentions are to have the best possible vacation, and make sure she does too."

And if he was lucky, that was going to include lots of sex.

"And what about when you get back to New York?"

Ethan stood with the plate dripping in his hands.

He hadn't thought that far.

HARRIET CONSIDERED HERSELF to be reasonably fit, but after a week of skiing her muscles ached in places they'd never ached before. And every moment of the day had been filled with activity.

Some meals they'd eaten with his family, some with the O'Neils, and once they'd eaten in the privacy of their own cabin and then spent the rest of the evening in the hot tub watching snow layer the trees in the surrounding forest.

Tomorrow was the wedding, which meant that today was the last day and Ethan had told her he had a surprise for her.

He'd disappeared after breakfast and told her to dress in warm gear and meet him at the end of the path.

As she eased her aching limbs into her ski gear, she hoped it wasn't anything that required her to be too athletic.

She closed the door of the cabin—no one seemed to lock any doors here—and trudged through a fresh layer of snow to the gate where Ethan was waiting.

She reached the gate and stopped, staring beyond to the trail.

"You love dogs," Ethan said, "so I thought you'd love this."

"This" was a sled pulled by a dog team of eight huskies. They stamped the ground and howled and barked, impatient and excited.

Harriet felt a thrill of excitement too. "This is the best thing anyone could ever have done for me."

And the thrill she felt wasn't all a response to the dogs.

Ethan had arranged this for her. She knew there were endless activities on offer at Snow Crystal, but he'd chosen the one he knew she'd love.

Her heart gave an uneven thud.

This wasn't just thoughtful, it was—

What was it?

He introduced her to Dana, the young woman who owned the dog team, and then Harriet climbed into the sled beside Ethan and the dogs, on Dana's instructions, took off.

They weaved their way along the main trail and then Dana turned off onto a narrower trail that led directly into the stillness of the snow-covered forest. The trees stretched tall, white sentries lining the path. The overnight fall of snow had added a layer of soft powder to the groomed trail and the surface sparkled under the bright sun.

The only sounds were the rhythmic panting of the dogs and the rush of the sled as it moved through the snowy wilderness.

Cocooned in blankets, Harriet watched the dogs ahead of her and marveled at their energy and how happy they seemed. That and the raw beauty of the landscape took her breath away.

When Dana finally stopped and pulled off the trail it took Harriet a moment to catch her breath.

"This is the best thing I've ever done in my life."

Ethan smiled and helped her out of the sled. "Time for a little refreshment."

They were in a clearing and she noticed something that looked like a mountain hut.

"Where are we?"

"It's called the Chocolate Shack. And they serve great food, but they're famous for their whipped hot chocolate."

"Hot chocolate?" Harriet tried not to think of her thighs, which was almost impossible since she'd spent the week putting pressure on them while learning to ski.

"Trust me. It's delicious. And this place is great. Tyler, Jackson and I used to come here all the time."

She could understand why.

A curl of smoke rose from the chimney and a few ski-ers wrapped in warm layers were seated at tables outside, a slash of color against a background of white. The sky was Caribbean blue, the temperature arctic cold.

Despite that, Ethan picked a table outside. "Keep your coat zipped and you'll be fine."

Harriet settled herself in a chair and he was back moments later with brimming mugs topped with swirls of cream and a dusting of chocolate powder.

Dana had opted to stay with the dogs and Harriet was almost tempted to join her.

Ethan must have sensed it because he put the mug in front of her. "People ski for miles to sample Brigitte's Belgian hot chocolate. Taste it, and you'll see why." He straddled the chair next to her.

Sun glinted off his hair and Harriet noticed the group of girls at the table closest to them turn and look at him.

Ignoring it, she took a sip of her drink, tasted hot velvety sweetness and moaned.

His gaze flickered to hers, then dropped to her mouth.

In that breathless moment of unspoken intimacy, she knew he wasn't thinking about the hot chocolate. And neither was she.

He leaned forward and wiped away a drop of cream from her lips with his thumb.

The heat and the tension should have melted every last drop of snow and ice around them.

Never in her life had she felt anything like this.

She wanted to freeze time and stay in this moment forever. Blue sky and snow. The dog team waiting impatiently on the edge of the forest. Hot chocolate and Ethan.

Ethan, Ethan, Ethan.

A burst of sudden laughter from the girls at the table next to them cut through the tension and Ethan slowly pulled away and reached for his own hot chocolate.

She noticed his hand wasn't quite steady.

His dark brows met in a frown, as if he was puzzling about something and she looked away quickly, hoping that what she felt didn't show in her eyes.

Unlike her twin, she wasn't good at hiding her feelings.

And right now her feelings were overwhelming.

Did he know? Had he guessed that her feelings had changed?

And what exactly were his feelings?

He'd arranged for her to go dogsledding because he'd known she'd love it beyond anything. No one had ever done anything like that for her before.

She finished her hot chocolate, wishing that they didn't have to go back to New York. Whatever happened, it wasn't going to be like this.

"We have another hour with the dog team." His voice was casual. "After that I thought we'd go back to the cabin. As this is our last afternoon on our own, I thought we could relax."

She didn't care where she was, as long as he was there too.

"Is that an indecent suggestion?"

"Definitely." There was a wicked gleam in his eyes. "Just doing my bit to help you earn your bad-girl credentials."

Her heart pounded a little harder. She put her mug down and stood up. "So what are we waiting for?"

The rest of the sled ride was as idyllic as the first part and for a moment Harriet seriously considered giving up her job and coming to live here. She had to remind herself that she knew nothing about handling sled dogs, and that her life was in Manhattan.

And so was Ethan. He was there too.

And she was determined to make the most of their last day.

They barely made it through the door of the cabin before falling on each other.

Trying to remove ski gear wasn't easy, and there was much laughter and some swearing before finally their warm outer layers hit the floor.

He pursued her up the stairs to the shelf.

"It's still daylight."

"Good. I want to see you." He reached out, stripped off her underwear and tumbled her back onto the bed. "I love you naked. You should never wear clothes."

"You want me to show up at a wedding naked? That would be a first."

And she wasn't sure about making love in daylight. Not because she wanted to hide her body, but because it would make it harder to hide her feelings.

He buried his mouth in her neck and then followed a trail down her body, discovering secret places. Sensation swarmed though her, and she wriggled under him but his hands and his mouth were everywhere. He paid attention to every movement she made, every quiver, every tremor, every moan and every gasp. He drew out the pleasure until she was shivering and shaking with desire and then he was inside her, filling her. He surged into her, his hand beneath her bottom as he drove into her with a slow, relentless rhythm. His forehead dropped to hers and then he kissed his way to her mouth. His breathing was unsteady, his shoulders slick with sweat. She felt the rough scrape of his jaw against the sensitive skin of her throat, and then the erotic stroke of his tongue as he teased the corner of her mouth.

He demanded everything and she gave everything, not because she'd planned it that way but because she couldn't help herself. It wasn't possible to give this much and still hold back.

"I love you." The words left her lips without thought or design. She breathed the words against his neck, and then his mouth. "I love you."

She felt the tension rip through him. Felt the sudden rigidity of his shoulders as he absorbed her words. If she'd said it at another time it might have changed everything, but they were too close to the edge for him to stop now so he simply thrust deeper, drawing her closer, kissing her and smothering the words until they came together in a rush of heated pleasure.

Afterward he gathered her to him and held her tightly.

She waited for him to speak. To say something. Anything.

But he said nothing, and any secret dream she might have had that he felt the same way, that their relationship might have changed for him too, died right there and then.

HE FELT GUILTY, leaving the bed before she was even awake.

He also felt like a coward. After what she'd said to him the night before, she deserved an answer. She'd taken a risk, put her heart out there, willingly making herself vulnerable. She deserved something in return, but he had no idea what to give her. All he knew was that he couldn't give her what she wanted.

He trudged through the snow to the farmhouse, opened

the door of the kitchen and the heat hit him, melting away the cold.

It was early, but the room was filled with delicious smells of baking.

He saw bread rolls and small pastry cases. Gingerbread Santas lay in uniform rows on the cooling rack, waiting to be iced. He was transported back to a time when he and Tyler used to tumble into the kitchen, cold and elated after a day on the slopes, and eat their way through whatever treats Elizabeth had cooked.

The food and the cozy atmosphere were as much a part of his memories of Snow Crystal as the snow and the skiing.

Elizabeth was in the process of removing something from the oven. She placed it on a rack and turned.

"Ethan! You're up early."

"So are you."

"I have things to do." She pulled off her apron and gestured to the table. "Sit down. I'll make us a coffee."

And suddenly he felt guilty. It was her wedding day. The last thing she needed was his problems. "I'm disturbing you. I shouldn't have come."

"Having a chance to catch up with you is more important than anything I'm doing now."

She'd always been like that, he remembered. She'd always had time to listen.

"You shouldn't be cooking on your wedding day."

"I love to cook. I'm doing what I love. And anyway, Élise and the kitchen staff are doing most of it. So what are you doing here so early?"

"Couldn't sleep."

Elizabeth put a cup of coffee in front of him and then poured one for herself. "Do you want to talk about it?"

"What?"

"Whatever it is that has you wandering along frozen trails when the sun is barely up."

"I just—I have a problem. I haven't decided how to handle it. I thought walking might clear my head."

"And did it?"

"Not so far." He took a mouthful of coffee. "It's good. I wish we had this at the hospital."

She waited a moment and then sat down next to him, picked up the first Santa and started icing it. "How is the hospital?"

"Same as ever."

"Do you enjoy it?"

"I guess I must, or I'd be doing something else."

"Not necessarily. Sometimes we do things because that's what we've always done. We don't question it." Elizabeth placed the Santa on the rack to let the icing dry and picked up the next one. "I like Harriet. I'm guessing you do too, or you wouldn't have brought her here. Is she the reason you're awake so early?"

He put the cup down. He remembered being nine and sitting in this kitchen telling Elizabeth about his plans to be a doctor. Being sixteen and talking about a girl he liked. He loved his parents, but there were things he'd been able to tell his godmother that he would never have been able to talk about with his family.

"I shouldn't have brought her here. It was a mistake."

Elizabeth stroked icing onto the next Santa. "Why was it a mistake?"

Because she'd fallen in love with him.

"By bringing her here, I sent out the wrong signals. Harriet is a home and family person. That's what matters to her. She runs a successful business with her sister, not because she wants to conquer the world but because she loves dogs and because working with animals is something she's good at."

"I suspect conquering the world might be a little overrated." Elizabeth dipped her knife in the icing again. "There isn't one definition of success, just as there isn't one formula that will make everyone happy. The secret is to know what you want. To know what makes you happy and do it. It seems Harriet knows that. Smart woman."

"She is."

"And how about you?" Elizabeth's voice was casual. "Do you know what makes you happy?"

"I always thought it was my work that made me happy. I accepted that, which is why I haven't had a long-term relationship since Alison."

"What does work have to do with relationships?"

Ethan stared at her. "Everything."

"Since when did a person have to choose between work and a relationship? Is there a law I didn't know about? Or has Harriet issued you with an ultimatum?"

"No!" He frowned. "Harriet would never do something like that. She's not an ultimatum kind of person."

"Then what's the problem?"

He thought about everything they'd shared the night before. "She told me she loves me."

Elizabeth put the knife down. "Just to clarify, the bad news is that a warm, smart, kind, incredibly lovely woman loves you?"

He eyed her, feeling like a jerk. "It's not as simple as it sounds. I enjoy her company. I like being with her, that's true. But—" He picked up one of the gingerbread Santas and stared down at it. "I never should have started this, but I didn't expect it to get so serious so fast. And now I have to find a way to unravel it without hurting her badly."

"Why would you want to unravel it?"

"Because it has no future."

"Are you sure about that? You don't feel the same way? You don't love her?"

He waited a beat. "No."

"Are you sure? Because watching you together I thought—" Elizabeth put the iced gingerbread back on the rack. "Ignore me."

"You're thinking that I love her too, but I don't. Honestly? I think there's something missing inside me—" He put the gingerbread down untouched. "I don't feel deeply anymore. I taught myself to switch off and detach and now I can't switch it back on again. And Harriet deserves more than that."

"So you're not making this decision for you, you're making it for her? Why don't you let her decide what she needs?"

"I don't want to see her hurt."

"I've known you since you were a little boy and you've always been the same. Always first there to save anything injured or damaged." Elizabeth reached across the table and took his hand. "I knew when I gave you your first Superman costume that you were going to try and save the world."

"Yeah, well even Superman struggled to save the world and have a relationship. Relationships are complicated."

"Anything that involves people is complicated. That doesn't mean we should walk away. Have you talked to her about it?"

"No." And he realized that while Harriet was constantly

forcing herself to face challenges head-on, his own approach was less impressive.

He'd walked out.

Elizabeth smiled. "It seems to me, an honest conversation would be a good place to start."

"You're right." He stood up, gave her a hug and walked out of her kitchen.

No matter how hard it was for him to say, and how hard it was for Harriet to hear, he needed to be honest.

Challenge Ethan.

HARRIET WOKE FEELING EXHAUSTED. She'd lain awake for half the night, thinking about what she'd said, and finally fallen asleep as the first fingers of light had poked their way through the trees.

The bed next to her was empty and cold, indicating that Ethan was long gone. For a moment she wondered if he'd packed and left, but then she saw his things strewn around the shelf.

She flopped back against the pillow, staring at the trees.

Way to go, Harriet. How to drive a man out into a blizzard.

He seemed to think that what he did, who he was, wasn't compatible with love and family life. He blamed himself. Felt responsible. She disagreed, but it wasn't what she thought that mattered.

You couldn't make someone love you. That wasn't how it worked. And a relationship between two people whose feelings were unevenly matched could only ever end in disaster. Feelings became a fault line, which would crack under pressure.

All her life she'd wanted love. To suddenly find it and know that it wasn't returned was the most exquisite agony.

Was this how her father had felt? Had he lived through every day knowing that his deeply felt emotions weren't returned? How hard must that have been to deal with?

It wasn't an excuse, but it was an explanation.

Harriet realized there could have been any number of reasons why her father hadn't loved her. Maybe she reminded him too much of her mother, the woman he loved so deeply and who didn't love him back. Maybe loving deeply had hurt him so badly that he'd been afraid to love again, even a child. She didn't know his reasons but what she did know was that his reasons had nothing to do with her. She wasn't responsible for the fact that his feelings for her weren't what she wanted them to be. If she could have gone back in time and spoken to the child she'd been then, she would have told her to stop trying so hard to please other people. She would have told her that life was hard enough without twisting yourself into knots trying to be someone you weren't, or trying to live up to some ridiculous standard that you weren't part of making.

Deciding that she was going to attend Elizabeth's wedding even if she had to go by herself, she took a shower and dressed in the outfit she'd bought for the occasion. It was a wool dress with a high neck and narrow sleeves. It had looked good the first time she'd tried it on in the store, but now she'd had her hair cut it looked fantastic.

Ethan appeared as she was wrapping the gift she'd bought.

From the way he was dressed, it seemed that he'd been skiing.

"I'm sorry I disappeared early—" He closed the door

against the blast of cold air and she smiled at him, forcing down all the emotions that tumbled inside her. Those emotions weren't his problem. They were hers.

"It's your vacation," she said. "Of course you want to ski. Was it fabulous out there?"

He shrugged off his coat, his gaze fixed on her face as if he was trying to work out what was going on. "Perfect powder. And now I have less than eight minutes to get ready for the wedding."

Which gave them no time for conversation.

And maybe that had been his plan.

Harriet looked at the snow clinging to his dark hair, the roughness of his jaw, the incredible blue of his eyes. She loved him so much it was hard to look at him and not want to tell him.

"It's the perfect day for a wedding, and it's not like we have far to go." The wedding was taking place at Snow Crystal. A small wedding with family and friends in one of the barns on the resort.

It was a five-minute drive away, but they made it in good time.

Elizabeth and Tom stood side by side, hand in hand, exchanging vows they'd written themselves.

Watching them together, Harriet thought about all the time she'd wasted wishing her family could have been different. Her family would never have been any different. To build something strong, you needed solid foundations and her parents had lacked that solid foundation of love.

It didn't matter what she felt for Ethan. It didn't matter how much she loved him. If he didn't return those feelings, then that was the end of it.

She wouldn't build a future on anything less than solid foundations. She didn't want that.

Back in the cabin, she packed her things, vowing that she'd come back to this beautiful place again one day, even though Ethan wouldn't be there.

She'd bring Fliss, and maybe Daniel and Molly. Maybe they could book a few cabins and invite her friends Matilda and Chase. Maybe Susan would come.

And they'd definitely go dogsledding.

Her love might not have a future, but life hadn't ended.

As she dragged her case into the living room, she saw Ethan standing there.

"Have you been waiting for me?" She let go of the case. "I'm all done. Ready whenever you are."

His gaze held hers. "We didn't get much of a chance to talk today."

"It was a wonderful day. I've never seen two people so happy."

"I wanted to talk about us. About last night."

She could have pretended not to know what he meant, but what was the point of that? "It's okay, Ethan. We don't have to talk about it."

"It's not okay." He spoke softly. "I didn't say what you wanted me to say, I know that. You're a wonderful person, Harriet—"

Oh no, not that!

Horror rippled through her. "Please—" She lifted her hand. "Spare us both the awkwardness. We do *not* have to discuss this."

"I think we do."

"Discussing it is a choice, and I choose not to."

"I'm not the perfect man, Harriet. I'm so far from the perfect man."

She stared at him, bemused. Was that what he thought? That she'd fallen in love with some false image of him? "I know you're not perfect. How could you be? There is no such thing as perfect. Strengths and weaknesses are as much a part of being human as the bones, blood and muscle you deal with every day. And here's the thing—I don't want perfect, Ethan." *Oh what the hey, she might as well say it one more time.* What did she have to lose that she hadn't already lost? "I didn't fall in love with you because I thought you were perfect. I fell in love with you for a million other reasons."

He looked pale and tired. "I like you, Harriet. I like you a lot. I care about you."

All good words, but not the one word she needed.

"I know. You don't have to explain."

"Everything has happened so fast—"

"Yes." She was surprised by how calm she felt. "Yes, it has."

"When we get back to New York we should spend more time together, and—"

"No." The word came out sharper than she intended, maybe because she was panicking. Spend more time together? Not in this lifetime. "Once we're back in Manhattan, we won't see each other again."

He looked bemused. "But you said—"

"I said that I love you, and I do. But you don't love me, and I'm not going to be one of those people who stays around in the hope it will happen, losing a little part of myself every day. I won't fight for your love, Ethan. I did that once before with my father, and I'm never doing it again. If someone can't love me the way I am, then it's not enough for me."

"Wait a minute—" He looked shocked. "You're ending it? That isn't what I want. I still want to see you—"

"That isn't going to work for me. If there is one thing living with my father taught me, it's that expecting someone to love you back just because you love them, is a shortcut to misery. It took me a long time to accept that my father didn't love me, and never would. A long time to stop trying to force myself into being a person I thought he might like more. These past weeks, with you, I've been me for the first time in my life. And I want to carry on being me. If we carry on seeing each other I'll be twisting myself into knots trying to get you to love me. And you'll be feeling guilty that you don't, and anything that develops from there will be shaky and unreliable. I can't do that to either of us."

"Harriet—"

"It's okay." She managed a smile. "Really. You can't choose who you love, but you can choose to be honest about it. You've been honest and I appreciate that. But I hope you understand when I tell you I can't see you anymore. I'd start to want things. Hope for things. And don't think for one moment that I regret any of this, because I don't. I've learned a lot over the past few weeks. You taught me how to be more relaxed on a date. Being with you has boosted my confidence. Being with you has taught me I have so many more resources at my disposal than I thought I had."

"Because I made you nervous. I made you stammer."

"And because of that I learned that stammering wasn't the end of the world. Life carries on." And her life would carry on. And at some point, hopefully, her heart would stop feeling as if it had shattered into pieces, each one inscribed with Ethan's name.

Knowing what she had to do, she picked up her case and walked to the door, her heart aching and her legs shaking, and realized that of all the challenges she'd set herself over the past few months, nothing came close to this one.

She was walking away from love.

That, she thought, was the biggest challenge of all.

CHAPTER TWENTY-FIVE

SHE ARRIVED BACK at her apartment to find the door ajar.

Great.

She'd been looking forward to a good session of wallowing in her own misery and now she had an intruder to deal with.

Misery turned to anger. This was her home. Her *home*. Someone else didn't get to break into it and take her things. That wasn't right.

Dragging a bottle of perfume out of her bag, she kicked open the door.

"If you're planning on taking something that doesn't belong to you, you picked the wrong day and the wrong woman."

Fliss flew off the sofa and Harriet stared at her sister, the perfume in her hand.

"What are you doing here?"

It was hard to know which of them was more surprised.

Fliss stopped too. Her jaw dropped. "Your *hair*!"

Harriet dropped the perfume and they flung their arms round each other, laughing and talking at the same time.

Fliss was the first to pull away, but only so that she could take a closer look at Harriet.

"I would never have dared have mine cut that short. It looks fantastic. We look so different."

We are different, Harriet thought. *Always have been.* But it was only now that she was starting to appreciate those differences. "I've stopped trying to be like you."

"If you were about to clock me with a heavy object, you're more like me than you think." Fliss picked up the abandoned perfume bottle. "What were you going to do with this? Make sure your intruder smelled good before you killed him? Nothing more guaranteed to dampen the Christmas spirit than the scent of rotting corpse."

Harriet grinned, ridiculously pleased to see her sister. "What are you doing here? Tomorrow is Christmas Eve. You're supposed to be on your way to stay with Seth's family."

"I wanted to see you. When you sent me that text saying that you'd broken up with Ethan I couldn't possibly go away and leave you alone over Christmas."

Harriet felt a rush of warmth. Ethan's family circle might be larger than hers, but there was nothing in the world, *nothing*, that came close to the sheer good fortune of having a twin.

"I appreciate you showing up here, but I'm fine." She retrieved her suitcase from outside the apartment and pushed the door shut.

"How can you be fine? You haven't said much, which I hate by the way, but I really had the impression you were in love with him."

"I am in love with him." Harriet hauled her suitcase through to the bedroom, wondering if it was ever going to get easier to say that. "But he doesn't love me." She glanced at her sister, who was still standing in the middle of the living room watching her.

There was anxiety in Fliss's eyes. "You've not been together that long. Maybe in time he'd—"

"No." Harriet said it firmly. "Don't do that. Don't say that. You're trying to make me feel better, but kidding myself that one day he might return my feelings isn't helpful. Trust me."

"I get it. I do. You don't want to be like Mum and Dad."

Hearing the shake in her sister's voice, Harriet discovered she wasn't as fine as she'd thought she was. "Do you mind if we don't talk about this?"

"Usually you like to talk about things that are bothering you."

"I'm getting better at handling them by myself. Where is Seth?"

"He had to do some last-minute shopping. You know what men are like with gifts." Fliss walked toward her. "You don't have to handle everything by yourself. I may not still be living here, but I'm still your sister. Your twin. And your business partner. I'm only a phone call away."

"I know that. And of course I'll call if I need to." Harriet hugged her. "But I like knowing I can handle it. It gives me a sense of security, knowing I can handle it. And speaking of the business, I've decided that if you want to add dog sitting into the mix for established clients we know and trust, then I'm on board with that."

Fliss pulled away. "Seriously? Because you didn't think you could handle that."

"That was then and this is now. I can handle it."

Fliss hugged her again. "I'm so proud of you. You're strong and smart and amazing. I came here expecting you to be a mess. Finally you fell in love, and—sorry, sorry. I'm not talking about it."

"I am a mess. Truly, I feel completely and utterly crap."

"Never heard you say 'crap' before."

"Lately I've said a lot of things I've never said before." Like *I love you*. "Right now I don't feel strong or smart. I feel really bad, but I'll handle it. This is just another obstacle and that's what life is all about. It's a series of obstacles." She pulled away from Fliss and walked across the room to switch on the Christmas tree lights. "Over Thanksgiving I decided I was going to force myself to do a challenge a day and I planned to end that at Christmas."

"You're not ending it?"

Harriet lit the candles she kept around the living room, thinking how much she loved her apartment. "For years I've been thinking 'if only I was more like Fliss,' or 'if I was braver life would be easier,' but every day brings challenges and obstacles, and you can either dodge them or deal with them. For years I dodged them. I chose to take the route with no obstacles. No way was I going to make that awkward phone call, or stand up to clients when they were rude because that made me feel uncomfortable. I dodged and I hid behind you and Daniel and thanks to you I lived a safe, protected life."

"And then we both abandoned you." Fliss looked stricken.

"You didn't abandon me. You're living your lives, which is how it should be. And you moving out is the best thing that has happened to me."

The anxiety faded from Fliss's eyes. "Should I be offended?"

"No. If you'd stayed I probably would have carried on taking the easy road. The one with no obstacles. But a road without obstacles is a parking lot and I don't want to live my life in a parking lot. Am I brokenhearted about Ethan?" She stood for a moment, feeling the heaviness in her chest and the lethargy that threatened to send her to bed for a month. "Yes. In fact I am. And later, once you've gone, I'm going to cry until my face looks like a tomato and bake a large batch of chocolate chip cookies, which I will probably eat all by myself."

Fliss stared at her. "You don't look brokenhearted."

"The damage is on the inside."

"You're hurting, and I can't bear it. I want to go down to the ER and punch Dr. Hot so hard he needs to practice medicine on himself."

"It's not his fault."

"What will you do?"

It was a question she hadn't even dared ask herself. "I don't know. What I always do. Walk dogs. Bake cookies. See my friends. Keep going and hope that one day I wake up and find it's not hurting anymore."

Fliss sniffed. "So you're okay then?"

Harriet thought about Ethan. "No," she said. "But I will be."

She'd already decided to get a dog. It was ridiculous that she loved dogs so much and didn't have one of her own. True, it meant that she was free to do things like dog sit at a moment's notice and foster animals when the animal shelter needed her help, but it also meant she didn't have a dog of her own. And she wanted one. She wanted a dog of her own.

And she was going to find a way to make that work.

SHE SPENT THE whole of Christmas Eve cooking.

The apartment was filled with the smells of baking and when she finally fell into bed, she was exhausted.

It was the first time she'd woken up to an empty apartment on Christmas Day.

For a moment she wished she'd accepted Fliss's invitation to join them.

What was so great about spending Christmas without your family? Was she suddenly some sort of martyr? This wasn't a challenge, it was just plain stupid.

She was wondering whether this might be the craziest thing she'd ever done, when Susan arrived. She was wearing a red sweater with black jeans and clutching an armful of parcels.

"I'm early, but I thought you might need help in the kitchen. Okay, I'm lying. I didn't want my own company anymore. I'm driving myself insane."

Harriet had never been more pleased to see anyone. "I'm so glad you're here. You have no idea. Come in. How are you feeling?"

"It's possible I will live. Thanks to your chicken soup." Susan put her parcels under the tree and then took a closer look at Harriet. "Dammit, what the hell happened to you? The man is an idiot. I need to scan his brain."

"Excuse me?"

"You're here on your own, you're pale and you obviously didn't sleep last night. Assuming that bout of insomnia wasn't caused by excitement over Christmas, it can only be about Ethan. Where is he?"

"I don't know. At work I assume."

Susan scowled. "You had a week together in a log cabin

in a forest. That should have been romance central. What went wrong?"

"Nothing." Harriet returned to her cooking, hoping they could move away from this subject. "We had a wonderful week. Everything went right."

"If everything had gone right, you wouldn't be on your own here now."

Harriet shook her head. "Can we talk about something else?"

"In a minute. When we're done talking about this. Does he know you love him?"

Harriet gave a crooked smile. She didn't bother asking how Susan had guessed. "I'm not one to hide my feelings so the answer to that is yes. But it's not mutual."

"If that's true then the man doesn't just need a scan, he needs surgery."

"You can't force someone to love a person."

"Mmm." Susan frowned. "You've never seen what I can achieve with a scalpel in my hand."

Harriet winced. "Promise me you won't say anything to him."

"Can't promise that." Susan wandered into the kitchen. "Any of that delicious coffee on offer?"

Harriet made her a coffee and handed her a tin. "Chocolate chip cookie?"

"Are you sure you can spare one?" Susan took the lid off the tin. "Holy smokes. How many people are coming today? The entire population of Manhattan?"

"Just you and Glenys."

Susan stared into the tin. "So by a rough calculation, I reckon that's about four thousand cookies each. What happened?"

"I may have gotten a little carried away yesterday. Baking cheers me up."

"Well, don't apologize for that." Susan took two cookies out of the tin. "I'm here for you. Anything you need, even if it requires me to consume my body weight in sugar."

Harriet managed a laugh but she had no idea how. Her whole body felt heavy. She was pretending she was coping well but the truth was she felt awful. Lethargic. Sad. And it hadn't even been forty-eight hours yet. "Tell me about you. Have you been in much pain?"

"No." The shadows under Susan's eyes told a different story. "They think I should be back at work mid-January. I'm starting physical therapy next week."

Glenys arrived with Harvey, having taken a cab the few blocks from her apartment. She and Susan immediately bonded and Harvey made himself at home in Harriet's apartment.

They swapped gifts, and Harriet served lunch and tried not to think about Ethan and what he was doing. Glenys and Susan were good company and Harriet was relieved that they were there.

"One more game of Scrabble," she announced, a few hours later. "Festive Scrabble this time. Only words relating to the holidays are allowed. And it's only fair to warn you about my competitive streak and my killer instinct."

"Killer instinct? You?" Glenys glanced at Susan, who shook her head quickly.

"You go, girl."

They were almost at the end of the game when there was a knock on the door.

"ALCOHOL is not a Christmas word." Glenys waggled her finger. "It doesn't count."

"Try working in the ER on Christmas Day. Alcohol is definitely a Christmas word. It's your turn, Harriet," Susan said. "I'll get the door." She walked to the door and pulled it open while Harriet made a word out of her own letters.

"FESTIVE." She put the letters down carefully. "And on a triple word score. Take that! You'll never catch me now. You might as well surrender."

Realizing that Susan wasn't responding in her usual way—in fact she wasn't responding at all—Harriet glanced across to the door. "Who is it?"

"It's Santa," Susan said faintly.

"Very funny."

"He has a gift for you."

"If this is an elaborate trick to distract me so that you can switch my letters when I'm not looking, it's too late. I've already won." Harriet took a last look at the board before going to the door. "I assume it's a charity thing—"

She stared at the tall, broad-shouldered Santa standing in her doorway. "Ethan? What are you—" She swallowed. "Why are you dressed as Santa?" And then she realized why, and what it meant, and her heart swelled in her chest. "You did it. You agreed to dress as Santa for the kids. Why? What changed your mind?"

"Someone once told me that they always do the one thing they don't want to do. I thought it sounded like a good idea."

"So this is Challenge Ethan?"

"Maybe. And I kept the costume on, because no one can turn away Santa, right?"

"Manipulative," Susan muttered and Ethan reached into the sack he was carrying and handed her a gift.

"This seems to have your name on it."

"Bribery is not going to work." But Susan took the gift from his hands. "Or maybe it will. Possibly."

Harriet was too busy thinking through the implications. He'd agreed to be Santa. Whatever part of him had thought he was too cynical to be Santa, he'd put it aside. Buried it. "Were they thrilled? Or were they too sick to be happy?" She hated thinking about the kids in hospital on Christmas Day. But at least they'd had a visit from Santa.

"They were all pretty happy to see me, you were right about that."

"Do you want to come in?" Her mind was racing with a thousand questions. *Why are you here? How have you been?*

He stepped inside and peeled off his beard. "Ouch."

Susan covered her eyes. "Carry on like this and you'll have me thinking that Santa isn't real."

"He's real, but right now he's overheated." He smiled at Glenys. "I'm interrupting your game. I apologize."

Without the beard, Harriet was able to take a closer look at him and realized he looked exhausted. As if he hadn't slept in days.

"Don't apologize. Harriet just thrashed us both and Susan and I were about to leave, weren't we, Susan?" Glenys was on her feet and whistling for Harvey.

"I was about to leave, but now I think it might be more entertaining to stay." Susan sent Ethan a look. "You'd better be about to say something worth hearing."

"I'm not going to be saying anything while you're standing there."

Susan grumbled and picked up her coat. "Make her cry and I'll hunt you down and fillet you."

"I've missed you at work. No one abuses me the way you do. Please come back soon."

Susan hesitated and then stood on tiptoe and kissed his cheek. "I plan to."

Glenys took Susan's arm. "Share a cab, Doctor?"

"Sounds good to me."

"Wait. You're both leaving?" Harriet felt a lurch of anxiety. She had no idea why Ethan was here, but she wasn't sure she wanted to be left alone.

"Thank you for a wonderful Christmas." Susan hugged her and so did Glenys.

"Best Christmas ever, although I may never forgive you for getting FESTIVE on a triple word score." They left, and suddenly she was alone with Ethan.

She wondered how it was, after all the intimacies they'd shared, she could feel awkward and uncomfortable being in the same room as him. "Have you eaten? Can I fetch you something?" She wanted to ask why he was so tired, but knew she shouldn't be asking questions that personal.

"Later. First there are things I need to say to you." He took her hands and pulled her against him. "That night in the cabin when you told me you loved me, you scared me."

"I know. You felt a responsibility to love me back, but—"

"I do love you back, and it has nothing to do with responsibility."

She stared at him, wondering if she'd heard him correctly. "But you said—"

"I know what I said and when I said it, I believed it. When it comes to relationships, you've set the bar high. I was afraid I couldn't be what you wanted me to be."

"Oh, Ethan—" Her eyes filled. "I've only ever wanted you to be who you already are. I don't want a fake version of you. I want you."

"I know. I've had time to think about that, and other things. Like how much I love you."

"Really? You were sure that you didn't have those feelings." She felt shaky and unsteady. "How do you know?"

"Over the years I've learned to switch off my emotions. It's almost become easy for me. I thought that was why my marriage didn't work. I thought that was why I couldn't give any relationship what it needed. When you ended it, I told myself I'd switch off what I was feeling, same as I always have. But it didn't happen. That was when I realized that what we have is nothing like any relationship I've had before. My feelings are nothing like I've ever experienced before."

"Ethan—"

"What I feel for you is too powerful to be buried. And it's certainly too powerful to be ignored. I know, because I tried."

She lifted her hand and touched his cheek. "Is that why you look so awful?"

"Turns out I don't sleep well when you're not in my life." He cupped her face in his hands. "You're not the sort of person who switches love on and off, so I'm assuming I'm not too late?"

She stared into his eyes, hardly able to believe this was real.

"Of course not. I love you."

He groaned and pulled her against him. "I love you too. I want to be your forever family, or whatever it is you call it when you find permanent homes for those animals you foster."

Forever family.

Merry Christmas, Harriet.

Her throat thickened and she leaned her head against his chest. "I want that too."

"Are you sure? You said you knew my strengths and weaknesses. I want to make sure that you do, because I'm not easy to live with. There will be days when I'm so focused on working I'll forget to call home."

She lifted her head and smiled. "I already know that. I know *you*. But while we're confessing all, you should probably know that I intend to get a dog. Are you okay with that?"

"Funny you should say that," he said, his tone conversational, "because my Christmas gift to you is going to be a puppy but I thought that, given you're the dog expert, you'd prefer to choose it yourself."

"We'll do it together." She slid her arms round his neck. "We'll go to the shelter and find a dog that needs a home."

He kissed her and it was at least five minutes before she was able to speak again.

"I'm glad you decided to be Santa."

"You do something you find hard every day. I figured that the least I could do was give this a try. It worked, I think." He looked pleased with himself. "I was a hit with the kids."

"I never doubted you would be."

"And it occurs to me that I had something to give all of them, but nothing to give you." He smoothed his hand over her hair. Kissed her mouth. "I came rushing over here because I couldn't wait another moment to talk to you. I don't have a ring. I don't have anything. All I brought is the promise of a puppy. This is not the romantic proposal you deserve."

"Are you kidding?" She almost choked on the words. "You're giving me love. That's the best gift of all."

"Are you sure?"

"If you know me as well as I think you do, then you know I'm sure." Her heart felt full. "Ethan, you brought yourself. The only thing that matters is that you're here. That you came. That you love me."

He wrapped her tightly in his arms. "So what's the next challenge?"

She leaned her head against his chest, breathing him in, feeling her future opening up like a bright shining path. There would be obstacles at some point, she knew that. But she also knew she'd deal with them. "I don't know what's next. But what I do know is that when you love someone, and they love you back, everything seems like less of a challenge." And she knew that wherever life took them, they were going there together.

* * * * *

THANK YOU

THANKS AND BIG hugs to my talented editor Flo Nicoll, who has worked with me for the past four and a half years and who always pushes me and demands the very best. This is our twelfth book together and I like to think we're a perfect team.

It takes a village to put a book on the shelves and I'm always nervous of thanking people individually because I will miss someone out, but my thanks go to everyone at HQ in the UK and HQN in the US. I'm so grateful to everyone for all the thought and effort they put into making sure my books reach readers. It's a tough job and they do it brilliantly.

My agent, Susan Ginsburg, is simply the best. I don't know where I'd be without her invaluable advice and input.

After three books with a large cast of dogs as secondary characters, I was struggling to find names so my thanks to all my patient and enthusiastic readers on Facebook who kindly contributed.

A special mention to Natalie Smith, who bid to name a character in this book to raise funds for the wonderful charity CLIC Sargent, whose work helps support children and young people with cancer. Natalie, your generosity is much appreciated and I hope you like "Nat."

My family and friends are endlessly supportive. Thanks to Joe, Ben and Kim for valiantly tasting batch after batch of chocolate chip cookies as I worked to perfect Harriet's recipe. Your dedication to the cause is appreciated. Now get back to the gym!

I owe the biggest debt of gratitude to my readers who continue to buy my books, thus ensuring I can continue with my dream job, writing them. Thank you. You're the best.

Sarah
xxx

Lauren's picture-perfect life is built on a secret she's worked hard to hide for years, a secret her teenage daughter has just discovered.

Jenna secretly longs for a family, but knows she must rebuild her relationship with her mother first.

Nancy knows the time has come to reveal her secret pain to her daughters...

A family built on secrets. A summer spent together. Their perfect chance to find hope, forgiveness and love.

Turn the page for a sneak peek of the captivating and emotional new book from Sarah Morgan, available in spring 2018!

ON HER QUEST to make a romantic dinner, Jenna stopped at the store on her way home and bought food. It always took a while because she bumped into so many people she knew. The sense of community was one of the things she loved about living on Martha's Vineyard. It was also one of the things she hated. Like today, for example, when she wasn't feeling sociable. She was still wound up after her encounter with her mother and wasn't in the mood for small talk.

It was unlikely she'd make it through a shopping trip without having at least three lengthy conversations, but that didn't mean she couldn't try.

She kept her head down and didn't look at anyone.

"Jenna? *Jenna!* I thought it was you."

Surrendering to her fate, Jenna glanced up from the apples. "Hi, Sylvia."

She'd been at school with Sylvia, but their lives had diverged. Jenna had gone off to college and Sylvia had stayed on the island and proceeded to pop out children as if she was on a personal mission to increase the number of year-rounders (personally Jenna was relieved to see half the population decamp to warmer climates in the winter months. The roads were clearer, the beaches were empty and you didn't have to stand in line for ages at the bakery).

Jenna put field greens, tomatoes and bell peppers into her basket. "How are the children?" Why had she asked that question? There were six kids. She could potentially be here for hours. The Denton family could make up a class by themselves.

Six kids?

Where was the fairness in that? Not that Jenna wanted six. She wasn't greedy.

If she could just have one she would never complain again.

She only half listened as Sylvia talked about the stress of ferrying the children from piano lessons, swimming lessons, art class and football.

"Time you and Greg started a family," Sylvia said, as if producing babies was simply something Jenna might have forgotten to do in the day-to-day pressure of living their lives.

Jenna fingered an overripe tomato, wondering whether the pleasure of pulping it against Sylvia's perfect white shirt would outweigh the inevitable fallout.

Probably not. That was the downside of being a teacher. Islanders would no doubt decide that someone with so little self-control wasn't fit to have responsibility for impressionable minds.

Regretfully she dropped the tomato into her basket with the others, made a vague comment about being busy and then imagined how Sylvia might interpret that. If she wasn't careful it would be all round the whole island that she and Greg were too busy to have sex.

"Greg and I love being just the two of us." She pinned a dreamy look on her face, hoping she wasn't overcompensating. "I'm cooking a romantic dinner."

"I envy you," Sylvia said. "If Mike and I want to be romantic we have to pay a babysitter. And he and I only have to look at each other for me to get pregnant, so I daren't touch him. He's quite the superstud."

Mike was a mild mannered, overweight accountant who left the talking to his wife in most social situations. The idea of him as a "Superstud" challenged even Jenna's overactive imagination.

She resisted the temptation to ask Sylvia if she had any sex secrets that might increase the chances of conception. She was too afraid of hearing the details.

"I must get home. Dinner to cook." She grabbed a bottle of wine and then hesitated. Did wine have a negative effect on fertility? Maybe. On the other hand, it was excellent for encouraging relaxation and there was no doubt they both needed a hefty dose of that.

She left the wine in the basket.

After her earlier encounter with her mother she needed it.

"By the way," Sylvia's voice was casual, "I was driving through Edgartown half an hour ago and I happened to see a pickup truck parked outside your mother's house. Guess who was driving it? Scott Rhodes." She glanced over her shoulder and spoke in an undertone, as if the mere mention of that name might be enough to get her arrested. "He looked as bad and dangerous as ever. I swear the man never smiles. What is his problem? I didn't know he knew your mom."

She hadn't known, either.

What was he doing calling on her mother? And if Sylvia had seen him half an hour ago then that meant Jenna must have missed him by minutes.

Scott Rhodes?

She remembered the summer she'd first seen him. He'd been working on a boat when she and Lauren had walked to the harbor to pick something up for their mother. He'd been stripped to the waist and across the powerful bulk of his shoulders she'd seen the unmistakable mark of a tattoo. That tattoo had fascinated her. Her mother wouldn't even allow her to have her ears pierced, and yet this man openly flaunted the ink on his skin.

She frowned. *Flaunted* wasn't the right word. On the contrary, he appeared supremely indifferent to the opinions of others and that, to Jenna, had been the coolest thing of all.

As someone who was constantly being reined in (*don't do that, Jenna; don't say that, Jenna*) she'd always felt envious of his complete disregard toward the opinion of his fellow man. Take this conversation for example. She couldn't imagine Scott Rhodes stopping to have a conversation with someone unless he wanted to.

She, on the other hand, did things like that all the time. *Hi, Angela, great to see you* (not great at all in fact), *Hi, Elise, of course I'd love to come to your fund-raising supper* (I'd rather pull my eyelashes out). She sometimes felt as if she was trapped in a web of other people's expectations. Scott Rhodes, however, answered to no one but himself and she envied that. There was something deliciously dangerous and forbidden about him. Even looking at him made her feel as if she was doing something she shouldn't, as if by stepping into his space you made a statement about yourself. About who you were. Danger by association. She expected to feel her mother's hand close over her shoulder any moment.

Not that she'd been *that* interested. Not really. She was in love with Greg and had been her whole life. Greg, who she knew so well he almost seemed like an extension of her. Greg, who smiled almost all the time.

Scott Rhodes didn't seem to smile at all. It was as if he and life were on opposing sides.

While she'd been watching that day he'd paused to wipe the sweat from his brow and she noticed that his forearm was strong, deeply tanned and dusted with dark hairs. He had the same dark hair on his chest and she was studying it with rapt attention (Greg's chest was smooth) when he glanced up and caught her looking. There was no smile, no wink, no suggestive gaze. Nothing. He was inscrutable. When his attention had shifted from her to Lauren she'd felt a sense of relief, as if she'd somehow escaped from making a mistake of monumental proportions. After a few seconds he'd turned back to the boat as if neither of them existed.

Jenna remembered nudging Lauren. "That guy is super hot."

"What guy? I didn't notice."

Jenna had wondered at the time why her sister would lie about that. And she *had* lied, she was sure of that. Not just because every passing female had noticed Scott, but because Lauren had answered a little too quickly.

Scott never stayed on the island for long. No one ever knew where he went or when he'd be returning. As he'd never been the sort to grow roots or drop anchor, no one expected him to stick around.

And he never stayed on the island itself. He slept on his boat, anchored offshore.

Why would Scott Rhodes be visiting her mother?

That promised to be an interesting conversation.

Hi, Mom, I hear you had the devil on your doorstep...

Aware that Sylvia was still waiting for a response, Jenna shrugged. "My mother knows everyone on the island. And she still plays a role in the yachting community. Scott knows boats."

Sylvia nodded. "That's probably it." It was obvious that she didn't think that was the reason at all, and neither did Jenna.

It nagged at her as she drove the short distance home, enjoying the last of the daylight.

The cottage she shared with Greg between Chilmark and the fishing village of Menemsha had a view of the sea from the upstairs windows and a little garden that frothed with blooms in the summer months.

It was, in her opinion, the perfect place to raise a child.

She pushed that thought aside along with all the questions she had about Scott Rhodes, and parked her car.

In the summer this part of the island teemed with tourists, but in the winter months you were more likely to see eiders congregating near the jetties, riding the current and sheltering behind fishing boats. The sky was cold and threatening and the wind managed to find any gaps in clothing.

Jenna fumbled her way into the house, grateful for the warmth.

She lit the wood burning stove in the living room, unpacked the shopping and started cooking.

She made a chicken casserole from scratch (beef was Greg's favorite but she'd read somewhere that red meat reduced fertility), threw together a salad and set the table.

Then she tidied the cottage, took a shower and changed

into a wool dress she'd bought to wear at Christmas two years before. It had looked good on her then. It didn't look so good now. It clung in places it wasn't supposed to cling. Had she really put on that much weight? She was going to eat less, she really was. She was going to stop baking. Do more exercise. Try and get a bikini body by the summer. In the meantime she needed to order some of that control underwear.

She dragged the dress over her head, stuffed it in the back of the wardrobe along with all the other clothes that didn't fit and instead pulled on her favorite pair of stretchy jeans and a sweater Greg had bought for her birthday. It was a pretty shade of blue shot with silvery thread and it fell soft and loose to the top of her thighs, concealing all evidence of her dietary transgressions.

She was checking the casserole when she heard the sound of his key in the door.

"Something smells good." Greg walked into the house and dropped his keys on the table. "You look gorgeous. Is that sweater new?"

"You bought it for me!"

"I have great taste." He kissed her on the mouth. "How was your mother? Are you in need of therapy?"

"Yes, but I decided on the sort you can pour into a glass. It was that or chocolate chip ice cream."

"That's what I call a dilemma." Greg hung up his coat. "Walk me through your decision-making process."

"Wine is made from grapes and grapes are fruit, which makes it one of your five a day. So it's healthy." She handed him a glass of wine. "And if I'm not pregnant, I might as well drink. How was your day?"

"If I tell you my day was good are you going to take this away from me?"

She grinned. "No, because by the time I've finished whining you're going to need it."

"Wine for whine. Sounds like a reasonable deal." Greg took a mouthful of wine. "I'm braced. Hit me with it. What was today's gem?"

"Nothing new. She reminded me about the painting incident and held me personally responsible for her gray hair."

"Her gray hair makes her look distinguished. She should be thanking you."

"She praised you, of course." She lifted her glass in a mock toast. "You, Greg Sullivan, are the all-conquering hero. A gladiator among men. A knight in shining armor. I was lucky you were there to save me from my wicked ways."

"She said that?" Greg put the wine down and gave her a sympathetic look. "Maybe it's time the two of you had a frank, adult conversation."

"Frank, adult conversations don't happen in my family. At least, not with my mother. There's something about being with her that turns me into—I don't know—I regress about two decades in her company." She shrugged. "I'm weird around her. We are so dysfunctional as a family."

"All families are a little dysfunctional."

"We're a lot dysfunctional."

It was easy to talk to him, but being with Greg had always been so easy. When people talked about marriage as something that had to be "worked at" she didn't understand what they meant. She and Greg just *were*. They fitted like hand in glove or foot in shoe. They didn't need to work at anything.

They ate dinner at the table in their cozy kitchen, while the winter wind lashed at the window. After they'd finished the meal and cleared up, they curled up on the sofa.

Jenna topped up Greg's wineglass and he raised an eyebrow.

"Are you trying to get me drunk?"

"Maybe. I'm a wild child, remember? Just living down to my reputation." She slid off her shoes, curled her legs under her and moved closer, pressing her body against the solid strength of his.

Unlike her, his body hadn't changed much in the past decade. Greg believed exercise helped control mood and set an example to the community by spending time in the gym and running on the beach. As a result his body was as good as it had been at eighteen.

Jenna still found him really attractive, but if she was honest unbridled lust wasn't what drove most of their sexual encounters these days.

"Let's go to bed."

He turned his head and looked at her quizzically. "It's not the right time of the month for you to get pregnant, is it?"

Did he really think that was the only reason she'd suggest it?

She felt a flash of guilt, and that guilt was intensified by the knowledge that she'd done those calculations too. And he was right, it was the wrong time of the month. But sometimes sperm hung around, didn't it? Or maybe her ovaries would be so excited they'd pop out an egg spontaneously. At least having sex meant there was a *possibility* she could get pregnant. If they didn't have sex, there was no possibility.

"It's not the right time for me to get pregnant, but that's not the only reason to have sex."

"Isn't it?" He spoke so softly she wondered if she'd misheard.

"What's that supposed to mean?"

"Nothing. Only that lately that's all you think about." He cupped her face in his hands and kissed her again.

Greg had been the only guy she'd ever kissed (she didn't count that one session behind the bike sheds with Nick Jones because that had been part of a dare). Sex had changed over time. Being with him didn't give her the same dizzying thrill she'd had when they'd first got together (*take that, Mom. Saint Greg and I had sex before we were married*), but in many ways it was better. Familiar. Intimate.

As he deepened the kiss, his other arm came round her waist and Jenna tried to suck in her stomach, regretting the cupcake she'd eaten at breakfast. She shifted closer to him and felt something hard dig into her hip. "Is that your phone?"

"No it's my giant penis and the reason you married me." There was laughter in his voice as he nuzzled her neck but she shoved him away.

"Wait! Greg—why is it in your pocket?"

"My penis?"

"Your phone!"

He sighed and eased away a little. "Because that's where I always carry my phone. Where else would it be?"

"Anywhere else! You're supposed to be keeping your testicles cool and your phone out of your pocket. We agreed."

Greg swore under his breath and released her. "This is crazy, Jenna! Next you'll be asking me to see clients in my boxer shorts."

"That's a great idea. Could you do that? I'm kidding," she said hastily. "Of course I don't expect you to do that. You're overreacting. Although if you sat behind a desk I guess you could—"

"No I could not! You're obsessed."

"I am not obsessed! I'm focused, which is not the same as obsessed. Focused is good. Focused gets things done."

He eased away from her. "Jenna, getting pregnant is *all you think about*. We don't talk about anything except babies."

"That's not true." Was that true?

"When was the last time we talked about something *not* sex or baby related? And I don't count talking about your mother."

"Over dinner." She smiled triumphantly. "I didn't mention babies once. We talked about decorating the upstairs bedroom."

"Because you want to turn it into a nursery, even though you're not pregnant."

Oops. Guilty as charged. "Last week we had that long conversation about politics."

"—and the impact it might have on any children we have."

That was true, too.

So basically she was boring. *Fat and boring.* "It's possible that I might be a little overfocused on pregnancy, that's true. It's what happens when you really want something you can't have. Like being on a diet. If you can't eat a chocolate brownie, all you think about is eating the chocolate brownie. I'm talking figuratively—" Of course, figuratively. Nothing to do with the entire tin of brownies she'd devoured the week before. "That brownie invades your head space until you can't think about anything else. You dream about brownies. Brownies become your life. You're a psychologist. You're supposed to know this!"

Greg pressed his fingers to the bridge of his nose and breathed slowly. "Honey, if you could just—"

"Do *not* tell me to relax, Greg. And don't call me 'honey' in that tone. It drives me batshit crazy."

"I know, but Jen you really *do* need to relax. If something is taking over your mind, then the answer is to focus on other things. The way to forget the brownie, is to think about something else."

"Cupcakes?"

His expression was both amused and exasperated. "One of my clients is opening a new yoga studio in Oak Bluffs. Maybe you should go. You might find it calming."

"Or I might find it annoying. It will be full of serene people with perfect figures who are all in control of their lives. I'd have to kill them, and that wouldn't be calming for anyone."

Greg sighed. "Okay, no yoga. Tai Chi? Kickboxing? Book group?"

"Book group? My mother goes to book group."

"Go to a different book group. Start your own. Do *something*. Anything to take your mind off babies."

"You're saying you don't want babies?"

"No, I'm not saying that." He sucked in a breath. "I do want babies, but I don't think all this angst is going to help."

"But—" She was about to ask him how he felt about the whole thing when her phone rang.

She ignored it.

Whoever it was could wait.

Of course Greg wanted babies. Didn't he?

He glanced from her to the phone. "Aren't you going to answer that?"

"No. This conversation is more important than my phone." Her phone stopped ringing but started again a moment later and Greg reached down to pick it up.

"It's Lauren."

She stared at him stupidly. "What?"

"Your sister." He thrust the phone at her. "We can wish Ed a happy birthday."

"But isn't it the middle of the night in London?"

"It was obviously a great party. Answer it." He walked toward the door and she frowned.

"Where are you going?"

"To pack. If you're going to talk to your sister, I have time to take a six-month sabbatical."

She pulled a face. "We're not *that* bad."

"No, you're right. A two-week vacation should cover it. In the meantime I'll make us coffee." Greg walked to the kitchen and Jenna watched him go.

He always made her laugh. And he was so *calm*.

She felt less anxious just being around him. Who the hell needed yoga when they were married to Greg?

Stretching her legs out on the sofa, she settled in to have a long chat with her sister (not that she was going to let Greg get away with that comment about the length of their phone calls. Maybe *one* call last month had reached the two-hour mark, but she and Lauren lived thousands of miles apart! What did he expect?). "Hi, Lauren. Happy Birthday to Ed! How was the party? I was going to call you tomorrow. Did our gift arrive?" She smiled in anticipation and because she was expecting everything to be perfect it took her a couple of minutes to absorb what her sister was saying. "What?" She sat up suddenly, spilling her wine over her jeans. "Say that again!"

By the time Jenna ended the call she was in shock.

Her hand was shaking so badly she almost dropped her phone.

Greg walked back into the room and put two mugs of coffee on the table. "Did you lose the signal or something?"

"No."

"Then why so quick? I was going to speak to Ed."

"You can't." Her lips felt strange, as if they didn't want to move. "Ed is—" She broke off and he looked at her.

"Ed is what?"

Her eyes filled. "He's dead. How is that even possible? Today was his fortieth birthday. People don't die on their fortieth birthday. My sister. My poor sister." This time she didn't even try to hold back the tears. "I have to go to her."

"Of course you do." Looking shaken, Greg took the empty glass from her hand and tugged her to her feet. "Go and pack. I'll call the airline."

"We can't—I can't—" She couldn't think straight. "There's school, and—"

"I'll call them while you're packing. I've got this, honey."

"What about the money? We already decided we couldn't afford to go away in the summer."

"We'll manage. Some things are more important than money."

She didn't argue.

Only hours before she'd been envying her sister, and now her life was shattered.

It was unbelievable. Unfair.

And to think she'd been about to offload her own problems.

She sleepwalked to the bedroom and pulled out her suitcase. Without thinking about what she was packing, she stuffed random clothes into it. All she could think about was her sister, her big sister, who had always been there for her through thick and thin.

There was nothing her sister didn't know about her. Not a single thing.

"It's all booked." Greg appeared in the doorway, his phone in one hand and his credit card in the other. His face was pale and his expression serious. "Take sweaters. And a coat. It's cold in England."

"What? Oh, yes. Sure." She pushed some thick socks into the case and paused, helpless. "What do I do, Greg? What is the right thing to say to someone who has lost their husband? I wish you were coming with me."

But they both knew he couldn't. He had people counting on him, and no one who could cover him.

"You'll be there with her, that's what counts. I'll call you every night."

Jenna glanced round her bedroom and tried to work out what she'd forgotten. Lauren would have made a list. She probably had a list ready to use entitled "for emergency travel." Everything would be checked off. Red ticks for the outward journey, blue ticks for the return journey.

There were no ticks on Jenna's list. Jenna didn't have a list to tick.

She was the disorganized one. Lauren was the perfect one.

Except that her perfect sister's perfect life was no longer perfect.

Loved this book?

Visit Sarah Morgan's fantastic website
at **www.sarahmorgan.com** for
information about Sarah, her latest books,
news, interviews, offers, competitions,
reading group extras and much more…

…and connect with her online, at:

 @SarahMorgan_

f **facebook.com/AuthorSarahMorgan**

g **goodreads.com/SarahMorgan_**

 instagram.com/sarahmorganwrites

 pinterest.com/SarahMorgan_

MORGAN_SM

Fall in love with New York City...
and fall in love with Sarah Morgan

Let Sarah Morgan whisk you away to the Big Apple
with her *From Manhattan with Love* series!

One Place. Many Stories